'Demonic, demented and truly ferocious and a flat-out joy
to read. In other words, a total feast. Like it?...
I plain worshipped it' – Ken Bruen

Lights Out

'*Lights Out* has the New York sound, the energy, dialog that's
on the beat... read it and you'll go hunting for Jason Starr's
other books, I promise' – Elmore Leonard

'Jason Starr is hypnotically good – if you miss him, you're
missing some of the best new writing there is' – Lee Child

'Jason Starr is a leader of the new noir movement'
– George P. Pelecanos

'A fast, furious page-turner from the git-go...
This book is a huge treat'
– Jefferey Deaver

The Follower

'A classic old-fashioned stalker novel, full of plot twists'
– *Sunday Business Post*

'This generation's *Looking for Mr Goodbar* and a crackling-hot
beach read' – *New York Post*

'Jason Starr's masterpiece' – Bret Easton Ellis

'*The Follower* puts Starr up there with some of the greats
of psychological suspense' – Joseph Finder

Panic Attack

'*Panic Attack* is the ultimate page turner' – Michael Connelly

'Completely brilliant' – Jerry Stahl

Novels by Jason Starr from No Exit Press

Panic Attack

JASON STARR

NO EXIT PRESS

This edition first published in the UK in 2016
by No Exit Press,
an imprint of Oldcastle Books
PO Box 394, Harpenden,
Herts, AL5 1XJ, UK
noexit.co.uk
@NoExitPress

A CIP catalogue record for this book is available from the
British Library.

ISBN
978-1-84344-709-2 (print)
978-1-84344-710-8 (epub)
978-1-84344-711-5 (kindle)
978-1-84344-712-2 (pdf)

Type   RT
in 10pt Palatino

in Great Britain by Clays Ltd, St Ives plc

For more   information about Crime Fiction go in   .co.uk

For Chynna and Sandy

The ego is not master in its own house
– SIGMUND FREUD

1

A DAM BLOOM WAS having a nightmare. It was the one he'd had before where he was in his office in midtown, treating a female patient, maybe Kathy Stappini or Jodi Roth – both of whom, interestingly enough, suffered from agoraphobia – when his office suddenly became a white, square-shaped room, the size of a prison cell, and Kathy or Jodi turned into a large black rat. The rat had long fangs and kept chasing him around, jumping at him, making a loud hissing noise. Then the walls started closing in. He tried to scream but couldn't make any sound, and then a long, narrow staircase appeared. He tried to run up it but couldn't get anywhere, like he was trying to go up a down escalator. Then he looked over his shoulder, and the rat was huge now, the size of a Rottweiler, and it was coming at him, baring its long fangs, about to bite his head off.

He felt a yanking on his upper arm. Startled, he tried to turn away, onto his other side, when he heard, 'Mom, Dad, wake up, wake up.'

He opened his eyes, disoriented for a moment, terrified of the giant rat, then realized that he was home in bed in his house in Forest Hills Gardens with his wife, Dana, lying next to him. He had the comforted, relieved feeling he always had after a nightmare. It was a rush of reassurance that everything was going to be fine, that thank God the world wasn't such a horrible place after all.

But then he heard his daughter whispering, 'Somebody's downstairs.'

Marissa had graduated from Vassar last year with a degree in art history – Adam and Dana hadn't been exactly thrilled about that choice – and was back living at home, in the room she'd grown up in. She'd been acting out lately, exhibiting a lot of attention-seeking behavior. She had several tattoos – including one of an angel on her lower back that she liked to show off by wearing halter tops and low-rise jeans – and had recently dyed pink streaks into her short light brown hair. She spent her days listening to awful music, emailing, blogging, text messaging, watching TV, and partying with her friends. She often didn't come home until three or four in the morning, and some nights she didn't come home at all, 'forgetting' to call. She was a good kid, but Adam and Dana had been trying to encourage her to get her act together and get on with her life.

'What is it?' Adam asked. He was still half-asleep, a little out of it, still thinking about the dream. What was the significance of the black rat? Why was it black? Why did it always start out as a patient? A *female* patient?

'I heard a noise,' Marissa said. 'Somebody's in the house.'

Adam blinked hard a couple of times, to wake himself up fully, then said, 'It was probably just the house settling, or the wind –'

'No, I'm telling you. There's somebody there. I heard footsteps and stuff moving.'

Now Dana was up, too, and asked, 'What's going on?'

Like Adam, Dana was forty-seven, but she'd aged better than he had. He was graying, balding, had some flab, especially in his midsection, but she'd been spending a lot of time in the gym, especially during the last year or so, and had a great body to show for it. They'd had some marriage trouble – they'd nearly had a trial separation when Marissa was in high school – but things had been better lately.

'I heard somebody downstairs, Ma.'

Adam was exhausted and just wanted to go back to sleep. 'It was nothing,' he said.

'I'm telling you I heard it.'

'Maybe you should go and check,' Dana said, concerned.

'I'm really afraid, Daddy.'

The daddy part got to him. He couldn't remember the last time she'd called him daddy, and he could tell she was seriously frightened. He was awake anyway and had to go pee, so he might as well go check.

He breathed deeply, then said, 'Fine, okay,' and sat up.

As he got out of bed, he cringed. He'd had on-and-off-again lower back pain and stiffness for the past few years, an overuse injury from running and golf. His physical therapist had given him a list of exercises to do at home, but he'd been busy lately with a couple of involved patient crises and hadn't been doing them. He was also supposed to ice his back before he went to sleep and after he went running or worked out, and he hadn't been doing that either.

Massaging his lower back with one hand, trying to knead out the stiffness, he went across the room, opened the door, and listened. Total silence except for some faint wind noise outside.

'I don't hear anything,' he said.

'I heard footsteps,' Marissa stage-whispered. 'Keep listening.'

Dana had gotten out of bed and was standing, in her nightgown, next to Marissa.

Adam listened again for around five seconds, then said, 'There's nobody there. Just go back to bed and try to –'

And then he heard it. The house was big – three stories, five bedrooms, three and a half baths – but even from where he was, on the second floor, at the end of the hallway, the sound of maybe a dish clanging or a vase being moved was very clear. It sounded like the person was either in the kitchen or the dining room.

Dana and Marissa had heard the noise, too.

Marissa said, 'See, I told you,' and Dana said, 'Oh my God, Adam, what should we do?'

They sounded terrified.

Adam was trying to think clearly, but it was hard because he was suddenly worried and frazzled himself. Besides, he always had trouble thinking when he first woke up, and he never felt fully functional until after his third cup of coffee.

'I'm calling nine-one-one,' Dana said.

'Wait,' Adam said.

'Why?' Dana asked, the phone in her hand.

Adam couldn't think of a good answer. There was someone downstairs; he'd heard the noise clearly, and there was no doubt what it was. But a part of him didn't want to believe it. He wanted to believe he was safe, protected.

'I don't know,' he said, trying to remain calm and logical. 'I mean, it's impossible. We have an alarm system.'

'Come on, Dad, I know you heard it,' Marissa said.

'Maybe something fell,' Adam said.

'Nothing fell,' Marissa said. 'I heard footsteps, you have to call the police.' Then from downstairs came the clear sound of a cough, or of a man clearing his throat. It sounded closer than the other noise Adam had heard. It sounded like the guy was in the living room.

'Okay, call the cops,' Adam whispered to Dana.

While she was making the call, Adam went to the walk-in closet, flicked on the light, reached to the top shelf and grabbed his Glock .45. Then he bent down, moved some things out of the way, and opened the shoe box where he kept the bullets.

'What're you doing?' Marissa asked.

Adam was still bending down, loading the clip, and didn't answer. He'd bought the gun four years ago after a couple of houses in the neighborhood had been robbed. He practiced shooting once in a while in the city, at the West Side Pistol Range. He enjoyed shooting, and it was a great way to relieve stress and safely express anger.

He came out of the closet with the gun in his hand, and Marissa said, 'Are you fuckin' crazy?'

Dana was still on the phone, finishing up the conversation with the 911 operator, whispering, 'Yes, we think he's in the house right now… I don't know… please hurry… yes… please hurry.' Then she ended the call and said, 'They're coming.' She put an arm around Marissa, then saw the gun in Adam's hand and said, 'What the hell're you doing with that?'

She hated the idea of having a gun in the house and had been asking Adam to get rid of it.

'Nothing,' Adam said.

'Then why're you holding it?'

He didn't answer.

She said, 'Just put it away, the police'll be here any minute.'

'Keep your voice down.'

'Adam, the police're coming. There's no reason to have a –'

She cut herself off when there was another noise. There was no doubt this time – there were footsteps, the guy was heading upstairs.

'Oh my God,' Marissa said, covering her mouth, starting to cry.

Adam was trying to think again, focus, but his brain was overloaded and he said, 'Hide in the closet.'

Dana said, 'What're you –'

'Nothing. Just go, goddamn it.'

'Come with us.'

'Just hide – *now*.'

Dana seemed hesitant. Marissa's crying was getting a little louder.

'He'll hear her,' Adam whispered urgently.

Dana and Marissa went into the closet and hid. Adam went to the door, holding the gun up by his ear, pointed at the ceiling. For several seconds, he listened, but heard nothing. He hoped this meant the guy had decided to go back downstairs. Maybe he'd heard Marissa crying and would simply leave the house and run away.

But then there was another creaky footstep on the stairs – the son of a bitch was coming up. It hit Adam as if he were realizing it for the first time – *someone was inside his house*.

He'd grown up in this very house, and then his parents had given it to him when Marissa was a baby, when they moved to Florida. He'd loved growing up in Forest Hills Gardens, with all his friends so close by and the houses with the big backyards, but the neighborhood was safer now than it had been back then when he was ten years old and an older kid stole his bicycle –

just came up to him with a knife one afternoon and said, 'Give it up.' As a teenager, he'd been mugged on Queens Boulevard twice, and when he was in his twenties – living in Manhattan while he was going for his doctorate at the New School – he was once robbed at gunpoint in the vestibule of a friend's apartment building in the Village.

Standing with the gun drawn, listening to the intruder take another step up the stairs, he remembered how awful and helpless it had felt to be a victim, and how he didn't want to be a victim again. His thoughts were frantic, but he was trying to be logical. He thought, *What if the guy has a gun? What if he's a total maniac? What if, any moment now, he charges up the stairs and starts shooting? What if he shoots* me?

Adam imagined getting shot, lying dead in the hallway, and then the guy finding Dana and Marissa in the bedroom. The guy could be some crazed rapist. There were always stories in the news about home invasions, men breaking into houses and raping women, but he'd never thought it could actually happen to him, in his own house.

But it could be happening now.

The guy was on the staircase, getting closer. In a few seconds he could be at the top of the landing, and then it would be too late.

All of this was going through his mind at once, and he didn't have time to think it through clearly. If he'd had more time, if he were in a calmer, less scattered state, he might've realized that the police would be arriving any moment. There was a private security company in Forest Hills Gardens and there was supposed to be a response time of less than five minutes. If he locked himself in the bedroom, hid with Dana and Marissa, the guy probably wouldn't be able to get to them. He might try the locked bedroom door, but then he'd give up, and the police would arrive.

But Adam wasn't thinking about any of this now. He was only thinking about how he wanted to protect his family, how he didn't want to be a victim again, and how some son of a bitch had broken into his house, the house he'd grown up in, the house that his father had bought in 1956.

He heard the guy take another step on the staircase, and then another. Was Adam imagining it or was the guy approaching faster? There was only a night-light on in the hallway, a little candle-shaped orange light plugged into a socket at ankle level. Adam's eyes had adjusted, but it was still hard to see very clearly. At any moment, though, the guy would appear. After he took another step or two Adam would see his head, or the guy might rush up and attack him.

Adam was standing by the entrance to his bedroom, and then, an instant later, he was in the hallway, running with his gun drawn, yelling, 'Get the fuck out of here!'

It was darker near the stairway than it had been near the bedroom door. Now Adam could tell that the guy wasn't as far up the staircase as he had thought. He was maybe halfway up, and Adam could tell that he was a big guy, but that was about it.

Then he saw the guy's hand reaching for something. It was a sudden movement, and Adam knew that it had to be a gun. He even thought he saw a glimmer of something, shininess near the guy's hand. If he waited any longer the guy would shoot him first. Then he'd shoot his way into the bedroom, find Dana and Marissa, and kill them, too.

The guy started to say something. Later Adam would dwell on this moment and remember that the guy had said, 'Please don't –' but at that moment everything was happening so fast that he wasn't even aware that the guy had spoken. He was only aware of the danger he and his family were in as he started firing his gun. He wasn't sure if the first shot hit the guy, but the second one did, high up, in his neck or head. The guy was falling backward, starting to tumble, and Adam remembered his shooting instructor saying, *Always go for the chest, not the head* – and he emptied the rest of the clip, the other shots going into the guy's chest or midsection. Then the guy fell out of view, into darkness, but Adam heard his body land with a loud thud at the bottom of the staircase.

There was silence for a long moment, and then there was noise from downstairs, but it had nothing to do with the guy Adam had shot.

There was someone else in the house.

There were footsteps, then deep breathing. Adam was out of bullets. If the other guy came upstairs or started shooting, he was screwed.

'Get the hell out of here or I'll shoot!' Adam yelled.

That was smart, brilliant maybe. Make the guy think he still had bullets. Why wouldn't he think so? Adam had fired off the shots so quickly the guy couldn't have possibly counted the shots. And even if the guy had counted them, knew Adam had shot ten rounds, how would he know he didn't have more ammo?

The strategy worked, or maybe the guy just panicked. Adam heard him running away, knocking into something – the console? – and then the front door opened and closed and the guy was gone.

'Adam.'

He turned suddenly, feeling a sharp jolt in his chest. Then he registered Dana and Marissa standing there.

'Are you okay?' Dana asked.

'Back to the bedroom!' Adam shouted.

'Are you okay?' Dana asked again.

'Just get back!'

Dana and Marissa went into the bedroom, and Dana shut the door. Adam was worried about the guy on the stairs. What if he was still alive?

He reached toward the wall at the other end of the landing and put his thumb on the light switch. He hesitated, wondering if this was a great idea. Maybe the guy was aiming his gun up the stairs, waiting for a clear shot.

Adam flicked on the light, relieved to see that the guy, wearing a black ski mask, was crumpled at the bottom of the stairs, not moving at all. He headed downstairs, going slowly, not taking his eyes off the guy's body.

As Adam got closer, he could tell that the guy had darkish skin, looked Latino, maybe Puerto Rican. His chest and face were a bloody mess, there was a big hole and oozing blood and gray stuff where his left eye used to be, and a big chunk of his jaw was gone.

Adam stared at the body for a while, trying to process what he'd done.

He'd shot a man. He'd shot and *killed* a man.

Then he looked toward the guy's right hand. There was a flashlight two stairs above the guy's head, but Adam didn't see any gun. There was no gun on the staircase or on the floor at the bottom, either. Maybe the guy had fallen on it and it was under his body.

Adam remained, staring in a daze at the man he'd killed until the police started banging on the front door.

2

IT WAS ALMOST four in the morning, about two hours since the shooting, and the Blooms' house was still filled with cops. Dana and Marissa were in the downstairs den with Dana's friends Sharon and Jennifer, who had come over during the commotion. Adam was at the dining room table, sitting across from Detective Clements, a weathered, gray-haired guy who reeked of cigarettes.

'So you saw Sanchez on the stairwell?' Clements said.

The cops had found a New York state driver's license and other ID in the dead guy's wallet and had learned that the victim was thirty-six-year-old Carlos Sanchez from Bayside, Queens. They'd already done a search on Sanchez and discovered that he was a career criminal with a long rap sheet and had been released six months ago from Fishkill, where he'd been serving a sentence for multiple drug-dealing convictions. Adam had already described everything that had happened prior to the shooting at least once, but Clements was still digging for details.

'Well, I didn't *see* him,' Adam said. 'I saw a figure. You know, a shadow.' Adam was exhausted, so out of it that it was hard to focus. The whole night seemed surreal – the nightmare about the giant black rat, waking up, the shooting, and now sitting here with this detective. He knew it would take a while before he could process and accept what he'd done. Meanwhile, he had a splitting headache, and three Advils hadn't made a dent.

'Yet you could tell it was a man?' Clements said.

'Yes,' Adam said. 'I mean, I heard the noise from downstairs, him coughing or clearing his throat or something. There was no doubt it was a guy. My wife and daughter heard it, too.'

'And then you shot him?'

'No, it didn't happen that quickly. I mean...' He had to think; for a moment he actually couldn't remember what had happened, the exact sequence of events. It was all blurry, disorganized. Then he said firmly, 'I didn't just *shoot* him. I saw him make a move first, like he was going for a gun.'

'Did you see a gun?'

'I thought I did, yes.' He felt uncomfortable, like Clements was trying to catch him in a lie. 'I mean, I could see his arm. He was coming up the stairs and I was afraid any second he'd start shooting. Look, what was I supposed to do? The guy was in my house, coming up the stairs, and my wife and daughter were in the bedroom. I didn't have any choice.'

'Did you give him any warning?'

'What do you mean?'

Adam had heard the question; he just wasn't sure how to answer it. He was also getting frustrated by the discussion in general.

'Did you tell him you had a weapon and did you ask him to drop his?' Clements asked.

'No, but I told him to get the hell out of my house, or something like that.'

'And how did he respond?'

Adam remembered that the guy had said something, started to speak, might have said, *'Please, don't –'* Adam hadn't told Clements about this because he didn't see the point. What difference did it make either way?

'I don't think he said anything,' Adam said, 'but, look, that part happened very fast. I thought he was about to start shooting, he was in my house. Why? I had a right to defend myself, didn't I?'

'Yeah, you did,' Clements said.

'Then why do I feel like you're interrogating me?'

'I'm not interrogating you, I'm questioning you.'

'What's the difference?'

Clements almost smiled, then said, 'Look, I don't think you have anything to worry about legally, all right, Dr Bloom? You were in a tough situation and you did what you had to do. You got B and E and, yeah, that gives you the right to protect yourself. As long as your gun license checks out I don't think you'll have a problem. But I just gotta say, it's a good thing you're not a cop.' He turned a page in his pad, then asked, 'What about the other intruder?'

'What about him?'

'Him. You said that before, too. How do you know it was a guy?'

Adam thought about it for a moment – it was still hard to think clearly – and said, 'I guess I don't know that. I just figured it had to be two guys.'

'But when you fired your gun you were unaware there was a second intruder?'

'Correct,' Adam said.

'So I guess that's why you spent a whole clip, huh? You didn't think you had to save any bullets for anybody else?'

Clements had already raised this issue of why Adam had fired ten shots, and Adam had explained that he'd done it because he wasn't sure he'd hit the guy, that he was just trying to defend himself. But Adam didn't like how Clements was bringing it up again, like he was trying to get to the bottom of something.

'I just wanted to make sure I...' Adam was going to say 'killed him' but modified it to '– got him before he got me.'

Clements, shaking his head while looking at the pad, said, 'It's a good thing you're not a cop, Doc. It's a good thing you're not a cop.'

Adam had had enough. He asked, 'Is it okay if we pick this up later, or in the morning? I'm exhausted and my head's killing me and I've been through a lot tonight, obviously.'

'I understand, but there're still a few things I need to be clear about, okay?' Adam breathed deeply, then said, 'For instance?'

'For instance,' Clements said, 'the issue of how exactly the intruders got into the house.'

They'd been through this already, too, at least a couple of times. The police had found no visible signs of a break-in, but both the back door in the kitchen and the front door had been unlocked, and the alarm system had been disarmed. Adam had told Clements that he was positive that he'd set the alarm before he went to bed, the way he did every night.

'Didn't we cover all of this already?' Adam asked.

Acting like he didn't hear this, Clements said, 'Are you sure you locked and chained the front door before you went to sleep?'

'Yes,' Adam said.

'Is it possible you went out, or your wife or daughter went out, maybe to take out the garbage or something, and forgot to –'

'No, I was the last one to go to bed last night, and I chained the door. I always lock and chain it if I'm the last one to go to sleep, it's part of my nightly routine. I make sure the gas is off in the kitchen, lock all the doors, set the alarm, and go to bed.'

'So assuming all this is correct, the other intruder must've unlatched the chain on the front door on his way out of the house.'

'That has to be what happened,' Adam said. 'I heard the front door slam.'

'So that means the intruders likely entered the house through the back door.'

'Yes,' Adam said, squeezing the back of his neck, trying to relieve some of the tension.

'And are you positive you set the alarm and no one else disarmed it after you set it?'

'I'm positive.'

'But the alarm wasn't set when we arrived, is that correct?'

'If the alarm was set the guy,' – Adam caught himself – 'the *person* would've tripped it on the way out.'

'That seems to make sense,' Clements said. 'So who –'

'I have no idea,' Adam said.

Clements glared at Adam, seeming irritated that he'd been

cut off, then continued, a little louder, 'So who except you and your family know the code to the alarm?'

'No one else knows it,' Adam said.

'Did you ever give anyone the code, on any occasion?'

'No.'

'Did you ask your wife or daughter –'

'You asked them directly, and they said no, didn't they?'

'Now I'm asking you.'

'Asking me what? If my wife and daughter lied to you?'

'Or weren't being entirely truthful.'

'What's the difference?'

Clements was smiling sarcastically, like he was enjoying the exchange, but Adam stayed deadpan.

'They didn't tell anyone the code,' Adam said. 'No one told anyone the code.'

'Sorry to play devil's advocate, Dr Bloom, but unless Houdini robbed your house, somebody got ahold of that code.'

'Maybe it was stolen,' Adam said, 'from the alarm company. Maybe they hacked into the system or something.'

'We'll explore that possibility,' Clements said, 'but nobody stole a set of keys from the alarm company. Did you or anyone in your family loan a set of keys to anyone?'

'I already told you, we only have three sets of keys to the house and one spare set, and the spare set is still where it always is.'

'Maybe someone got access to the keys. A worker in the house?'

Adam thought for a moment, then said, 'We had some painting done a few weeks ago, but those guys had nothing to do with this.'

'Your wife gave me the names of the painters, the electrician, your maid, your gardener. Can you think of anyone else we should check out?'

'No,' Adam said.

'I noticed the keys to the back door weren't Medecos or ones that couldn't be easily duplicated,' Clements said, 'What I mean is they looked like normal keys.'

'Yeah?' Adam asked. 'So?' His eyelids were heavy, and he felt like he could pass out at any moment.

'So it's possible somebody could've duplicated the keys at some point,' Clements said.

'It's possible,' Adam said, 'but no one knows where we keep the spare keys.'

Clements turned a page, then said, 'Your wife told me you'd been planning to go away to Florida for several days, right?'

'That's right,' Adam said, 'to visit my mother.'

'You canceled the trip because of a storm?'

'That's right. We heard there was a tropical storm off the coast down there. They said it could turn into a hurricane and might hit Florida, so I thought we might as well go some other time.'

'When did you decide not to go?'

Adam thought about it for a moment, rubbing the back of his neck again, then said, 'Two days ago.'

'Who knew you changed your plans?'

'Nobody,' Adam said. 'I mean, I had to notify a few patients, to reschedule appointments, and I guess Dana and Marissa told a few people, but we didn't take an ad out in the paper.'

Clements, not amused, asked, 'Do you ever have any patients who are prone to violence?'

Adam immediately thought of Vincent, a patient he'd been seeing for about a month who'd told him about how he'd beaten up some guy during a bar fight a few weeks ago. There was also Delano, a guy in his forties, who had stabbed his brother – non-fatally – when he was a child.

'Yes,' Adam said, 'I have a few.'

'Has anyone threatened you lately?'

'No,' Adam said. 'Actually I've rarely if ever had any situations like that. I'm a psychologist, not a psychiatrist. If I have a patient who shows signs of that kind of volatility I'll refer him elsewhere.'

'So I guess you're pretty good at that, huh?' Clements said. 'Telling if somebody's volatile or not?'

Adam wasn't sure why Clements was asking this – whether there was any point to it or he was just trying to be a wiseass.

'I think I am pretty good at it, yes,' Adam said.

'Then maybe you're in the wrong profession,' Clements said,

'maybe you should be doing my job.' He smirked, then asked, 'Does your daughter have friends over?'

'Of course,' Adam said. 'She lives here.'

'Is there any drug or alcohol use in the house?'

'Excuse me?'

Adam didn't like where this was going.

'Sanchez had multiple priors on drug charges. Perhaps your daughter was an acquaintance of Sanchez's, or a client of his.'

'There's no way she knew that guy, okay?'

'Maybe she has a friend, or a friend of a friend, or someone she may have invited into the house, someone who knew the place, who could've –'

'My daughter had nothing to do with this.'

'Dr Bloom, I'm only –'

'And she has no friends who'd steal a key or rob a house. Her friends are all normal, nice kids, just like her.'

'I noticed the bong in her room, Dr Bloom.'

Again this felt like more than 'routine questions.'

'What're you trying to say?' Adam asked.

'I'm trying to figure out how the intruders got into your house.'

'Yeah, that's funny, because it sounds like you're trying to say something else. My daughter had nothing to do with this, okay, so let's leave her out of it.'

Clements seemed unconvinced, but he asked, 'What about your relatives?'

'What about them?'

'Any animosity in the family? Anybody with a grudge?'

Adam thought about Dana and her brother, Mark, the manic-depressive. They were on bad terms and hadn't spoken in years, but Mark lived in Milwaukee and obviously had nothing to do with any of this, so Adam didn't see the point in even mentioning it.

'No,' he said. 'Nothing like that. This had nothing to do with my family. Zero. Zilch. Nada.'

Clements closed his pad – finally – and said, 'That should do it for now. But I want you to think about who could've gotten ahold of the keys and the code to the alarm. Right now this does seem to have all the makings of some kind of inside job. Not only did the person, *persons,* have access to the house, they also seemed to know the house very well. I mean, they knew you didn't have a chain on the back door and they could enter that way, so it seems like at least one of the perps had been in the house before. Maybe he was a repairman or a plumber, a mover, he delivered a rug, something like that. So if you can think of any times when someone could've had access to the key and the alarm code, can you let me know as soon as possible?'

'I'll let you know right away,' Adam said, standing up.

'I'm gonna have to talk to your wife and daughter again now,' Clements said.

'Are you kidding me?' Adam said.

'It won't take long, but I need to talk to them.'

'Why can't it wait till –'

'Because it can't, all right?' His tone left no room for discussion.

Adam and the detective went out to the living room, where Dana and Marissa were sitting on the couch, across from Sharon and Jennifer. Being around Sharon, especially when Dana was in the same room, was always awkward for Adam to say the least.

About five years ago, when Adam and Dana were having serious marital problems, Sharon and her husband, Mike, were also having trouble in their marriage. Sharon called Adam one day at work and asked if she could come by his office for some advice. Adam said that would be fine and arranged to see her at seven o'clock, his last appointment of the day, when the other therapists were out of the office. Adam gave Sharon some informal marital counseling, and then he hinted that things weren't going so well in his own marriage. He knew exactly what he was doing – exposing his own vulnerability as a way of letting Sharon know that he was interested in her – and he already knew that she was attracted to him, because she had been flirty with him for years. They commiserated with each other about their marriages for a while, and then Sharon confessed that she'd often fantasized about 'something happening' between her and Adam. Adam, who counseled people having affairs practically every day, knew that getting involved with Sharon would be a huge mistake and could create a rift in his own marriage that would be impossible to repair. But knowing what to do and actually doing it are two very different things. He was as human as anyone else and had been flattered by the interest from another woman and simply couldn't resist her.

They only had sex that one time, on the therapy couch. There were no ethical issues because he wasn't actually treating Sharon, but he didn't want to get into a full-blown affair with her or deal with the pain and drama that would inevitably follow, so he wisely told her – and she agreed – that they had to consider this a one-time thing and go on with their lives. She wound up working things out with her husband, and Dana and Adam went into counseling and managed to improve their marriage – well, for the most part. Adam still felt there were serious underlying problems in their relationship, mainly a lack of closeness, and he considered confessing the affair to Dana. Normally he advised his patients to confess infidelity because he believed it was the only way to truly heal and re-establish closeness and trust in a marriage. But in this case, because he didn't feel any emotional involvement with Sharon, he decided that confessing the affair would only hurt Dana and do more harm than good. So instead he worked on exploring his reasons for the affair and developed strategies for becoming a better husband. While he regretted what he'd done, he refused to blame Dana or himself. Marriage had ups and downs, and his minor lapse had hardly been atypical. He had done the best he could under the circumstances, and if he got into a similar situation in the future he would try to make a better decision.

He would have preferred to cut off contact with Sharon completely, but, of course, this was impossible. They often saw each other around the neighborhood or at parties, and Sharon and Dana were good friends, and so were Marissa and Sharon's daughter, Hillary. Adam and Mike occasionally played golf together at Adam's country club and got along well. Sharon and Adam were always friendly with each other but, although they avoided discussing the affair, there was a simmering attraction between them that would probably be there for the rest of their lives.

Detective Clements asked Marissa if she'd come with him into the dining room.

Marissa, looking exhausted, asked, 'Again?'

'It's okay,' Adam said, glaring at Clements. 'It won't take long.'

When Marissa and Clements left, Dana said to Sharon and Jennifer, 'You two should go home now, it's late.'

'Are you sure?' Sharon asked. 'Because if you want us to stay –'

'No, it's okay, really. I'll talk to you guys tomorrow.'

'I know,' Jennifer said, 'we'll bring over bagels and coffee in the morning.'

'You don't have to do that,' Dana said.

'No, we want to,' Sharon said.

Sharon and Jennifer took turns hugging Dana and then came over and hugged Adam. Trying not to notice the very familiar scent of Sharon's perfume and how it was starting to give him an erection, Adam said, 'Thanks so much for coming.'

He meant it, too. It was very thoughtful of her to come over in the middle of the night to give her support. She didn't have to do that.

'Of course I was going to come,' she said. 'Why wouldn't I?'

When Sharon and Jennifer were gone and Dana and Adam were alone in the living room, Dana asked, 'Why does he want to talk to Marissa again?'

Adam didn't want to tell her that Clements had mentioned the bong in Marissa's room, knowing it would only upset her. He figured he'd tell her about it tomorrow.

'I think it's just some more routine-type questions,' Adam said. 'He knows how tired we are, so I think it'll only take a few minutes.'

Adam could tell that Dana knew he was keeping something from her – a woman always knows; well, almost always knows – but she let it pass.

'So how're you doing?' Dana asked.

'Okay, considering,' Adam said.

'Maybe you should talk to somebody.'

Earlier, Detective Clements had asked Adam if he wanted to talk to a psychologist, which Adam had thought was a slightly strange question to ask a psychologist.

'I'll have a session with Carol,' Adam said.

Carol Levinson was one of the therapists with whom Adam shared office space. He wasn't in formal therapy with her, but he talked to her on an as-needed basis.

'Don't worry about me, I'll be fine,' Adam said. 'How're you doing?'

'I'm okay,' she said. 'I guess.'

There was a coldness in Dana's tone, an undercurrent of distance, and Adam knew it had to do with the gun. She'd been opposed to having it in the house, and she'd asked him to get rid of it on several occasions. He'd explained to her that he felt it was necessary, that he felt too vulnerable and unprotected without it, and finally she'd agreed that as long as they kept it hidden she was fine with it. But now he knew she was harboring resentment and secretly blamed him for the shooting. Of course, she wouldn't actually say something about it – not now, anyway. No, that wasn't her style. In these situations, she always avoided confrontation and was frequently evasive and passive-aggressive. She'd let it simmer for a while first to create more drama, and then, maybe a couple of days from now, she'd bring it up.

'I'd tell you to go to sleep now,' Adam said, 'but I think Clements is going to want to talk to you again, too.'

'I just want all these cops out of the house.'

'Me, too. But it can't be much longer now.'

'Is the body still there?'

'I don't know, I didn't check.'

'Are the reporters still outside?'

'Probably.'

'I don't want to be in the newspapers,' she said. 'I don't want my name, your name, and I definitely don't want Marissa's name in there.'

'I don't think there's any avoiding it.'

'My God, do you think it'll be front-page news?'

Adam thought it could make the front page of all the major

papers – a shooting in an affluent New York City neighborhood had to be a major news story – but he wanted to placate her and said, 'I doubt it.'

'It'll definitely be on the TV news,' she said, sounding not at all placated. 'I saw all the cameras out there. New York One, for sure, and probably all the local news shows.'

'You never know,' Adam said. 'By tomorrow there'll probably be other big news stories, and this one'll get buried.'

He could tell Dana still wasn't buying any of this. Well, he'd given it a try, anyway.

'What about the other guy?' she asked. 'Did the detective say they think they were gonna find him?'

'I'm sure they'll find him soon, probably before morning,' Adam said. He could tell how upset she was, so he kissed her and hugged her tightly and said, 'I'm so sorry about all of this. I really am.' He held her for a while longer, and he knew that she was thinking about saying something about the gun again, that it took all her self-control to not lay into him about it.

Instead they let go and she said, 'I just want this all to go away. I want to go to sleep and wake up and find out none of this ever happened.'

Several minutes later, Marissa returned from talking to the detective, and then Dana went into the dining room to answer a few more questions. Marissa looked distraught, which made Adam feel awful. She'd called him daddy earlier, and he realized how, despite all her acting out lately, she was still his little girl. He hugged her tightly and kissed her on top of her head and said, 'Don't worry, kiddo. Things'll be back to normal soon, you'll see.'

There were still cops and other police personnel in the kitchen, in the living room, and especially near the staircase, dusting for fingerprints and apparently looking for other forensic evidence. He looked out a window and saw that news trucks were still there, and reporters were milling around on the lawn; and some neighbors were there, too. He knew the reporters were probably waiting to talk to someone from the family, to get a few good sound bites, so he figured he might as well get it over with.

He went outside and it was very surreal – standing in front

of his house at four in the morning with all the lights in his face and the reporters shouting questions. He recognized a couple of the reporters – What's Her Name Olsen from Fox News and the young black guy from Channel 11. Somebody was holding a boom with a mike over his head, and people were sticking mikes from ABC, WINS, NY1, and other stations in front of his face. He wasn't used to this kind of attention; he normally tried to avoid being in the spotlight. For years he'd suffered from glossophobia, a fear of public speaking, and he usually tried to stay in the background, to be an observer. At psychology conferences, he never made a presentation unless he absolutely had to, and then he had to use a number of cognitive-behavioral strategies to overcome his anxiety.

'Why did you shoot him?' the guy from Channel 11 asked.

'I didn't have any choice,' Adam said, already sweaty. 'He was coming up the stairs in the middle of the night and when I shouted for him to get out he didn't leave. I think anyone in my position would've done the same thing.'

'Did you know he wasn't armed?' What's Her Name Olsen asked.

'No, I did not,' Adam said.

'Would you do it all over again?' a guy in the back shouted.

'Yes,' Adam said. 'If I was in the same situation, if someone broke into my house and I thought my family was in danger, I think I would. Absolutely.'

There were a lot more questions, and they all had a similar vaguely accusing tone. Adam was surprised because he'd thought that he'd be treated more sympathetically by the press. Instead he felt like he had when Clements was questioning him, like the reporters were trying to put him on the spot, trying to draw out some hidden truth that didn't exist.

But he remained out there for a half-hour or longer, fielding every question the reporters asked him calmly and politely. He used the techniques he sometimes suggested to his patients – focusing on his breathing, speaking from his chest rather than his throat – and gradually he felt more relaxed, almost normal. When the reporters were out of questions, he thanked them for their time and went back into the house.

3

W HEN MARISSA HEARD the gunshots, she was convinced
her father was dead. God, it had been so stupid to go out
there with the gun and start shooting, what the hell had he
been thinking? But that was just the way her dad was – when
he made his mind up to do something he got totally possessed.

Hiding in the closet with her mother, Marissa had started to
scream, but her mom put a hand over her mouth, shutting her
up, and said, 'Shh.'

She could tell how angry her mother was about the gun, too.
It had all happened so fast, there was nothing either of them
could do to stop him.

The gunfire ended very quickly – it seemed to last for only a
few seconds – and the house was silent.

Her mom said, 'Wait here,' and went to see what was going
on. Marissa, afraid her mother would get shot, too, went to try
to stop her, but then they saw her dad standing there at the
top of the landing, holding the gun. He looked so terrified and
panicked, and then he lost it and shouted for her and her mom
to get back to the bedroom.

A few minutes later, he joined them.

'Did you kill him?' her mom asked.

'Yes,' her dad said.

'Is he dead?'

Her dad swallowed, clearing his throat, then said, 'Yes, he's dead.'

When the police arrived, her dad went down to talk to them and explain what had happened. Then they heard more sirens, and more cops arrived. Marissa and her mom stayed upstairs for a while longer, talking to some cop who grossed her out the way he kept smiling at her and checking out her boobs; then they took the back staircase downstairs. On her way past the main staircase, Marissa took a peek over her shoulder, looking down toward the bottom of the stairwell, and saw the blood and one of the guy's legs – his jeans and a black high-top sneaker. God, this was so fucked up.

Downstairs, a cop took Marissa and her mom into the living room and asked them questions. Her mom was much more together than she was, or at least she seemed more together. She was able to describe everything that had happened, but when Marissa spoke it was hard to keep her thoughts organized, and she thought she sounded scattered.

After what seemed like forever her dad came into the living room and said, 'How're you guys doing? You two okay?'

She could tell he was trying to put up a front. He was trying to take charge, be Mr Strong, Mr In Control, but he had never been as in touch with his emotions as he thought he was. Just because he was a shrink didn't mean that he wasn't as screwed up as the rest of the world. She could tell that inside he was terrified, a total mess. She felt sorry for him, but she also knew that he'd gotten himself into this situation. No one had made him get that gun. No one had made him pull the trigger.

'A detective just got here,' her dad said. 'He's gonna want to ask us some questions.' He sounded removed, deadpan.

'Are you okay?' her mom asked her dad. She was obviously furious but trying to restrain herself.

'I'll be fine, don't worry about me,' her dad said. Then, without emotion, he added, 'So they didn't find a gun.'

Now her mom was raging, seething. Her dad seemed oblivious, but how could he be? It was so obvious.

'Are they sure?' she asked.

'Yeah,' her dad said, 'but it's not my fault. I saw him reach for something. What was I supposed to do?'

She could tell he wanted reassurance, but there was no way he was going to get it from her mom.

'I have to sit down,' her mom said.

A few minutes later, when her dad left the room to talk with the detective who'd just arrived, her mom said to her, 'What the fucking hell was he thinking?'

It wasn't like her mom to curse. It was kind of scary actually.

'I know, right?' Marissa said. 'When he got the gun I couldn't believe it. I was, like, what the hell're you doing?'

'I'm so angry right now I just want to… I just want to strangle him.'

Her mom's face was red. Marissa couldn't remember the last time she'd seen her mom so angry. Maybe she never had.

Although Marissa was pretty angry at her dad herself, she felt like she had to take on the role of calming her mom down and said, 'I guess he was just doing what he thought he had to do.'

'He thought he had to go shoot someone?' her mom said. 'Come on, give me a break, okay? I was on the phone with nine-one-one, how long did it take the police to get here, five minutes? We could've locked ourselves in the bedroom, hidden in the closet. He didn't have to take the gun out, and he sure as hell didn't have to shoot somebody.'

'Maybe it was like he said, he thought he was defending himself.'

'I don't care what he *thought*,' her mom said. 'How many times did I tell him to get rid of that stupid gun? Just a few weeks ago I told him I didn't feel comfortable with it in the house, and he hit me with his usual' – she tried to imitate Adam, making her voice deeper – '*It's just for protection. I'll never actually use it.*' Then in her normal voice she said, 'I knew something like this was going to happen, it was just a matter of time.'

Detective Clements came into the living room to talk with

Marissa and Dana. They pretty much told him what they'd told the first cop, Dana doing most of the talking. Then Clements and Marissa's dad went back into the dining room for another round of questioning. Sharon Wasserman and Jennifer Berg had come over. Marissa was best friends with Sharon's daughter, Hillary, who had graduated from Northwestern last year and was now living in the city. Jennifer's son, Josh, was going to GW Law School and in seventh grade had been Marissa's first boyfriend.

After what seemed like at least an hour, Clements and Marissa's dad returned, and Clements said he wanted to talk to Marissa, alone this time. Marissa was exhausted and just wanted to get into bed and crash, and she didn't see why she had to answer the same questions all over again.

She went back into the dining room with Clements and sat across from him at the table.

'I know it's late,' Clements said, 'but there are a few more things I need to run by you.'

'Okay,' Marissa said, crossing her arms tightly in front of her chest.

'Your friends,' he said, 'any of them have a criminal background?'

'No.'

'I'm not necessarily talking about jail time. I'm talking about anyone who might've stolen something in the past, or talked about wanting to steal something, or –'

'If you think one of my friends broke into our house with that guy, you're crazy.'

'What about drug users? Any of your friends do drugs?'

Of course her friends did drugs. Well, some of her friends. She was twenty-two years old, for God's sake – but what was she supposed to do, rat out her friends to some cop?

'No,' she said.

He seemed incredulous. 'Sorry,' he said, 'but you're gonna have to answer these questions honestly.'

Thinking, *Yeah, right, I'm not under oath*, she asked, 'What do my friends have to do with our house getting robbed?'

'Where do you get your pot, Marissa?'

Now, not only was she upset, but she was starting to get seriously scared. She had a bong in her room and a dime bag of pot in the back of her underwear drawer. She didn't know if Clements had been up to her room yet, but he probably had. Still, she wasn't dumb enough to admit drug use to a police detective.

'What're you talking about?' she asked.

'I was in your room,' he said.

Her heart was beating so fast and so hard, she felt like it was making her rock back and forth.

'Look, I'm telling you,' she said, 'none of my friends had anything to do with this, that's crazy.'

'I'll ask you one last time. Where do you get your drugs?'

She wanted to cry, but she wouldn't let herself. 'I don't do *drugs*,' she said.

'I saw the bong in your –'

'A friend left it here, okay? I'm just watching it for her.'

'Watching it, huh?' He smirked.

She was a shitty liar and knew she couldn't keep this going, so she said, 'It's mine, okay? What're you gonna do, arrest me for having a bong?'

'Possession of marijuana *is* illegal.'

'It's not mine,' she said desperately.

'This is the last time I'm going to ask you,' he said. 'Where do you get your pot?'

'My friend Darren.'

'How do I get in touch with him?'

This guy was such an asshole.

'Why do you have to –'

'What's his phone number?' he asked.

Darren was a guy she'd gone to Vassar with – an on-again, off-again boyfriend – who was now back living with his parents on the Upper West Side. If he got busted, he was going to fucking kill her.

She gave Clements Darren's number and said, 'But please don't call him. I'm telling you, he has nothing to do with this.'

Clements ignored her and asked, 'Have any of your friends committed any crimes or talked about committing crimes or served any time for a crime?'

Immediately she thought of Darren, who'd once spent a night in jail in Poughkeepsie when he'd gotten pulled over and the cops had found a joint in his car, but how much trouble was she going to get the poor guy into?

'No,' Marissa said. 'No one.'

'I know we've been through this already, but did you ever meet Carlos Sanchez?'

'Never.'

'How do you know?'

'Because I just know, that's why.'

He put a small plastic bag on the table with a driver's license inside it. 'Look familiar?' he asked.

She glanced at the picture – scruffy guy, kind of ugly, with cold, detached eyes. She'd never seen him before in her life.

'No, never,' she said.

Clements didn't seem satisfied. He asked, 'Ever lend anyone a key to the house or –'

'No, I've never lent anyone a key, ever.'

'Are you telling me the truth?'

'What do you think, I gave somebody a key and said come rob my house?'

'Is that what happened?'

'No, of course not.'

She couldn't believe this.

Then Clements stood and said, 'Okay, you're gonna have to come with me now.'

'Come with you where?'

'Out to the staircase for a second. I want you to take a look at Sanchez.'

Suddenly she felt sick. 'You mean look at his body?'

'The driver's license photo was several years old,' Clements said, 'he'd gained a lot of weight. I want you to see if you recognize him.'

'Do I have to?'

'Yes, you have to.'

Although she'd never seen a dead body before – well, except at a few funerals she'd been to – she just wanted to get to sleep and didn't really care one way or the other.

She went with Clements out to the foyer. The body was still at the bottom of the staircase, splayed the way it had been before, except now Marissa could see all of it. There were technicians working near the body, maybe collecting DNA evidence or looking for fingerprints or whatever, and there was blood – it looked purple – on the bottom stairs and on the floor in front of the staircase. There was much more blood than Marissa had expected to see, which made her queasy enough, but then as she got closer, she looked at the dead guy's face. His eyes were half-open, and there was blood leaking out of his nose. Something looked weird about his mouth, and then she realized that most of his jaw was missing.

'Oh my God,' she said.

Misunderstanding her response, Clements said, 'You recognize him?'

Starting to back away, she said, 'No, I have no idea who he is. Can I go now? Can I just go?'

When she returned to the living room, Clements wanted to talk to her mom, so she and her dad were left alone.

First he hugged her and assured her things would return to normal soon – *yeah, right* – then he asked, 'So how'd it go in there?'

She didn't answer right away, then said, 'He made me look at the body.'

'What?' She could tell he was seriously upset. 'Why the hell did he do that?' She didn't feel like talking to him about it. Things had been tense and awkward between them, well, for years, but since she'd graduated from college their relationship had become even more strained, what with him constantly on her case about getting a job and moving out on her own. Her plan had been to live at home temporarily, until she could support herself, so she'd gotten a part-time job at the Metropolitan Museum of Art through a contact from an art history professor. But she didn't like her boss, and the job had had practically nothing to do with art – her main duty had been renting out tour headphones – and after about a month she couldn't take it anymore and quit. She'd been sending out résumés and going on interviews, but her father wouldn't let up about the 'big opportunity' she'd blown, and it was hard to even be in the same room with him sometimes.

'He wanted to see if I recognized him,' she said. 'Whatever.' She was exhausted and really didn't feel like talking anymore.

But her dad couldn't let it go and said, 'This is getting ridiculous now. There's no way he should've made you do that, I mean what's the point of that?' He shook his head, brooding, then asked, 'Did he ask you about your bong, too?'

God, Marissa didn't want to be having this conversation right now, especially not in the middle of the night when she was so exhausted.

'Yeah,' she said, 'but it was no big deal.'

'How many times have I told you to get rid of that thing?'

'You've never told me to get rid of it.'

'I told you I don't want you smoking in the house.'

'I think I've smoked in the house twice since graduation, but if it bothers you so much I'll stop.'

'And I don't want you drinking in the house anymore either.'

'When do I drink in the house?'

'The other night – when you had Hillary and that guy over.'

'That *guy* was Hillary's friend Jared, who's in med school, and we were drinking wine. I think we had one glass each.'

'Well, I don't want any drinking in the house anymore. Is that understood?'

'This is ridiculous,' Marissa said. 'I didn't do anything wrong. You're just taking everything out on me.'

'Excuse me?' he said, raising his voice slightly.

'Like this has anything to do with my bong or drinking wine. This has to do with you and your gun.'

Her father looked at her the way he had so many times lately, like he hated her.

'Just go to bed,' he said.

'See?' she said. 'I didn't do anything wrong and you treat me like I'm ten years old.'

'When you act out like you're ten I'll treat you like you're ten. Just go to bed.'

Realizing there was no point in arguing with her father when he got like this, she left the room. There were still a lot of cops near the front of the house, though it looked like they'd finally removed the body. Avoiding the commotion and, worse, another confrontation with that asshole Clements, she took the back staircase up to her room.

Lying in bed, trying to fall asleep, she suddenly remembered she'd given Detective Clements Darren's contact info. She called Darren, leaving a frantic message, telling him that the cops had found pot in her room and he had to get all the drugs out of his apartment ASAP.

Back in bed, she put in her iPod earbuds and listened to tracks by Tone Def, this new alternative/punk/postgrunge band she was into. She was still angry at her father for laying into her, and she just prayed that somehow all of this would blow over quickly. Living at home had been difficult enough lately; she couldn't handle it if things got any worse.

4

WHEN ADAM WOKE up he felt much better. He'd gotten
several hours of solid sleep, and it was a bright, sunny
day; bars of sunlight were coming through the venetian blinds,
spreading into the room. He glanced at the clock – 9:27. He'd
decided to cancel his patient appointments for today, but he felt
well enough to work and planned to have a few phone sessions.

He didn't think about the shooting at all until he went
downstairs, passing the spot on the staircase where the body
had fallen. He didn't look very closely, but it seemed like the
police technicians or ambulance workers or whoever had done
an excellent job cleaning up all the blood and even repairing
some of the wall damage. It was almost like it hadn't even
happened.

Dana wasn't in the kitchen, but there was evidence that she'd
been there: a coffee mug in the sink; some crumbs – probably
from a bagel – on the countertop; the *Times*, folded open to the
crossword puzzle, on the kitchen table. There was no sign that
Marissa had been downstairs yet, not that he expected there
to be. On most days she slept until at least eleven o'clock,
sometimes past noon. Today she'd probably sleep till one or two.

He poured his own cup of coffee, then opened the newspaper. Although he'd spoken to a *Times* reporter at some point last night, as well as to reporters from the *News* and the *Post*, he knew the story about the robbery and shooting couldn't have made it into today's papers. But it would be in all of the major papers tomorrow for sure.

He skimmed the front page, reading about the latest bombings in Israel and Iraq, then went right to the sports section. The Jets were playing the Patriots on Sunday and he read about the game. After finishing his coffee and skimming an article in the *Times* on a promising new drug to treat schizophrenia, he went online with his BlackBerry and emailed a patient, Jane Heller, asking her if she wanted to have a phone session this afternoon at four. He also emailed Carol, his colleague, to see if she had time for a session sometime this week.

He didn't hear any fuss outside and wondered if there were still neighbors in front of the house. He went into the living room and parted the shades. A Fox News truck was parked across the street, but that was it.

As he headed upstairs to shower and get dressed, once again he had to pass the spot where the body had been. What had Clements said his name was, Sanchez? Yeah, Sanchez, Carlos Sanchez. Adam stared at the spot for a while, feeling remorseful until he reminded himself that it was Sanchez who'd made the decision that had led to his death, not Adam. If he'd killed someone for no reason, *murdered* someone, or even if he'd killed someone accidentally, by a mistake he'd made, he'd have something to feel guilty about. For example, if he'd killed someone in a traffic accident, he would've had to accept responsibility. But this situation had been completely different. This hadn't been an accident; this had been self-defense.

Adam went into the shower, and under the hot spray he was able to relax. He remembered the dream he'd had, about the black rat. He wondered why the dream had begun in his office. Was it really work related, or did his office symbolize a familiar place where he felt comfortable? And what was the significance of the black rat beginning as Jodi Roth or Kathy Stappini? The rat was threatening, but Jodi and Kathy were hardly threatening.

He thought it might have to do with the therapist-patient relationship in general. As a therapist he was in a position of control, but then he lost control when he was attacked by the rat. So perhaps the dream was about losing control or, more specifically, being attacked. When had he ever felt attacked? He thought of his overbearing mother, his distant father, the bullies who'd tormented him throughout elementary school and junior high, and how in his marriage he sometimes felt attacked by Dana. Maybe the rat was actually Dana, symbolically attacking him, smothering him.

He made a mental note to bring all this up in his session with Carol.

When he came out of the shower, wrapped in a towel, Dana was in the bedroom, fully dressed in jeans and a long-sleeved black scoop-neck top. She was looking for something in the top drawer of the dresser.

'Good morning,' he said.

She waited a couple of beats, then said, 'Good morning,' and he could tell she was still angry about the gun. He always knew when she was angry and exactly what she was angry about, though she rarely expressed her anger in an appropriate, productive way.

But he didn't feel like getting into a big discussion with her about her anger so he said, 'Looks like they're pretty much gone, huh?'

'I talked to a couple of reporters this morning,' Dana said. Her voice was a monotone; she was definitely repressing rage.

'Yeah?' Adam asked. 'From where?'

'I don't know.' She was still searching in the drawer. 'TV, newspapers, wherever.'

Adam tossed the towel into the hamper and was naked. He caught a glimpse of himself in the mirror and, as usual, sucked in his gut a little. He wasn't in such bad shape for his age – only about ten, okay, fifteen pounds overweight – but he was self-conscious about the flab in his midsection. He really had to start running again, get a regular tennis game going at the country club. He played golf frequently, but riding around in a golf cart wasn't doing much for his waistline. He had to do more crunches, get serious about it. In three years he'd turn fifty, and he wanted to be thin in his fifties.

'Well, it seems to be blowing over,' he said distractedly.

She closed the drawer, then turned toward Adam – still avoiding eye contact – and said, 'It's not here.'

Adam was no longer looking in the mirror, but he was still distracted. 'What's not?'

'The paper I wrote the code to the alarm on.'

Now she had Adam's full attention, and he looked at her and asked, 'What're you talking about?'

'This morning when I woke up I remembered I had the number, the code, whatever, written down on a little piece of paper. Remember, I wrote it down when we first got the alarm because you had the code on that card they gave you, but I didn't know it?'

'Okay,' Adam said. Actually, he didn't remember any of this; he was just egging her on.

'So I thought I put it in the drawer in the bureau in the den, you know, where we keep the old bills, but I checked this morning, and it wasn't there. And now I've checked all over and I can't find it anywhere.'

'Maybe you threw it out.'

'Maybe, but I really thought it was in the drawer downstairs.'

Dana, unlike Adam, was a very organized person and usually didn't misplace things.

'Did you check thoroughly?'

'Of course I checked thoroughly, but it wasn't there.'

'Okay, calm down.'

'I am calm,' she said, but she obviously wasn't. She was making eye contact with him for the first time this morning, glaring at him in a very cold, very distant way.

'So where else can it be?' Adam asked.

'Well, obviously, I thought it was in the drawer up here.'

'Did you check the kitchen?'

'I definitely didn't put it in the kitchen.'

'What about under the drawer in the bureau? Sometimes things spill out over the top and fall through the –'

'I already checked and it wasn't there. Should I call Detective Clements and tell him?'

'I think that's a little ridiculous.'

'Why is it ridiculous? He thinks somebody had the code to the alarm and a piece of paper with the code's missing.'

'Okay, fine,' Adam conceded. 'If you want to call him, call him. It doesn't really matter one way or another, but I'd just look around once more before you waste his time, that's all.'

Adam was pulling on his jeans; his damn back was bothering him again. He wasn't facing Dana, but he could tell she was still in the room. She was probably looking at him angrily with her hands crossed in front of her chest. He turned around for a moment just to see if he was right. Yep, he was.

'So have you talked to Marissa yet today?' she asked.

'I don't think she's up yet. Guess she didn't have any job interviews this morning,' Adam said, smirking.

'So do you really think one of her friends could've been involved?'

'That's ridiculous,' Adam said.

'I think so, too,' Dana said, 'but the detective kept asking about it. I don't think he'd be asking if he didn't think there was some possibility that –'

'Come on,' Alan said, 'the guy's name was Carlos Sanchez. I've never heard her talk about any Carlos Sanchezes, have you? Besides, he was an older guy. No, it definitely has nothing to do with her.'

'Maybe he was her drug dealer or something,' Dana said.

'Oh, come on, I really doubt that.'

'Why? She's smoked pot in her room, and the pot has to be coming from somewhere.'

Adam considered this as he opened the drawer to his dresser, looking through a stack of folded shirts. It wasn't totally beyond the realm of possibility that the break-in had something to do with Marissa. She'd had friends coming and going in the house since graduation, and occasionally Adam had seen her with people he'd never met before. One guy last week had looked pretty shady – long hair, tattoos up and down his arms. If it didn't have to do with drugs, it could've had something to do with some guy she was dating.

'Last night I told her I don't want her drinking and smoking in the house anymore,' Adam said. 'If this had anything to do with her or not, I think we have to make it clear, if there're any drugs in this house, she has to move out. That's it, no bending, no negotiations.'

'And don't you think that's just a teensy bit hypocritical?'

They'd had this discussion before, so Adam knew exactly what she was implying: how could he tell his twenty-two-year-old daughter not to smoke pot in the house and have guys up to her room when as a teenager he'd gotten high and had sex with all his girlfriends in this very house, starting when he was sixteen years old?

'That was the seventies,' he said. 'It was a different time.'

He was going to add, *We know more now than we knew then,* but he already felt like he was beating the clichés to death.

'If she was your son I don't think you'd have a problem with it.'

'That's not true,' Adam said. He pulled on a navy long-sleeved shirt with a Fresh Meadow Country Club logo, remembering that he had a 7:24 tee-off time on Sunday with his friend Jeff. 'I wouldn't want my son to make the same mistakes I made.'

'Well, I still think there's a double standard going on here,' Dana said.

Adam recognized that tone in her voice again. He knew that she wasn't upset about what she pretended she was upset about. She was just looking for the right opening, dying to blame him for the shooting.

'Didn't you want to call Clements?' he said, not exactly dismissing her, but the implication was there. Now fully dressed except for shoes and socks, he picked up his BlackBerry and checked his email. He'd gotten two new emails – one from Carol suggesting Friday at four for a session, and one from his assistant, Lauren, saying that Jane Heller could do the phone session at three today, not four.

Dana, still standing there with her arms crossed, asked, 'Aren't you worried?'

'Worried about?' Adam asked. Darn it, Lauren had also

written that his session with Dave Kellerman couldn't be rescheduled. Dave was a newish patient who was just starting to make substantive progress, and Adam hated to have two weeks between sessions.

'The other guy, or person, whatever,' Dana said. 'The one who got away.'

'Why would I be worried about him?'

He started typing a message: *Hi Lauren, Please tell Kellerman I'll call him personally to try to sched* – then he stopped punching the keypad when he heard Dana say, 'Can you pay attention to me instead of that stupid thing for one second?'

'This is important,' Adam said.

'And what happened last night isn't?'

Adam rolled his eyes, then said, 'What is it?'

'You shot somebody, and his accomplice, partner, whatever you want to call it, obviously knows where we live,' Dana said. 'I find that very disturbing.'

Adam stared at her for a moment. She wasn't exactly blaming him for the shooting yet, but she was oh so close.

'Don't worry about it,' Adam said.

'How can you say that? How do you –'

'Because the cops know the dead guy's name. These criminals, they're always repeat offenders. They're probably wanted for robberies all over the neighborhood. They probably made a list of whatchamacallits – known associates. It's just a matter of going through the list and arresting the guy. If they didn't arrest him already, it's only a matter of time before they do.'

'I didn't hear Clements mention anything about known associates,' Dana said. 'He made it seem like they had no suspects at all.'

'That's just the way cops are,' Adam said semi-distractedly as he typed: *ule. I'll try him later today, if I can get hold of him at work.*

Dana said, 'I hope you're right, but I didn't get that vibe. I think if he had any suspects he would've – can you please listen to me for God's sake?'

'I'm sorry,' Adam said, still looking at his phone. 'I have important stuff to take care of.'

'I don't get it,' she said. 'Why do you even care about work right now?'

'What am I supposed to do? Not go on with my life?'

'You act like... I don't know... like you don't care. I mean, I'm telling you I'm worried. I'm afraid he's going to come back tonight and –'

'He's not coming back.'

'How do you know?'

'Because why would he? That's a surefire way to get caught, rob the place you already robbed.'

'Yeah, and what makes you think the guy's a freaking Rhodes scholar? We're talking about a criminal here, for God's sake. He's not necessarily thinking logically.'

Adam considered this, then said, 'Even if he does come back, he's not getting in. We're changing the locks in an hour, the alarm guy's coming down later to change the code. There's no way anybody's getting into this house again.'

'You don't know th – and can you stop staring at that thing?' she nearly screamed. 'It's so goddamn rude.'

Now he looked at her and said, 'What? What do you want me to do?'

'I'm scared,' she said. 'I don't think it's enough.'

'It's a state-of-the-art alarm system.'

'That didn't help us last night.'

'Okay, I have an idea, let's get a watchdog.'

He was saying this facetiously. She was allergic to dogs, and he knew she had no intention of taking immunotherapy shots for the rest of her life.

'Maybe we should move,' she said.

'What?' He couldn't believe she was even suggesting this. She knew how much he loved the house, how much it meant to him.

'The house is worth a lot now,' she said. 'Marissa's out of school, will be on her own eventually, and I've been wanting to move anyway. We could move someplace small, a condo maybe in the city or –'

'You're out of your mind,' Adam said.

'Why does wanting to move mean I'm out of my mind?'

'Because our house was robbed,' he said, 'it's not like it's been contaminated with nuclear waste. How many other houses in the neighborhood have been robbed over the past couple of years? Did everybody else just pack up and move?'

'Everybody else didn't kill one of the robbers.'

Adam glared at her hard and said, 'Okay, here we go, finally, I knew this was coming. I'd appreciate it if you stopped it with your passive-aggressiveness and evasiveness. If you have something to say, please just come out and say it.'

'You know exactly what I want to say.'

'Then what're you waiting for? Come on, let's go, I want to hear it.'

Her lips moved and her mouth started to open a few times, as if she were about to speak, but she kept catching herself. Then she finally let out a deep breath and said, 'This is ridiculous,' and marched out of the room melodramatically.

'Brilliant,' Adam said, and he picked up a pillow off the settee and flung it across the room. Then his BlackBerry started ringing and he saw LAUREN on the caller ID. Snapping into his upbeat work persona, he said, 'Hey, Lauren, what a coincidence, I was just about to shoot you off an email.'

5

From the very beginning, the Blooms had been very good to Gabriela. Twelve years ago, when she came to New York from Ecuador, she was just nineteen and very shy, and she spoke only a few words of English, and she didn't think she'd ever find a good job in America. But the Blooms hired her because Gabriela's sister, Beatrice, who was working for another family in Forest Hills Gardens, told them that Gabriela was a good maid and asked them to please give her a chance. Gabriela was very grateful to the Blooms for giving her a good job when no one else would, and she always told them how she hoped to repay them someday.

Although Gabriela had worked as a maid for two years at home in Quito, she'd never had to clean a house the size of the Blooms'. The first day she felt like such a fool; she didn't even know how to turn on the vacuum cleaner. Some families might've lost patience and fired her right away, but the Blooms were very kind and understanding. The first few days, Mrs Bloom cleaned the whole house with her, explaining how everything was done and where everything went, and she didn't lose patience at all even though Gabriela couldn't understand most of what she was saying.

When Gabriela started to work for the Blooms, Marissa was just ten years old, in fourth grade. Marissa had a babysitter who still took care of her part of the time, but sometimes when the babysitter was sick Mrs Bloom would ask Gabriela to go pick Marissa up from school or take her to play with her friends. Gabriela liked Marissa, she was such a sweet little girl, and she liked Mr Bloom, too. Sometimes he sat down with her in the kitchen and helped her with her English, teaching her new words. He was a very good man who worked hard and who loved his family very much. She hoped that someday she could find a man for herself like Mr Bloom and have a family as nice as his.

Her first few months in New York, Gabriela was living with Beatrice and her family in Jackson Heights, Queens, sharing a room with Beatrice's daughter. But then at a party one night she met a Mexican man named Angel. He was very handsome and a very hard worker. He was a waiter at a diner in Manhattan, but he had big dreams. He wanted to open his own restaurant one day. He took her dancing in the Village a few times, and he knew how to do the mambo. They started doing everything together – going out all the time, going to Jones Beach, or just staying home at his apartment – and that summer he got her pregnant. He didn't want to get married, which was okay with her. He was young, just twenty, and she knew how scared young guys got. She thought she'd have the baby and then in a couple of years they'd get married.

But when Gabriela was getting ready to have her baby, Angel disappeared. At first she thought something bad happened to him; maybe he got hurt or something. The people at the diner said they didn't know where he was, he just stopped coming to work. She got Beatrice's husband, Manny, to go looking for him, but he couldn't find him anywhere, and then she called the police. They said that chances were he probably just ran away. She couldn't believe that Angel would do something like that, but then, a few days before she had to go to the hospital, Manny found out from one of Angel's friends that Angel was living in the Bronx with a new girlfriend.

Gabriela had her baby, a beautiful girl, Manuela, named

after Gabriela's grandmother. She was worried that it would be hard to work and take care of her baby at the same time, but the Blooms were so nice, letting her take Manuela to work with her every day. The Blooms got her more work with other families in the neighborhood, and pretty soon she was working five days a week, making enough money to move into her own apartment in Jackson Heights. For the next few years, Gabriela was working hard, making money, but it was hard not having a man in her life and a father for Manuela.

When Manuela was about five years old, Gabriela met Juan. He was forty-two, his wife had died of cancer, and he had two boys. He wasn't very handsome – he was fat and had a big crooked nose – but he was a very good man and he loved Gabriela and always bought her flowers and told her how beautiful she was. When he asked her to marry him, she said yes.

Everything seemed so happy; she finally had a good man to take care of her and her daughter. Then, one morning, she was working at the Blooms' when she got a phone call from her sister. Beatrice was screaming hysterically, 'Dios mio, Dios mio, Dios mio!' and then she told Gabriela that a taxi had hit Juan while he was crossing a street in Manhattan. Mrs Bloom took Gabriela to the hospital, but when they got there Juan was already dead.

Gabriela knew that Juan had been her true love and that she would never find such a good man ever again. She was sad for a long time, and even though the doctors gave her medicine to make her mind feel better, it was still hard to get out of bed. She used to laugh and smile all the time, and people had always told her how funny she was, but after what had happened to Juan it seemed like there was nothing to laugh about anymore. Some days she didn't feel like going to her job, so she just didn't go. Many families would've fired her, but the Blooms were very kind. They sent her flowers and called her every day to check on her and tried to get her to talk to the doctors and take her medicine.

About a month after Juan was killed, Gabriela was finally able to get out of bed and go to work every day again, but she didn't feel the same and she didn't take care of herself the way she used to. She didn't care how she dressed or how her hair looked, and she stopped putting on makeup and she got very fat. If she wasn't so sad and so lonely and feeling so bad about herself all the time, she probably would never have wanted to be with a man like Carlos.

She met Carlos on the subway. He was sitting next to her and he asked her if she wanted a piece of gum. She said no thank you, and then he said, 'Then how 'bout we go to dinner instead?' She didn't think he was very handsome, but at least he made her smile, so she gave him her phone number.

The next night he took her to a very nice Chinese restaurant, and during the meal he held her hand and told her how pretty and sexy she looked. They went out a few more times, and then she went back to his apartment. In bed he asked her to do coke with him. She'd never done any drugs before, but she was a little drunk so she decided to try it. It made her feel good and – for a little while at least – like she didn't have any problems at all.

She started going out with Carlos a few nights a week. He didn't have a job, and she knew he was probably some kind of criminal, but she didn't want to ask where all his money was coming from. She was just happy to not be alone anymore and she liked how Carlos bought her presents all the time – jewelry, clothes – and she liked having a man in her life again. They did coke sometimes, and then one night he asked her if she wanted to try heroin. She'd seen the marks on his arms and legs, so she knew he liked to shoot up, but she was afraid of the needle. But he kept asking her, saying, 'You got no idea how good this shit feels, it's gonna blow you away.' So she tried it one time, just to see what it felt like, and after a couple of weeks she got hooked.

Everything was good for a while. She was seeing Carlos all the time and getting high a lot and forgetting about all of the tragedy in her life. But then she started seeing Carlos's bad side. It was like she was sleeping the whole time she knew him and then woke up and saw who he really was. It started that night they were fighting about something when they were getting high and he suddenly hit her hard in the face. No man had ever hit her before, and she couldn't believe that this was happening to her. She couldn't tell anybody about it, feeling too much shame, and she was also afraid it would only make Carlos hit her even harder next time. Instead she made up a story that Manuela had swung the bathroom door into her face. She just couldn't leave Carlos, even though she wanted to, because she needed the drugs so bad. He started yelling at her and beating her and one night broke her arm. She had to make up another story to tell the Blooms and the other people she worked for, saying she fell on the street, but she knew she couldn't keep making up lies forever. She also knew she had to get away from Carlos, but she couldn't leave him no matter how hard she tried.

Then she got sick with a high fever and a bad rash all over her back and chest. She knew what was wrong with her, but she didn't want to believe it. She went to church and begged God not to let this happen to her. She screamed, 'I don't deserve this, God! I don't deserve it!' Then she went to a clinic, and they told her she had HIV. She was crying for days and couldn't get out of bed. She was afraid of getting sick and dying, but she was also angry at herself for being so stupid, for believing that Carlos was clean. When she told Carlos she was sick, he still wouldn't tell her the truth, saying he wasn't sick and she must've caught the HIV from some other man. Then he beat her again, and she screamed at him to go away and stay out of her life forever.

Gabriella knew she had done such a bad thing to her daughter, ruining her life, too, and she felt like she wanted to kill herself. She almost did it one night. She had the bottle of pills, and she wrote a letter telling Manuela how sorry she was and asking Beatrice and Manny to please raise her daughter good. She put the pills in her mouth and was about to swallow them when she decided that she couldn't do this to her daughter, that killing herself now would be even worse.

She was still young and healthy, and maybe if she took her medicine she'd live for a very long time.

The next day she went to the police and told them how Carlos was beating her, and the judge gave her a restraining order so Carlos couldn't come close to her or her daughter ever again. Then she sent Manuela to stay with Beatrice and she went away to a center on Long Island to get clean. It was very hard at first, but she listened to what they said and she got off the drugs for good. She went back to her life of working hard every day and helping Manuela with her homework and decided this was how she was going to live the rest of her life – being the best mother she could be.

She kept her HIV a secret from everybody, even her daughter. She didn't want her daughter to think her mother wasn't strong, that she wouldn't be there for her someday, and she was worried that if people she worked for found out she was sick they would be afraid and want to fire her. She was good at hiding it from people, even her own family, but it got hard sometimes, like when Beatrice would say to her, 'What's wrong with you, Gabriela? Why do you stay home alone every night? Don't you want to find a man?' Gabriela would say that she didn't want a man in her life right now, that she just wanted to be alone with her daughter and be happy.

But sometimes it was very hard to be alone and she called Carlos and told him to come over. They were both sick, and even though she hated him for getting her sick and hitting her so much, she felt like he was the only man she could ever have. But then he'd start treating her bad and hitting her, and even hitting Manuela a few times, and she'd tell him to get out of her life for good or she was going to call the police. She'd stay away from him for another year or two, until she'd start to feel lonely and scared again and forget how bad he'd made her feel and how much he'd hurt her, and she'd call him up and start the whole thing all over again.

Gabriela was thirty-one years old. She knew her life would never change, that she would never be happy all the time, but her doctors told her her HIV was doing okay and she would live for many, many years. Manuela was eleven years old, in sixth grade, and was turning into such a beautiful young lady. Gabriela taught her daughter to stay away from drugs and the bad boys and to wait to meet somebody someday who would treat her good, the way she deserved to be treated. Gabriela just wanted her daughter to have a good, happy life; it was the only thing she cared about.

Then one day Gabriela was riding the bus home from work

when Beatrice called her and was screaming and crying. It reminded Gabriela of that terrible day Juan had died, and she was afraid something bad had happened to Manuela.

'No mi hija!' Gabriela screamed. 'No mi hija! No mi hija!' Gabriela screamed so loud that everybody was looking over, and the driver even stopped the bus.

Thank God, Beatrice wasn't calling about Manuela, but it was still very bad. It was their father in Quito. He was very sick and needed a new kidney or he was going to die, but the doctors said he was too sick to get a new kidney from the hospital, so the only way was if they bought one on the black market.

Crying, Gabriella asked, 'How much do they need?'

'Twelve thousand dollars,' Beatrice said. 'That's crazy money. What're we gonna do?'

Gabriela didn't have money to send to him. The money she made from cleaning houses was just enough to pay for rent and bills and food. Sometimes she didn't even have money to buy new clothes for Manuela.

'How much money you have?' Gabriela asked.

'We only have two thousand in the bank,' Beatrice said, 'and we need it for rent and bills.'

Gabriela had no idea what to do. Twelve thousand dollars was more money than she'd ever seen.

When she got back to her apartment, she called home and it was sad to hear her mother crying and her father sounding so sad, and she felt so bad, knowing there was nothing anybody could do to help him. They just had to let him die.

'How much time does *papi* have?' Gabriela asked her mother.

'If they don't do nothing, maybe a month or two,' she said. 'They don't know.' Gabriela spent most of the next few days crying. She and Beatrice were planning to go to Ecuador, to be with their father for the last time. They wanted their whole families to go, but they didn't have the money for the plane tickets.

Everything seemed so bad, and she didn't know what to do, and then she was cleaning the Blooms' house one morning when she saw a little piece of paper in a drawer in the dining room. The paper had some numbers on it, and on top she saw the words CODE NEW ALARM.

Mrs Bloom was home, right upstairs, and Gabriela heard footsteps in the hallway. Gabriela didn't even think about it and put the paper in the pocket of her apron.

Later, at home, she felt bad. She didn't even know why she took the paper, because the Blooms had been so good to her and there was no way she could ever steal from them.

Then, in the middle of the night, she woke up and thought: What if she gave Carlos the code? She didn't ask about where he got his money, but she knew he probably knew how to rob places. And if he stole from them it would be different than if she stole from them. She didn't want to do something bad to the Blooms, but she didn't want her *papi* to die, either, and she didn't know what else to do.

She called Carlos and told him to come over.

After she told him about the code, he said, 'You got the key to the house?' Gabriela hadn't even thought about this. She was so worried about her *papi* and getting money that she hadn't thought about anything else.

'No, but I can get it,' she said.

The next day, at the Blooms', when she went out to get lunch, she took the keys from the drawer in the kitchen and went to a locksmith. She found out she couldn't copy the keys to the front door because they were some kind of special locks they couldn't copy without some kind of card.

She thought that was it, her *papi* would die, but then the locksmith told her she could copy the keys to the back door. This was okay, maybe even better, because it was darker in the back of the house and nobody would be watching.

Everything was looking good, but not for long. When she got back to the Blooms' she remembered that Carlos still had the paper with the code on it. She'd been so busy talking to Carlos and thinking about the keys that she forgot to ask for the paper back.

When Mrs Bloom went out to do something, Gabriela called Carlos and asked him to bring the paper to her apartment later on.

'Too late,' Carlos said. 'Threw it out.'

'Why'd you do that?' Gabriela said. 'I have to put it back in the drawer.' Again Gabriela felt like the whole plan wouldn't work. They wouldn't be able to rob the house, and her *papi* would die.

'I thought the paper was yours,' Carlos said. 'I thought you copied the shit down. I thought that's why you gave it to me.'

Gabriela, starting to cry, said, 'Why'd you have to throw it away, Carlos? Why'd you have to do that?'

'I didn't wanna be walking around with the code to the alarm of the house I'm gonna rob in my pocket. So I just memorized it, got it all up here now.'

'Where'd you throw it out?' Gabriela said. 'Maybe it's still there.'

'I don't remember,' he said, 'near the subway or whatever. Garbage man probably picked it up already.'

'That's it,' Gabriela said, crying. 'We're going to have to forget the whole thing now.'

Carlos laughed and said, 'Damn, you gotta stop all your worrying 'bout everything and shit. Let me do all the worrying, all right, baby?'

'But if they see the paper is gone they'll know I took it.'

'Why they gonna know that? Use your head, baby. You know how many people they probably got coming into their house? Big house like that, they probably got people coming and going all day.'

This was true, Gabriela thought. Men were painting the downstairs bathroom and were in the house all day long, and sometimes the plumber and the electrician were in the house, too, and what about all of Marissa Bloom's friends? Why would the Blooms think she took the code when she'd been working for them for so many years and they had so much trust in her? Maybe not putting back the paper was even *good* because maybe they'd think for sure that some stranger must've taken it.

She didn't know if this really made sense or she just wanted it to make sense, but it made her feel better anyway.

That night she and Carlos talked about the rest of the plan. The Blooms were going to be leaving for Florida next Tuesday, all three of them, so it would be a good time to rob the house. Gabriela knew where the Blooms kept all their expensive things, their rings and jewelry. After Carlos stole everything he was going to sell it to somebody called a fence.

'Is the fence okay?' she asked.

'Hell yeah,' Carlos said. 'My man Freddy's cool, know him forever, gonna give us a good price, too. Third what the shit's worth.'

'And then you're gonna give me half the money, right?'

'Nah, we're gonna split it three ways,' Carlos said.

'Three?' Gabriela didn't know what he was talking about. 'How does it make three? Me and you's two, not three.'

'You think I'm crazy?' Carlos said. 'I ain't gonna rob the place alone. That's the way you get caught, wind up back upstate and shit. I ain't goin' in there without no backup.'

Gabriela didn't like the way this sounded at all. She'd already been feeling very bad, stealing from the Blooms who'd been so good to her. But it seemed more okay when it was just her and Carlos because she knew Carlos, and even though he'd gotten her sick, she felt like she could trust him. But she didn't like trusting some man she didn't even know.

'Who is he?' she asked.

'You don't gotta know,' he said. 'If the cops come around, it's gonna be better that way. Can't talk about what you don't know.'

She still didn't like it, but she knew nothing she said was going to change Carlos's mind.

'I don't care what you do,' she said, 'long as I get the money for my *papi*.'

On the day of the robbery, Gabriela had to go to work for the Seidlers, another family in Forest Hills. Carlos didn't want her to call him all day, or even later on. He'd said, 'Don't do nothin' stupid, just sit by the phone and wait for me to call. Cops track calls and shit. We don't want them seein' we been talking the day the house got robbed. *Comprendes?*'

Not talking seemed like the right thing to do, but it was hard, working all day long, keeping all the wondering and worrying in her head.

Later, she came home and had dinner with Manuela and called her parents at the hospital in Ecuador. Her mother said that *papi* wasn't doing very good, and then she put Gabriela on the phone with him. Gabriela could hear it in his voice, how sick he was. He just didn't sound like the *papi* she knew. She kept telling him to hold on, that she was gonna get the money for him real soon. He told her don't worry, he was gonna be fine, but she heard the lying in his voice. That's the way her *papi* was, always wanting to be strong.

Manuela spoke to him, too, and after, she was crying and said to Gabriela, 'How come you told him you were gonna get the money soon? Where you gonna get it from?'

Gabriela hugged her daughter and said, 'God is going to get us the money. You'll see.'

Around eleven Manuela was asleep and Gabriela was alone, waiting for Carlos to call, even though they weren't supposed to rob the house till the middle of the night, like two in the morning. She didn't know how long it was gonna take to rob a house, but she didn't think it would take too long. Maybe by three they'd be all done, but then how long would it be before he called her? Knowing Carlos, he'd want to do drugs after. She wished she had some heroin right now; that stuff used to keep her very calm.

She tried to watch TV, but it was too hard, so she spent the whole night just walking back and forth in her living room. She'd never seen a clock move so slow. It seemed like it took forever till midnight came, and then one and two o'clock came even slower. But finally it was time – the house was being robbed, and soon, hopefully tomorrow, she'd have her money and her *papi* would be having his operation and everything would be okay.

The only problem was she had a horrible empty feeling in her stomach, like something was gonna go wrong. She kept telling herself, *Don't think about that. That's stupid. Nothing's gonna go wrong. They're gonna get the ring and the necklace and all the jewelry and sell it, and soon you're gonna have the money for papi.* She kept telling herself this, but she didn't believe it. The bad feeling was still there; it wouldn't go away.

At three thirty, she knew it should be all over by now. They should be out of the house, back at Carlos's or wherever. Then how come he wasn't calling her? He'd said he'd go to a phone booth after the house was robbed and call her with a calling card so the police couldn't find out. Maybe he didn't have a chance to make the call yet. Maybe he was just making sure they were safe and everything was okay; *then* he'd call her.

But when four o'clock came, Gabriela didn't believe that Carlos had forgotten about anything. He and his friend were ripping her off, that's what was happening. They weren't going to split the money three ways. That had just been more of Carlos's lies. They were going to split it two ways, and one of the ways wasn't going to be hers. She didn't know how she'd been so stupid, trusting a man who'd already lied to her so badly, getting her so sick and ruining her whole life.

A few times, she was about to call him on his cell, but each time she stopped herself at the last second. She knew if he was going to steal from her, he wouldn't answer his phone when she called, and she was still hoping she was wrong, that something happened, like he didn't have a chance to get to a phone yet to call her, and everything would turn out okay.

Then, at five in the morning, she was still in the living room, waiting for the phone to ring, when Manuela came out and said, 'Mami, what's wrong?'

'I just been worried about your *abuelo*,' Gabriela said.

'I thought you said God was gonna save him?'

'I don't know anymore, baby,' Gabriela said. 'Maybe God's too busy today.' Gabriela made Manuela breakfast and lunch, then kissed her goodbye. She was so glad she had such a beautiful daughter, and she knew if it wasn't for her daughter she probably would have killed herself a long time ago.

Manuela went back to sleep, and Gabriela turned on the TV, just to keep her mind busy. She watched *Cada Día* on Telemundo for a while and then switched to an English news channel, hoping to find out something about the robbery. She didn't think there'd really be anything about it on TV, she thought she was just being crazy, so she couldn't believe it when she saw the reporter standing in front of the Blooms' house.

It was very hard to understand what was going on. Not because her English wasn't good enough – she didn't speak fluent but she could usually understand most of the news on the TV – but because she didn't believe that a house getting robbed was such a big news story, on the TV news, it just didn't make any sense. But then she heard what the lady was saying, how one of the men who'd broken into the house had been shot and killed by Adam Bloom. Mr Bloom himself was on TV, talking about why he used his gun. Gabriela still couldn't believe it – she thought she had to be asleep, having a bad dream. Then she heard the reporter saying, 'Police are identifying the dead man as thirty-six-year-old Carlos Sanchez of Queens.'

Sitting on the couch, she stared at the TV for a long time – maybe for seconds or minutes or hours, she had no idea. Finally she was able to think. She couldn't understand how this could have happened. The Blooms were supposed to go away; the house was supposed to be empty. And why did Mr Bloom shoot Carlos? She knew he had a gun – she'd seen it in his bedroom closet when she was cleaning, and sometimes he even left it out on the little table near his bed – but she couldn't imagine that kind man killing somebody even if his house was being robbed. It just didn't make any sense.

Then it hit her, what this really meant, and she started crying like she was at a funeral, but she wasn't crying for Carlos. She didn't go to church very much lately, but she still believed in Jesus Christ and that even bad people like Carlos had some good in them somewhere. But she still couldn't feel bad that Carlos was dead, not after all the bad things he had done to her. The one she was crying for was her *papi*. Carlos wasn't the only man Mr Bloom had killed with his gun, because now her *papi* was going to die, too.

Gabriela was still sitting on the couch crying when Beatrice called and said, 'Did you hear what happened at the Blooms' house last night?' Beatrice said she was in Forest Hills, at work in another house, and everybody was talking about it.

'Yes, I saw it on the news,' Gabriela said.

'The guy who was killed,' Beatrice said. 'They said his name is Carlos, Carlos Sanchez. It's not your old boyfriend Carlos, is it?'

'Don't tell anybody you know that,' Gabriela said. 'Please.'

'Why?' Beatrice asked. 'What's going on?'

'Nothing,' Gabriela said. 'I just don't want the police coming, asking me questions, when I'm so worried about *Papi.*'

'You okay?' Beatrice asked. 'You don't sound good. I'm worried about you.'

'I'm fine,' Gabriela said, crying. 'But please, please don't say anything to the *policía.* I'm begging to you.'

Gabriela was scared, even more scared than she was when she found out she had HIV. At least there was medicine she could take for HIV, but she couldn't think of any way to make this okay. So many people knew that Carlos was her ex-boyfriend. The Blooms and the other people she worked for didn't know because she never wanted them to find out about the drugs and the HIV, but Beatrice and her whole family knew, and Manuela knew, and neighbors in Gabriela's building knew. And what about all the times over the last couple of weeks that Gabriela had talked to Carlos on his cell phone? There was no way the *policía* wouldn't find out.

Gabriela was thinking about killing herself again – she could jump off a bridge or take pills. Pills would be very easy. She had a new bottle of sleeping pills and could take all of them and be dead very quickly. If she was dead it would probably be better for Manuela, too. It wasn't going to do her any good having a mother in jail. Beatrice could raise her good and give her a happy life.

At seven thirty, after Manuela left for school, Gabriela got the sleeping pills out of the cabinet. She was planning to text-message Beatrice, to tell her what she was going to do, so Beatrice could discover her body and not Manuela. She just hoped that she died before Beatrice arrived at her apartment. The worst thing would be if she woke up alive in some hospital bed.

She was about to type the text message when the doorbell rang. She looked through the peephole and saw a man with dark hair.

'Who's there?' she asked, and the man said, 'Police.'

She was surprised. She knew the police would come, but she didn't think they would come this fast. She was going to lock the door and take the pills, but she was afraid the police would break the door down and call an ambulance and save her.

She opened the door, hoping she could convince him to go away so she could have a chance to kill herself.

'Yes?' she said.

'You Gabriela?' he asked.

He was in a leather jacket and was wearing dark sunglasses. He didn't look like police.

'Yes,' she said. She couldn't remember ever being so scared.

The man reached into his jacket for something. She thought she'd see a badge, but it was a gun. She looked into the dark hole and saw her poor *papi*'s face.

6

MARISSA GOT OUT of bed at around noon and headed down the main staircase. She was about halfway down when she suddenly stopped and couldn't get herself to go any farther. Although it looked like the blood was all gone, she remembered what that guy had looked like, with that big piece of his jaw missing and all the blood, and got so grossed out she felt like she was going to throw up. She took the back stairs instead and went right into the kitchen. She was planning to ignore her father, give him the silent treatment after their argument last night. She didn't see him downstairs, and her mother wasn't around either.

'Ma!' she called.

No answer. Usually she loved it when she had the house all to herself, but after last night the idea of being alone kind of freaked her out.

'Mom! Dad!'

Her dad came out of the den, finishing a call on his BlackBerry. 'Okay, Lauren, I'll check back with you later on that. Byebye now.'

At first Marissa was kind of surprised that her dad was

acting so normal, that he was able to get back to work so quickly after going through so much trauma, but then she decided it made perfect sense. After all, he wasn't exactly in touch with his emotions. She remembered how he didn't cry at all at his father's funeral – even at the cemetery, when they lowered his father into the ground, he was stone-faced – and then a few months later he was a mess, snapping at everybody all the time, drinking too much. It would probably take him a few weeks before he realized how he actually felt about the shooting, and in the meantime he would take his anxiety out on her and her mom.

When her dad came into the kitchen Marissa was at the counter, pouring a cup of lukewarm coffee.

'Hey, good morning,' he said, sounding inappropriately upbeat. 'How'd you sleep?'

She waited several seconds before mumbling, 'Shitty.'

'Aw, that stinks,' he said. 'Maybe you should take a nap later or something. Oh, and by the way, I'm really sorry about last night. I was just feeling exhausted and stressed and I shouldn't've taken it out on you.'

'Whatever,' she said, not ready to forgive him yet.

'No, not *whatever*,' he said, mimicking her. 'I was wrong and I'm sorry. Friends?'

He extended his arms, inviting her to hug him.

'Friends,' she said grudgingly.

They hugged loosely; then she took a sip of the coffee. It tasted sour and murky.

'Hey, so I was thinking,' he said. 'Maybe instead of going down to Florida I'll just fly Grandma up here instead.'

'Can she travel?' Marissa asked.

'She said she's been feeling a lot better lately and that she could handle the flight. She could just sleep downstairs on the pullout and use the downstairs bathroom so we don't have to worry about her going up and down the stairs.'

'Sounds good to me,' Marissa said.

She was always up for getting out of a trip to Florida. She used to like going down there when she was a kid, mainly because she and her parents always stopped at Disney World on the way back, but for the last ten years or so going to her grandma Ann's condo in North Miami had been torture. It was always nice to see her grandma, but at her condo Marissa was basically a prisoner, hanging around all day, playing Rummy Q, watching game shows, and waiting for the main activity: going to the early bird dinner at four o'clock.

'Yeah, I think I'm just gonna call her and suggest it,' her dad said. 'Maybe next weekend or the weekend after.'

'So,' Marissa said, 'is there any news?'

'News about what?'

Was he serious?

'The shooting,' she said.

'Oh, no,' he said. 'I mean, I don't know what news there would be since last night. I mean, they removed the body right after you went to bed, and I was up for maybe another hour or so. I've been getting a lot of calls and emails, of course. It's amazing the way news spreads. Remember my old friend Stevie Lerner? Big guy, dark curly hair? Anyway, you met him when you were about eight years old, I think, and the last time I saw him was at a wedding maybe ten years ago. Anyway, *he* called to see if everything was okay.'

'Did they figure out how the burglars got in yet?' Marissa asked.

'No, I don't think so,' he said, like he really didn't care one way or the other. 'But the lock guy was here already, and we have brand-new locks for the back door, Medecos. There're new keys. The alarm guy should be here at around –' He checked the time on his cell phone. 'Actually, they should've been here a half-hour ago.'

Marissa took another sip of the gross coffee, then said, 'I'll talk to you later,' and started to leave the kitchen.

'I was thinking,' her dad said, 'maybe we could all go out to dinner tonight. You know, as a family.'

'I'm supposed to hang out with some friends,' she said.

This wasn't really true. She had no set plans with her friends; she just didn't feel like spending a whole night with her parents.

'Oh, then maybe we should do something over the weekend, just the three of us. Maybe go into the city to see a movie or a show? When was the last time we went to a Broadway show? It's been ages.'

'Are you sure you're feeling okay, Dad?'

'Fine,' he said, smiling unusually widely. 'What do you mean?'

'The way you're acting. It's… I don't know… not normal.'

'What do you mean?' he said. 'I had a phone session with a patient. I'm taking care of stuff around the house. I think I'm acting very normal.'

'Yeah, but it's not normal to act normal. I mean, you're allowed to be upset.'

'Upset about what?'

'You shot somebody,' Marissa said. 'If that happened to me, I mean, if I was the one who shot him, I'd be a total mess right now. I mean, you wouldn't even be able to talk to me.'

'Everybody handles things differently,' he said.

'*Anybody* would be upset,' she said.

'Look, I was upset at first, okay? I mean, you saw me last night, right? I was expressing my anger then, but I'm okay with it now, I really am. I mean, I'm not going to beat myself up over it. I was in a difficult situation, and I did the best I could under the circumstances. I wish it hadn't happened, but it did happen, and it could've happened to anybody – that's the important thing. You know how many people in this neighborhood have guns? The Zimmermans have a gun, the Stenatos have a gun, the Silvermans have a gun, the Coles have a gun. I bet there's a gun in every other house on this block, if not in every house, and I think any other father would've done what I did. I protected my family, that's all. It's not something to feel bad about, it's something to feel good about.'

God, he was so deep in denial it was hopeless.

'Look, Dad, if I were you, I'd talk to somebody. Your therapist, some other counselor, whoever. I really think you're still in shock right now but you don't realize it.'

'Shock?' he said, like he'd never heard the word before. 'Why do you –'

'Hello?' her mom shouted. It sounded like she was in the foyer, near the front door. She sounded totally panicked, like something horrible had happened. 'Who's home?'

Marissa and her dad looked at each other with concerned expressions, then left the kitchen together and met her mom in the living room. Her mom looked frantic and went right up to Marissa and wrapped her arms around her and wouldn't let go.

'What is it, Mom? What's wrong?'

Her mother was crying now, but it was worse than the way she'd been crying last night. Last night she was just upset. Now she looked devastated.

'Yeah, what's going on?' her dad asked, concerned yet calm.

Marissa's mom let go of her. Tears were streaming down her cheeks, leaving smudges of mascara, and her lips were trembling.

'I-I just spoke w–w-w-with that d-d-detective... c-c-c-clements.' She had to catch her breath. 'I c-c-alled him about the paper... he called back and... and... she's d-d-dead.'

Marissa was lost. 'Who's dead?'

'G-g-gabriela,' her mom said. 'Somebody shot her. She's dead.'

Marissa was confused. The only Gabriela she knew was their maid, but that was impossible. Marissa must've misunderstood something. Her mother must've meant some other Gabriela. Maybe someone from the neighborhood or a friend of a friend. Something like that.

'Gabriela?' Marissa asked. 'Gabriela who?'

Her mom couldn't speak for several seconds, then blurted out, 'Our Gabriela.' The room seemed like it was spinning, and then Marissa wasn't sure where she was anymore. Her father had to actually grab her to keep her from falling. Somehow they all wound up on the living room couch, Marissa sitting between her mom and her dad.

Her mom was asking her if she was okay, and Marissa, crying, was saying, 'It's not true. Please tell me it's not true.'

'It's true,' her mom sobbed. 'It's true, it's true, it's true.'

'How do you know it's true?' her father asked. 'Maybe there's some mistake.' Her dad wasn't crying at all, and he didn't even seem very upset. He sounded weirdly calm, in control.

'He told me,' her mom said. 'The detective. He said she was shot this morning in... in her apartment.'

'Maybe there was a screwup,' her dad said. 'Maybe it was some other Gabriela.'

'No, I asked,' her mom said emphatically. 'He said it was Gabriela Moreno, and he gave me her address in Jackson Heights. It's not a mistake. She's dead. Somebody shot her.'

Marissa was still sobbing. Last night had been one of the scariest times of her life, but this was like a total nightmare. Gabriela had been so young, so happy, so healthy. How could she be dead? This wasn't possible.

Then it hit Marissa, and she said, 'Oh my God. You don't think it has something to do with last night, do you?'

'It has nothing to do with last night,' her dad cut in quickly. 'Okay, come on, let's not get all hysterical before we know all the facts. I want to talk to Clements, find out exactly what's going on here.'

He was trying so hard to sound in control. Like people were getting shot left and right, but of course he could handle it, it was no big deal.

'He said he'll be over,' her mom said, 'later.'

'Good,' her dad said. 'I'm sure there's a lot we don't know right now.'

'Didn't Clements say he was gonna go talk to Gabriela?' Marissa asked. 'Isn't that what he said last night?'

'He didn't have a chance to talk to her,' her mom said. 'He said he was planning to talk to her today when –'

'Then it has to have something to do with it,' Marissa said. 'It's too coincidental.'

Her father stood up and started making a call on his BlackBerry. 'Let's just see one thing, okay?' he said.

'What're you doing?' her mom asked.

'Let's see if she picks up her phone.'

'What's wrong with you?' her mom said. 'I'm telling you, she's dead.'

Her dad ignored her, with the phone to his ear. Then after several seconds he clicked off and said, 'Voicemail.'

'Of course her voicemail picked up,' her mom screamed. 'What the hell's wrong with you?'

'Can you guys please just stop fighting?' Marissa asked.

'What's Gabriela's cell?' her dad asked, and her mom leaned over her lap, grabbed fistfuls of her hair as if she were trying to pull it all out in total frustration, then made an infuriated gravelly sound in the back of her throat.

'What were you saying before about a paper?' Marissa asked.

Still looking down, her hands still clutching her hair, her mom said, 'I had the code to the alarm written on a piece of paper. I realized it was missing this morning, that's why I called Clements.'

'Okay, think about what you're saying,' her dad said. He was standing in front of them, looking down at them. 'Just think about it for a second without getting hysterical. You know Gabriela, right? You know how wonderful she is, how loyal she is, how trustworthy she is. How many times has she been in this house alone? How many times did she babysit for us, or pick up Marissa from school? She's worked for us for how many years? Twelve? Thirteen? And in all that time she's never stolen anything from us. I'm talking not even a dollar bill from on top of my dresser. I mean, there's probably been hundreds of times that she had total access to my wallet, your pocketbook, your jewelry, and she's never stolen a cent from us. But now you're positive, there's no doubt in your mind, that she conspired with that criminal Sanchez to rob our house? Why? Because they're both Spanish? I mean, just think about how absurd that is before you start screaming your head off at me, okay?'

Her father ended his speech, seeming proud of himself, as if he'd just delivered a Shakespearean soliloquy or something. But, Marissa had to admit, the idea that Gabriela was part of the robbery did sound ridiculous. She couldn't imagine any scenario where Gabriela would do something to hurt Marissa's family.

'He's right, it does sound pretty crazy,' Marissa said. Then she said to her dad, 'So what do you think it was, a big coincidence? She gets shot the morning after our house is robbed, right before the detective has a chance to talk to her?'

'Look, there's a lot we don't know right now,' her dad said. 'Maybe it has something to do with her daughter, some guy she was dating.'

'Manuela's eleven,' Marissa said.

'What I'm trying to say,' her dad said, 'is let's just confirm she's actually dead.'

'It's confirmed!' her mom suddenly shouted. Her face was red, and her eyes were very big. 'How many times do I have to tell you before it gets through your thick skull? She's dead! She's fucking dead!'

Her dad shook his head in frustration and exited to the kitchen.

'You're so goddamn impossible,' her mom said and left, going toward the front of the house.

'Ma,' Marissa called and followed her.

She watched her mother head up the main staircase, hesitate for a moment as if suddenly remembering what had happened there, and then rush upstairs.

Marissa couldn't believe how absolutely screwed up everything suddenly was. Gabriela had always been so warm, so friendly, and had probably been one of the kindest people Marissa had ever met. Marissa remembered all the times Gabriela played with her and took her places when she was growing up. In high school when she had boyfriend problems, she never felt comfortable talking to her parents, and Gabriela was always there to give advice. Marissa had helped Gabriela learn English, and Gabriela had helped her with her Spanish. She had been a combination big sister and close friend, and Marissa just couldn't accept the idea that she was gone, as dead as the guy on the stairs last night, that she'd never see her face or hear her voice again.

Standing in the foyer, Marissa started to cry again. Then her dad came in and put an arm around her and in that pseudo calm voice said, 'It's gonna be okay, sweetie. I promise.'

Marissa couldn't take it anymore. If he was in denial before, now he was hopeless.

She broke away and said, 'Please, Dad, just stop it already,' and went upstairs, not even realizing she'd passed the spot where the body had been until she was in her room.

She checked her phone and saw that she'd received a bunch of emails and texts from her friends as news of the robbery had been getting around. She felt like she really needed to vent, let out her anger, so instead of replying individually she went online and posted a long entry on her Artist Girl blog, which most of her friends – her closest friends, anyway – read every day. She described the robbery as dramatically as possible, focusing on how terrified she'd been when she woke up and heard the intruders in the house and everything that had happened with the shooting and how the police had questioned her and her family for most of the night. She left out the part about how Clements had questioned her about her drug use in the house, paranoid that this would somehow incriminate her. Although she didn't mention anything about Gabriela specifically, she hinted at it, ending with 'Now things seem to be getting even more fucked up. This is the craziest day of my life.'

After she posted the blog, she searched Google News for 'Gabriela Moreno,' hoping to find nothing, but there were two news items about the shooting. Marissa read them, feeling devastated and numb. The items gave pretty much the same minimal information that Marissa's mother had already reported: Gabriela had been shot to death in her Jackson Heights apartment this morning by an unknown assailant. The motive for the shooting was also unknown.

'Goddamn it,' Marissa said, and she picked up the keyboard and banged it against the desk. It sounded like something cracked, but she didn't care.

She hoped that whoever killed Gabriela rotted in hell for it, but she still couldn't believe that Gabriela had actually been involved in the robbery. Maybe her dad was right about it being a coincidence. Maybe Gabriela was shot for some crazy random reason. It seemed far-fetched but not any more far-fetched than her having anything to do with that dead guy, Sanchez.

'Marissa.' Her father knocked on the door. 'Marissa, can you come downstairs for a sec, please? Detective Clements is here.'

Great, just what Marissa needed.

'Coming,' she said, nearly whispering.

'What?'

'I said I'll be right there!' she shouted.

She took her time, answering a few more emails, then went downstairs. Her mom, her face still smeared with mascara, was at the dining room table with Clements. Her dad looked more serious than he had before.

'What's going on?' Marissa asked.

'Please… join us,' Clements said.

Marissa sat in the empty chair, noticing that her mom and dad were avoiding eye contact with each other.

'I guess you heard the news,' Clements said.

'About Gabriela, yeah,' Marissa said. 'Why? Nobody else died, right?' She was only half-joking.

'No one else died,' her dad said in a monotone.

'I was just filling your parents in on a few of the latest developments,' Clements said.

'Oh, no, what now?'

'She was involved in the robbery,' her mom said.

'You know that for sure?' Marissa asked.

'It's very likely she was involved,' Clements said. 'We've established a connection, a very definite connection, between her and Carlos Sanchez.'

'What kind of connection?' Marissa asked.

'They had a history,' Clements said. 'They dated for several years and there was a history of domestic violence. She'd even gotten a restraining order against him.'

Marissa looked at her mom, then her dad, in disbelief. 'Did you guys know about this?'

Her mom shook her head. Her dad didn't have any reaction.

'She'd been in contact with him by cell phone numerous times in the days prior to the robbery,' Clements said. 'A neighbor also thinks he saw Sanchez at her building one day last week, but that hasn't been confirmed yet.'

'Wait, that doesn't make any sense,' Marissa said. 'If she had a restraining order against him, why would he've been at her building?'

'We're not sure,' Clements said. 'Her sister said their father in Ecuador is ill and needs money for an operation, so that may've been the motive.'

'Tell her about the AIDS,' Dana said.

'Her father had *AIDS*?' Marissa asked.

'Not her father – Sanchez,' Clements said. 'And he didn't

73

have full-blown AIDS. He was HIV positive.'

'I don't see what that has to do with anything,' Marissa's dad said.

'We all have to get tested now,' her mom announced.

'That's ridiculous,' her dad said.

'His blood was all over the staircase,' her mom said, suddenly looking and sounding maniacal. 'It could've splattered on you.'

'Oh, stop it,' her dad said, waving a hand at her dismissively.

Marissa couldn't believe her parents were actually arguing about HIV transmission. They'd officially hit a new low.

'The risk for HIV transmission in this type of situation is minimal if not non-existent,' Clements said. 'The virus dies almost immediately when it's exposed to air.'

'See?' her dad said to her mom, like he was so proud of himself.

'I don't care,' her mom said. 'The blood was everywhere, I want to get tested.'

'If you want to get tested, get tested,' her dad said. 'I can't stop you.'

'Okay, so let me get this straight,' Marissa said to Clements. 'You think Gabriela took the code to the alarm so she and her ex-boyfriend could rob our house?'

'It seems logical,' Clements said. 'Your mother says she believes Gabriela had access to the code.'

'What about the keys?' Marissa asked.

'She could've copied them at some point,' Clements said. 'We're talking to area locksmiths, and my guess is we'll find out that she copied the keys to the back door.'

'I don't believe it,' Marissa's mom said. 'If Gabriela robbed the house, then who killed her? Explain that.'

'It's too early to speculate,' Clements said.

As Marissa's mom rolled her eyes, Marissa said to her dad, 'I thought you heard another guy in the house.'

'I'm not sure about that,' he said. 'It could've been a woman.'

'According to your parents,' Clements continued to Marissa, 'Gabriela wasn't aware that you'd canceled your trip to Florida, so she may have believed the house would be empty. Did you tell her you weren't going to Florida?'

Marissa didn't say anything, she just shook her head.

It was starting to set in – *Gabriela had been involved in the robbery of their house. She'd actually been involved.*

'Oh my God,' Marissa said, 'I don't think I can handle any more of this.'

Her dad, suddenly all protective, said, 'If you don't have any more questions for her, why does she have to be here?'

Ignoring him, Clements said to Marissa, 'I understand you were close with Gabriela.'

'Yes,' Marissa said, trying her hardest not to cry. 'I was.'

'Did you talk to her at all during the last few days?'

'Monday,' Marissa said. 'I saw her Monday.'

'Did she mention anything to you about how she needed money, or about how she'd gotten back with her old boyfriend?'

'I had no idea she even had a boyfriend.'

'So there was nothing unusual in her behavior?'

'Nothing at all. She was her usual happy, smiley self.'

'Well, she was apparently very good at keeping secrets,' Clements said. 'Did she ever mention anything to you about drug use?'

'Gabriela?' Marissa said, shocked. 'Are you kidding? She was totally antidrugs.'

'Sanchez had a history of heroin addiction,' Clements said. 'It's likely that since he had a relationship with Gabriela she was using as well, at least when they were together.'

'That's hard to believe,' Marissa's dad said.

'I can't believe that either,' her mom said. 'The money's one thing. Anybody can get desperate, make a mistake, but drugs? I don't think she'd be able to hide that from us.'

'You'd be surprised what people can hide when they put their minds to it,' Clements said.

There was an awkward silence in the room for several seconds – Marissa noticed that her mom and dad both seemed uncomfortable – then her dad asked, 'So's that it?'

'Yeah,' Clements said, getting up. 'For now.'

Marissa and her dad stood, too.

'You've got to be kidding me,' her mom said, remaining seated. '*That's it?* There's a killer out there, a killer who was probably inside our house last night, and you say *that's it*?'

Her dad said, 'You don't know –' and her mom shouted at him, 'We *do* know! Why do you think she got shot today? Because somebody was trying to shut her up, that's why! And you shot the other guy! You killed him and you think he's not gonna come back here?'

'Okay, try to calm down,' Clements said.

'Why the hell should I try to calm down?' her mom said. 'Do you have any leads? Do you have any idea, any idea at all who shot Gabriela?'

'We're working on it,' Clements said.

'Oh, you're working on it,' her mom said. 'That makes me feel so much better. You're just so good at reassuring us. Meanwhile, you could've saved her life. Last night, if you weren't here asking us about my daughter's bong you could've talked to Gabriela sooner, stopped her from getting killed, and found out who the other guy is. Now you'll never find him, and he knows who we are, he knows where we live, he's been in our house!'

'I'm sorry,' Marissa's dad said to Clements.

'You don't have to apologize for me, you son of a bitch!' her mom screamed. 'You caused all this – you and your stupid gun! How many times did I tell you to get rid of that stupid thing?'

'Here comes the blame,' her dad said.

'I'm blaming you all right!' she screamed. 'Who else should I blame?'

'See? I knew you couldn't hold back forever. You've been dying to blame me. Go ahead, keep going, let's hear all that rage.'

'I told you if you had that gun in the house something horrible would happen someday. You didn't listen to me, and, what do you know, something horrible happened. What a shock!'

'Horrible!' her dad shouted. 'That's a good one, I love that. No, *horrible* would've been if you and Marissa got killed, that would've been horrible. You should be thanking me instead of yelling at me!'

'You wanna be thanked? Okay, thank you! Thank you for fucking up my life!'

'Can both of you just stop it already?' Marissa screamed as loudly as she could.

Finally there was silence as Marissa's parents remained glaring at each other, breathing heavily. Then Clements announced, 'I'll keep you informed, and you let me know if anything comes up on your end.' Then he looked at Marissa's mom and said, 'And despite what you think, Mrs Bloom, we do know how to do our job, and I think we do it very well.' He put his pad away in his pocket, then said, 'Sorry again for your loss,' and left.

Marissa remained with her parents in the dining room, watching them exchange looks. Then her father said, 'That was brilliant, insult the whole NYPD, why don't you?' and that set her mom off again. Marissa couldn't take it anymore and went up to her room. She heard her mother shouting, 'You still think everything's okay? You think it's going to all miraculously blow over?' – and then she turned up her stereo – more Tone Def – to drown her parents out.

She hoped this wasn't just the beginning, that her parents weren't going to start having marital problems again. In high school, it had seemed like her parents were on the verge of divorce, at each other's throats 24/7, and they always argued about the stupidest things. Like her dad would leave some dirty dishes in the kitchen sink or pee on the toilet seat, and her mom would lay into him about it. Or her dad wouldn't like a look her mother had given him or her tone of voice, and it would lead to a huge fight. And, because her dad was a psychologist and they were in marriage counseling, they would both go into this weird therapy-speak in their arguments that only led to more fighting. Like during a fight her mother might say, 'You're so annoying' and her father would say, 'You're generalizing' or 'There you go with your rage again,' and then *that* would lead to a fight. Or sometimes they would be arguing and her mother would say, 'You're being defensive,' and her father would fire back, 'There you go, projecting again,' and they'd be off, shouting at each other in their ridiculous mumbo jumbo about who was projecting and who was being defensive. Of course there was never any resolution to their fighting; no one ever won or conceded. It seemed like they had the same argument over and over again, like an annoying song stuck on repeat play. Marissa never understood why they bothered to stay together. If they couldn't get along, why make each other miserable? Why not just get divorced? She'd hoped they weren't staying together for her, because she would've preferred that they just split up and move on with their lives. What kid wanted unhappy parents?

Marissa turned down the music, and she could still hear her parents going at it; it sounded like they were in their bedroom now. She took a quick shower and was toweling off when she heard her mother shout, 'What're you gonna do then? Get your gun again? Shoot him?'

God, were they still arguing about the gun?

Marissa headed back to her bedroom, passing her father in the hallway. He marched by and went downstairs. He was in sweats and sneakers, probably on his way to the gym.

Sitting on her bed, Marissa texted Hillary, who worked in midtown. They arranged to meet for drinks at five thirty. Marissa typed:

cant wait I SO have to get out of this crazy fucking house

She got dressed quickly – skinny jeans, a black lace cami, and the cute little leather jacket she'd bought last week at UNIQLO in SoHo. As she left the house, she saw her father on the sidewalk, talking to several reporters. They'd probably come back to ask him questions about Gabriela and she could tell he was into it, furrowing his eyebrows and moving his hands a lot as he talked, acting like he was a movie star giving a press conference.

Marissa walked several blocks, through the gates of Forest Hills Gardens to the subway on Queens Boulevard. Riding on the R train, she wore her sunglasses because she was crying and didn't want anyone to see. She still couldn't believe that Gabriela was actually *dead*.

When she arrived in Manhattan, she had some time to kill, so she went to the Whitney to see the Man Ray exhibit. She'd sent a job application to the Whitney, as she had to practically every other museum in the city, and hadn't heard anything yet. She'd been applying to a lot of galleries, too, and had gone to an interview to be the 'events coordinator' at one downtown, but she'd gotten no job offers so far. Her father had probably been right about how she'd made a mistake by quitting the job at the Met. She should have stuck it out for at least six months to use it as a reference, or until she found something else. She just hoped she found *something* soon; she wanted steady money coming in so she could afford the rent for her own place, or even a share. She hated not having her own money and being so dependent on her parents.

After the museum, she walked to midtown, feeling out of place around all of the oppressive office buildings and stressed-out working people. Downtown was cooler, though all of Manhattan seemed so uppity and into itself that Marissa felt like she just couldn't connect. She liked Brooklyn a lot better – especially Williamsburg, DUMBO, and RAMBO – but most of her friends were working in the city and always wanted to meet at midtown bars or go out in Murray Hill or, the worst, the Upper East Side.

At five thirty, she met Hillary at McFadden's at Forty-second and Second. It was the typical midtown after-work bar – lots of suits and ties, lots of uptight people desperately trying to let loose, businessmen calling each other 'bro' and 'dude.' Marissa felt like she was on a different planet, but Hillary, who had an entry-level marketing job at some ad agency, seemed right at home, smiling, waving, saying hi and even *hugging* people as she entered. Marissa and Hillary had been best friends for years, but lately Marissa felt like they'd been drifting apart. She hoped it was just a phase, though, that Hillary would eventually get over this whole trying-to-act-like-a-yuppie kick and return to acting like her normal self.

Hillary hugged Marissa hello; then Marissa said, 'God, I need a drink so badly. Something strong.'

They found seats at the bar and ordered cosmos, 'heavy on the vodka.' Hillary had already read about the robbery on Marissa's blog, but Marissa retold the story anyway.

'Oh my God, that must've been so horrifying,' Hillary said.

'It gets worse,' Marissa said, her voice cracking.

Hillary, like all of Marissa's friends, had known Gabriela. It was almost like Gabriela had been a part of the Bloom family.

When Marissa told Hillary about Gabriela being killed and probably being involved in the robbery, Hillary started to cry, and Marissa cried with her. Hillary said all the expected things – *I can't believe it, it's not possible, she was so* young – as they continued to sob together.

Finally Marissa said, 'Maybe we should stop crying, this *is* a happy hour after all,' but the attempt at an icebreaking joke didn't even get a smirk from Hillary.

'It's so horrible that you have to go through all of this,' Hillary said.

'Yeah, I know it sucks,' Marissa said. 'My mom's worried that the guy who shot Gabriela's still out there, but I'm not really worried about that. I'm sure the cops'll catch him.'

'God, I certainly hope so,' Hillary said.

Marissa sipped her drink, then said, 'I was so happy when you said you could meet up. It's been a total nightmare at home. My mother's angry, so she's snapping at my father, and, of course, my father's taking it out on me, as usual. He actually said I have to stop drinking and smoking in the house, treating me like I'm some kind of party animal or something. Meanwhile, I barely smoke or drink at all. But their fighting, that's the worst. I swear, it was like when I was a teenager all over again. I really don't know what's wrong with them. If they can't get along and can't stand the sight of each other, why don't they just get divorced?'

Suddenly Hillary's eyes widened, and Marissa could tell something was wrong. 'What is it?' Marissa asked.

'Nothing, never mind,' Hillary said and took a sip of her drink.

'Come on, what is it? Is it about Gabriela?'

'No.'

'Then what is it? Come on, you have to tell me.'

'It's really not important.'

'Come on, just tell me.'

'It's nothing,' Hillary said. 'I shouldn't've said anything.'

'You didn't say anything yet. Come on, now you *have* to tell me.'

Hillary took another sip of her drink, breathed deeply, then said, 'It's just… it's about your mother.'

'My mother?'

'See? I shouldn't've opened my big mouth.'

'What about her?'

'I mean, with what you're going through now and every –'

'Come on, just tell me already.'

Hillary waited several seconds, as if trying to organize her thoughts, then said, 'I heard her and my mom talking the other night. They didn't think I was home, but I heard them from upstairs.'

'What were they talking about?'

'I'm sorry. I mean, I didn't want to tell you, but –'

'Is it something bad?'

'No. I mean, not *bad* bad.'

'Is my mom sick?'

'No, God no, nothing like that.'

'Then what is it?'

'It's just she's… well, she's… cheating on your dad.'

Marissa couldn't believe it. 'My *mother*?'

'Sorry, I didn't want to tell you, especially not now when –'

'You sure you didn't misunderstand something?'

'Positive. She was talking about how it's been going on for months and she keeps wanting to break it off but she can't.'

For months?

'With who?' Marissa asked.

'You know him,' Hillary said.

'Oh God, who?'

'Tony.'

'Who's Tony?'

'You know – Tony, that trainer guy at New York Sports Club.'

It took a few moments to register, then Marissa said, 'You mean that big guy with the thick Bronx accent?'

Hillary nodded uncomfortably.

'You're kidding me, right?' Marissa said.

'Swear to God,' Hillary said. 'See? I shouldn't've told you.'

Marissa saw a flash of her mom and Tony together – naked. It was kind of funny.

'Who would've thought?' Marissa said. 'My mom and a bodybuilder. Good for her.'

'Wait, you're not upset?'

'Upset? Why would I be upset? If I was my mom I would've cheated on my dad years ago. Maybe my parents'll finally get divorced, put all of us out of our misery.' She finished her cosmo in one gulp, then added, 'Honestly, this is by far the best news I've heard all day.'

7

J OHNNY LONG WAS walking uptown on Eighth Avenue, on his way back from Slate, a pool hall in Chelsea where he'd hustled a hundred-something bucks off some drunken stockbroker, heading toward the touristy bars around Times Square, where he hoped to find a decent-looking woman to screw and rob, when the rain started. It was coming down hard, lightning and thundering, and didn't seem to be letting up. He waited it out for a while under an awning, then dashed across the street to the Molly Wee Pub on Thirtieth and Eighth, figuring he'd wait out the storm there.

When he entered the Irish bar, he noticed five women checking him out. This wasn't unusual; women checked him out wherever he went. His looks had always been his biggest asset and his biggest liability. It was great to look hot when he wanted to pick up a woman, but during a stretch at Rikers being known as 'Johnny Pretty,' 'J Lo,' and – the worst – 'Jenny from the Block' had caused him seven and a half months of total hell.

Johnny often got mistaken for Johnny Depp, and not just because they had the same first name. He was bigger than Depp, more muscular, but their faces looked alike – both had that sleepy, washed-out look – especially when he let strands of his longish, greasy dark hair fall over his light blue eyes. He also got mistaken for Jared Leto every once in a while, or one of the other guys in 30 Seconds to Mars.

He sat at the bar, ordered a club soda with a wedge of lime – he didn't touch alcohol – and checked out his options. Two of the women were with guys – not impossible, but it made things a little harder, and he wasn't in the mood for hard. So it was down to the thin girl with dark hair who was at the table with a group of friends, the girl with dark curly hair or her blond friend at the end of the bar, or the older blonde who was alone at a table near the door. He wasn't attracted to any of the women, not that that mattered.

He sipped his club soda and looked up at the basketball game on TV, deciding to let fate decide for him. It would save him some work, and besides, the odds of picking up a woman were much better when he let the woman make the first move. If he went over to one of the women his chances would still be very good, but it would require much more charm and effort, and if it turned out the woman was married or had a serious boyfriend there was a chance Johnny wouldn't be able to pull it off. But he knew if he did nothing, just sat and waited for a woman to come over to him, he would almost definitely score.

Although he wasn't looking at any of the women, he could feel their eyes on him. He just knew that they wanted him so badly, that they were just dying to be with a hot guy like him, a Johnny Depp lookalike, for chrissake. At one point, he looked casually beyond the bartender and in the mirror behind the bar saw that the blonde and the girl with the dark curly hair were still looking in his direction, obviously talking about him. The dark-haired girl was probably saying something like 'God, he's so cute,' and the friend was egging her on, saying, 'Go ahead, talk to him, what're you waiting for?' That was the way it always happened. It was so predictable it was almost boring.

Sure enough, about a minute went by, and then Johnny heard, 'Excuse me?' He looked over and saw the girl with the dark curly hair. She was overweight, and there was nothing particularly attractive about her face. She was someone Johnny would normally pass on the street and barely notice.

'Did anybody ever tell you you look just like Johnny Depp?' she asked.

She was blushing badly and looked even less attractive closer up in brighter light. Her makeup looked caked on, especially around her eyes, which weren't blue or even green. He could tell that she was terrified and it took all her nerve to go up to a guy as good-looking as he was and actually say something. He also knew that his initial reaction to her was key: she wasn't just going up to him to hit on him; they were actually hooking up unconsciously. He had to show her instantly that he was attracted to her, but more importantly that he was a good guy, someone she could trust.

He smiled widely, letting her see his perfect white teeth, and looked right in her eyes like he was totally enamored with her. He knew humble was the way to go and said, acting totally blown away and flattered, 'You really think so?'

'Yeah,' she said. 'Haven't you heard that before?'

'Never,' he said. 'Wow, you really made my day.'

He maintained eye contact, letting her notice his light blue eyes, which women often complimented. In fact, just last night the woman he'd picked up in Brooklyn told him that he had the most beautiful blue eyes she'd ever seen. He wound up screwing her, but he'd gotten away with only about a hundred bucks and no jewelry. Hopefully this woman would be a bigger score.

'By the way, I'm Gregory,' Johnny said and held out his hand.

She was so taken by him she waited an extra beat, then said, 'Oh, I'm Theresa.'

He held her hand for a few seconds longer than necessary, letting her know that he liked her, that he was *interested*. It was so easy to pick up women; at least for him it was. He knew he didn't have to come on strong and try to impress them with a fancy job and make them laugh nonstop. Women wanted to be *noticed*, and they wanted to be *respected*. All you had to do was be attentive, listen to a woman, show her that you cared about what she was saying, and you were halfway there. It was so simple that it always amazed Johnny when he saw guys blow easy lays by going on and on about themselves. What were they trying to do, scare the women away? Yeah, Johnny knew his looks helped him out a lot, made him even more irresistible, but even an ugly guy could pick up practically any woman he wanted, if he could make her feel special, like she was the only person in the world that mattered.

Johnny made small talk with Theresa – *Where are you from? Do you live around here? What do you do for a living?* – but instead of just firing off the questions machine-gun style like the average guy, he really listened to the answers and of course, he maintained eye contact the whole time. She said she worked as an office manager at a PR agency, which disappointed him because it didn't sound like she had big bucks. Still, she seemed pretty well off – middle class at least – and he was encouraged when she dropped that she lived alone. Roommates were always problematic.

He didn't say a word about himself until she asked him; then he did his best to tell her what she wanted to hear. Since she'd mentioned she lived in Queens, he told her that he was born in Queens and still had a lot of family there. He was actually from Brooklyn and was an orphan, but he wanted to have a connection to her, and it seemed to work. Because she was an office manager, he told her he was 'a consultant for a financial services company.' If she'd had a lower- or higher-level job, he would've told her he did something else for a living, but he wanted to have a career that was on her level. In other words, he didn't want to be too far above her or too far below her. Also, whenever he met women with white-collar jobs he loved saying he was 'a consultant for a financial services company' because the job title sounded so ambiguous that he could easily bullshit about what he actually did on a day-to-day basis if the women happened to ask any questions. But the women rarely questioned him about his job, at least not right away, and these were usually one-night stands anyway.

His other brilliant move – which practically sealed the deal – was playing the Catholic card. He noticed she was wearing a crucifix, so he casually mentioned that he had gone to church last Sunday. Her eyes brightened and she said, 'Wow, I go to church all the time.' He gave her some crap about how important spirituality was in his life and how sad it was that the country was 'getting away from all that.' Then a few minutes later she actually said, 'God, it's so great to meet a guy who goes to church,' as if she seriously believed she'd met her Catholic Prince Charming on a rainy night in an Irish bar around the corner from Penn Station. At times like these, Johnny's lies amused him to the point where it was hard not to start laughing hysterically, but as always he managed to contain himself.

Johnny knew Theresa was dying to screw him now, that in her mind he was the greatest guy she'd ever met and she couldn't wait to introduce him to her parents and all her friends. Of course, she might give him a hard time about having sex tonight, doing the whole playing-hard-to-get/wanting-to-take-it-slower routine, but he knew that with a little gentle persuading and pouring on a little more charm at the appropriate moment – this was where his good looks and trustworthy eyes really paid off – she wouldn't be able to resist him.

Then her friend, the blonde, came over and said she had to get home. This was the last hurdle, and it was a major one. If Theresa had driven her friend to the bar (unlikely, since she'd mentioned she'd gone out tonight right after work) or her friend was staying at Theresa's place (also unlikely, because she would've brought this up already) then Johnny's pickup attempt could be shot. If this were to happen it wouldn't be any big deal really, because he could simply pick up someone else – or, let's be serious, let someone else pick *him* up – at this bar, or, now that the rain had stopped, he could continue on to Times Square and pick up a tourist at a bar around there. He knew he could find a more attractive victim, though it would be a shame because he was oh so close with Theresa.

'Gregory, I'd like you to meet my friend Donna,' Theresa said.

'It's great to meet you,' Johnny said. 'I love that jacket. Where'd you get it?' Actually it was a cheap-looking denim jacket that looked like it was from a thrift shop.

'Oh, thank you so much,' she said, blushing the way Theresa had. 'Actually, I got it at Daffy's.'

'Really? Wow, I love it.'

That was perfect – complimenting the friend, getting her

to like him, too. Predictably Donna told Theresa that she was ready to leave. She said something about how she had to get up early tomorrow, which sounded to Johnny like a lame excuse since tomorrow was Saturday and odds were she didn't have to work. She probably just felt self-conscious, sitting at the bar by herself not getting hit on, and wanted to leave, even if it meant taking her friend with her and – as far as she knew – ruining a budding love connection.

Theresa seemed disappointed and torn, and Johnny knew exactly what she was thinking: *would he have more respect for me if I left?* But the fact that she wasn't leaving told Johnny that she one hundred percent wanted to stay; she just needed a way to justify it to herself.

'Hey, if you'd like to stay I'll make sure you get home safely.' Maybe anyone else delivering this line would've come off as a sleazeball, a player, but not Johnny. He always seemed sincere and caring.

'Wow, that's so nice of you,' Theresa said.

Again Johnny had to resist the urge to burst out laughing.

The girls talked it over for a few moments while Johnny looked away, sipping his club soda, giving them space, and then Donna announced, 'Well, I'm going home, it was really nice meeting you.'

'You, too, hope to meet you again sometime,' Johnny said, thinking, *Yeah, like that's gonna happen.*

Donna left, and Johnny knew the last obstacle had been removed – it was pretty much home free from here.

And he didn't waste any time. After he said something funny and she laughed, he leaned in and kissed her. He didn't slobber over her with an open mouth. It was a simple, classy kiss. He kept his lips against hers for several seconds and then pulled back and said, sensitively yet with passion, 'Do you want to get out of here?'

A few minutes later, they were in the cab. He was a total gentleman – kissing her, of course, but not trying to get in her panties or anything like that. The cab ride to Astoria might cost him about thirty-five, forty bucks, and he hoped that it was worth his while, that he wasn't wasting a whole night with this woman.

During the cab ride she said everything he expected her to say. *I don't usually do this. Are you sure we're doing the right thing? Maybe we should wait.* Playing the game, he kept saying things like 'Hey, if you don't feel comfortable, I can go home.' Giving her every opportunity to back out of it. Yeah, right.

In Astoria, he was disappointed when they pulled up in front of a modest two-family house. He was hoping she lived in one of the new yuppie condos they'd put up out there; it would've been an indication that this was going to be worthwhile. Still, he was trying to be optimistic, not acting in any way disappointed.

As soon as they entered her apartment, he switched on his passion button and began to give her the full Johnny Long lovemaking treatment. He kissed her lips softly, pushing her hair back away from her face, telling her over and over how beautiful she looked. They went into the bedroom and began to make love. He asked her if she had candles and incense, knowing that women always loved that crap. She said she didn't have incense but had candles and went to get them.

She returned to bed, the candles lit, and Johnny began to make love to her the way only Johnny Long could. He knew he was the best lover in the world, and not only because women often told him he was. One day he'd gone to the library and read books by the so-called Casanovas, and those guys didn't know anything he didn't know. In one book, some French guy claimed he'd been with over a thousand women and had satisfied all of them. Johnny laughed when he read that – no one could give a woman more pleasure than Johnny Long. The last time he'd counted he estimated that he'd been with 450-plus women, but he was only thirty-one years old and planned to be in the thousands by the time he was thirty-five.

Johnny knew that writing a book about his own sex techniques would be impossible because he had no techniques. He couldn't tell people to do this or do that and you'll get a woman off every time, because nothing worked every time with every woman. Women were like trees: they were all different. It was all about instinct, getting into the woman's head, feeling what she was feeling.

He kissed Theresa very slowly and softly on her mouth and

her neck, then moved to her breasts and stomach and inner thighs and finally worked his way lower. The entire time, like when he was talking to her at the bar, he was very attentive, picking up on the cues she gave him and playing off them. Like a super sex computer he instantly processed the information she was giving him and transformed himself into her ideal lover, the man of her dreams. He pleasured her for a long time with the perfect intensity, and then he began to make love to her at the exact pace she wanted. She climaxed easily, moaning, 'Oh, Gregory, oh, Gregory.' For a moment he'd forgotten he was Gregory and thought she'd confused him with somebody else.

He got her off four times, and he knew there was no chance she was faking. No one could fake orgasms with him because he knew, he always knew. Afterward, he held her in his arms and gently stroked her hair and kissed her ear, gently sucking on her lobe for a while.

Later, when she finally fell asleep, he got out of bed, dressed silently, and got to work robbing her apartment.

He started with her purse, scoring $237 – not bad at all for purse money; it more than covered the cab ride, so already the night was a success. He easily found her jewelry box in the top drawer of her dresser and took everything, noticing a couple of necklaces, both sterling, and rings that he thought would get him several hundred dollars for their gold value alone. With a little luck this would turn out to be a great score, and he knew that as long as he got away cleanly, he had almost no chance of getting caught. Theresa had no real information about him, and she probably wouldn't even report the crime to the police. Johnny wasn't sure why the women he screwed and robbed almost never tried to rat him out. Part of it probably was that they felt so ashamed and embarrassed about what had happened that they didn't want their friends and family to find out about it, but Johnny liked to think that it was mainly because he'd left them so satisfied, giving them the best sex of their lives, so that in the morning they'd decided that, yeah, losing their money and other valuables sucked, but what did they *really* have to complain about?

He was about to leave the bedroom when he noticed, on the

night table, the gold crucifix Theresa had been wearing at the bar. He snatched it and, on his way out, smiled, thinking how he'd have to go to church later and confess. He was still giggling about that one as he left the building and headed toward the subway station.

night table, the gold crucifix Theresa had been wearing at The bar. He snatched it and put his way out, sighed, thinking how he'd have to go to church later, and confess. He was still antsy about that one as he left the building and headed toward the subway station.

8

'JOHNNY LONG. THAT you?'

The voice came from behind Johnny as he was entering the Astoria Boulevard subway station. He was surprised to hear his name spoken at three in the morning in Astoria, where he didn't think he knew anyone.

For a moment he worried it was a cop. Just in case, he started reaching into the pocket of his jacket where he had a Kel-Tec .380.

But then he looked over his shoulder and actually had to blink, doing a double take.

'Carlos?' he asked.

He hadn't seen Carlos Sanchez, his old friend from St John's, in how long? Eight, nine years? Nine years, but Carlos looked like he'd aged twenty. He was only four or five years older than Johnny, but he looked fifty with all of that gray in his hair, and his face looked old and drawn, too. Johnny had heard through Rayo, another guy from St John's, that Carlos had been away for dealing.

Carlos came over and gave Johnny a big hug. He reeked of booze and pot smoke, and Johnny couldn't wait for the hug to end.

'It's been a long time, bro,' Carlos said, finally letting go. 'Been a long, long time. The hell you doin' 'round here?'

'I should be asking you that question,' Johnny said. 'I thought you were away.'

'Naw, man, that's ancient history,' Carlos said. 'Got out six months ago, and I'm livin' here now, bro. Well, not here, here, I mean Queens, Bayside. I'm just here in Astoria on some business, know what I'm sayin'?'

Johnny wasn't surprised Carlos was dealing again; the guy had been dealing since he was thirteen. Johnny had never touched drugs, not even pot, which was the main reason why he'd only been away one time. When you weren't whacked out on drugs and could think clearly, it was easy to stay one step ahead of the cops.

'Where you living now?' Carlos asked.

'Still in Brooklyn,' Johnny said. 'Got a little place out in Red Hook.'

'Yeah, how you gettin' by?'

'I'm doing okay.'

'Yeah, you still a pretty boy. I bet you gettin' all the ladies, right?'

'I can't complain.'

'Can't complain? Yeah, I remember the times, we'd point to any girl in the schoolyard or wherever, pay you twenty bucks or whatever and bet you couldn't go pick her up, and you'd take our money every time.'

'Not every time,' Johnny said.

'Not every time,' Carlos said. 'Check this guy out. You still got that sense of humor goin' on. You still make me laugh.'

Johnny heard a subway pulling into the station above them. 'Well, that's my ride,' he said. 'It was really great seeing you again, man.'

'Come on, hang out,' Carlos said. 'Where you rushin' to at three in the morning?'

'Long day,' Johnny said. 'Gotta crash.'

'Come on, man. You ain't seen your ol' bro in how many years and you can't sit down and have a drink?'

Johnny really wanted to get home and away from Astoria.

It was unlikely that Theresa would call the cops, but after he hustled a woman he didn't like to stay in her neighborhood.

'I don't drink,' Johnny said.

'Johnny Clean, that's right,' Carlos said. 'Remember everybody used to call you that shit? Never drank, never did nothin'. That's how you stayed a pretty boy, right?'

The train was pulling into the station, the brakes screeching.

'Hey, I've got an idea,' Johnny said. 'Why don't you give me your cell? We'll hang out some time.'

'Nah, come on, sit down with me right now,' Carlos said. 'We can get some coffee and cake. I got something I gotta talk to you about anyway, somethin' where you can make some serious cash, know what I mean?'

Johnny wasn't interested in hearing Carlos's idea, but he knew he couldn't just blow him off. You didn't do that to a guy from St John's. Growing up, those guys had been Johnny's whole family. He'd spent every Christmas with them, every Thanksgiving.

'Okay, let's go,' Johnny said, 'but I can't stay out long.'

They went to the corner, to the Neptune Diner, and sat in a booth by a window with a view of the Grand Central Parkway, still a lot of traffic this time of night. Johnny was starving – a night of hustling and sex had built up quite an appetite – and he ordered a bacon cheeseburger with everything on it. After a couple of bites, he realized it wouldn't fill him up, so he ordered another one.

Carlos caught Johnny up on guys from the old neighborhood. Everybody, it seemed, had gotten into some kind of trouble. Pedro was doing fifteen for manslaughter. Delano was at Attica for dealing. DeShawn had been stabbed to death in a fight outside a bar in Philly. Eddie had OD'd on smack.

'Sounds like me and you are the big winners, huh?' Johnny said, smiling.

'Yeah, I'm doing okay,' Carlos said. 'Not in jail anyway, and I got my HIV under control.'

'Oh, shit,' Johnny said. 'Sorry to hear that, man.'

'Eh, it's okay,' Carlos asked. 'The fuck you gonna do, right? And with the medicines they got, I'm gonna live longer than you.'

Carlos was sobering up, and Johnny started to have a good time bullshitting with him about the old days at St John's. Johnny had forgotten how much he'd needed Carlos back then. The courts had sent Johnny to St John's when he was nine years old after his mother was killed. They'd told Johnny she went in a car accident, which hadn't made sense to him because she didn't own a car, and then he found out a few years later that his mother wasn't really a secretary, she was a hooker, and she'd been stabbed to death by one of her clients. Johnny felt like an outcast at St John's because all the other kids were a lot tougher than him and had known each other all their lives. He got picked on a lot – it seemed like every day somebody wanted to kick his ass – and Carlos had been the only one who always had his back.

So when Carlos looked at Johnny seriously and said, 'So the thing I got goin' on...' Johnny knew he couldn't say no right away even though he also knew this wasn't going to lead to anything good. He had to at least listen to his old buddy, see what he had to say, give him a little respect.

Surprisingly, Carlos's plan didn't seem so bad – rob some fancy house in Forest Hills while the family was away in Florida. Carlos's ex-girlfriend, the maid, had the keys and knew the code to the alarm system.

'Shit's gonna be so easy,' Carlos said. 'The house is gonna be empty and we gonna go in and out. Gabriela, my girl, she said the lady in the house got a diamond ring. It's so expensive she doesn't wear it, but she keeps it right out in her bedroom. My girl's gonna tell us where everything's at so we can go in, out, and then we got fifty thousand dollars, twenty-five each.'

'What about your girl?'

'That's the funny shit.' Carlos was laughing. 'She was on my ass the other day, sayin' she wanted the money split three ways, going it gotta be equal and shit or she won't give me the keys. So I was telling her, yeah, don't worry, baby, it'll be three ways, anything to shut her fat ass up, right? But when we get the money, that's it, we gone. She never gonna see our asses again.'

Carlos was still laughing, wiping tears out of the corners of his eyes with his index finger.

Johnny had to admit the plan sounded good, but that's what worried him. In his experience, when something sounded too good it usually meant it was bad.

'How do you know the family'll be in Florida?' he asked.

'Because my girl works there,' Carlos said. 'She knows everything.'

'And when we don't give her a cut, how do you know she won't rat us out?'

'Why'd she rat us out and get her own ass sent to jail? The cops, they're gonna know she got us the key and the code. Naw, trust me, the bitch is gonna keep her mouth shut.'

Johnny had some more questions, but he couldn't find any obvious holes in the plan, and he didn't see how he could say no. Twenty-five Gs was some serious cash – beat the hell out of the kind of pocket change he'd been making lately, a few hundred bucks here and there on the good days. The summer was coming, and he could use a break. It would be nice to take a couple of months off, go to the beach down the shore, work on his tan. How hot would he look with a tan? How many women would want to screw him then? He'd pass that thousand mark in four years, no problem.

'So,' Carlos said, 'you in or out?'

Johnny looked across the table at his old buddy and smiled.

The night of the robbery, Johnny and Carlos, wearing backpacks, met where Carlos had parked his car, outside a pizza place on Austin Street in Forest Hills. Johnny had come by subway, but Carlos had taken his car, a beat-up Impala. Not the best getaway ride, but if things went right they wouldn't be in any rush. They'd just casually get in the car and drive away.

'Ready to do it?' Carlos asked.

'Hold up,' Johnny said, looking around. He didn't like this at all. Yeah, it was better meeting here than in front of the house they were gonna rob, but it still felt too out in the open. It was 1:30 AM, and almost all the stores were closed, but there were still cars passing by, and right across the street and down the block a little, there was a homeless-looking guy hanging out.

'What's wrong?' Carlos asked.

'Maybe we should've met at the house,' Johnny said.

'You told me to park here.'

'The car's okay. I'm talking about us. It's not good if somebody sees us together.'

'So what if somebody sees us?' Carlos said. 'We're just two people. What did we do?'

'I mean if somebody remembers,' Johnny said. 'After.'

'After what? The people're in Florida. It's gonna be like a week before they find out the joint got robbed.'

Johnny didn't care, he still felt uncomfortable. The homeless guy seemed to be looking right at them. Johnny still had a bad feeling about the whole thing. He'd been on a roll lately – picking pockets, picking up women, hustling a little pool. It wasn't big money, but it was steady, and it was safe. Why was he getting in on a robbery with a drug addict?

He was ready to back out. He was going to say to Carlos, *Sorry, man, I don't like it,* and go back to Brooklyn, but he knew he'd be letting Carlos, his brother, down, and was there really a reason to? Maybe he was just overthinking it, making it more complicated than it really was. Maybe it was like Carlos said, an easy twenty-five K. He'd go along with it, see how it went. If it didn't feel right at the house, he could bail then.

They went past Austin Street under the Long Island Rail Road tracks and through the big gates into Forest Hills Gardens. Johnny had only been to this neighborhood once or twice, driving by, and he'd forgotten how fancy all the houses were. They were like mini mansions, with front lawns and backyards and driveways, and they had to go for, what, three, four million dollars, maybe even more nowadays. It reminded him of the houses in Rockaway in Brooklyn. One summer, when Johnny was eleven or twelve years old, he stole a bicycle, and every day he biked all the way to the beach. He'd pass all the fancy houses out there, watch all the families – the dads playing catch with their kids in the street, or the kids playing on their front yards and shooting hoops in their backyards. He'd wonder what it would feel like to be one of those kids, just for one day, to have everything instead of nothing.

As they walked, they didn't talk at all. This had been Johnny's

97

rule – no talking. They went about three blocks, made a left, and there was the house. Jesus, it was one of the nicest ones on the block – three stories, brick, front lawn. When Johnny was a kid he would've killed to live in a place like this. He hoped the people appreciated what they had, that it wasn't just all normal to them and they didn't give a shit.

Johnny and Carlos looked around to make sure the coast was clear, then nodded to each other and walked up the driveway to the backyard. One thing struck Johnny as wrong, and he'd kick himself about it later: a shiny black Mercedes was in the driveway. There was a garage in the back, so if the people were away, out of town, wouldn't they put the car in the garage? Or why not drive it to the airport and leave it there? Johnny was going to say something to Carlos, even suggest they go back to their car, but then he thought maybe there was nothing so strange about it at all. Lot of rich people have two or even three cars. Maybe the other cars were in the garage and the people had left the Merc in the driveway. Maybe they'd taken a limo to the airport. There were a lot of reasons why the Merc could be there.

At the end of the driveway, it was dark, just like Carlos had said it would be. They opened their backpacks and put on their ski masks and gloves and took out their flashlights. Then they went around to the back door. Carlos turned on his flashlight and opened the door with the keys. So far so good, but now they had to disarm the alarm. Carlos went right to the keypad and punched in the numbers, but the red light was still blinking. Fuck, in maybe a minute or less the alarm would start blaring, and they'd have to run as fast as they could back to the car and get the hell out of Forest Hills.

'Come on,' Johnny stage-whispered. He was holding the door open, ready to take off.

'Wait,' Carlos said, and he started punching the numbers in again.

Jesus, Johnny knew he should've made Carlos write the code down, but he swore he had it memorized. Carlos typed in several numbers, then hesitated, as if thinking, using all his concentration, then punched in the last two.

The red light turned green.

Carlos smiled widely, and Johnny wondered, *Had the guy been fucking with me all along?* It was the type of prank Carlos would've pulled at St John's, trying to scare the shit out of somebody and getting a big kick out of it.

But they were in the house, that was the important thing. Now they had to get what they needed and get the hell out.

Shining their flashlights ahead of them, they went through the kitchen – it was huge, with brand-new-looking stainless steel appliances – and into some kind of big pantry. Then they went into the living room – man, these people were loaded; they had a plasma TV on the wall, looked like a sixty-incher – and entered the dining room, where Carlos started coughing. He bent over for a few seconds, like he was trying to prevent a full-blown coughing fit. Then he straightened up and said in a loud whisper that was almost like his normal speaking voice, 'Gotta stop smoking, man.'

'Shhhh,' Johnny said, shining his flashlight at his own face to show Carlos how serious he was.

Carlos smiled, and Johnny wondered if the cough was just for show, too, to get a reaction.

Carlos's attitude was starting to piss Johnny off. He'd been cool on the way to the house, but now that they were inside he was acting like this was all a big game or something.

They continued to the foyer, to the staircase. The plan was Carlos would go up and get the jewelry and whatever cash there was, and Johnny would be the lookout. Johnny knew he was putting a lot of trust in Carlos. Carlos could come down and say he couldn't find the jewelry, and meanwhile pocket all of it, but Johnny didn't want to believe Carlos would ever do that to him. They were brothers for life, and they'd never rip each other off. They had a bond that nothing could break.

Or did they?

Carlos started upstairs. The stairs were creaking, more than Johnny liked, and then they heard the noise. Johnny knew Carlos had heard it, too, because he suddenly stood still and cut off his flashlight. Johnny did the same and immediately stuck his hand in his pocket and gripped his piece.

Johnny tried to convince himself that it was just the wind, the house settling, but he knew exactly what he'd heard: footsteps. Somebody was up there.

Carlos wasn't packing. Johnny had wanted him to, but Carlos had said, 'Why do I need a piece when there's gonna be nobody in the house to shoot?'

Johnny was aiming his gun toward the top of the staircase. His eyes hadn't adjusted yet, and he could barely see. If he saw someone, anything, and had a clear shot, he was going to take it.

The only light in the room was coming from the streetlights outside and maybe some dim light from a night-light or something upstairs. Now Johnny could see the front door, the windows, and the outline of the staircase. He couldn't see anything upstairs yet, but he was just starting to see Carlos, standing there, about halfway up the stairs.

Then Carlos started heading up again.

Johnny wanted to scream, *What the fuck're you doing?* The guy wasn't carrying, and somebody was up there. He had to know somebody was up there.

Then Johnny heard movement, maybe the floor creaking. Shit.

Carlos said, 'Please don't shoot me,' and then the shots came. Two first, then a bunch all at once. Jesus, the shooter was opening up on Carlos, *the fuck was going on*? Johnny saw Carlos fall back a little, trying to steady himself by grabbing the railing, but then he lost his balance and fell to the bottom of the stairwell.

The whole thing had happened so fast, maybe like *three* seconds total, that Johnny didn't have any time to think about what to do. He was about to fire at the staircase – he saw somebody there now, looked like a guy in a T-shirt and boxers – but did he really want to get into a shootout?

He took a couple of steps toward the door then heard, 'Get the hell outta here or I'll shoot!'

It sounded like some rich, middle-aged white guy trying to be tough. Johnny would've bet any amount the guy was full of shit; he'd probably spent his whole round and was standing there shitting bricks with nothing but a handful of metal. If Johnny had taken a few seconds to think it over, he would've blown the guy away, but his instincts told him to get the hell out before this thing went from bad to worse.

Instead of going all the way back through the house to the back door and then having to go through the backyard, all the way around to the driveway, he went toward the front door. His eyes had adjusted more, and there was enough light there from the streetlights outside to see what he was doing as he unbolted two locks and unchained the door. He wasn't afraid the guy would shoot him in the back because he knew, he just knew, the guy had been bullshitting.

A few seconds later Johnny was sprinting down the block, and then he turned onto the main street and ran toward the Forest Hills gates. He heard sirens and immediately slowed, taking off his ski mask and gloves and walking at a normal pace as a police car sped by in the opposite direction.

Johnny felt like shit for ditching Carlos. Yeah, it looked like those bullets got him, probably got shot in the head the way he fell back, but what if he was wrong and Carlos had just gotten hit in the arm or something? Maybe if Johnny hadn't taken off, if he'd opened up on the middle-aged guy instead, he could've pulled Carlos out. Instead Johnny had saved his own ass instead of trying to help his brother, a guy who'd helped him so many times before.

Johnny went down to the subway. The platform was pretty much empty – just a homeless guy, sleeping sprawled out on a bench. It wasn't the same homeless guy he'd seen earlier on the street, though. Johnny was going to take the first train that came, but at this time of night, past two in the morning, he had no idea how long that would take. He listened for a rumbling in the tunnels, but there was nothing. He had to get the hell out of Forest Hills. The cops were definitely at the house now; how long would it be before they checked the subway station? Johnny figured he had five, ten minutes, if that.

He wasn't going to take any chances. He jogged to the end of the platform, then jumped onto the tracks and headed into the tunnel. He hadn't been in a subway tunnel in years, but as kids he and his friends used to walk the tracks all the time. One New Year's Eve, he and Carlos and a couple of other guys from St John's had walked along the 6 train tracks from Grand Central to Union Square. When trains came they'd stood in the space between the tracks and the wall.

Johnny walked along the tracks as fast as he could, occasionally jogging and even running. There was enough light to see anyway, but to make his path even more visible he shined his flashlight ahead of him, scaring away rats here and there.

It only took him about ten minutes or so to reach the Sixty-seventh Avenue station. He was going to continue through the tunnel to the next station, but he heard a train coming from behind him and climbed onto the platform. It was an R – heading toward Manhattan and Brooklyn. Johnny got on and sat in a seat in the corner, finally able to catch his breath.

Less than an hour later, he arrived at his tiny studio apartment in a walk-up tenement on Van Brunt Street in Red Hook, all the way out near the river. He still felt bad about ditching Carlos, but he kept telling himself that he'd done the right thing. Even if Carlos had been alive he would've been seriously injured, bleeding like hell, and it would've been impossible to get him out of the house. But no matter how hard Johnny tried to rationalize and reassure himself, he couldn't help feeling like a big wimp.

He took a long shower, thinking about all the ifs. If it hadn't started to rain that night in the city, if he hadn't gone into the Molly Wee Pub, if he hadn't picked up that girl Theresa, if he hadn't gone to the diner with Carlos, if he'd just said 'No thanks' at any point. He felt like a total idiot, but now his biggest concern was not messing up his life even more. He knew that with his pretty-boy looks he couldn't survive jail again – especially a long stretch. He'd kill himself before he had to be a sissy for all those guys again.

Johnny didn't think the cops would find a connection between him and Carlos. Before running into each other in Astoria that night, they hadn't seen each other in years, and Johnny had been careful to not talk to Carlos on his cell or any other way that could be traced. Assuming Carlos had been smart enough not to shoot his mouth off about the robbery – and Johnny didn't think he had – the only one Johnny had to worry about was Carlos's girlfriend, Gabriela.

What had Carlos said her last name was? He'd mentioned it the other night, when they got together in the city, on that bench in Battery Park, and went over the robbery plans for the final time. Was it Madena? Madano? Madeno? With the hot water beating down on his head, Johnny racked his brain, trying to remember the name, and then he thought, *Moreno.* Yeah, that was definitely it.

There were probably dozens of ways the cops could connect Gabriela to Carlos. Carlos had sworn to Johnny that Gabriela didn't know anything about Johnny, that she didn't even know his name, but what if Carlos had been bullshitting just to get Johnny to go along with the robbery? Was Johnny supposed to take Carlos's word for it now, when he'd been wrong about the house being empty tonight, when Johnny's ass, literally, was on the line? And if Gabriela did know about Johnny, what was to stop her from ratting him out to the cops, making some kind of deal with them?

Johnny got out of the shower and, with a towel around his waist, called 411 and got the address of Gabriela Moreno in Jackson Heights. That was easy. He put on his usual outfit, the Johnny Long uniform – dark jeans, skintight black tee, worn black leather jacket – tucked his piece under his jeans, safety on – didn't want to blow his dick off; what would he do without it? – and was out the door.

The sun was starting to rise when Johnny stood on the subway platform, waiting for an F train. To get to Jackson Heights in Queens, he had to change trains twice in the city. It would've been faster to steal a car or take a livery cab, but as always Johnny played the percentages. Getting busted for grand theft auto or having a cabdriver finger him in the courtroom would have been the stupidest ways to go down. He figured he had a little time to play with anyway. The cops would have to ID Carlos, figure out exactly who he was, then make the connection to Gabriela. Johnny had told Carlos to be careful, not to talk to Gabriela on his cell, et cetera, so hopefully the guy had listened.

Johnny got out at Eighty-second Street in Jackson Heights. He had Gabriela's address, but he had no idea how to get there. He had GPS on his phone, but he knew the cops could trace that shit. So he asked a guy outside the station for directions. The guy – he was old with very thick glasses, so Johnny thought he would have a hard time ID-ing him later – told Johnny where to go. It was farther than he'd thought, sounded like it would be a ten-minute walk at least. After walking for about twenty minutes Johnny knew something was wrong. He asked a teenager, a black kid on his way to school, for directions, and the kid kind of laughed and told Johnny he'd walked way out of the way. Johnny had to jog back about ten blocks and ask somebody else for directions before he finally found Gabriela's apartment building.

It was past seven thirty – about five hours since the robbery. The cops, if they'd moved fast, could've already gotten to her. A good sign: Johnny looked around and didn't see any police cars, marked or unmarked. *Unmarked*, that always cracked Johnny up. The cops always thought they were so undercover in their unmarked cars; meanwhile the unmarked cars were always black Impalas or Chargers that screamed 'cop.' If they wanted to be unmarked, why didn't they drive beat-up Chevys with Puerto Rican flags all over them? Sometimes Johnny thought cops had to be the biggest bunch of idiots in the world.

Johnny pressed the apartment buzzer with G MORENO next to it – didn't anybody ever tell her not to put her name on it? – and when she answered he said, 'Police,' and she let him right up.

On the stairwell he stopped and attached the sound suppressor to the end of the barrel, then put the gun back in his inside jacket pocket and continued up to her apartment. He rang the bell, and she answered, looking scared, like she thought she was about to get busted. Well, she was about to get busted, just not the way she thought.

Johnny was surprised, though; she was actually a really good-looking woman.

Yeah, overweight, but she had a pretty South American look and big light brown eyes. How had Carlos gotten a woman this hot?

'You Gabriela?' Johnny asked.

She nodded, and he shot her in the face. She fell back a little, then crumpled onto the floor, the blood puddle spreading around her mouth. He checked to make sure none of her blood was on him, and then he stood back and put a couple into her chest to make sure she was gone for good.

He took a quick look around, spotted her pocketbook. He took twenty-three dollars, then tossed the pocketbook onto the floor and got the hell out of there.

Heading back toward the city on the 7 train – it was crowded with commuters – Johnny stood at the end of the car, facing his reflection in the door, replaying the shootings. He thought it had all gone pretty well. He didn't think he'd been seen entering or leaving, and he'd been careful not to leave any evidence behind. He knew that because of Gabriela's job the cops would try to make a connection between her shooting and the shooting and robbery in Forest Hills, but he didn't see any way the police could get to him. There was no way that Gabriela and Carlos would've talked about the robbery with anybody else, and hopefully the purse on the floor would be enough to throw the stupid cops off.

It felt so good to finally be able to relax. Johnny had been on edge pretty much nonstop since meeting Carlos in Forest Hills, and he was looking forward to getting back to Brooklyn, maybe stopping at a diner for a big breakfast, and then getting into bed and sleeping for as long as possible.

But then, when he was switching for the F train at Thirty-fourth Street, he got all tensed up again, thinking, *What if Carlos is still alive?* Maybe Carlos was in a hospital, hooked up to machines, and the police were questioning him right now. Johnny didn't think Carlos would talk to the cops – St John's brothers didn't rat each other out – but then again you never know what a guy will do when the cops start hanging twenty-five to life over his ass.

In Brooklyn, Johnny realized he had lost his appetite and decided to skip the diner and head straight home. He turned on the TV to the local news station, and there it was, the top story, the robbery and shooting in Forest Hills. The reporter said Carlos Sanchez had been shot and killed by the owner of the house.

'Thank fucking God,' Johnny said, and he leaned back on his sofa and relaxed again.

He was totally in the clear. There was no way the cops would ever catch on to him. All he had to do was lie low for a while and everything would be okay.

On the TV, they were showing the guy, Dr Adam Bloom. Johnny thought, *Doctor? What kind of doctor is he?* Johnny hated the way the guy was acting all smug and proud of himself, talking about how he did the right thing shooting Carlos, saying, 'I'd do it all over again' and 'I think anybody in my position would've done what I did.' Man, Johnny wished he'd just shot the guy last night, blown him away.

The report ended, and Johnny shut off the TV and got into bed. He tried to fall asleep, but he kept thinking about the time when he was fifteen years old and these gangbangers were kicking the shit out of him in a schoolyard and everybody was standing around letting it happen, except Carlos. He came right over, pulled a blade, put it up to the biggest guy's face, and said, 'Mess with my boy, you mess with this.' It wasn't the only time Carlos had saved Johnny's ass from a beating – Johnny might not've survived being a teenager if it wasn't for Carlos. So now it just didn't seem right that Carlos was going into a box in the ground, probably in Potter's Field, where the city buried people who had no families, and that cocky bastard, Dr Bloom, got to go on living with his happy family in his big, fancy house.

Yeah, Johnny knew he had to do what Carlos would've done for him.

He had to give that uppity son of a bitch some payback.

9

BEFORE THE ROBBERY and the shooting, Dana Bloom thought she had gotten back in control of her life. She'd told Tony that she wanted to end their fling and, although he didn't take it very well, and it had been hard for her to let go, too, she'd made it three days without any contact with him and she felt like she'd made it over the hump, that she was ready to put the past four months with Tony behind her and rededicate herself to her marriage.

But now, suddenly, everything was falling apart again, and it was all because of that stupid gun. She had no idea why Adam had to go and shoot that guy – why couldn't he listen to her for once in his life? – and now Gabriela was dead and she couldn't help thinking that it was all Adam's fault, too. That he wouldn't take any responsibility or admit any fault for anything he'd done infuriated her more than anything. Why was it so hard for him to say *I'm sorry*?

After Detective Clements left, Dana felt completely helpless. Not only couldn't she get through to her husband, but she felt like the police couldn't protect them, and she didn't feel safe in her own house.

They were walking along the hallway past Marissa's room – she was in there blasting her stereo again, some god-awful music – and Dana was saying, 'Let's go to Florida, just to get out of the house for a few days or a week or whatever.'

Adam, heading into the bedroom, said, 'That's ridiculous. I'm not running away.'

Following him, Dana said, 'Don't call me ridiculous.'

'I'm not calling *you* ridiculous. I'm saying running away is ridiculous.'

'Who's talking about running away? I'm just saying I'd feel a lot safer if we weren't here, in this house, while that killer's still out there, that's all.'

'What killer?' Adam said. 'Think about what you're saying. It just doesn't make any sense.'

'What doesn't make any sense? What planet are you on? Gabriela was killed, and –'

'And that has absolutely nothing to do with us.' He was raising his voice to talk over her. She hated it when he did that; it was so demeaning and disrespectful. 'You're just making up stories, trying to scare yourself,' he added and turned away from her, changing into his sweatpants. Another thing she hated – when he gave her his back.

'I can't believe you,' she said. 'You really can't be this stubborn. You're just doing it to get a reaction from me.'

'Really? And why would I want to do that?'

'Because you like it, you like provoking me. You like the way it makes you feel.'

'That's it, you have me figured out, all right. I woke up today and I said, *You know what, I think I'll provoke my wife today. That'll be so much fun.*'

'That's exactly what you do.'

'Oh, for Christ's sake, stop it. Your problem is you just refuse to see anything any other way. You know everything. You have all the answers. You even know more than the police, apparently. I still love that, by the way, telling off the NYPD. That was just brilliant.'

'You're doing it again,' she said.

'Doing what again?'

'Spinning everything I say into something I'm not saying instead of just listening to me.'

'I'll listen to you if you start making some sense.'

She was so angry at him she couldn't even remember what they were arguing about anymore. She took a few moments and then said, 'So what if I'm right? What if it is all related? What if whoever killed Gabriela comes back here, tries to break into our house?'

'He won't get in.'

'What if he does? What're you going to do then? Get your gun again? Shoot him?'

'If he breaks into our house and heads upstairs in the dark, yes, I'll shoot him.'

Dana stared at her husband, slack jawed, her hands on her hips. 'Who the hell are you?' she said. 'I feel like I don't know you at all anymore.'

'Oh, stop it with your melodrama.'

She continued, 'You shoot one guy and you suddenly think you're so tough, you're some kind of Mafia hit man or something? Acting so rational, so in control. You're not afraid, and you won't run away, you're just gonna keep shooting people with your gun – your gun'll keep us all nice and safe.'

Shaking his head, he said, 'I'm going to the gym,' and left.

That was so like him – just walking out of the room in mid argument with everything unresolved, leaving her all pent up and frustrated. It was so controlling, so manipulative, and she knew exactly why he was doing it – to push her buttons. She used to complain about it all the time when they were in marriage counseling, but he kept on doing it anyway. If that wasn't an indication that he didn't care about her, what was?

A little while after Adam left, Dana heard Marissa going downstairs, and the door slammed again. Dana was alone in the house, and she *felt* alone. She just wanted some emotional support at a difficult time; was that too much to ask for? Things were going to get worse, she just knew they were going to get worse, and no one was going to be able to help her, not the police, and not even her own husband.

Then she did something that she knew she'd regret – she got her cell phone from her purse and called Tony.

He picked up and said, 'It's so great to hear your voice, baby. I miss you so much.'

She thought, *What the hell am I doing?* She wanted to hang up – she knew that it was the right thing to do, that this wasn't going to solve anything, that in fact it was going to make things even more complicated – but she heard herself say weakly, 'I miss you so much, too.'

'I've been waiting for you to call,' he said. 'Where are you?'

She wanted to feel his body against hers so badly. She wanted to feel him inside her.

'When do you get off?' she asked.

'I'll get off for you anytime,' he said.

If any other man had said that to her, she would have assumed he was making a bad pun, but she knew even a bad pun was beyond Tony. It was usually hard for her to hold conversations with him that didn't involve bodybuilding, protein supplements, or sex. Not that Dana usually had any objection to this, especially the sex part. She was interested in Tony for sex and sex only, and she'd made this very clear to him.

They arranged to meet at four at his place. Dana didn't want to have to see Adam again when he got back from the gym, so she left the house early and killed time at the Starbucks a few blocks from Tony's. She was dressed casually, jeans and a black turtleneck, but underneath she was wearing a hot pink satin halter from Victoria's Secret. Adam didn't like lingerie – one time she'd worn sexy underwear to bed and he'd actually told her that it looked silly on her; way to make a woman feel great about herself – but it always turned Tony on.

Heading toward Tony's building, she tried to talk herself out of going. She knew that she was jeopardizing her marriage, and did she really want to lead Tony on more than she already had? Although she'd told him many times that they had no future together, that she had no intention of ever leaving Adam for him, when he said things to her like 'Wouldn't it be great if we were living together?' or 'Imagine if it could be like this forever,' she'd felt like she wasn't getting through to him at all.

It was still hard for her to believe she'd gotten into this situation. For years with Adam, even when things weren't great, she'd never even thought about cheating on him. She'd seen the way affairs had destroyed families in her neighborhood, and she imagined growing old with Adam, for better or for worse.

But she'd had opportunities to be unfaithful. Mr Sorrentino, Marissa's fifth-grade science teacher, used to flirt with her at parent-teacher conferences, and a few years ago, Scott Goldberg, an old boyfriend from college at Albany, had contacted her. He'd recently gotten divorced and was going to be in the city on business, he said, and he asked her if she wanted to meet at the bar of his hotel for a drink. She made up an excuse and didn't go. There were other opportunities now and then, but any time she sensed a guy was coming on to her she always maintained boundaries and let him know she was married and not interested.

But over the past several years her attitude had gradually changed. Part of it, she had to admit, may have had to do with empty nest syndrome. When Marissa went away to college, Dana and Adam had more time to spend together, but it was hard for her to shift gears, to become just a wife again instead of a wife and mother. It was hard to remember what she liked about Adam, hard to remember what they used to talk about, and they actually spent less time together than they ever had before. Adam always seemed to be wrapped up in work, and she started to realize how lonely she was. For years she'd defended her life as a stay-at-home mom – she refused to use the word 'housewife' – by telling her working friends, 'I love doing nothing,' but secretly she regretted not going back to work years ago and was jealous of her friends who had careers. She was bored at home, and it was getting harder to fill her days. Last year menopause had started setting in, so she had to deal with the emotional ups and downs, and for a while she'd been on Prozac for what her psychiatrist had called 'a mild depression.' When Marissa graduated and decided to move back home, Dana was actually thrilled. Things had been getting tense with Adam, and it was nice having her daughter around again.

Around the time Marissa moved back in, Tony started working as a trainer at the New York Sports Club. He was very friendly and flirty with Dana from the get-go, smiling at her all the time and saying hi, or coming over when she was using machines and saying things like 'What you want to do is get some more extension,' or passing by smiling, commenting, 'You look sensational today.' She thought he was just being nice and there was nothing more to it, but she had to admit, it stroked her ego to hear those compliments, especially from a guy in his twenties. She looked good for a forty-seven-year-old woman who hadn't gotten any work done. She was slim, still had nice legs, and though she sometimes felt self-conscious about the lines around her eyes and mouth, most people who met her thought she was in her early forties, even late thirties. But it had been years since a man had paid any attention to her. When she was younger and passed a construction site, guys would whistle at her and make crude comments; yes, it had felt like harassment back then, but now she missed getting male attention, even the negative kind. She liked how when she was using the elliptical StairMaster she'd look in the mirror ahead of her and see Tony checking out her ass and then looking away quickly when their gazes met.

The most attractive thing about Tony was that he was attracted to her. He wasn't bad-looking – he had a cute, pudgy Italian face – but his interest in her, the way he made her feel like a young sex object, was irresistible. When was the last time Adam had told her she was pretty or paid attention to her the way Tony did? She felt like Adam took her for granted and barely listened to her half the time. She'd be telling Adam about something that had happened during the day, or something interesting she'd read about in the paper or seen on TV, and she'd see his eyes wander and she'd know that even though he was answering her, saying 'Really?' and 'Okay,' he was thinking about something else and couldn't give a shit about her. She started looking forward to going to the gym and seeing Tony, craving his flattering comments and the feeling she got whenever he smiled at her.

Then one day she was on the exercise mat, stretching, when Tony came over and asked her if she'd lost some weight. She'd actually gained a few pounds, but she said, 'No, I'm the same,' and he said, 'Well, you look sensational.' She noticed his eyes pan toward her breasts for a moment – she loved when he did that, and she was glad she was wearing that new exercise bra with that great support – then he said, 'Hey, I'm getting off at seven, want to get some coffee or somethin'?' She had nothing planned – Adam had said he'd be in the city seeing patients and wouldn't be back till late – but she said, 'Sorry, I can't.'

It was the right thing to do. Tony was a nice fantasy, but that was how she had to keep it – a fantasy.

But the next time Tony asked her out for coffee, a few days later, she said yes. Coffee had somehow evolved into a drink at a nearby sports bar. As she'd expected, they had zero to talk about, but she loved the way he looked at her, like she was the most beautiful woman he'd ever seen – he actually said, 'You're the most beautiful woman I've ever seen' – and she wanted him to kiss her. Into their second round of margaritas he asked her if she was happily married, and she said, 'We've had some problems,' purposely leaving the door open, wanting to keep this flirtation or whatever it was going, loving the way it made her feel, terrified to give it up. There was a long moment when they looked into each other's eyes, and she saw his shift downward slightly, toward her lips. She checked the time on her cell phone and said, 'I should really get –' and he reached out and held her hand – when was the last time a man besides her husband had held her hand in a romantic way? – and said, 'Come back with me.' She told him she was extremely flattered but she couldn't, and she insisted on paying for the drinks and left.

She barely slept that night. It hit her how truly unhappy she had become at home, and she couldn't stop thinking about Tony and wishing she'd gone back to his place with him. She fantasized about him doing things to her until she couldn't take it anymore and had to go into the guest bedroom and use her sex toy.

The next day Adam said he was working late again, and at around four fifteen Dana arrived at the gym, remembering Tony telling her he would be getting off work at five. Working out on the elliptical StairMaster, she looked in the mirror and saw Tony get distracted, checking out her ass several times while training a client.

At five to five she went up to Tony and said, 'So does that offer still stand?' About ten minutes later, they were at his place, screwing against the wall, then on the living room floor. It was by far the hottest, rawest sex Dana had ever had. God, it had been more than twenty years since she'd had sex anywhere other than a bed. She'd never been with a guy so strong, so powerful, and it felt good to feel his strong hands pinning her down, squeezing her ass. The fact that he wasn't very bright and they had nothing in common made him even sexier. It reduced him to being a total sex object. He was just man – raw, simple man who gave her pleasure. She'd thought that so many things were missing in her marriage, that she and Adam had such underlying problems, but under that grunting bodybuilder, she felt like all she'd needed all along was to get laid.

In a few hours she had more sex than she'd had in the last two years with Adam. Pathetic, but true.

She felt very guilty and conflicted afterward. She'd felt great with Tony, but now she felt like a horrible person, a liar, a slut. In the past she'd watch a movie and see a woman cheat on her husband and think, *What a total idiot,* and now, somehow, she'd become that woman. She'd been faithful to Adam for twenty-seven years, including the time they'd been dating, and now she'd have to go through the rest of her life knowing that she'd been unfaithful. Making it worse, she knew this was totally one-sided; Adam would never even consider cheating on her. She didn't plan to ever tell Adam, but how did she know Tony wouldn't go bragging about his conquest in the gym? For all she knew he was sleeping with dozens of other unhappy married middle-aged women. Tony and Adam saw each other at the gym all the time; they weren't very friendly, but they said hi to each other. She knew that if Adam somehow found out he'd never forgive her, and she was angry at herself for getting into this position. With one phone call, some young muscle-head trainer from the New York Sports Club had the power to ruin the rest of her life.

But this didn't stop Dana from seeing Tony again. She met him a couple of days later, and then they started to see each other regularly, three or four times a week. She couldn't stop thinking about him when they were apart, about how good it had felt to be taken away to a place so foreign that her normal life seemed dull in comparison. Sometimes they text-messaged each other or talked on the phone; although they had very little to say to each other, she got excited every time she saw his name flash on her phone or heard his voice. She felt like she was a teenager again, in her first relationship, and everything was fresh and exciting. To deal with her guilt, she told herself that she was having a fling, which somehow seemed more harmless than an actual affair. A fling felt like something she could compartmentalize, something that wasn't potentially destructive. A fling was like a star that would shine briefly and brightly and then gradually peter out. She'd use the fling to help her get through this rocky period in her marriage, and then everything would return to normal.

Some days she was so sore from sex with Tony that if Adam came on to her she'd have to make up stories. *I'm too tired. I think I'm coming down with something.* The constant lying was the worst part and was beginning to wear on her, overshadowing all the positives of the fling. Then Tony did something that told her it was really time to end it.

She came home from shopping one afternoon, and Gabriela, who was cleaning in the kitchen, said, 'I think somebody like you, Mrs Bloom.'

Typically, since she'd gotten involved with Tony, Dana feared the worst, and her fight-or-flight mechanism kicked in. 'What're you talking about?' she snapped.

'Look in the dining room,' Gabriela said.

Oh shit, had Tony been to the house?

Dana went through the swinging doors, ready to scold Tony, tell him it was over, and then she saw the large, tacky bouquet of flowers on the dining room table. Well, it wasn't as bad as him showing up, but it was almost as bad.

She read the computer-printed note:

**Hey you were fucking great last night baby
You got a sensational body baby
Love T-Bone!!!!**

She called him up, furious, and he said he didn't think he'd done anything wrong because he'd made sure the flowers would be delivered during the day when her husband was at work.

'How'd you know he'd be at work today?' she said. 'What if he was home?' He admitted that, yeah, that probably hadn't been such a great idea and promised he wouldn't do anything like that again, but she saw this as a major wake-up call. He'd been getting reckless lately – texting her dozens of times a day and calling her a few times when Adam was home. She had a marriage to protect, but he was a single guy with nothing at stake, and it was starting to feel too unbalanced. Besides, he was getting too hooked on her, even saying the other night when they were lying in bed, 'I think I'm falling in love with you.' There was no doubt about it – she definitely had to end the fling now, or things were going to spiral out of control.

She said to Gabriela, 'Promise me you won't say a word about this to Adam.'

'Don't worry,' Gabriela said. 'You can always trust me, Mrs Bloom.'

The next day Dana went to the gym and told Tony there was something important she needed to talk to him about, and they went into the sales office. She knew he'd be upset and hoped that telling him in the gym would prevent a big scene. He got melodramatic, told her she was doing the wrong thing and he couldn't live without her, but she managed to leave before the real begging started.

The breakup was hard for her, too, surprisingly hard. She didn't miss him as much as she missed the idea of him, of having something exciting and unpredictable in her life. Suddenly being home with Adam felt excruciatingly dull; she felt like a prisoner serving a life sentence with no possibility of parole. She was back in her old rut, in her empty, meaningless, lonely life, living day to day, with nothing to look forward to.

Tony had left two phone messages and six text messages on her cell. He wasn't taking the breakup well, and she wanted to call him, tell him she'd made a mistake, but she resisted and deleted all the messages without playing or reading them. God, this was even harder than when she'd quit smoking, but she knew she had to treat it exactly the same way, like she was breaking an addiction. The first days of getting over the addiction were always the hardest, and the trick was to stay strong, not give in. She was glad that she and Adam and Marissa were planning to go to Florida to visit Adam's mother. Getting away from New York for a few days would be a huge help.

The next day she was home alone, and she felt the familiar intense urge to call Tony and arrange to meet at his place for a quickie during his lunch break. She fought it and called her friend Sharon instead and went over to her house a few blocks away for coffee. Keeping the fling a secret for so long had become draining, and Dana needed to talk to someone about it.

Opening up to Sharon was a big help. It made her feel like she'd done the right thing, ending it when she did, before it snowballed out of control.

Sharon told her, 'You and Adam have invested so much time together, whatever you do don't throw it away, especially for some guy you don't even really like.'

Sharon's words were like a refreshing blast of reality. Dana continued to delete all of Tony's messages and managed to make it through the most difficult first few days. She spent more time with Adam; she met him in the city one night and they went out to their favorite Spanish restaurant in the West Village, and another night they stayed home and watched a movie together, cuddling on the couch.

They had to cancel their trip to Florida because of the tropical storm, but Dana didn't feel the desperate need to get away anymore. Tony had gone a whole day without trying to contact her, and she was starting to think of the fling in the past tense. It had been fun for a while, but it had ended, and now it was time to repair her marriage.

Then the robbery happened, and now here she was, relapsing, going back to Tony, about to mess up her life all over again.

She knew that restarting something that had been so hard to

end was a huge mistake. It was wrong to take her anger about the shooting out on Adam in this way, and it definitely wasn't going to accomplish anything. Despite everything they'd been through and how angry she was, she loved Adam and wanted to improve their marriage and work out their differences. She knew that if she didn't get herself to turn back she could ruin her life, but the pull to be with Tony and screw things up was so intense. She felt like something beyond her was controlling her, making her decisions, and she was just a witness to it all.

On the stairs, going up to his apartment, she was still trying to talk herself into turning back, reminding herself how much Adam meant to her, how this wouldn't resolve anything, how it could make things worse, much worse, and then she saw Tony – in tight black boxer briefs and nothing else – and a few seconds later they were in his apartment and he was kissing her neck, pushing her up against the back of the front door. Her pants and turtleneck were off and he was sliding his hands up under her red lace panties, over her ass, saying, 'I love when you wear this shit,' and she was moaning, 'Oh, God, baby. Oh, God...'

Then, afterward, under his body on the floor, she thought, *What the hell am I doing?*

Tony looked into her eyes, smiled, and asked, 'You want some Gatorade or somethin'?'

'I... I have to go,' she said, bending down, reaching for her jeans.

'What's the hurry?' Tony said. 'We got all night.'

'This was a mistake,' she said out loud, but to herself. 'This was a huge mistake.'

'What're you talking about?' He sounded seriously confused. 'I thought you said you missed me.'

She pulled her jeans on, not bothering to zip or snap them. She was muttering to herself like a mantra, 'Gotta get home, gotta get back, gotta get home, gotta get back...'

When she was about to put her turtleneck on Tony grabbed her wrist hard and said, 'Come on, what're you doing?'

'Please let go of me,' she said.

'Why? I don't get it.'

He let go of her wrist, and she finished getting dressed.

'Was I too rough on you?' he asked. 'I thought you like it like that.'

When she left his apartment and was going downstairs he screamed after her, 'When am I gonna see you again? Don't do this to me, baby! You know how much I love you, baby!'

She walked fast, saying to herself, 'What an idiot, what a fuckin' idiot.' She didn't know if she was talking about herself or Tony, but she couldn't believe she'd done such a stupid, impulsive thing. What the hell was she doing? She was forty-seven years old, acting like she was seventeen. It was no wonder Marissa had been giving them so much trouble lately – look who she had for a role model.

Several minutes later, as she approached her house, she was a little calmer – less emotional, anyway. Okay, so she'd had one minor slipup, but she could forget it ever happened; it didn't have to mean anything. She just wondered about Tony. There was a tone in his voice, anger she'd never heard before. He'd already sent those flowers; what was he going to do next?

Damn it, she usually showered after having sex with Tony, and now she reeked of his cologne.

She opened the front door quietly, hoping Adam wasn't home. 'Honey, that you?'

'Fuck me,' she muttered.

10

WHEN ADAM SAW all the news trucks and reporters out in front of the house, he thought, *Oh, no, not again*. He just wanted to get away from the house for a little while, de-stress, *not* have another pointless argument with Dana. He didn't want to go through all of that having-to-defend-himself-to-the-reporters nonsense again.

He was planning to be curt, answer a question or two, then say, *Sorry, in a hurry*, and walk away. But surprisingly, the questioning today seemed to have a much different tone than last night. Even while asking questions like 'Do you think your maid's murder was related to the break-in last night?' and 'Who do you think killed your maid?' and 'Do you think your maid robbed your house?' the reporters seemed almost apologetic.

One reporter asked, 'In the wake of the shooting this morning in Jackson Heights, do you feel vindicated, Dr Bloom?'

'No, I don't feel vindicated,' Adam said. 'I feel justified, yes, but I felt justified yesterday, too. In my mind, nothing's changed.'

Adam didn't feel nearly as self-conscious as he had during last night's questioning. He even ended making an impromptu speech, looking right into the camera, saying, 'My family's very saddened by the death of Gabriela Moreno. I don't know if she was involved or wasn't involved in the robbery of our house, but she was a wonderful woman, and I hope whoever killed her is brought to justice as soon as possible.'

Walking to the gym, he was proud of the way he'd handled himself. If there was a bright side to all of this, he was definitely overcoming his glossophobia. He thought he came off as confident and well-spoken, and the last bit was a perfect touch, not publicly blaming Gabriela, showing people that, despite everything, he was compassionate and forgiving. Okay, so maybe he was letting his ego take over and he was enjoying the attention a bit more than he ought to, but was there really anything so wrong with this?

As he walked along Austin Street in the main commercial area of Forest Hills, he couldn't help looking around to see if anyone was recognizing him. No one seemed to be, but he expected people at the gym to come up to him. He didn't know very many people there – most of the regulars were in their twenties and thirties – but they had seen him around and might have seen him on the TV news earlier and made the connection.

The girl at the front desk who scanned his membership card didn't have any unusual reaction, and in the main part of the gym people were in their own worlds, watching TV, reading magazines or newspapers, listening to their iPods, or just focusing on their workouts.

After Adam did a half-hour on an exercise bike, he headed toward the weight room. He passed Tony, one of the trainers. Tony was a nice guy, always talking to Adam about the Knicks, the Mets, and the Jets. He thought Tony might say something to him about the shooting, but he didn't, and he wasn't particularly friendly either. He glanced at Adam, then looked away and kept walking. That was weird. Eh, maybe he was just in a bad mood.

Adam finished his workout, breaking a nice sweat. He'd only lasted sixteen minutes on the treadmill, but maybe he could get up to twenty or twenty-five next time. He was looking forward to showering at home and making a few calls for work, and then maybe he and Dana could watch a movie together. He felt bad about fighting with her before, especially about the way he'd ended the argument, just walking out on her like that. He felt like he'd been manipulative. He knew how much his being dismissive bothered her, and it was wrong of him to try to push her buttons that way.

But then, when he arrived back at the house, he found a note:

Went to Sharon's. Be back later. D

The way she'd signed it 'D' and not 'Love, D' or even 'XO D,' the way she normally would've, showed she was seriously upset, which annoyed Adam.

He could understand why Dana would be angry at him, but it seemed like she was taking it too far, going out and leaving a curt, nasty note. After all, had he done something *so* awful? He'd walked out on her in the middle of an argument and, oh yeah, he didn't want to get rid of his gun – the gun that she had agreed to let him keep in the house, the gun that had saved their lives last night. He didn't see why any of that warranted this kind of reaction, and, come to think of it, he didn't like what she'd said to him before, how he was ruining their lives. What was that supposed to mean, anyway? Up until today he'd thought things had been pretty good between them lately. Okay, they needed to start spending more time together – what couple didn't? – but they'd been expressing their anger well and hadn't been arguing as much as they used to. But now, just because something horrible had happened to them last night, because they'd been through a tragedy, she was making him out to be this horrible person, this tormentor who was ruining her life?

The more Adam thought about it, the more upset he got. And to think, he'd actually been considering coming home and apologizing to *her*. He was the one who deserved the apology, damn it. He'd been traumatized, and all he got from her was what, blame? Where was the support? Where was the love? How come he hadn't heard, 'Don't worry, honey, everything's going to be okay?' Or even a little hug would've been nice. He knew this was just another example of how Dana twisted things whenever they had a disagreement, making him feel like everything was his fault when in actuality he'd done nothing wrong.

He crumpled up Dana's note and threw it toward the wastebasket near the front door. It didn't go in, but he didn't bother to pick it up.

He took a quick shower, then saw he'd gotten a call from Jen, a thirty-four-year-old patient with a history of clinical depression who was in an emotionally abusive relationship. He'd also gotten a text from her: *please call me back doctor*. Adam returned the call immediately, and Jen was extremely upset – sobbing, barely able to speak. She eventually explained that her boyfriend, Victor, had walked out on her for good. Adam talked to her for a long time, mainly listening to her and giving her a chance to express her feelings but also calmly pointing out the advantages of the relationship ending and reminding her how unhappy she'd been with Victor. Meanwhile, he was really probing for signs of a deeper depression. She'd once tried to kill herself in college, and he was particularly looking for signs that she was suicidal, such as extreme self-loathing, worthlessness, and hopelessness. But he decided that she was in the midst of an acute reactive depression and didn't pose any immediate danger to herself. By the end of the conversation, she sounded much calmer and in control of her emotions, and she promised she'd call him first thing in the morning to let him know how she was doing.

Helping people get through difficult times in their lives always lifted Adam's mood and reminded him of his real purpose in life. What was the famous Jackie Robinson quote? The only meaning your life has is the effect it has on other lives? Something like that. Anyway, Adam was looking forward to getting back into the swing of things at work, resuming his normal life. He sat down with his laptop for a while and answered his email; most of it was work-related, though a couple of friends had heard about the robbery and shooting and wanted to offer support and make sure everything was okay.

At around four, the guy from the security company arrived and programmed a new code, and Adam made him check and double-check to make sure the system was working properly.

'Don't worry, sir,' the guy said. 'As long as the system's armed, nobody's getting into this house.'

Adam wasn't concerned. They had the alarm system and the new Medeco locks on the back door, and of course he still had his gun. He felt they'd be very well-protected if, on the off-chance, someone – perhaps Sanchez's accomplice – decided to rob the house again, though he doubted that would happen. There was just no way that a burglar, no matter how stupid or angry he was, would try to rob a house where a shooting had taken place, a house that had been crawling with cops and reporters. Why not rob another house in the neighborhood, or in a completely different neighborhood, someplace totally off the radar? Besides, there was still a chance that Gabriela's murder had nothing to do with the robbery. Maybe Gabriela herself had been the second intruder last night and then had been killed in some random robbery attempt. Although Adam couldn't imagine any logical scenario where he or his family could be in danger, he was glad he would be prepared for the worst nevertheless.

He microwaved leftover chicken and string beans and was eating at the kitchen table while rereading the sports section of the *Times* when he got a call on his BlackBerry with the ID FOX BROADCASTING. He figured it was another reporter with a follow-up question, but it turned out it was Karen Owens, a producer from *Good Day New York*. She asked Adam if he would like to appear as a guest tomorrow morning.

'You're kidding,' Adam said. 'Why do you want me?'

'Why do you think?' she said. 'You're a big local news story, Dr Bloom.' Adam couldn't think of any reason not to go on, so he said yes, figuring, *What the hell?* She told him how much she was looking forward to meeting him, and they arranged for a limo to pick him up in front of his house at six tomorrow morning and take him directly to the studio on the Upper East Side.

A few minutes after he got off the phone with the producer from Fox, he heard the front door opening. Still blown away by the call – was he really going to be a guest on *Good Day New York*? – for a moment he forgot he was angry with Dana and called out, 'Honey, that you?'

He went into the foyer, noticing right away that she didn't

seem very happy to see him. Then he remembered the way they'd left off before and how angry he was at her and he said, 'You're back early,' tempering his enthusiasm.

'Why's it early?' she asked, avoiding eye contact, taking off her coat.

'I don't know. Usually when you go to Sharon's you don't get back till ten or eleven.'

'We just had coffee,' she said flatly, hanging up her coat in the closet.

'So anyway, you wouldn't believe it,' Adam said. '*Good Day New York* wants me on tomorrow.'

'Great,' Dana said in a monotone.

Adam didn't expect her to be excited, but he didn't feel like playing their usual I-can-be-cold-and-distant-longer-than-you game either.

'I really think we need to talk,' he said.

'Later, okay?' she said.

'Wait a second,' he said, and she stopped and stared at him. Her expression was so void of emotion she could've been staring at a piece of wood.

'I don't think it was right what you said before,' he said.

'What did I say?' she asked.

For a moment he couldn't remember himself; then he said, 'About how I'm screwing up your life or however you put it. How exactly do you think I'm screwing up your life?'

She let out a breath, looking down, and said, 'You're right, I'm sorry. I didn't mean it that way at all.'

Was she actually giving in? She almost never admitted any fault in an argument, or at least not until after hours of not talking to each other.

'Well, I accept your apology,' he said, 'and I'm sorry, too. I shouldn't've just left like that. I know how much you hate it when I do that.'

'It's okay,' she said and took a couple of steps toward the stairs.

'No, it's not okay,' he said, and she stopped. 'I was wrong and I'm sorry. Forgive me?'

She nodded tentatively, now looking like she might start to

cry. She didn't usually get so emotional during their arguments; he figured it probably had to do with Gabriela and not him.

'Hey, come here,' he said.

She didn't budge, but he went over to her, kissed her quickly on the lips, and then hugged her. She seemed uncomfortable, pulling back a little.

'Is that a new perfume?' he asked.

'What?' She seemed a little startled. 'No… I mean, not really.'

'I like it,' he said as his cell started ringing. He took the phone out of his pocket and looked at the display, which was showing an unfamiliar 212 number.

'The hell is that?' he asked, squinting at the phone.

As he answered the call – 'Yes?' – Dana rushed upstairs.

'Mr Bloom?' a woman said.

'Who's this?' Adam asked.

'Grace Williams. I'm a reporter for *New York* magazine. Do you have a moment?'

The woman explained that she wanted to interview him for a feature story. Adam couldn't believe it – what was going on here? He arranged to meet her tomorrow afternoon in midtown; then he ended the call and went to tell Dana the news. She was in the shower – he heard the water running – but when he tried the bathroom door it was locked. This was strange – Dana almost never locked the door when she showered.

He knocked on the door and said, 'Dana, you okay in there?' No answer.

He banged harder and shouted, 'Dana!'

'What is it?' she shouted back.

'Nothing,' Adam said. 'I'll talk to you when you come out.'

'What?'

'Never mind!'

Adam emailed his assistant, Lauren, asking her to move his lunch appointment to another day, and he started looking through his closet for something to wear tomorrow. Normally he dressed professional-casual – shirts, slacks, and sport jackets – but on *Good Day New York* he didn't want to come off as some stuffy psychologist. He wanted to look cool, relaxed, hip. Maybe he'd go for the sweater-and-jeans look, or was that *too* casual?

He laid out dark jeans and a black crewneck sweater on the bed, but he wasn't sure. Maybe he'd wear a black button-down shirt with a black sport jacket over it – the Hollywood player look, show people that he was a successful psychotherapist but wasn't trying to show off about it.

Dana came out of the bathroom in a robe, her hair wrapped in a towel. 'You won't believe the call I just got,' he said. 'Now *New York magazine* wants to interview me.'

'Did Clements call?' she asked as if she hadn't heard him.

'No,' Adam said.

'That's not good.'

'It's not good or bad,' he said, 'but isn't it crazy? First TV and now a magazine interview?'

'Sorry,' Dana said flatly, turning away. 'I guess I just can't get as excited about your fifteen minutes of fame as you are.'

'I'm not excited,' he said, ignoring the not so subtle put-down. 'I'm just surprised. I really didn't think this would get this kind of attention.'

'Is that what you're looking for? Attention?'

'Of course not,' he said.

Dana glanced at the outfit laid out on the bed.

'So I want to look good on TV,' he said. 'What's wrong with that?'

'Nothing,' she said. 'I just don't understand why you have to go on the show in the first place.'

'What do you mean? They asked me to. It's helping me emotionally, with my glossophobia. And, besides, it could be some good publicity. Maybe I'll get a few new patients out of it.'

'You could've said no. I don't know why you want to bring more attention to us, I don't see how that's going to help make things any better.'

Adam, frustrated because he knew she was making sense but he didn't want to hear it, said, 'I thought we made up downstairs. Can we just stop this nonsense?'

'That's a good idea, let's stop the nonsense,' she said. 'I've been through a lot today, and I really don't want to get into this again right now.'

Adam was thinking, *And what was that supposed to mean? I*

haven't *been through a lot*? It was so typical – making him out to be the bad guy – but he didn't want to argue anymore so he took the high road instead, taking a long deep breath, then saying, 'Look, I understand how you feel, okay? You're afraid, and I'll admit it, I'm afraid, too. I mean, I think it's highly unlikely anything's going to happen, but I admit I won't feel one hundred percent safe until it all blows over. But, honestly, I really don't think running away to Florida is necessary, and I'm not even sure we could do that with a police investigation going on. Besides, the house is secure now, I'm confident about that.'

'What about the gun?' she asked.

He breathed deeply again, then said, 'Okay, I'm willing to compromise. Right now I want it in the house, just in case, but when this blows over, when the police make an arrest and figure out exactly what's going on, I'll get rid of it.'

'You really mean that?' she said.

'Promise,' he said, raising his right hand as if he were on a witness stand. 'I still think the gun saved our lives last night, but if you really don't want it in the house, if it makes you this upset, I'll get rid of it, okay?'

She was teary eyed again.

'Thank you,' she said.

'Aw, come here,' he said, and he hugged her.

Now she was crying. He had no idea why she was so upset. Maybe she was just letting out stress.

'Come on, don't be sad,' he said. 'Everything's going to be okay. We're going to get through this, I promise.'

She cried even harder, and then he moved his hands lower, around her waist. She seemed like she'd lost weight; felt a lot firmer, too. He couldn't remember the last time they'd had sex. Jesus, had it been a month? Two months?

He undid her robe with one hand and started to slide his other hand up over one of her breasts.

'Not tonight,' she said quickly, pulling away a little. 'I'm just so worn out. I mean, because of the long day and everything.'

'I understand,' he said, moving his hand away, 'but let's definitely do it tomorrow night, okay? It's been too long, you know?'

He stayed with her for a while longer, holding her, and then went downstairs to let her get some rest.

Adam was tired, too, but there was no way he was missing watching the news later tonight. He set the upstairs TiVo to record the Channel 5 news at ten and the Channel 4 news at eleven, and the downstairs TiVo to record the Channel 11 news at ten and the Channel 2 news at eleven. Meanwhile he planned to watch the Channel 9 and Channel 7 news on the downstairs TV.

At around nine thirty Marissa came home.

'I was just about to call you to see when you were gonna be back,' Adam said. 'We have a new code for the alarm, I'll give it to you in the morning.'

'Cool,' she said, and he could tell she was drunk.

'Went out drinking again tonight, huh?' he asked, trying his hardest not to get angry at her and have a repeat of last night.

'I met Hillary at a happy hour,' she said flatly.

'Seems like a happy five hours.'

'I'm allowed to have a few drinks at a bar with a friend, Dad.'

'I want you to cut down on the drinking, okay?'

She shook her head and went upstairs.

'Hey, I'm talking to you,' he said. She didn't stop, and he added, 'No smoking tonight, and I mean it.'

A few seconds later he heard her bedroom door slam. He didn't care if she got angry at him; he was going to stay on her case, keep giving her tough love until she got the message and straightened out her life.

At ten o'clock he watched the Channel 9 news. He'd thought his story would be the lead, but it was the third story, after a water main break in downtown Manhattan and a three-alarm fire that had killed three people and one firefighter on Staten Island. There was footage of a female reporter in front of the house, probably taken this morning. The reporter explained how during an attempted robbery Carlos Sanchez, who was unarmed, had been shot and killed by the owner of the house, 'forty-seven-year-old Adam Bloom.' Then the reporter commented that Adam claimed he had believed Sanchez was

129

armed when he shot him. Adam didn't like that word – 'claimed' – but he felt vindicated when Detective Clements, of all people, said in footage taken in front of a police precinct, 'I believe Mr Bloom acted appropriately in this situation. He has a license for the gun he used, and the man he shot, Carlos Sanchez, was an intruder in his house who had a history of violence.' Adam was hoping they'd show some of his interview from this afternoon when he thought he'd sounded so good, but instead the reporter was talking about how Gabriela Moreno, who'd worked as a maid at the Blooms' house, had been gunned down early this morning at her apartment in Jackson Heights and police were investigating a possible link between the incident and the robbery in Forest Hills. Then the reporter was shown again in front of Adam's house, and finally there was footage of Adam from this afternoon. He was disappointed, though, that they didn't show his speech to the cameras. Instead they went to a sound bite of him saying, 'I feel justified, yes,' and then cut back to the anchor desk. Adam was also disappointed with how he looked on TV. His hair looked okay – his bald spot wasn't visible from the head-on angle, and the gray didn't seem *too* prominent – but he looked older than he did in person, and he especially didn't like the deep dark circles under his eyes. He'd thought the camera was supposed to add five pounds, not five years.

During the next hour or so he watched the other newscasts, including the ones he'd TiVo'd. They all covered the story similarly, with only minor variations. The Channel 4 news didn't include any comment from Detective Clements, and unfortunately none of the segments showed any of Adam's great speech. Channel 5 and Channel 11 didn't include any statement from Adam. On the Channel 7 and Channel 2 news, both reporters paraphrased his quote about feeling justified, but they seemed to take it out of context. Adam didn't see why all the reporters seemed to love that quote so much, why they'd all chosen to include it in one way or another, while he could think of several other comments he'd made that had sounded equally good. Also, he was surprised that none of the stations had portrayed him incredibly heroically. He'd thought he would be, given the change in the reporters' attitudes this afternoon and the new interview requests. Then again, the shooting of Gabriela was relatively fresh news, so he might not get the full hero treatment until the morning papers. Certainly after the interviews with *Good Day New York* and *New York* magazine ran people would have a more complete picture of what had *really* happened last night.

As he replayed the Channel 9 newscast for the second and third times, Adam wondered if any old friends and girlfriends were watching the news tonight. At least a few people in his past must have seen him, and they'd probably said to themselves or to the person next to them, 'Adam Bloom? Wait, I know that guy.' He especially hoped Abby Fine had been watching. He'd dated Abby during his freshman year at Albany until he found out that she was cheating on him with his roommate, Jon. He'd read in an alumni newsletter that Abby lived with her family in Manhattan, so there was at least a chance she'd seen him on TV tonight. Adam felt like he looked good for his age and was probably better-looking now than he'd been in his early twenties when Abby had last seen him. He hoped she was watching tonight with her husband – hopefully he was dull and prematurely aging – and felt like she'd missed out.

As Adam shut down the house for the night, making sure all the doors were locked and checking and double-checking to make sure the alarm system was armed, he imagined what tomorrow would be like. After all the media exposure today and the likely stories in tomorrow's papers, he would have to be recognized on the streets. Just for the hell of it, he might walk to work from the Fox studios to see what kind of reactions he got.

He had to admit that Dana had been right – he *was* enjoying this attention. He often told his attention-seeking patients that wanting attention was childish. He'd tell them, 'Children want attention, adults want respect.' In his own case, although he was aware that he was acting childishly, he also knew that the media interest was fulfilling a deep-seated need in his psyche. While he had a successful practice as a psychotherapist – he made a good living and had helped dozens of people through the worst periods of their lives – one of his big issues was that he felt he hadn't gotten enough recognition for his work. His doctoral degree from the New School hung on the wall in his office, but he'd never received any other honors or acclaim. He occasionally contributed an article to a journal but, unlike many of his colleagues, hadn't published any books in his field. Carol, for example, had written several books, and sometimes it was hard not to feel jealous about her achievements. For the most part, Adam had become resigned to the idea that when he died he wouldn't leave behind any legacy, but he still had a void in him, a strong need for attention that this whole situation was satisfying.

He got into bed and spooned Dana from behind for a while as she slept, then turned in the opposite direction. It was hard to fall asleep. He was so absorbed, replaying bits from the newscasts in his head and imagining what tomorrow would be like, that after about an hour he was still wide awake. He was about to get up to take an Ambien when he thought he heard a noise downstairs.

He sat up in bed and listened again but didn't hear anything. He knew rationally that no one was there, but he figured he might as well make sure just for peace of mind.

He was on his way to the door when Dana asked, 'What is it?'

He looked back and saw her sitting up in bed. The lights were off in the room, but the bedroom door was half-open, and there was enough light from the light in the hallway – which Adam had left on – to see her clearly.

'Nothing,' he said quietly. 'Everything's fine, go back to sleep.' He didn't want to alarm her, so he was trying to talk in an overly calm voice, like an airline pilot trying to relax his passengers during a period of heavy turbulence.

But Dana knew him too well to be fooled, and on the verge of panic, she asked, 'What's going on?'

Trying to put it as casually as he could he said, 'Nothing, I just... I think I heard something downstairs.'

'Oh my God.' Her voice was trembling, and she was covering her mouth with her cupped hand.

'Relax,' Adam said. 'I'm sure it was nothing, but lemme go check just in case.'

'Don't go anywhere,' Dana said, and she reached for the phone.

'Wait, don't call the police,' Adam said. 'I'm sure it was nothing.'

'What did it sound like?'

It had sounded like footsteps, but he didn't want to tell her this, especially when he wasn't sure that he hadn't imagined it.

'It was probably just the house settling or something. Just wait a second, okay?'

He went to the door and listened for several seconds but didn't hear anything. He looked back at Dana and held up an index finger and mouthed, 'Wait,' and then he walked as quietly as possible toward the staircase.

Unlike last night, when it had been almost pitch-dark, tonight he could see the staircase clearly because of the light in the hallway and a light he had left on downstairs in the foyer. He had a flashback to nearly twenty-four hours ago – firing off those shots. It was so vivid he could feel the gun in his hand, hear the shots, see Sanchez's body falling. It felt like it was actually happening all over again. But what if it *did* happen all over again? Without his gun, how was he supposed to defend himself? He felt extremely vulnerable and defenseless. He didn't care what he'd promised Dana; there was no way he was ever getting rid of the gun. If they were going to get rid of the things that protected them, why not get rid of the locks on the doors and the alarm system? Hell, why not just keep the doors wide open?

He went to the top of the stairs and bent down to get a view of the front door. It was chained, just as he'd left it.

Then he heard, 'Dad.'

It was just that one word, but it might as well have been a rifle fired right next to his head. He was so startled he jerked forward, lost his balance, and almost fell down the stairs. He had to grab onto one of the wooden posts on the railing to steady himself.

'You okay, Dad?'

He managed to stand up and turn around. His pulse was pounding.

Looking at his daughter, who was by the door to her room, holding a glass of maybe diet soda, he said, 'For God's sake, Marissa.'

'Is everybody okay?' Dana had come out to the hallway.

'What're you freaking out for?' Marissa said. 'I just went downstairs to get something to eat.'

Adam took a few moments, trying to catch his breath. Then he couldn't restrain his frustration and snapped, 'Just get the hell to bed right now, okay?'

'What did I do?' Marissa asked.

'Just go,' Adam said.

She returned to her room, slamming the door. Adam shook his head in frustration and disgust and marched past Dana and got back into bed.

'Are you okay?' Dana asked as she got in next to him.

'Fine,' Adam said. 'Let's talk about it in the morning, okay?'

They lay in the dark silently for a few minutes.

Then Dana said, 'Thank God you didn't have your gun. You might've shot her.'

Eventually Adam fell asleep.

11

A T FIVE IN the morning Adam got out of bed, wide awake. He decided to go the Hollywood route – the black button-down shirt with the black sport jacket and jeans. He checked himself out in the bathroom mirror and thought he looked great, though he wished he'd had time to stop at his barber and get a little trim. Ah, well, his hair still looked nice and thick and healthy. As a last touch, he grabbed his sunglasses – the ones he'd bought for eight bucks on the street – and put them in the pocket of his jacket. It was cloudy out, and he wasn't going to wear them on the air, but he thought they looked cool with just the tip sticking out.

He was waiting in the living room, looking out the parted venetian blinds, waiting for the limo to arrive. The woman from Fox had said it would be here at six, and it was already five after. He couldn't remember the last time he'd been in a limo, especially a big, fancy one. It would probably have a widescreen TV and a fully stocked bar. He normally took the subway to and from work, and it was going to be fun – well, a nice change of pace, anyway – to ride into the city in style, to feel like a celebrity. Then after he was on TV he'd probably get phone calls nonstop, from old friends – wouldn't it be a kick if Abby Fine called? – and there'd probably be more interview requests. At noon he had his *New York* magazine interview. This one hadn't fully set in yet – *New York* magazine was interviewing him. Wasn't *Saturday Night Fever* based on a *New York* magazine article? Okay, maybe he was getting a little far-fetched now, but so what? It was fun to fantasize. He wondered who they'd get to play him in the movie, Hanks or Crowe? Hanks was too sincere, too hokey, but Crowe had the right combination of vulnerability and toughness. Yeah, he could definitely see it: Russell Crowe as Adam Bloom, a working guy, just going about his life, when somebody breaks into his house one night. It's Bloom's moment of truth, his life is on the line, but he does what he has to do to defend his family and in doing so becomes a local hero. The movie would probably make millions at the box office. Who doesn't love a good courage-under-fire story?

Then Adam, on a roll, wondered, And why not a talk show? He could be the next Dr Phil. Dr Phil wasn't even a real psychologist, or he'd had his license revoked, or something like that. Dr Adam could take over for Dr Phil in no time. Even if he couldn't land a TV show, Adam knew he'd be a natural for radio. He was so well spoken and articulate and could talk on any subject, and he'd be great with guests, get very introspective and personal. His show wouldn't be just fluff. No, Dr Adam would tackle serious issues.

Adam was looking forward to riding in the limo, relaxing, sipping coffee and nibbling on a croissant, or maybe having a Bloody Mary to loosen up before going on the air. He was so caught up in his fantasies that he barely noticed when the navy sedan pulled up in front of the house.

At first he thought the driver, a stocky black guy, was looking for a parking space, but then he got out of the car.

Adam came out and said, 'Can I help you?'

He really thought the guy must have the wrong address.

'You order a car?'

'Yes, but it was supposed to be a limo.'

The guy laughed, like this was a joke. Adam felt the letdown, naturally, but he didn't let it get to him. Okay, so there wasn't a limo. Limos were overrated anyway. They were too cheesy, too Donald Trump. He was still looking forward to his big moment, getting the most out of his day in the spotlight.

When he arrived at the Fox studios a producer – a girl who looked Marissa's age – greeted him and told him how happy they were to have him on the show. Then she took him to a room where a makeup artist powdered his face. Okay, now the star treatment was starting. When the makeup was done Adam looked in a mirror and thought he looked thirty-five, tops. God, he hoped Abby Fine was watching.

The producer returned and told Adam that he would be going on in about a half-hour and led him to the greenroom. Adam wasn't nervous at all. There was another guest waiting – a leggy blonde.

'Hi, I'm Annie,' she said, smiling. She explained that she was the star of a new Broadway musical, then asked, 'Why are you here?'

'Oh, I'm a local hero, I guess,' Adam said, trying to sound modest, like he was almost embarrassed about it.

'Really?' she asked, impressed, her face brightening. 'What did you do?'

'Oh, it was no big deal,' Adam said. 'My house was robbed the other night, and I... well, I shot one of the robbers.'

She cringed and said, 'You mean you *killed* somebody?'

Somehow this wasn't the reaction he was expecting.

'Yeah, unfortunately,' he said, 'but I didn't have any choice. It was the middle of the night, and he broke in. He was coming up the stairs.'

She still seemed almost horrified and asked, 'Oh my God, did he have a gun?'

'No,' Adam said, 'but I thought he did. I mean, he was reaching for something.'

He was waiting for her to start getting impressed, but her expression didn't change. Maybe she didn't understand the real danger he'd been in.

'My daughter woke us up in the middle of the night,' he said. 'Oh, and the guy I killed, he was a hardened criminal. He'd spent like ten, fifteen years in prison.'

The last part had been a pure exaggeration, but at least Annie got a little sympathetic. She said, 'Wow, that must've been really scary.'

'It was,' Adam said. '*Is*. I'm sure it'll take months before I get over it completely.'

The producer came in and told Annie that it was her turn to go on and Adam that he would be next.

Adam remained in the greenroom, rehearsing in his head what he was going to say. He couldn't wait to get out there.

Annie seemed to be on for a long time, segueing from talking about her musical to talking about fund-raising work she was doing for PETA.

During the commercial break, the producer returned to the greenroom, looking upset, and said, 'I'm so sorry, Mr Bloom. We went over today, and I'm afraid we won't have time to talk to you.'

'I'm sorry?' Adam had heard her, but he hadn't quite absorbed what she'd said. Did she mean he was going on *later*?

'We can't have you on,' she said. 'I'm so sorry for the inconvenience. If there's someplace you have to get to, I can arrange to have a car service take you.'

'Wait,' Adam said. 'You mean I'm not going on at all?'

'I'm afraid not,' she said.

'Well, that's ridiculous,' he said. 'I got up at the crack of dawn today, came all the way down here, juggled my schedule –'

'I know, it really sucks,' she said, 'but people get bumped all the time. It's not personal or anything. It just happens.'

'Can I talk to the producer?'

'I am the producer.'

'I mean the head producer.'

'I am the head producer.' She sounded snippy, insulted. 'I'm sorry, Mr Bloom, but there's nothing we can do.'

She left the room. Adam was upset and was about to go after her and continue complaining when he realized that there was nothing for him to complain about. Yeah, he'd been looking forward to going on the show, and it would've been fun to be the center of attention for a while longer, but it wasn't like the show owed him anything.

He left the studio and went right to a newsstand on Lexington Avenue and bought copies of the *Post, News,* and *Times* and read them while standing in the vestibule of a closed shoe store. His story didn't make the front page of either of the tabloids – the *Post* and the *News* – but both gave it space several pages in.

It wasn't exactly what he expected.

The *News* headline was TRIGGER HAPPY. The *Post*: GUN CRAZY.

What the hell was going on? Adam skimmed the articles, getting increasingly upset, wondering if he should call his lawyer, threaten a libel suit. Both articles were totally skewed and misleading, making it sound as if Adam had acted impulsively, shooting an unarmed man who posed no danger to him. The *News* article reported that Adam confronted Sanchez on the stairs and fired 'without warning,' shooting the unarmed man 'multiple times.' The *Post* called Adam 'the new Bernie Goetz,' comparing him to the vigilante who'd shot four unarmed teenagers on the subway in the eighties. Neither paper included any quotes from Adam, and while both acknowledged that Sanchez had a criminal background, they made this seem incidental compared to what Adam had done. Both also left out the quote from Detective Clements that had played on the TV news last night, about how Adam had been justified in his actions. The *Post* actually wrote that the police 'weren't able' to press charges against Adam in the shooting, implying that they wanted to charge him but, for legal reasons, couldn't.

Even the *Times* didn't get it right. Although the *Times* article wasn't as sensationalized, it was still written from the angle that Adam had acted impulsively and irrationally, not in self-defense, and it didn't include the supportive quote from Detective Clements, either.

After Adam read the three articles twice, he remained outside the shoe store, stunned. He couldn't believe that this was actually happening to him. It was bad enough to have had his house broken into, to have been forced to kill someone, but now he felt like he was being victimized all over again. Had the *Post* actually compared him to Bernie Goetz? That was insanely ridiculous. Adam hadn't acted like a vigilante, carrying his gun around, trying to clean up the scum of New York. He'd been asleep in his bed, for God's sake.

He glanced at the articles again, as if to confirm to himself that he'd actually read what he'd read, that it hadn't all been some nightmarish hallucination, and then, in a daze, he headed downtown toward his office.

Unlike yesterday and earlier this morning, now he didn't want people to recognize him. He felt embarrassed, ashamed. He couldn't believe that he'd actually been looking forward to today, that he'd talked himself into believing that he was going to be treated like a hero, wearing his sport jacket with the shades sticking out of the pocket. He felt like the punch line of a bad joke.

He just wanted to disappear, be anonymous again, like he normally was in New York, but was he imagining it or were people staring at him? That guy in the suit walking toward him with the earbuds looked like he was thinking, *Don't I know you from somewhere?* The mother and daughter waiting to cross the street ahead of him – they were looking at him, too, knowingly and judgmentally. Adam tried to look straight ahead, to avoid the intrusive stares, but it was impossible not to notice them. That young black guy was looking at him; the old lady pushing the shopping cart filled with groceries was looking; the Arabic guy at the pretzel cart was looking. They all seemed to know exactly who he was and what he'd done and why he'd done it. There was no room for negotiation.

When he entered his building on Madison off Fifty-eighth, he expected Benny, the building's security guard, to give him his usual warm smile and say, 'Morning, Dr Bloom,' or at least make a polite, banal comment about the weather, like 'Gettin' colder out there, huh?' Instead he barely looked at Adam as he walked past, and Adam knew why. There was a copy of the *Post* on Benny's desk.

On Adam's floor, when Lauren looked at him, he saw her do a double take. She said, 'Hi, Adam, how are you?' but there was no sincerity in her tone, no sympathy for what he'd been through. The coldness surprised Adam. He thought he'd at least get some sympathy and understanding from his colleagues. After all, if the people who know you best won't stick by your side during a crisis, then who's left?

'Okay, considering,' he said.

'That's good,' she said, still avoiding eye contact and seeming tense and distracted. 'Alexandra Hoffman called, and I forwarded her to your voicemail. And Lena Perez called; she said she has to reschedule her appointment next week.' When the phone rang she seemed eager to answer it, to have an opportunity to end the conversation.

On his way to his office Adam passed Robert Sloan, one of the other therapists in the suite, but Robert wasn't exactly Mr Supportive either. He asked some questions about the shooting, but, like that woman Annie in the greenroom, he didn't seem to get that what Adam had done had been heroic. He even seemed judgmental, as if he'd already decided that Adam had done something wrong and nothing could change his opinion.

Throughout the morning everyone in the office seemed to be avoiding him. Even Carol, his own therapist and mentor, seemed to be ignoring him. Adam passed by her office several times, hoping to have a chance to talk to her and process everything that had happened, but her door was closed all morning even during times when Adam knew she didn't have any patients scheduled.

There was no flood of phone messages from patients and old friends, but Adam was relieved about this. He hoped it meant that no one had seen him on the news or read about him in the morning papers. Oh, God, he hoped Abby Fine didn't buy a newspaper today.

When Lauren came into his office to let him know about some correspondence regarding a patient's insurance claim, Adam felt he had to set the record straight and said, 'Look, what the papers said is total crap. That's not what happened at all, okay? The guy broke into my house, and the police think there might've been somebody else in the house with a gun, and that that person might've shot my maid. So I did the right thing, okay?'

'I believe you,' Lauren said, but it was obvious she was just saying this to end the conversation as quickly as possible.

Adam felt like locking himself in his office and spending the rest of the day alone, but he had an eleven o'clock appointment with Martin Harrison. Martin was what Adam and his colleagues called a professional patient. Adam had been seeing him for nearly two years but except for exhibiting mild symptoms of OCD and perhaps some generalized anxiety disorder, there was nothing really wrong with him. He was happily married with two kids and was doing well in his career as an advertising exec, but, for whatever reason – perhaps it was a subconscious emotional dependency issue, because his father had left his mother when he was five years old – he continued to pay out of pocket to see Adam two days a week. During most sessions, they rehashed topics they'd already discussed, and sometimes it was a strain to find anything to talk about. But what was Adam supposed to do, suggest that he end his treatment? What with managed health care restricting the annual visits of his insurance-paid patients, cash-paying patients like Martin were what made Adam's practice sustainable.

Martin's major personality flaw was that he had a very direct style of communication, almost too direct, bordering on inappropriate. When he entered Adam's office, he didn't even say hello but went right to, 'So I was reading about you online this morning.'

Oh, Jesus, Adam hadn't thought about this yet. The story wasn't just in the papers; it was all over the internet. Somehow that made it seem more permanent. People would throw out today's papers, but the story, with all those skewed, misreported facts, would be available online forever.

'What did you read?' Adam asked, trying his best not to sound overly concerned but probably failing miserably.

'Just about how you had to shoot that guy. Yeah, it sounds rough. Sorry you had to go through all that.'

Martin didn't sound very sympathetic. Adam considered pointing this out to him – maybe it could become an issue for today's session? – but instead he said, 'Just so you know, it didn't happen like that at all. My life was in danger, and I had to shoot that guy in self-defense, but of course they tried to sensationalize the whole thing.'

'I hear you, I hear you,' Martin said. 'I'm just glad to see you pulled through and you're okay.'

Adam got the sense that Martin really didn't care whether he was okay or not. No, to him, Adam was the typical guilty guy who would swear he was innocent ad nauseam till the day he died. Still, Adam wanted to keep things as professional as possible – this was a therapy session, after all – so he tried to minimize the whole situation, saying, 'Well, I can't complain that the last couple of days have been uneventful.'

Adam laughed, trying to get Martin to laugh with him, but Martin was unusually serious. Throughout the rest of the session, he seemed very agitated – fidgeting a lot, avoiding eye contact. Adam confronted him about his behavior a few times, but he insisted that everything was fine. Then, as he was leaving, he said that he wouldn't be able to make it to his appointments next week. Adam asked him if he was going on vacation, and he said, 'No,' but didn't give any other explanation for the cancelations.

Adam wondered if this was just the beginning. Maybe even his oldest, neediest patients would have second thoughts about seeing him and there would be a mass exodus from his practice. He was trying to decide whether he should do some damage control, or *pre*damage control, maybe have Lauren contact some of his regulars and make sure all was well, when he remembered that he had a noon meeting with the reporter from *New York* magazine.

He rushed over to the Starbucks on Madison and Forty-ninth, looking forward to the chance to set the record straight and to tell the public what had really happened the other night. When he entered, an attractive young black woman came over and said, 'Dr Bloom, right?'

'That's me,' Adam said.

'Nice to meet you, I'm Grace Williams. I'm sitting right over there.' She pointed to a table behind her. 'Do you want to get something?'

Wow, not only did she want to meet him for coffee, rather than lunch, she wouldn't even *pay* for the coffee.

'That's okay,' Adam said. 'I had a cup today and don't want to be overcaffeinated.'

He sat across from her, and she took out a pad, turned on a digital recorder, and said, 'This shouldn't take long.'

'I want to tell you, I'm really glad I'm getting a chance to talk to you. I've been kind of shocked, actually, by how this whole story has been misreported.'

'Really?' she asked, barely interested.

'Yeah,' he said. 'I mean, they've been making me out to be a vigilante or something, but that isn't the case at all.'

'I'm just going to ask you a few questions, Dr Bloom, okay?'

'Okay, but –'

'Did you ever fantasize about using your gun to kill someone?'

Was she serious? It seemed like she was.

'No,' Adam said. 'Of course not.'

'Even someone you really hated. Like a boss or an ex-lover.'

'One time at the range, just for fun, a guy put a photo of Osama bin Laden on the target, but –'

'Did you ever feel like you want to blow all the bad guys in the city away?'

'No,' Adam said firmly. 'And see, this is exactly what I'm talking about, how this whole thing has gotten distorted. I never felt that way at all.'

'So you don't condemn the man who broke into your house?'

'Of course I condemn him,' he said. 'He was trying to rob my house.'

'Why did you shoot him ten times? Wouldn't once have been enough?'

He hated her sensational tone.

'Do you want the facts,' he asked, 'or do you just want to write a provocative story?'

'I want the facts, of course,' she said, looking right at him.

'It was dark,' he said. 'I didn't know if I hit him or not, so I had to keep firing to make sure I got him.' He wasn't sure this was true, because he vaguely remembered knowing that the first shot had hit Sanchez, but he continued, 'And it happened very fast. When you're in that type of situation you don't think, you just react. It's like a soldier in battle. You're in fight-or-flight mode. You have to listen to your instincts, follow your gut. Oh, and since it seems very likely that my maid, who was killed yesterday morning, had something to do with the robbery, I feel like I absolutely did the right thing.'

'What do you mean?' Grace asked.

'You heard that my maid was killed, didn't you?'

'You killed your maid?'

'No, I didn't kill her. Jesus, whatever you do, don't write that. No, it was another shooting.'

'In your house?'

'No, not in my house, but there was definitely someone else in my house the night of the shooting, and that person could've had a gun. The police know the guy I killed, Sanchez, was involved with my maid. They were lovers, boyfriend-girlfriend, whatever. It was either my maid with the gun or someone my maid knew. So it was just by chance that Sanchez wasn't armed. You get what I'm saying?'

She didn't seem to get it, or want to try to get it, and asked, 'But doesn't it bother you that you killed an unarmed man?'

Adam took a few moments to collect his thoughts, choosing his words carefully, then said, 'Of course it bothers me. I didn't ask to be in that situation, it wasn't something I sought out. I'm sure I'll be thinking about it for the rest of my life. But that doesn't make me an aggressor, a vigilante.'

'So you're saying you'd kill him all over again?'

'Kill is a strong word. You know, I really think you're –'

'Would you shoot him all over again?'

'Yes,' he said. 'I mean, I wouldn't do anything differently except –'

She turned off the recorder, put it away in her purse, then stood up and said, 'That should do it, Dr Bloom.' She stuck her hand out to shake. 'It was really nice meeting you.'

'That's it?' he asked.

'Yeah, sorry to run, but I have to get back to the office and write this up so we can post it this afternoon.'

'Post it?' Adam was confused. 'Isn't it going to run in the magazine?'

'No, it's for Daily Intel, our online blog. But I got everything I needed, it should be great. Thank you so much, Dr Bloom.'

On his way back to his office, Adam decided that it was better that the story was running online. He wanted to set the facts straight as soon as possible so he could start to put this all behind him and go on with his life.

Late in the afternoon, he went online to Daily Intel and saw the headline:

VIGILANTE ADAM BLOOM WANTS TO BLOW AWAY ALL OF NEW YORK CITY'S BAD GUYS

'That fucking bitch,' he nearly shouted.

The story was even more skewed than the ones in the morning papers. It made him sound like a gleeful white-collar sociopath who'd been brooding for years, waiting for an opportunity to blow somebody away. Everything he'd said during the interview was taken out of context, and the article was filled with misquotes. She wrote that he 'often fantasized' about using his gun to kill someone and that he had a lifelong disgust for crime and criminals. She added that he claimed he was 'following his gut' when he unloaded ten shots into the unarmed intruder and observed that he expressed no remorse for the shooting. She ended with the completely fabricated line '"I'd love to shoot him all over again," Bloom boasted.'

Adam called Grace Williams up, ready to give her hell. Of course he got her voicemail, and he left a message. 'This is Adam Bloom. If you don't take that bullshit off your site I'm gonna sue you and your fucking magazine!'

He must've been screaming into the phone, because Lauren rushed into his office, asking, 'Is everything okay?'

'Just leave me alone!' he yelled, and when she left he picked up his phone's handset and flung it across the room. It hit the filing cabinet, and part of it broke off.

This day was rapidly turning into the day from hell. And to think, he'd been convinced he was going to be the next Tony Manero in *Saturday Night Fever*.

He didn't hear from Grace, and the story was still online. No big surprise there. Why would they care about what he thought?

He rode the subway in rush hour back to Forest Hills. On the crowded R train, he felt like strangers were looking up from their newspapers and noticing him, scrutinizing him. At Northern Boulevard, a group of laughing teenagers got on. Adam didn't know if they were making fun of him or not, but he felt like they were.

Adam decided there was nothing he could do to control what other people thought. If the press wanted to keep attacking him, and the public wanted to keep judging him, that was beyond his control.

In Forest Hills, he stopped at Duane Reade and picked up some stuff for the house – toilet paper, paper towels, dishwashing liquid – and then he went to the wine store around the corner and bought a bottle of $6.99 merlot. He felt bad for arguing so much with Dana over the last couple of days, and he was looking forward to having a nice, relaxing evening at home. Maybe they'd order in some Chinese, have a couple of glasses of wine, and then make love. He had so much going for him in his life, and he wanted to start appreciating what he had instead of constantly wanting more. He didn't need to be hailed as a local hero and be the basis of a Russell Crowe biopic in order to be happy.

When Adam turned onto his block in Forest Hills Gardens, it was starting to get dark. There were several teenagers playing touch football in the street, and as Adam got closer he recognized a few of them – Jeremy Ross, Justin Green, Brian Zimmerman. It brought back memories of when he was their age and used to play football on the street with his friends, not going inside until it was pitch dark.

'Hey, right here,' Adam said, and Jeremy tossed him the ball. Then Adam said to Brian, 'Okay, go deep.'

Brian sprinted down the block, and Adam faded back and shouted, 'To win the Super Bowl!' and then unloaded a bomb. Well, he tried to. The wobbly ball bounced off the windshield of a car about twenty feet in front of Brian.

'Next time,' Adam said, smiling, and headed up the walkway to his front door. When he went in he announced, 'I'm home!' Then he saw the piece of paper on the floor. It was plain white, eight and a half by eleven, folded in half. He opened it and saw, written in Magic Marker in block letters:

YOU THINK YOU'RE SOME KIND OF HERO, HUH?
YOU THINK YOU'RE A BIG SHOT. I'M GONNA MAKE
YOU WISH YOU WERE NEVER BORN, YOU LITTLE
COCKSUCKING SON OF A BITCH.

He went into the living room and saw Dana watching TV.
Her feet were on the ottoman, a throw covering her legs. She
looked very tired, maybe depressed.

'Did you see the note on the floor?' he asked.

She was slow to respond. Eventually, in a monotone, she said,
'Note?'

He handed her the paper, watched her growing concern as
she read it.

'I think we have a situation here,' he said.

148

12

MARISSA'S GOAL FOR the foreseeable future was to spend as little time with her parents as possible. It was getting to the point where it was hard to be around them, even to be in the same house with them. It was bad enough with their arguing, but now her father was getting on her case because she went to a happy hour with Hillary? What, now she wasn't allowed to hang out with her friends? What was he going to do next, lock her in a tower like Rapunzel? Oh, and how about her mom having an affair with Tony the trainer, of all people? It explained why her mom had been acting so uptight and distracted lately. If it wasn't so annoying it would've been funny, hilarious actually, that her parents were always telling her how she had to grow up, get her life together, when she felt like she was the adult and they were the kids.

In the morning, after Marissa checked out her friends' blogs and MySpace and Facebook pages, she posted an entry on her own blog entitled JUST WHEN I THOUGHT THINGS COULDN'T POSSIBLY GET ANY MORE FUCKED UP. She wrote about Gabriela's murder and how yesterday had officially been the worst day of her life. She was in a very nihilistic mood and ended with *I'm so fucking sick of this stupid fucking world and I just don't give a fucking shit about fucking anything anymore.* She read the entry twice – she thought it was one of her best ever; maybe she should've majored in creative writing – then posted it and went downstairs. She brewed some coffee and was pouring a cup when her mom came in and said, 'Dad got bumped.'

'Huh?' She had no idea what her mother was talking about. She also had no idea why her mom was wearing her robe and had no makeup on at – what? – one in the afternoon.

'He was supposed to be on *Good Day New York* this morning, but I fast-forwarded through the show and he wasn't on. They must've bumped him.'

'Oh,' Marissa said, surprised her mom cared after the way she and her dad had been arguing yesterday.

'If I were you I wouldn't read the *Daily News* today. It's not exactly a flattering portrayal of your father. Expected, I guess, but still not very enjoyable to see in print.'

'Did they say anything bad about me?' Marissa asked. She didn't really think there would be anything bad; it was just instinctive insecurity coming out.

'They mention us,' her mom said, 'but no, nothing bad.'

'Thank God,' Marissa said, then added, 'That sucks for Dad, though.' She stood at the counter, sipping her coffee, trying to wake up. Her mother, meanwhile, started scrubbing the stove with a Lysol Wipe. 'So,' Marissa asked, 'are you feeling okay today?'

'I'm fine,' her mom said. 'Why?'

'You didn't get dressed yet.'

Her mom continued scrubbing, then finally said, 'I have no place to go.' What was going on now? Was her mom *depressed*? Marissa was tempted to blurt out, *What's wrong, Ma, boyfriend trouble?* She managed to keep this to herself but couldn't help smirking.

'What's so funny?' her mom asked.

'Nothing,' Marissa said. 'Why?'

Her mom gave her a look, then continued scrubbing – too hard, like she was trying to sand a piece of wood. Finally, maybe to herself, she said, 'We have to find a new maid.'

Marissa had been trying not to think about Gabriela; it was too sad. 'Is there anything new about that?' she asked.

'No,' her mom said, and she finally stopped scrubbing and dropped the wipe into the garbage. 'But can you believe her sister called and asked me if we'd pay to have the body shipped to South America?'

'What did you say?'

'She was so upset, I didn't want to be rude. I said I'd have to discuss it with my husband.'

'That was nice of you, I guess. I mean, we still don't know for sure Gabriela had anything to do with the robbery, right?'

'Oh, come on, you sound like Dad now. She was dating that guy Sanchez, for God's sake.'

She didn't know what was up with her mom's attitude, why she was acting so irritable. She wondered if it had to do with her affair. Maybe she was feeling guilty or something.

'I can't believe she and that guy were together,' Marissa said. 'I had so many talks with her about boyfriend stuff, you know, and I didn't think she'd been with a guy since her fiancé died. She'd never said anything about any guy named Carlos.'

'She obviously had a lot of secrets,' her mother said. Then she made a face, as if she'd caught herself saying something she hadn't meant to – *Gee*, Marissa thought, *whatever could that be*? – and said quickly, 'Anyway, the answer's no, I'm not paying to have her body shipped anywhere.'

'How much do they want?' Marissa asked.

'What difference does it make?'

'I mean if it's only, like, a thousand dollars –'

'I'm not giving them a thousand dollars, I'm not giving them one dollar, I'm not giving them one penny. That woman hurt us, don't you get it?'

Well, so much for trying to have a conversation with her mom. Marissa took her coffee and went back to her room, back to her PC. From now on maybe she should just stay in her room all the time, not even talk to her parents. Her parents should stay in different rooms, too. Maybe they'd all get along better if they never had to see each other.

She checked her blog and saw that she'd already gotten sixteen responses in the backlog, mostly from friends, but a few from random web acquaintances. Everyone was very supportive, writing about how sorry they were and how bad they felt, et cetera. Marissa added her own comment, thanking everybody and writing that she was 'feeling a little better today.' Then she checked Yahoo! Messenger and MySpace to see which of her friends were online and started IM-ing with Sarah, a friend from Vassar. Sarah lived with her boyfriend in Boston, but she said she was coming into the city tonight and planning to stay for a few days with her brother in Hell's Kitchen. Marissa was excited. Hanging out with Sarah would be a great distraction from all the crap that was going on in her life.

Sarah typed, *So you going to the party at D's tonight?*

'D's' meant Darren's, but Marissa didn't know about any party. Hmm, strange, what was up with that? She hadn't heard from Darren at all the last couple of days, come to think of it, and hadn't even gotten any response to the SOS phone message about how he had to get rid of his drugs before Detective Clements busted him. Now that Clements had found out that the break-in had nothing to do with Marissa or her friends, she doubted he'd wasted his time with some low-level drug dealer, which meant Darren was blowing her off because (a) he was pissed off at her for trying to rat him out or (b) he wanted to make her *think* he was pissed off at her for trying to rat him out. Darren had played immature, hot-and-cold head games with her before, so choice (b) was much more likely. He was probably trying to get her to contact him and be all apologetic and clingy.

Marissa thought about it for several more seconds, then typed, *What party?* Sarah typed, *You weren't invited????* and Marissa replied, *Nope.* Then Sarah typed, *That's such bullshit hold a sec.*

Perfect. Sarah was a big drama queen and loved stirring things up. If Sarah got Marissa the invite, at least it wouldn't look like she was desperate.

Waiting for Sarah to get back to her, Marissa checked out the *Daily News* article about the shooting, the one her mom had told her to avoid. God, it was like a freaking nightmare. Anyone who read it would think her father was a nutcase or something. She felt bad for her dad, but she was angry at him, too, for dragging her and her mom into this. Their names were right there in the paper, for the whole world to see. She wondered if it would blow over or if for the rest of her life when people found out she was Adam Bloom's daughter they'd hate her, treat her like she was Charles Manson's daughter or something. She was so panicked that she researched how to change her name. It was apparently complicated for post-9/11 security reasons, but it was doable. Her middle name was Suzanne, so she could be Marissa Suzanne. She was going to seriously consider doing it if things got any worse.

She was still reading the article when she heard a beep, announcing a new IM. She switched screens and saw that Sarah had invited Darren into their IM session. Darren was playing dumb, writing that of course she was invited to the party and he was so sorry he 'forgot' to tell her about it. Meanwhile, it was so obvious that he hadn't invited her on purpose to try to get her upset. What he was doing was so immature, so junior high school.

So, you going? Sarah typed. Marissa replied, *Yeah I'll be there*, and Darren wrote, *Sweet*.

Marissa was nauseous.

The rest of the day, Marissa browsed job listings and sent out a few résumés, but she wasn't hopeful. She thought she had a great cover letter that she tailored for each job she applied to, but no one seemed interested in hiring her, and she was running out of places to apply to. Suddenly afraid she was going to be unemployed and living with her parents forever, she downloaded grad school applications for master's programs in art history from a number of schools including Yale, Bard, and Brown. She doubted she'd actually apply to the schools – she wasn't sure if she wanted to go to grad school at all, and she definitely didn't want to go for a year or two – but at least it made her feel like she had a fallback plan.

Her mom had gone out shopping, and when she returned Marissa wanted to avoid another depressing conversation, so she stayed in her room and locked the door. She read an email from her friend Jen. *Don't know if you saw this yet, this really sucks but thought you'd want to read it anyway, sorry.* Marissa clicked on the link to Daily Intel, where there was another scathing article about her dad. This one was an interview, and her dad sounded like he was boasting about the shootings, like he was so proud of himself. God, what the hell was wrong with him anyway? Weren't things bad enough? Did he really have to go ahead and make an even bigger ass of himself? People actually read that blog; people Marissa *knew* read that blog. This was starting to get seriously embarrassing. Jen had already read the article, and she loved to blab and would probably tell everybody she knew, and Marissa and Jen knew pretty much the same people.

At around seven, Marissa left to meet Sarah for drinks at some new bar in midtown. As Sarah went on about how happy she was in Boston with her boyfriend in their great new apartment, Marissa couldn't help feeling a little jealous. She'd hooked up a few times with Darren and one night with the bass player from Tone Def, but she hadn't had a serious boyfriend since junior year of college, in, God, almost two years.

Later, in the cab to the party, Marissa felt so desperate that she was seriously considering sleeping with Darren tonight. But then she weighed all the pros and cons and only came up with a long list of cons. The only reason she'd gotten involved with Darren at all over the past few years was because she hadn't had much choice. The ratio of girls to guys at Vassar had been high to begin with, and the ratio of girls to straight guys had been even higher. Things were so bad for girls that a lot of Marissa's friends had been lesbians in college, or at least bi, but the idea of being a LUG – lesbian until graduation – hadn't appealed to Marissa so whenever she got really hard up she wound up settling for Darren. It wasn't that he wasn't good-looking, because she actually thought he was pretty cute – tall and lanky with short curly hair and big brown eyes; goofy, but in a cool way, like Josh Groban. The problem was she didn't feel any real connection with him. They didn't have a lot in common, and whenever she tried to have a conversation about movies or art – or anything she was into – she could tell he was zoning out. She'd made it clear to him many times that she was interested in him for sex only, and he'd always say he was cool with that, but then after they'd hook up a few times he'd start getting possessive, calling her all the time and getting weirdly jealous about any guy she even mentioned in casual conversation, and she'd have to cut him off. She knew if she slept with him tonight it would just start the cycle all over again, and she didn't feel like dealing with all of that.

As the cab pulled up in front of his parents' building, she decided she definitely wouldn't have sex with him. She'd just hang out for a while and call it a night.

Marissa had been to Darren's parents' apartment a few times before. The space was awesome – three bedrooms, high ceilings, crown molding, hardwood floors – and it was extremely well furnished. She even liked the borderline-tacky Pizza Place–esque oil paintings of Venetian scenes in the dining room. She didn't know where his parents were tonight, but she knew it was highly unlikely that they knew anything about this party.

As she'd expected, the apartment was infested with Vassar people – i.e., people she'd hoped she'd never have to see again once college ended, but in the four and a half months since graduation it seemed like she was running into them on a regular basis. It amazed her how this could happen. New York City had like twelve million people, and sometimes it felt like she was still in a college town and it was impossible to meet anyone new.

She hung out for a while talking to Megan and Caitlin, who'd lived in her dorm freshman year. They were both from Scarsdale – 'nough said. Then this guy Zach Harrison came over and lamely started hitting on her. Zach had dated one of Marissa's old housemates; he was one of those boisterous, heavyset guys who laughed loudly and sprayed saliva when he talked, especially when he was drunk, like right now. He cornered Marissa – literally, backing her into a corner in the dining room, blocking her escape with his huge stomach – and told her stories about people from school whom she either didn't know or didn't care about. Of course he thought the stories were hilarious and kept belly laughing, spitting in her face. Finally Drew McPhearson came over and said something to Zach, and Marissa jumped at the opportunity to escape and

155

headed down the hallway, past more Vassar people and some non-Vassar people, toward Darren's room.

Darren and several others were sitting around, chilling, listening to Daughtry, getting wasted. Aside from Darren, the only other Vassar person in the room was Alison Kutcher – sadly no relation to Ashton. The non-Vassars all looked skanky, and one woman looked burnt-out and in her thirties. Marissa figured they were some of Darren's drug clients.

'Hey, there she is,' Darren said, and he got up, his eyes glassy and bloodshot and kissed her on the lips. She didn't have a chance to turn her head or she would've.

Marissa sat – purposely *not* next to Darren – and someone passed her the bong.

'It's Northern Lights,' Darren said proudly.

Marissa took a long, deep hit, closing her eyes, savoring it, and then she exhaled and her brain moaned, *Thank you*.

'Awesome shit, right?' Darren asked.

She didn't answer, just leaned back and smiled, enjoying the rush of mellowness.

They passed the bong around a few times, then Marissa suddenly had to pee and went to the bathroom. When she came back everyone was gone except Darren. Did he really expect her to believe that this wasn't planned, that everyone had just left on their own?

He was sitting on his bed with the bong and waved her over and actually said, 'Come on, come over here, I won't bite.'

She really wanted another hit, so she sat next to him and lit the bong and inhaled deeply, holding it in her lungs until she started feeling dizzy and then letting it out very slowly through her mouth and nostrils.

Then she realized that Darren was kissing her neck, under her jaw.

She shifted away and said, 'This is a bad idea. I just want to be friends.'

She was aware that she was talking extremely slowly, or at least she felt like she was.

Something about her delivery must've seemed funny to Darren because he started giggling. Then he said, 'We are friends,' and tried to nibble on her ear again.

'I mean *friends* friends,' Marissa said, moving away again.

'It'll be just sex,' he said.

'You can't have *just* sex,' she said.

'Oh, yeah,' he said and tried to touch her crotch.

She stood up and said, 'Stop it.'

'Come back here,' he said and unsnapped his jeans.

She tried to leave, and he grabbed her arm.

She turned and said, 'Get the fuck off me.'

'Okay,' he said, letting go. 'Chill.'

Marissa left the room and walked, very unsteadily, into the living room. She tapped Sarah on the shoulder and said, 'I wanna go.'

'Now?' Sarah asked. It was obvious she wasn't budging.

'It's okay, stay,' Marissa said. 'I'm just gonna take a cab to Penn Station, there's an LIRR train I can catch.'

Darren was heading down the hallway saying, 'Hey, come on, just chill,' and she just wanted to get away. She went through the dining room and left the apartment.

She knew Darren was following her, so she didn't want to wait for an elevator and took the stairs instead. After two or whatever flights she felt dazed – from the alcohol and pot, though she also had mild vertigo – and she had to stop for a few seconds to steady herself. Then she continued down to the lobby and out to the street.

She went to Broadway and hailed a cab downtown. What was up with the way the Jamaican-looking cabdriver kept eyeing her in the rearview? Shit, he was going to drive her someplace and try to rape her, she was sure of it. She'd read some article online, linked to somebody's blog, about how a fake cabdriver in Manhattan had picked up this woman and taken her to Connecticut or Long Island or someplace and raped her. What could she do to stop him? He looked like he was a big guy, and she had no way to protect herself.

'Stop the fucking cab!' she screamed.

He was looking back at her with his rapist's eyes again, saying, 'What you want to do?'

'I said stop right now!'

He seemed to be driving faster, zigzagging, saying, 'I can't stop in traffic, lady.'

Shit, he was really going to do it. It was really *happening*.

She gripped the door handle, figuring she'd jump out when the car was moving if she had to, and the cab screeched to a halt. She got out, and the driver said, 'Hey, where's my money?'

She reached into her purse, grabbed some crumpled bills, and threw them through his window.

'Crazy lady,' the driver said and drove off.

Shaken and on the verge of tears, she rushed along the sidewalk. As she waited to cross a street a woman asked her, 'Are you okay?' and Marissa ignored her and crossed against the light, a car nearly hitting her.

After going a few more blocks she started to realize how ridiculous she'd acted. Had she really gotten out of the cab? That cabdriver hadn't done anything wrong; he hadn't even been looking at her, for chrissake. It had been a normal cab ride, and she'd totally freaked out. It was all Darren's fault; his goddamn pot had made her paranoid. This was officially the shittiest week of her life.

She took another cab to Penn Station and caught the train to Forest Hills. She could've taken the subway, but late at night she usually took the Long Island Rail Road because she felt safer and the ride only took twenty minutes. Walking home from the station she felt a lot less wasted but still a little drunk. She was dreading what her dad would say to her when she walked into the house. Of course, this time she actually had been drinking and smoking, so he'd feel even more justified in attacking her. Maybe he'd hit her with *You really need to get focused, Marissa* or *It's time you start setting your priorities straight.*

When Marissa turned the corner onto her block, she saw a police car double-parked in front of her house. What the hell? There were two cops in the car, and they looked at her as she turned up the walkway.

In the house she heard voices – her mom was talking and, oh no, it was Detective Dick Clements. She didn't know if Dick was his actual first name, but that's what she'd been calling him in her head.

She entered and saw Clements, her mom, and her dad at the dining room table.

'Who died now?' Marissa asked. She was trying her hardest not to look or sound wasted. Though she knew she could never pull this off, it didn't stop her from trying.

'Everything's okay,' her dad said.

Then he looked at her more closely, probably noticing how bloodshot her eyes were. Clements and her mom were giving her looks, too.

'Why don't you go upstairs?' he said, sounding embarrassed, disappointed. Yeah, like he should be the one to talk.

But she gladly left. She figured that nothing was going on, that Clements was just there to update them about the investigation.

She was in bed, starting to pass out, when her dad came into her room and said, 'Can we talk for a second?'

Here we go.

'I'm really tired,' she said.

'It's important,' he said, sitting in the chair at her desk. 'Unfortunately things have gotten a little more complicated.'

'What do you mean?' she said, surprised he wasn't laying into her about the drinking and pot smoking.

'Well, somebody... threatened me,' he said.

'What do you mean *threatened*?'

'There was a note under the door. Detective Clements isn't as concerned as Mom is.'

She sat up and said, 'I thought you said everything was okay?'

'Everything is okay. Nothing's changed.'

'Nothing except you're getting death threats.'

'Threat, singular – and it wasn't a death threat, or any type of specific threat, really. I mean, technically I don't know if you'd even call it a threat at all.'

'What did it say?'

'Just about how I'm going to pay for what I did, et cetera, et cetera. It was probably because somebody read those lies in the newspapers today.'

Marissa couldn't believe how deep in denial her dad was. What would it take for him to actually admit he was scared?

'So you think the same person who put the note under the door killed Gabriela?'

'No, I don't think that. And the police haven't found any link yet between what happened to her and the robbery.'

'Wait,' Marissa said, 'so what do they think? That it was all what, a coincidence?'

She saw her father's jaw shift a few times as he ground his teeth. Then he said, 'Possibly.'

'And you believe that?' Marissa asked.

'Look, there's no reason to panic,' her dad said, weirdly calm. 'The police are giving this case, *cases,* their full attention. It sounds like they have a lot of leads they're following up on, and I'm sure they'll have a suspect in custody soon.'

'Is that what Clements said or is that what you're saying?'

Her dad shifted his jaw again, then said, 'The other thing is the note could've been a prank. When I got home before, a bunch of kids were playing football in the street, right in front of the house. The police are talking to them to see if they saw anything, but one of them could've done it. Justin Green was there. I remember his parents were having some discipline problems with him a few years ago; he almost got expelled from school. They even asked me if I could suggest a good child psychologist and I gave them a referral.'

It was amazing how her dad could make up these stories; it was even more amazing that he actually believed them.

'I guess anything's possible,' she said and lay down again.

'But look,' he added, 'I just want you to know, there's nothing to worry about.'

She thought, *Yeah, nothing except that some maniac wants to kill you.*

He continued, 'You might've noticed the police car outside. The cops'll be there all night and all day tomorrow. Twenty-four-hour protection.'

'What about tomorrow night?' Marissa asked.

'They'll probably be out there for the next night or two. Mom wants to get private security, and maybe, just to make her feel better, we'll do that. But there'll probably be an arrest by then and this whole thing will be moot.'

He stood up, and she saw him noticing her bong, which was out in plain view on her desk, right next to her laptop.

'I threw out all my pot,' she said.

This was true. She'd thrown out the dime bag this morning.

'So, did you have fun tonight?' her father asked.

She remembered Darren grabbing her arm, her screaming at the cabdriver to pull over.

'Yeah,' she said. 'It was okay.'

'That's good,' he said. Then, after several seconds of awkward silence, he said, 'Well, good night,' and left her alone.

Marissa was still thinking about the cab ride, how she'd totally freaked.

She stirred for a long time and finally fell asleep.

She dreamed about Prague. She had never actually been there, but she'd seen enough pictures of the cobblestone streets, the buildings, the castle, the Charles Bridge, to know that she was specifically in Prague and not some other Eastern European city. She was happy in the dream, hanging out, playing guitar, getting wasted. So what if she didn't know how to play a single chord on a guitar – the dream still felt real.

She woke up, disappointed to be in her bed in her house in Forest Hills, and thought, *Why not just pack up and go?* What was stopping her from doing something radical like that? She had no job, no boyfriend, no responsibilities. And going to Prague would solve two problems: It would get her far away from her parents and all of *their* problems, and she'd be able to afford to live on her own. She still had about six thousand dollars left over from the trust fund her grandparents – her mom's parents – had left her. That was two months' rent at a decent apartment in Manhattan, but in Prague she could probably last six months or longer, especially if she lived in a hostel or some kind of cheap housing.

She went online and Googled 'moving to Prague' and viewed pictures of the city – eerily, her dream had been almost dead-on – and read all about relocating, becoming increasingly psyched. She was so sure of her plan that she posted a blog entry entitled I'M MOVING TO PRAGUE.

When she went downstairs, her mom was frantically

vacuuming. It was obvious that her mom had a lot of manic energy today, but Marissa didn't know if it was because she was worried about the break-in or if it had to do with her affair with Tony the trainer or both. When Marissa asked her if she was okay she mumbled, 'Fine,' but barely made eye contact. Later on, when Marissa went downstairs to do some laundry, her mom was lying on a couch, covered by a shawl, watching a soap opera. With her dad acting so deluded and her mom acting so weird, Marissa felt like she was living with two mental patients.

She couldn't wait to escape to Prague.

Marissa was still upset about Gabriela but was trying not to think about it too much and was resisting searching for information about the murder. She figured if there was any major news – if there'd been an arrest – her mother or father would let her know, and reading about it would only upset her even more. She also was afraid she'd stumble on some new embarrassing article about her father that would make her want to contemplate a name change. Instead she focused on happier things – Prague and, more immediately, her plans to go out tonight. Tone Def was playing a set at ten at Kenny's Castaways, and there was no way Marissa was missing it. She was planning to meet Sarah, Hillary, and Hillary's work friend Beth at the Bitter End for drinks at six. She'd also been exchanging text messages with Lucas, the bass player from Tone Def she'd hooked up with that one time, and Lucas had invited her and her friends to hang out at some place on the Lower East Side after their set. Marissa was looking forward to having a fun night out with her friends and then hopefully hooking up with Lucas, maybe going back to his place.

She left the house looking very sexy, very rock 'n' roll, in pre-ripped skinny jeans, a low-cut T-shirt showing her angel tattoo, knee-high black leather boots, chunky tribal wood earrings, and dark, gothicky lipstick, which contrasted nicely with her pale skin. She met her friends for drinks, and then a few people wanted to eat, so they went up the block to some cheap Vietnamese place and then over to Kenny's. Marissa had a nice buzz and didn't want to lose it, so she suggested doing shots of schnapps to celebrate.

'Celebrate what?' Hillary asked.

'Me moving to Prague,' Marissa said like it was obvious.

Sarah and Beth wouldn't do the shots, but Marissa and Hillary did. Now Marissa had a really good buzz going; she was even close to being drunk. An annoying retro punk band called I'm Bernadette was finishing their set, and the place was filling up for Tone Def, who had a big cult following. Marissa made her way through the crowd toward the stage, wanting to say hi to Lucas. Naturally there were a lot of Vassar people in the crowd – there was just no escaping them – and she stopped and had a short conversation with Megan, Caitlin, and Alison. Then she spotted Darren, sitting with Zach Harrison at a table off to the right. She couldn't believe Darren was actually here – what a total asshole. She knew he only came because he'd heard *she'd* be here; he didn't even *like* Tone Def. What was it going to take for him to get the freaking point?

She went past Darren's table toward the stage, where Tone Def had started setting up. She wanted Darren to see her with Lucas and get jealous as hell.

'Hey, where's Lucas?' Marissa asked Julien, Tone Def's drummer.

'Hey, how you doin'?' Julien said. 'Dunno, he's around somewhere.'

'I think I saw him going into the bathroom,' a guy plugging in an amp said distractedly.

Marissa went to the area outside the men's room and waited. A few guys went in and out, but there was no sign of Lucas. Meanwhile, there was a line forming outside the women's room. Marissa didn't want to go back to the area in front of the stage, knowing Darren would come up to her, so she remained outside the bathroom.

A girl banged on the women's room door, saying, 'Come on already.' Another couple of minutes went by, then Lucas came out of the bathroom with his arm around this drugged-out girl with long, messy red hair. His jeans were partially unzipped and her lipstick was all smeared, as if there was any doubt what had gone on in there.

Marissa would've walked away if she'd had the chance, but

Lucas and the girl were walking right past her. Lucas's eyes widened when he saw her, then he said, 'Hey,' and he and the girl continued toward the stage.

Marissa suddenly felt lightheaded, like she might pass out, a combination of shock and the schnapps hitting her system. She had to actually lean against the wall for a few seconds with her eyes closed to stop the room from spinning. Then she opened her eyes and saw Darren coming toward her.

'Hey, what's up?' he asked, smiling stupidly. Did he expect her to be, what, *excited*?

She tried to get past him, and he grabbed her arm like he had last night. 'Hey,' he said, 'where're you going?'

'Just leave me alone,' she said, yanking her arm free.

'What's wrong?' he asked.

'*You're* what's wrong,' she said, but he probably couldn't hear her because she was walking away and Tone Def's set had started. Her friends, standing in front of the stage, waved her over, and she had to stand there, watching Lucas play bass. It was hard not to notice how relaxed he looked post-blow-job. As soon as she got home she was *so* deleting all of the Tone Def tracks from her Mac and iPhone.

She was sick of looking at Lucas. She looked over to her left, but Darren was there, so she turned quickly to the right and saw this incredibly good-looking guy standing a few feet away from her watching the show. She thought she'd seen him somewhere before, and then she knew why – he looked so much like Johnny Depp. In fact, for a few seconds she thought he actually *was* Johnny Depp, but then she thought, *Would Johnny Depp really be watching some lame band in the West Village with a bunch of people from Vassar?*

She was checking him out more closely – he actually looked a lot younger than Johnny Depp – and then he looked in her direction and smiled. She thought he might be smiling at somebody next to her, but, nope, he was smiling at her. She smiled back at him and then looked quickly away toward the stage, where Lucas was doing a bass solo, making a face like he was having another orgasm. Did it really take that much energy to create such shitty music? She felt a tap on her shoulder, and the Johnny Depp guy was next to her saying something, which of course she couldn't understand because (a) she was nervous as hell and (b) the music was so damn loud. Then he made a drinking motion with his hand, and she nodded and then walked ahead of him through the crowd toward the bar. She hoped Darren was jealous, watching them leave. She also hoped Lucas was noticing but doubted he could with the spotlights on him and the way he was busy fucking his bass.

When they got closer to the bar area, where the music was lower, the Johnny Depp guy leaned closer to her and said, 'Hey, I'm Xan.'

He pronounced it 'Zan,' but she didn't think she'd heard him correctly and said, 'I'm sorry?'

'Xan,' he said. 'My real name's Alexander, but people call me Xan.'

He had bright blue eyes, long sideburns, hadn't shaved in a couple of days, and strings of greasy hair hung coolly over his face. His scruffiness and darkish skin somehow made his blue eyes seem bluer.

'I had a friend Scott in college and he called himself Scuh,' Marissa said. 'I thought that was stupid, but Xan, that's really cool.'

He smiled, looking into her eyes, and asked, 'So what's your name?'

'Oh,' she said, feeling like an idiot for not telling him on her own. 'Marissa.'

'Marissa or Rissa?' he asked.

She laughed and said, 'Rissa, I like that.'

'Then there you go,' he said. 'From now on I'm gonna call you Rissa.' *From now on.* She liked that. And he was looking into her eyes again – when was the last time a guy had paid so much attention to her? Especially a cool, hot guy like Xan? She loved his lips, too – she could tell they were really soft. She was dying to kiss him, not just to make Darren and Lucas jealous but because she really wanted to.

Finally she was able to clear her mind enough to think of a good question. 'So are you a big Tone Def fan?'

Okay, so maybe it wasn't a *good* question, but at least there wasn't dead air. 'I've seen them a couple times,' Xan said. 'What about you?'

Picturing Lucas coming out of the bathroom with the blow-job queen of the West Village, she said, 'Actually, I think they suck. My friends wanted to come, so I kind of got roped into it. Are you in a band?'

'Do I look like I am?'

'Yeah, kind of.'

'Actually I'm a painter.'

'You're kidding me.' She was excited. 'What do you paint?'

'Different stuff. Portraits, street scenes. Stuff out of real life.'

'Wow,' she said, 'that sounds amazing. I majored in art history.'

'Really?'

'Yeah, at Vassar. I also worked at the Met for a while over the summer.' She left out that she'd rented headsets and had lasted barely a month. Let him think she'd been some important curator.

'Really?' he said, still smiling. 'That's amazing.'

God, she was dying to kiss him. He was so hot – and also she'd finally met someone in New York she had something in common with.

'So who are some of your favorite artists?' she asked, realizing too late how stupid this question sounded.

'Oh, man, there are so many,' he said. 'I like a lot of different types of art, you know? I really like the Impressionists, like van Gogh, um, Monet, Cézanne, Degas, yeah, Degas's stuff is really great... but I like other stuff, too, like, um, Edward Hopper –'

'Oh my God, I *love* Hopper. His work is so simple, yet so deep. I love twentieth-century urban Americana.'

'I also like Picasso, Warhol, um, Jackson Pollock –'

'I can't believe it. You just named my favorite artists.'

'Oh, and I love Frida Kahlo, too.'

'Get out, I'm *so* into Frida Kahlo. I did this twenty-five-page paper on her senior year. I think she's amazing. Do you know that painting *Henry Ford Hospital*?'

'Yeah, that one's great, but I think my favorite's *Self-Portrait with Small Monkey*.'

'I know, I love *Small Monkey*. The use of animals in that is so powerful and so resonant. It really is the quintessential example of the angst in Kahlo's oeuvre.'

Angst in her oeuvre? Yikes, she wished she could shut herself up. She hoped she wasn't sounding too pretentious, too much like a know-it-all.

He took a sip of his beer but didn't stop looking right into her eyes.

'So what kind of stuff do you paint?' she asked.

'Hard to describe it,' he said. 'I'm into a lot of different, um, movements. I do some street-scene-type stuff, but I also paint mountains, people, a little of everything, you know?'

'Wow,' she said, impressed. 'So, if you don't mind my asking, do you do something else to support yourself or...'

'No, I'm just an artist,' he said. 'I believe you have to find what you love to do in life and keep doing it no matter what. You can't let money get in the way of happiness. You just have to do it, be passionate, follow your dream, you know?'

'I think that's amazing,' she said. 'I say the same thing all the –' Marissa spotted Darren with Zach at the edge of the crowd watching the band.

'What's wrong?' Xan asked.

'Oh, nothing,' she said. 'I just know that guy over there. He's just some guy I used to go out with, and I've been trying to blow him off and he won't get the message. It's so annoying that he's even here.'

Darren came over to Marissa and said, 'Can we talk for a sec?'

'I'm busy right now,' Marissa said.

'Excuse me,' Darren said to Xan, 'but I have to talk to my girlfriend.'

'I am *not* your girlfriend,' Marissa said. 'Can you just leave me the hell alone?'

'I just want to –'

'Hey,' Xan said to Darren. 'She asked you to leave her alone.'

'Am I talkin' to you?' Darren said.

Xan put his beer down on the bar, then calmly grabbed a fistful of Darren's jacket and pulled him away toward the front door. Marissa couldn't tell what Xan was saying to Darren because he had his back to her and the music was still very loud. But she could see Darren's face. At first he seemed angry, like he was ready to fight Xan, but as Xan spoke to him his expression gradually morphed. He looked confused, then concerned, then terrified.

Finally Xan returned to Marissa and said, smiling, 'I don't think he'll be bothering you anymore.'

Marissa watched Darren go over to Zach. They had a very short conversation; then Darren rushed out of the bar without looking in Marissa's direction.

'That was amazing,' Marissa said. 'What did you tell him?'

'I just gave him a little lesson about the right and the wrong way to treat a woman,' Xan said. 'Do you want to get out of here?'

Marissa thought, *Uh-oh, he doesn't want to sleep with me, does he? Please don't be that kind of guy.*

But then he added quickly, 'I mean out of this bar. Someplace quieter, where we can talk.'

'Yeah,' she said, 'that sounds great.'

Tone Def was still doing their first set. Marissa went over to Hillary and said she was leaving for a while and asked her to text her if they wound up going someplace else.

'Where're you going?' Hillary asked.

'I met a guy,' Marissa said.

'Really? Who?'

Marissa looked back toward where Xan was standing, and Hillary looked over, too.

'Oh my God, he's fucking *hot*,' Hillary said.

Marissa smiled proudly.

Marissa and Xan left the bar and went down Bleecker to Café Figaro. They sat at a table outside and drank cappuccinos and had a great conversation about art and New York, and then he mentioned that he hadn't gone to college but had traveled in Europe and used to live in Prague. He actually had *lived* in Prague. If that wasn't a sign from the gods, what was? She told him all about her plans to move to Prague, though in the back of her mind she was thinking, *Do I really want to go?* Prague had sounded like a great idea before she'd met Xan. If this turned out as good as she thought it would, if she and Xan started dating, maybe she'd bag those plans.

Okay, okay, so she was getting way ahead of herself, but it was fun to fantasize.

Then they discovered an even bigger coincidence. He mentioned that he'd traveled in England, and she told him that she'd done her junior year abroad in London, studying at University of the Arts. Then they realized that they had been in London at the same time.

'Where were you staying?' Marissa asked.

'With a friend in Hampstead,' he said.

'Oh my God, that's where I lived the summer after the semester ended. Where in Hampstead?'

'Um, lemme try to remember,' Xan said. 'I think it was Kemplay Road.'

'I was on Carlingford Road,' Marissa said. 'I can't believe it, I was living right around the corner from you.'

They had refills on the cappuccinos, and she had such a good time talking to him that they lost track of time. They were mostly talking about her – he was asking a lot of questions about school and her childhood and her plans for the future. It was so refreshing to be with a guy who was actually interested in her, a guy she had so much in common with. It didn't hurt that he happened to be gorgeous, too. She felt like she'd hit the jackpot.

It was getting late, so she checked her watch and yawned for effect and said, 'I should be getting home soon.'

She was hoping he'd ask for her number, but instead he said, 'I'll ride home with you.'

'That's crazy,' she said. 'You said you live in Brooklyn, right?'

'Yeah, so?'

'But it's so out of the way for you.'

'There's no way I'm letting you ride the subway home alone at this hour.' She said she took the subway home all the time, or could take the LIRR, which was safer, but he insisted on coming with her. She wasn't exactly opposed. She thought he was very romantic and thoughtful, and she couldn't remember a guy ever going out of his way to do something like that for her.

Darren would've ditched her hours ago on some dark corner in Manhattan.

When they got to the Forest Hills stop she thought that would be it, they'd say good night and he'd head back to Brooklyn. But, nope, he insisted on walking her all the way back to her house. This whole night had been reminding her of something, but she didn't know what, and then it hit her – that old black-and-white movie she'd seen on TV a few weeks ago, *Marty*. This was just like *Marty* – meeting a guy at a club, him taking her home late at night. Except in *Marty* they didn't kiss good night, and she was hoping Xan kissed her.

On her block she suddenly got nervous, fearing everything was going to get all screwed up. The police car was there again, parked across the street. She didn't know if Xan had heard about the shooting in the news or not, and she was afraid that he'd see the police car there and start asking her questions. She was afraid that if he knew she was the daughter of Adam Bloom, the crazed vigilante, he'd want nothing to do with her.

She was relieved when Xan didn't seem to even notice the police car. Maybe he was too nervous, distracted.

'Well, this is it,' she said, and they stopped in front of the house.

'Wow,' Xan said, admiring it. 'It's big. I bet you loved growing up here, huh?'

'It was okay,' she said.

Then he held both her hands and they stood facing each other. She'd already given him her number on the subway, and they'd talked about going out sometime.

'I'll call you tomorrow,' he said, and she said, 'That'll be great,' and then he was kissing her.

Finally she pulled back and said, 'I should really go.'

'Okay, it was great meeting you, Rissa.'

She told him it was great meeting him, too, and they said good night and waved goodbye to each other as he walked away, down the block.

As she entered the house the alarm started beeping. She typed in the new code she had memorized and then rearmed the alarm and went upstairs.

It was amazing the way life worked out sometimes – just when she thought things couldn't possibly get any worse, something amazing and unexpected happened. If this wasn't evidence that there had to be a God, or some higher power, what was?

She rushed upstairs and posted a blog entry on this very topic.

13

13

JOHNNY LONG HAD a chance to shoot Dr Bloom right in the head. It was a little after two o'clock in the afternoon on Wednesday, the same day Johnny killed Gabriela, and he was waiting in a stolen Honda on the corner of Bloom's block. Johnny had been in Forest Hills for about an hour, hour and a half. There were some people in front of the house, looked like reporters, but he didn't see any cops. He didn't know where Bloom was, if he was in the house or not, and he didn't even know if he'd get a chance to shoot him today. It would suck if he couldn't get it over with, because he was tired and just wanted to go home and crash.

Then the asshole doctor came out, no, *strutted* out, like he thought he was hot shit, but that didn't piss off Johnny as much as the way the guy was dressed – in sweats, sneakers, looking like he was what, going to the gym? About twelve hours ago the guy had shot Carlos in his house – no, not shot him, *unloaded* a whole clip into him at point-blank range, and the next day he's going out to exercise?

Johnny usually didn't enjoy killing people. He'd only killed three people in his life, well, four including Gabriela, and he only did it when he absolutely had to, when he had to save his own ass. But killing Adam Bloom was going to be different. It was going to be a blast shooting him in the head, seeing him fall down on the sidewalk, his blood and brains spilling out.

He watched Bloom talking to the reporters, holding court. Man, look at that guy, acting so proud of himself, using his hands to get a point across. Johnny could tell the guy was loving every second of this; he was getting off on it. Well, soon he was going to get a bullet in his head, too.

Finally Bloom stopped yapping and walked away alone toward the corner. Johnny waited several seconds, then started his car and drove slowly up the block. Bloom turned the corner, and then Johnny turned and saw Bloom about twenty yards ahead. Johnny had bought a clean .38 Special from his gun man, Reynaldo, and he had it in his right hand with the passenger-side window already open. There didn't seem to be any people around. When Bloom got to that space up ahead where there were no parked cars in the way, Johnny would speed up a little, then slow down again and get a clear shot at Bloom's head. Maybe, just for fun, he'd call out, 'What's up, doc?' right before he shot him.

Bloom was in the perfect spot, and Johnny hit the gas harder and was almost alongside him. He had the gun raised, aiming right at Bloom's left ear, but then he thought, *Why kill him now?* Yeah, he'd be dead, and Carlos would be able to rest in peace, but would it really be getting revenge? Killing wasn't revenge. Making a guy feel pain and *then* killing him was revenge.

Johnny continued tailing Bloom, staying about half a block behind him, trying to decide what to do – shoot him now, just get it over with, or fuck up his life first, and maybe make a few bucks at the same time? Johnny figured the guy had that big house and all that jewelry and that diamond ring. He probably had a lot of cash in there, too. It would still be nice to be able to kick back this summer, hit the beach down the shore for a month or two.

Then an idea came to Johnny – a way to get revenge, real revenge on Dr Bloom, and get the biggest score of his life at the same time. It was so obvious he couldn't believe he hadn't thought of it sooner.

He left Forest Hills, going down Queens Boulevard, the plan getting better and better.

Oh, yeah, this was gonna be fucking beautiful.

After he ditched the Honda on a side street in Kew Gardens, he rode the subway to Brooklyn – lifting a wallet from a guy in a suit along the way, making a cool hundred and eighty-six bucks – and went to a Burger King with internet terminals and started finding out as much as he could about Marissa Bloom.

The TV news reports had mentioned that it had been Adam Bloom's twenty-two-year-old daughter, Marissa, who had woken her parents up last night, telling them that their house was being robbed. Johnny was looking for pictures of this girl to see what he was dealing with, and he found a picture of a Marissa Bloom right away, but this had to be a different Marissa Bloom, because she looked like she was about forty and worked at some company in San Francisco. Another Marissa Bloom was too young, played goalie on a Little League soccer team in Parsippany, New Jersey, but holy shit, here we go – Marissa Bloom with some friends at a party at some uppity-looking college called Vassar. She wouldn't be the most beautiful woman Johnny had ever scored with, but compared to most of the women he'd been screwing lately she was a knockout – nice enough face, slim arms. The picture didn't show her legs, but usually if a girl's arms were fit it meant her legs were, too. If this Marissa Bloom was the right Marissa Bloom, he was in business.

He found some more pictures of her taken at Vassar. In a couple she had long hair; then her hair was shorter. In one her hair was spikier and she had a punk-type look. He was already starting to get an idea of who this girl was, imagining the guy he'd have to be to win her over.

But how did he know this was the right girl? He did a search for 'Marissa Bloom Forest Hills,' checked out a few results, and found nothing, but hold up, what was this, a blog called Artist Girl? There was a picture of the Marissa Bloom from Vassar in the upper left corner, and then he scrolled down and there it was, the title of a blog entry from only a few weeks ago: TEN THINGS I HATE ABOUT FOREST HILLS.

He felt like he'd hit the jackpot, like the goddamn stars were aligning. This was almost going to be too easy – everything he needed to know about her was right here in her blog. And she didn't have one of those blogs that went on and on, talking about shit in the news. This blog was all about her, like a freaking diary. She posted almost every day, and the archives seemed to go back for years, to when she was in high school. All Johnny had to do was read this whole blog a few times and he'd be the Marissa Bloom expert of the whole goddamn world.

He stayed at Burger King for three or four hours, reading Marissa Bloom's blog, finding out all about her, starting to feel like he'd known her all his life. He found out all about her past boyfriends, all the gossip with her friends, the classes she'd taken in school, her junior year abroad in London, her favorite artists and paintings. Usually when he was picking up a woman he had to get information as he was going along, try to figure out how to use it to his advantage on the spot. But in this case he had all the information he needed about her in advance, and he could think through every last detail, make sure there was no way he could slip up at all. This was almost going to be too easy.

He found more pictures of her on her blog and on her MySpace page, which she hadn't made private. In a couple of the pictures she was in a bikini, and she wasn't bad-looking at all. Her legs were as thin as he expected, and she had surprisingly nice tits. He had to rein it in – he was starting to get a hard-on, not a thing you want to do in a crowded Burger King – but, yeah, he could already imagine seducing this girl, making love to her, giving her mind-blowing orgasms.

He read more blog entries, trying to decide who he should be – a musician or an artist. He knew he could pull off either one, so it was only a matter of which one she'd be more likely to fall for. He'd used the 'I'm in a band' line lots of times to pick up women – he had a rock-star look to him, which helped, and any girl was a sucker for a hot guy with a guitar – but then he read that Marissa was into some band called Tone Def and had 'hooked up with' the bass player for the band. That KO'd the musician idea. He figured she'd want somebody different, somebody fresh. She'd never had an artist boyfriend, so that definitely seemed like the way to go.

He went to Wikipedia and read about the artists and paintings she'd mentioned on her blog. He didn't know shit about art, but after a while he knew enough buzzwords and basic facts to get the gist of what it was all about. Nobody could bullshit better than Johnny Long. All he needed was to know ten percent about something and he could fill in the other ninety and sound like an expert about anything.

He took in as much information as he could, then went home and crashed. In the morning, he got to work right away, knowing that this Marissa Bloom thing would be a lot more complicated than his usual pickup. If he wanted to do this thing right, really pull it off the way he wanted to, he'd need a whole new ID. For one-night stands he could make up any story about himself that he wanted because the girl never had a chance to check out any of it. But with Marissa he was going to have to build up her trust in him, get her to really like him and know him, or at least believe that she knew him. He might have to actually date her, even bring her back to his place, so everything would have to add up.

He went to Brighton Beach and met with this guy Slav who sold dead Russians' IDs. For three hundred bucks Johnny got a Social Security card and a driver's license and a brand-new identity: Alexander Evonov. Although Johnny was Irish-Italian, he had dark features and figured he could easily pull off the Russian story, say his grandfather was from Moscow or wherever.

Next, if he was going to say he was an artist, he was going to need some art stuff around his apartment. Made sense, right? He stopped at an art supply store and bought paint, an easel, a smock, and a bunch of drop cloths to spread around. He figured he'd need some art around the house, too, so he went to a Salvation Army and a couple of thrift shops and picked up whatever paintings he could find. Some were of mountains, others were of people and street scenes, and some were just shapes and colors and looked like they were by that guy Marissa had mentioned in her blog, something Polish-sounding, something-sky? Kalinsky, Kazinsky, no, *Kandinsky*. Yeah, that was it. Of course, the paintings Johnny bought didn't look like the same person had painted them, but he already had a story ready to explain that. He'd say he was into a lot of different – what was that word he'd seen in Wikipedia? – *movements*. Yeah, he'd say he was into a lot of different movements.

Johnny stopped at Blockbuster and took out *Frida* and *Pollock*. After he watched the movies he figured he'd be all set as far as art was concerned, but something about the name, Alexander Evonov, was bugging him. It just didn't sound cool enough. It was no Johnny Long, that was for sure, but he couldn't expect to come up with a fake name as cool as his real name. He was stuck with Evonov but figured he could fiddle with Alexander, come up with something more hip. Alex? No, there were a million Alexes in the world. Al? Nah, sounded like an old man. He thought about Xander, then thought, *Why not just Xan?* Yeah, Marissa Bloom, a girl who lived in an uppity house in Forest Hills but who was trying so hard to look cool with that jewelry and the pink streaks in her hair, was going to love meeting a guy named Xan.

On his way back to his apartment he passed a newsstand so he checked out the papers and saw the headlines TRIGGER HAPPY and GUN CRAZY. Reading the articles at the newsstand, Johnny couldn't help cracking up. At one point he had to catch his breath, he was laughing so hard. Adam Bloom was the joke of the city; they were comparing him to Bernie Goetz, for chrissake. Was this too beautiful or what? He was so glad he hadn't shot Bloom yesterday. If he had it would've been like doing the guy a favor, putting him out of his misery. But little did the guy know, his misery was only beginning.

Man, Johnny was loving this, imagining that cocky rich shrink, reading the papers today, feeling like the world's biggest idiot, probably wishing he'd never been born. Well, it was going to be like he'd never been born very soon, but first Johnny wanted to make that asshole really sweat, and he knew exactly what to do next.

He took the subway to Forest Hills. He walked right up to the Blooms' door and slid a note he'd written underneath. He loved this, being so close to the house, like he was rubbing it in the guy's face, showing the guy, *I don't give a shit, I can get as close to you as I want. I can even screw your daughter, you son of a bitch, and there's nothing you can do to stop me.*

There was nothing he liked more than screwing with people's heads, and this was going to be his biggest mindfuck ever.

Back at his apartment, he watched *Frida* and *Pollock*, fast-forwarding through the boring parts – okay, most of both movies – but he picked up some more good info. He spent the rest of the evening setting up his apartment to make it look like an artist lived there. On the paintings he'd bought, he added a signature – XAN – in thick black letters, over whatever signatures were there. He hung a few paintings on the walls, spread a drop cloth on the floor, and set up the easel with a canvas on it. He put the paints on the palette and then, trying to do what that guy Pollock did, spread some paint around, just kind of winged it at the canvas, letting it clump and drip. He used blue and yellow mostly, then threw in a little green and why not some red and black in the corners? He stood back and looked at it. Hey, he didn't think it looked so bad, at least as good as Pollock's shit.

Although he still felt like he had to work out a few details in his head, he didn't think he'd have any trouble convincing Marissa he was Xan Evonov, the up-and-coming artist.

In the morning he walked several blocks to a coffee bar that had internet terminals. He wanted to read more about Marissa, see if she mentioned where she was going to be over the next few days, but he started to panic when he saw a new entry up: I'M MOVING TO PRAGUE. He thought she was moving now, which would've screwed up all his big plans, but he relaxed when he realized that it was just something she was talking about doing. Then, toward the bottom of the page, he saw the heading WHERE I'LL BE TONIGHT, and underneath it Marissa had written: *I'll be checking out the greatest band in the world, Tone Def. They're on at ten o'clock at Kenny's Castaways! Everybody should come!*

Could she have possibly made things any easier for him? Not only did he know where she was going to be, he knew the exact time, no less.

For the next hour or two, Johnny read more of Marissa's blog, working out in his head things he'd say to her and his plans for what would happen after. He was so prepared and had so much more information than he had for his usual pickups that he was afraid he'd overdone it. He had to be careful to let stuff come out naturally, not to say anything to her or about her that he wasn't supposed to know.

At around ten, he showed up at the club, paid the five-dollar cover, and went inside. He looked around near the bar and didn't see Marissa, and then he went farther in toward where the band was playing. Man, what shitty music. Was she serious with that 'best band in the world' crap? Johnny knew if she wasn't screwing the bass player there was no way in hell she would've liked this garbage, and when Johnny saw the bass player up there, strangling the bass, trying to look like Kurt Cobain, burnt-out with the hair over his eyes, he couldn't help smiling. If that was the guy she went for, some wannabe like that guy, there was no way she'd be able to resist Johnny Long, the real deal.

Johnny looked toward the front of the stage, thinking she'd be up there with the other groupie types. He didn't see her – but wait, there she was, standing next to a few other girls. She looked better in person than she did in the pictures. She had a sweet little body and what looked like a pretty nice ass. He didn't look at her for very long, though, knowing how important it was for her to notice him first. He got into a good position, off to the side about ten feet away from her, and looked toward the stage. After a little while, although he was still staring straight ahead and couldn't see her at all, he could feel her eyes on him. He knew she was checking him out, noticing how hot and sexy he was, but he had to play this right. Timing was everything with a pickup, and he had to give her a chance to really notice him, build up a fantasy in her head about who he was. She didn't just have to like him, she had to *want* him.

At the perfect moment, when he sensed she was about to look away, he turned and gave her the Johnny Long smile. He knew that the way a woman reacted to his smile was as good as him asking her to have sex with him and her answering yes or no. If she looked away quickly the answer was no; the door was closed. If she didn't look away but reacted like she'd been caught doing something, the door wasn't completely closed, but it would take some work to open it all the way. Ah, but if the woman smiled back and didn't look away at all, then the door was open, and in Marissa Bloom's case there was no doubt about it. Her door was wide, wide open.

He went over to her, maintaining lots of eye contact, and asked her if she wanted to get a drink at the bar, and naturally she said yes. He let her walk ahead of him, loving the way her little ass looked in those tight jeans. He liked the little tee she was wearing, too, how it showed the angel tattoo on her lower back. Tattoos on the lower back were always a good sign. He'd never met a girl with one of those who didn't love to screw.

At the bar, he put his greatest asset to work – his irresistible charm. As he expected, she loved that he'd shortened his name to Xan, and saying that he'd call her Rissa from now on had been unplanned but ingenious. Having a pet name for her communicated to her that he wanted to see her again, that he *expected* to see her again, but he didn't have to come out and say it, which would've made him seem way too pushy so early on. He bet he was the only Casanova in the world who knew this trick.

When the conversation got into art, he really hit his stride. It was obvious that she was thrilled to meet an artist, and it impressed her more than if he'd told her his last name was Trump. He dropped all the names of her favorite painters but did it in a casual way, like *Wow, we both love the same painters, isn't that a big coincidence?* Man, she ate that shit right up. Every time he mentioned Pollock or van Gogh or Kahlo or whoever, he was one step closer to scoring. He knew so much about her, had so much information to drop, it almost seemed unfair. But then he reminded himself – she wasn't just some innocent girl, she was the daughter of Adam Bloom, the daughter of the guy who'd killed Carlos in cold blood. She deserved everything she had coming to her.

Things were going so well that he knew he could've scored with her tonight if he wanted to, but he had to stick to his game plan. This was a long con after all. Yeah, he was going to nail her good, but he had to build her trust completely to accomplish everything he wanted to accomplish.

So he kept the BS flowing, telling her everything she wanted to hear, and then her boyfriend came over. This was too perfect. Johnny figured it was that Darren guy she'd been blogging about. Johnny had been in this situation many times before and knew there was no better way to win over a girl than to get rid of her pissed-off ex. It helped when the ex was a skinny little weasel. So Johnny took Darren aside and squeezed his hand as hard as he could and told him very calmly that if he didn't leave Marissa alone he was gonna cut off his dick and feed it to him. He said this with steel in his voice, looking right into the wimp's eyes, and he could tell he was getting his point across. Finally he let go of the guy's hand and watched him hightail it out of there.

Johnny could tell Marissa was impressed, and he scored more points when she went to tell her friend that she was leaving. Her friend looked over at Johnny, and he grinned and read her lips: *He's fucking hot.* Now Johnny had gotten friend approval. Was he the greatest pickup artist in the world or what?

Johnny had to be careful not to get too cocky, not to shoot himself in the ass. At the café he almost went a little too far, saying that he'd lived in Hampstead at the same time she did. Of course, he'd picked up this info from her blog, and he'd been smart enough to do a little extra research about it earlier, checking out the neighborhood on a map of London and picking up the name of a street in Hampstead near where she lived. But that was all he knew about the area and he had to change the subject quickly before she asked too many questions.

He had to be more careful from now on, make sure he didn't get boxed in like that again. He saw her checking her watch, saying she had to get home. He knew she was just being the Good Girl, trying to make him think she wasn't the type who went home with guys she hardly knew. Yeah, right. He knew if he tried to get her back to his place, hit her with some more charm, he could've scored, no problem. He almost pushed for it because he was in the mood to bang her, but he knew that would be taking a risk. She might feel bad in the morning, freak out, not want to see him again, and he didn't want to take that chance.

So he insisted on taking her back to Forest Hills, and he could tell she was impressed. She'd met a hot guy who was nice and thoughtful, too. She probably felt like she'd struck gold. What woman wouldn't?

At the house, Johnny was glad to see the police car parked in front. He'd expected Bloom would panic when he found the note under his door and try to get some kind of extra protection, but little did he know this was gonna backfire right into his face. This was exactly what Johnny wanted, for the cops to see him coming home with Marissa, kissing her good night, and walking away. Now he could get as close to the Blooms and the house as he wanted to because as far as the cops were concerned he was clean.

He told Marissa all the right things, how he wanted to see her again, and he knew she wanted him to kiss her. He let her want it a little longer, making her really want it, and then he gave it to her. He was holding both her hands and was gentle with his lips and slipped in just enough tongue. She was pressing her body up against his in a way that told him she was ready for him, but he stuck to his plan and said goodbye, leaving her wanting more.

As he walked away, he saw the cop looking over at him. Johnny looked down, avoiding eye contact. Man, Johnny couldn't remember the last time he'd gotten a rush like this. He couldn't wait to see Marissa's blog tomorrow. She'd write about how she'd met this great guy named Xan and how excited she was. Just thinking about that name, Xan, cracked Johnny up. But nothing was funnier than picturing Dr Bloom sitting there in his fancy house. He'd probably jazzed up his alarm system, gotten new locks for the doors, and thought he was safe with the cops sitting out there. Yeah, like anything could protect him now. Pretty soon Johnny was gonna be inside his daughter *and* inside his house, and that would only be the beginning of the pain he'd make that man feel.

14

O N FRIDAY MORNING Adam decided that shooting Carlos Sanchez ten times had probably been a mistake. Shooting him the first two times had been necessary – he had no doubts about that – but he wished he could take back the other eight shots.

But, unfortunately, there was nothing he could do about that now. What was that Shakespeare quote, what was done can't be undone? It was so true. And ruminating about it incessantly was just causing anxiety and stress, so why not just let go?

Adam was getting dressed to go to work when Dana sat up in bed and said, 'I want to go to Florida.'

She had just woken up and her voice was deeper than normal, more gravelly.

'Come on,' Adam said, 'you know we can't do that right now.'

'We can do whatever we want. We're not trapped here.'

Buttoning a red pinstriped shirt, Adam said, 'Clements said he doesn't want us to leave.'

'I want to talk to a lawyer today. We're not criminals, for God's sake, we're not suspects in anything. We don't have to stay around here, putting our lives at risk, because he *wants* us to stay.'

'I think you're being a little melodramatic –'

'We can be available by telephone. We can be available by email. We can teleconference with him. This is the twenty-first century, for God's sake.'

Adam, sitting down in a chair, putting on his loafers, said, 'If there was a reason to go to Florida I'd go.'

'Your life was threatened,' Dana said. 'If that's not a reason to go, what is?'

'Okay, just relax, take some deep breaths,' Adam said. 'It's very difficult to talk to you when you get like this.'

Adam was looking down at his shoes, but he knew exactly what Dana's expression was – she was staring at him in mock exasperated disbelief.

'Fine, you do whatever you want to do,' she finally said. 'But I'm leaving, and I'm taking Marissa with me. If you want to stay here that's up to you.'

Adam stood back and checked himself out in the mirror. He didn't look the best he'd ever looked. He appeared tired, worn, burnt-out – the stress of the past few days was getting to him. He could see Dana behind him, sitting at the edge of the bed. She didn't look so terrific either.

'Let's discuss this later when you're calmer,' he said. 'I have to get to the office.'

'I'll let you know what hotel we're staying at,' Dana said.

'Oh, come on, can you please just stop it with the posturing?'

'He's using us as bait. I refuse to be bait.'

'There's no one to bait us. The note was a prank.'

'It was a death threat, Adam.'

'It said nothing about killing me. It said, what, I don't even remember. Oh, yeah, it said I was going to wish I was never born. Come on, that means nothing. It's something a kid in a schoolyard would say.'

'I don't understand why you're not taking it seriously.'

'Not taking it seriously? Come on, I had Clements down here right away, I had cops outside all night. I think I'm taking it very seriously, but I still think it was a prank.'

'A kid from the neighborhood wouldn't do something like that.'

'You don't know that. It sounded like a kid, I mean the language.'

'It sounded like somebody who's angry, who wants to hurt you.'

'Explain to me how that makes any sense. Please just try to explain it. Somebody who robbed our house would come here the next day and put a note under the door? Why? To scare me? If somebody's angry, wants revenge, why leave a note? See, so if you think about it, logically, it doesn't make any sense. It had to be a prank, maybe not a kid from the neighborhood but maybe some nut who read about me in the paper. I'm sure that happens all the time when somebody's front-page news. That's why, you noticed, Clements wasn't very concerned. He probably sees this kind of thing happen all the time. If our number was listed I bet we would've been getting threats all night.'

Dana had a strange look. She was zoning out, looking like she was barely aware he was in the room.

'What's wrong?' Adam asked.

She seemed far away for a while longer; then she focused and said, 'Nothing.'

'You see my point now, don't you?'

'Gabriela didn't rob our house.' She sounded oddly distant.

'What? What're you talking about?'

'She wouldn't do that,' she said. 'I could see her getting desperate, wanting to help her father, but I can't see her actually breaking into our house. That isn't something she'd do.'

'I disagree,' Adam said. He glanced at the clock – 8:26. Damn, he had to get going. 'She had a relationship with Sanchez, she made him copies of our keys and got him the code to the alarm. It makes sense that she broke in.'

'Then who killed her?' Dana asked.

Adam didn't have an answer to this, so he said, 'I agree there are some holes.'

'Oh, really,' she said sarcastically. 'You've come to that conclusion, huh?' Adam couldn't remember – was his appointment with David Rothman at nine or ten? If it was at nine he'd never make it.

Turning on his BlackBerry to check, he said, 'You have to give the police a little more time. Clements seemed confident last night that they'll get a break in the case. I bet you they'll make an arrest by the end of the day. Meanwhile, the cops are right outside.'

Dana said something, but Adam was distracted, looking at his BlackBerry. Shit, it was at nine. 'Sorry,' he said, 'what was that?'

'I said I think this is all about your ego. You think if you run away you'll be admitting you did something wrong.'

Adam considered this, then said, 'When I was in junior high and kids threatened to beat me up every day after school, I never had a problem at all running away from them. Trust me, if I believed I was in any danger at all right now, or you or Marissa was in any danger, I'd have no problem running away. But in this case I just don't think that's necessary.'

'Yeah? And what if you're wrong?'

It was 8:28.

'I know you don't like it when I leave in mid-discussion, but I have no choice,' he said. He gave her his usual quick kiss goodbye and then said, 'I'll call you in a couple of hours, okay?' and left.

Adam arrived at his office at a few minutes past nine. David Rothman was in the waiting area, reading *Newsweek*.

'Morning, David, I'll be with you in one sec,' Adam said and went toward his office. He passed Lauren in the corridor; they exchanged good mornings, and he noticed that she didn't seem quite as cold and distant as she had yesterday. Adam hadn't bought a newspaper on the way to work, but he'd glanced at other people's papers on the subway and knew that at least he wasn't front-page news again. Hopefully there were no mentions of him at all in today's papers and the whole story was starting to fade.

Adam got settled in, refilled the water pitcher, and then reviewed his notes on his previous sessions with David. Things had been going well in David's therapy lately. He had been seeing Adam for over ten weeks now with various issues, including some associated with middle age, as he had recently turned fifty. His wife had a drinking problem, and he had associated co-dependency issues, as well as difficulty expressing his anger, to his wife and in general. When he started seeing Adam, he'd been acting out by having a series of one-night stands with women he'd picked up at bars, and Adam felt he exhibited several telltale signs of sex addiction. They'd been working on techniques for expressing his anger, and, with Adam's guidance, he had managed to convince his wife to go to AA. While he still expressed the desire to philander, they had been working on various behavior modification techniques, and David hadn't cheated on his wife at all under Adam's care.

Adam returned to the waiting room and said, 'David, come on in.'

David entered the office and settled on the couch, and he and Adam exchanged their usual small talk. David worked in advertising, and his company had a skybox at Madison Square Garden, so they discussed the Knicks for a minute or so. Adam was hoping the shooting wouldn't come up, but those hopes were dashed when David said, 'Oh, yeah, so I heard about what happened. Is everything okay with that?'

'Yes, thank you,' Adam said. 'It was a difficult situation, but my family's handling it.'

He was trying to sound professional and curt and not to be at all evasive, though he was eager to get on to another topic.

'That's good,' David said. 'I imagine stuff like that gets blown out of proportion in the news.'

'It does,' Adam said flatly. 'So how're you doing?'

David began by talking about an ongoing issue he had with a co-worker he didn't get along with, and Adam noticed that he seemed particularly agitated – shifting around a lot, crossing and uncrossing his legs. It was hard for Adam to be as attentive as he normally was during a session. He couldn't help wondering if David's agitation had to do with what he'd heard about the shooting or if it meant he didn't feel comfortable with Adam as his therapist. Adam was mulling over whether to be assertive and ask David what was bothering him or to ignore the whole thing.

But then Adam realized he was way off base when David said, 'So anyway, I, uh, met a woman the other night.'

Well, that explained the agitation; this was a major setback for David. Wanting to keep his patient feeling reassured and at ease, Adam asked in a very normal, nonjudgmental tone, 'Where did you meet her?'

'Online,' David said. He crossed his legs, then uncrossed them again. His forehead was glistening with sweat. 'I mean, not online, I mean through an online service... Ashley Madison.'

Adam knew of Ashley Madison and other similar extramarital dating services. Several of his patients frequently met sex partners through these sites.

'Okay,' Adam said calmly, waiting for David to continue on his own. David explained how he'd registered with Ashley Madison and then had arranged to meet a woman, Linda – who was married with two kids – at a hotel and had sex with her. When he described what had happened, and especially when he mentioned the sex and how 'hot and raw' it was, David started talking faster and louder, and Adam could tell how exhilarating the whole experience had been for him. It was very similar to the way a drug addict would behave when describing the experience of doing drugs; in fact, in a previous session David had told Adam about the coke habit he'd kicked several years ago. This had hardly been surprising to Adam, since most sex addicts have other addictions and are frequently co-dependent. All in all, David was just about as textbook as they get.

As David finished telling the story, his lips started quivering, and then the tears came, flowing down his cheeks, and he said, 'I don't know why...' He was crying harder and had to get hold of himself. Finally he said, 'I don't know why I keep doing this. I don't know... I don't know what's wrong with me.'

David had cried before during sessions – he was a sympathy seeker – and Adam gave him tissues and reassured him, saying things like 'It's okay' and 'I know how hard it is.' David, as usual, was blaming himself for his behavior, playing the victim, saying, 'I feel like such a piece of shit. I don't know what the hell I'm doing with my life anymore.' Adam advised him not to beat himself up about it too badly and reminded him that the internet could be very tempting for anybody and that these things happened, using the same tactics he'd employ in any similar therapy session, trying to support and reassure his patient. All the time, though, he couldn't help feeling like a total fraud. Who the hell was he to counsel anyone when his own life had been such a mess lately? And trying to treat David for philandering was the biggest joke of all, what with David sitting on the very couch where Adam had screwed Sharon Wasserman. Adam was telling David, 'You don't have to feel like you always have to be perfect,' and meanwhile he couldn't help imaging Sharon on top of him, *riding* him, his hands on her breasts. Adam told David, 'Just because you want to have sex with another woman doesn't mean you have to actually do it,' remembering how he'd said Sharon's name again and again when he came.

When the session ended, Adam felt guilty for charging David. Normally Adam was extremely attentive and used his instincts to anticipate where a session was headed and find the right openings to challenge his patients' behavior, but he felt like he hadn't helped David as much as he could've. For example, instead of letting David go on with his self-loathing, Adam should have been tougher and said something like 'It sounds like you're ready to leave your marriage.' Adam knew that David had no desire to get a divorce, but this could have helped David begin to acknowledge his reasons for philandering. But today Adam had been so distracted with his own thoughts and self-doubt that he'd felt off, out of sync, like he'd missed all of the obvious openings.

He had two more morning sessions and, as with David, Adam felt out of sorts, off his game. He had no doubt that the shooting and related issues were seriously affecting his performance at work. If this continued and he couldn't work through it, he'd have to take some time off to clear his head, maybe go down to Florida after all.

During a break in his schedule, he went around the corner to the deli to get a cup of coffee and a muffin, and on his way back he checked his voicemail and saw that he had three messages and four missed calls from Dana. She had called and left a message on his work voicemail as well. Jesus Christ, what was going on now?

He called her, and she picked up during the first ring and said, 'I've been calling you.'

'I've been with patients all morning, what's going on?'

'She's HIV positive.'

He thought she was talking about Marissa. Feeling like he might pass out, he managed to say, 'What the hell're you talking about?'

'Detective Clements just called and told me they found out Gabriela had HIV. They found her medicine or whatever in her apartment.'

'Jesus,' he said, catching his breath. 'I thought you meant...'

'What?' Dana said.

'Never mind,' Adam said, still light-headed.

'Can you believe it?' Dana continued. 'Clements said even her sister didn't know. She might've been infected for years.'

Adam didn't understand why Dana was calling him so urgently to tell him about this. 'So is that it?' he asked.

'Aren't you shocked?' Dana asked.

Actually Adam wasn't shocked. Her boyfriend had had HIV, so why was it out of the realm of possibility that Gabriela had been infected?

'Oh, and that's not all,' Dana went on. 'They found out she was a drug addict, too, heroin, just like her boyfriend. Can you believe it? She was a junkie and had AIDS while she was working for us.'

'Let's not start with that again,' Adam said. 'That's not how AIDS, HIV, is transmitted.'

'I'm talking about the deceit,' Dana said. 'That woman lied to our fucking faces for years. I can't tell you how furious I am.'

'You have a right to be furious,' Adam said.

'Aren't you furious?'

'Of course I'm furious.'

'You don't sound furious.'

'I'm standing on the corner of Fifty-eighth and Madison,' Adam said. 'Sorry, but there's a limit to the amount of furiousness I can express right now.'

Dana didn't seem amused and said, 'Well, it was nice talking to you, too,' and hung up.

Several minutes later, as he rode in the elevator back up to his office, he decided that although hanging up on him had been melodramatic and childish, Dana had made a good point. Being so wrapped up in what was going on with the police and the media, and then, on top of everything, receiving that threatening note, maybe he hadn't been expressing his anger very effectively lately, and this was likely contributing to all the symptoms of anxiety and self-doubt he'd been experiencing.

His one o'clock appointment, Helen, didn't show up. Helen had never missed an appointment before, and Adam assumed that it was related to the shooting and that he had permanently lost another patient. His two o'clock, Patricia, a banker with panic disorder, showed up, but Adam felt he was as ineffective and off the mark as he'd been with his earlier patients. Patricia didn't seem pleased at the end of the session either, and when Adam asked her if she wanted to make an appointment for her next session now, she said in a somewhat distant tone, 'I'll call you,' even though she normally made her appointments in person. Adam knew that something had to change fast, because at this rate either all his patients were going to stop coming to see him on their own or he was going to drive them away.

At four o'clock, Adam went down the hallway to Carol's office for his session with her, and he felt like he seriously needed it. Carol, waiting in her chair, didn't say hello, just 'Come in.'

She was slim, in her late fifties, always wore her gray hair in a neat bun. She'd been a mentor to Adam and also a confidant. He often discussed patients with her, and she always had sound, rational advice. He was eager to talk to her about everything he'd been going through lately, but first he felt like he needed to express his feelings about her and his other co-workers, so he said, 'Before we start, I just want you to know that I feel incredibly attacked and judged by all of you.'

Carol, holding her pad, was sitting calmly across from him. 'Attacked?' she asked as if surprised. 'Why do you feel attacked?'

The problem with being in therapy as a therapist was that Adam always felt one step ahead of Carol. He always knew exactly where she was going with her questioning, what types of feelings she was trying to elicit from him. It was like being a football coach who had access to the other team's playbook. It was still worthwhile for him to see her – expressing how he felt was important in itself, and simply talking about his problems always helped him understand himself better – but he felt like he'd never be able to make true progress in therapy because he'd always be slightly guarded and would never open up fully. Right now, for instance, he knew that she knew exactly why he felt attacked, but she was asking the rhetorical question to get him to express his anger more fully. He knew what she was doing because it was the same tactic he would take with his own patients.

Going along with it, just to express himself for the sake of expressing himself, he said, 'I just felt incredibly judged by everyone, like I was guilty till proven innocent. I felt uncomfortable just being here yesterday.'

'Do you feel uncomfortable today?'

'Yes, I do. To a slightly lesser extent, but I feel like I'm... I don't know... an outcast.'

Adam knew that probably sounded very whiney – like his own patients sometimes sounded – but he already felt better, just from verbalizing how he was feeling.

'Well, I'm sorry if I made you uncomfortable,' Carol said. 'That certainly wasn't my intention.'

She was backing off, giving him space to continue to vent. She also wanted to re-establish trust in the therapist-patient relationship, to make him feel safe and relaxed.

'As you can imagine, this hasn't been an easy situation for me to be in,' he said.

'I'll bet,' she said. 'It's probably bringing up a lot of issues for you.'

He was surprised she was taking the session in this direction so quickly. 'What kind of issues?' he asked.

'Issues of control or lack of control,' she said. 'Issues with your family – your current family and your parents. You grew up in the same house you live in now, didn't you?'

'You're right.' He hadn't thought much about this connection to his past that now seemed so obvious. 'It is bringing up issues with my parents. It's a very familiar feeling of being blamed, of being judged.'

'And it's making you feel like the victim again,' she added.

He'd told her in previous sessions that he was often picked on as a kid and was unpopular in elementary school and junior high, and they'd talked about how these experiences had scarred him. He remembered that just this morning, with Dana, he'd brought up running away from the bullies in school. There had to be some significance to this.

He told her all about the night of the shooting, mentioning that he had been having the recurring dream about the giant black rat who'd transformed from a female patient when Marissa woke him up. He was able to describe all the events in a very clear, matter-of-fact way, and it felt good to talk about it in a safe setting, where he didn't feel threatened. It was much different than when he talked to the press and the police, when he felt like he had to choose his words carefully because everything was being scrutinized.

He told her the police believed his maid, Gabriela, had been involved in the robbery, and he made sure that he expressed his anger about this properly. He didn't just tell her he was angry in a detached way. He made sure that he *felt* the anger, that he was *experiencing* the anger.

'I can't believe she was able to deceive all of us for so long,' he said. 'I'm usually so perceptive, nothing gets past me. I feel so furious. I feel so wronged.'

This was good – he was expressing himself well, using 'I' statements.

'You didn't know,' Carol said.

'But I feel so hurt by what she did to me,' Adam said. 'If I'd just caught on sooner, I could've fired her and prevented all of this. They say she was a drug addict, and I don't know how she was able to keep that a secret. I can always tell when somebody's lying to me. It's my best skill.'

'Addicts can be very clever,' she said. He'd said the same thing many times to his own patients.

He went on, describing what had happened after the shooting

– how he'd expected to be treated like a hero and was shocked when he saw the way he was being portrayed by the media.

'I know how ridiculous this sounds now,' he said, 'but I thought I'd be famous because of this, famous in a good way. I mean, you can't believe how caught up I got. I thought I'd be the next Dr Phil. I thought they'd film a movie about my life.'

'It was an exciting feeling,' she said. 'It made you feel confident.'

'Yes,' he said, 'and my glossophobia subsided, which was a very exciting, seductive feeling, too. Also, I have to admit, I enjoyed the attention. I know that's childish, that as an adult I should want respect, not attention, but it felt very seductive – and addictive, which is strange for me because I don't have an addictive personality.'

'It's easy to feel seduced by your emotions when your self-esteem is low, when you're unhappy in other aspects of your life. You experienced a psychological high, it was a very powerful feeling. Do you think you don't get enough respect in your life?'

He knew what she was trying to do. She was challenging him, trying to draw out a defensive response, but he went with it, saying, 'Yeah, sometimes. As you know, this can be a thankless profession.'

'Well, your colleagues respect you.'

'I haven't been so sure about that.'

'You can't expect people not to feel a little awkward,' Carol said. 'It was an unusual situation, and I think everyone handles these sorts of things in their own way.'

He could see her point.

'What about at home?' she asked. 'Has your marriage been good lately? Do you feel respected and appreciated?'

He thought about his bickering with Dana and his problems with Marissa. 'No, I don't,' he said, 'and I know I probably haven't been doing a lot to change that. What happened the other night certainly didn't help.'

'You said you don't feel like you did anything wrong that night.'

'I don't. Well, except for shooting him so many times. I think that was a mistake.'

'Every decision you make can't be the perfect one, Adam. You can only try to do your best.'

'I know, you're right,' he said, 'but… there's something else.' He sipped some water, collecting his thoughts, then said, 'There's something… I didn't tell anyone yet. I didn't tell the police. I didn't even tell Dana.'

As a seasoned therapist who'd heard it all, nothing usually shocked Carol, but Adam noticed her growing concern. 'Something about the shooting?' she asked.

'Yes,' Adam said.

She was waiting intently for him to continue.

'I didn't lie to the police about anything,' Adam said. 'Everything I told them was entirely truthful, exactly as I remembered it. But I… well, I omitted something.'

He paused again, wondering if he was doing the right thing, starting to tell Carol about this. He wasn't concerned about her talking to the police – she wouldn't, *couldn't* violate their confidentiality – but he was afraid it could affect their professional relationship. Well, it was too late now, and if you couldn't tell your therapist about these sorts of things, who could you tell?

'Before I shot the guy, Sanchez, he said something,' Adam said. 'It all happened so fast, it was hard to process it at that moment, but I remembered it afterward. He said… I *think* he said, "Please don't." That's all I heard, those two words. I still know I did the right thing, because even if he was saying *Please don't kill me* or *Please don't shoot me* or whatever, there was no way in that situation I should've believed him. I mean, I did see him reach for something. It might've been his flashlight, but it looked like a gun, and he could've shot me. He could've shot my whole family.'

'So what exactly do you feel guilty about?'

'I don't know if guilt is the right word,' he said. 'I feel… regret. I feel like I made a mistake.'

'You've made mistakes before, haven't you?'

'None that involved killing somebody.'

'It happens every day, Adam. You think policemen and firemen don't regret their decisions from time to time? You have to do the right thing and be forthcoming with the police, but you can't blame yourself, and you can't let it interfere with other aspects of your life. Besides, you said you thought he had a gun, right?'

'Right,' Adam said.

'So yes, you heard him say those two words, but it happened very quickly, and you don't know for sure what he was trying to say or why he was saying it. It sounds to me like you're making a lot of assumptions.'

He was aware that she was just supporting him, that she didn't actually believe any of this. Still, the process was helping.

'I feel shame about what I did,' he said. 'I feel anger. I feel... foolish.'

'Everyone has regrets,' she said. 'You don't have to beat yourself up about it. You had a lot of unexpressed anger, and then an event happened, something beyond your control. Someone broke into your house and you had to make a fast decision, but it was the best decision you could've made at the time, under the circumstances.'

'I really need to reparent myself, don't I?' Adam asked.

The need for reparenting had been a major issue in previous sessions. Carol knew all about his emotionally withholding parents and his related propensity toward self-loathing and self-blaming.

'I think it could be useful to use some of your reparenting techniques,' she said. 'Just don't be so hard on yourself. So maybe you made a mistake, or maybe you didn't make a mistake. Remember, Adam – you're allowed to make mistakes once in a while. Every decision you make doesn't have to be perfect.'

Her advice was fairly generic and, almost verbatim, what he would have said to one of his own patients. Still, it had resonance for Adam and really seemed to hit home. He thought, *Every decision you make doesn't have to be perfect, every decision you make doesn't have to be perfect*, and he experienced a relaxed yet intense buzz, an emotional high he sometimes had after a particularly productive therapy session.

He had two more patients in the afternoon – he was supposed

to have three more but had another no-show – and he felt much more effective than he had earlier in the day, much more like his usual self. Whenever any self-doubt crept in he'd think, *Every decision you make doesn't have to be perfect,* and he'd feel instantly reassured.

But Adam knew that this was only a temporary ego boost, that he still had major issues to deal with if he wanted to keep his self-esteem high. He had to be easier on himself, not criticize himself as much, and – this was key – *he had to stop neglecting himself.* He was such a people-pleaser, so focused on patients and helping others, that he hadn't been paying nearly enough attention to his own needs. He had to start taking the advice he gave to his patients every day and apply it to his own life, and this started with his most important personal relationship – his marriage. He hadn't been expressing himself well to Dana at all lately, and he'd let too much anger and resentment go unresolved.

At the end of the day, when the other therapists had left, he went into his office and closed the door and turned on classical music – Bach's Brandenburg Concertos – very loud. Then he kneeled in front of the couch and started punching the couch cushion as hard as he could. Physical activity was a great way to vent and relieve stress, and he always suggested that his patients express anger in a safe way, like screaming or punching pillows. Imagining that the cushion was people who had done him wrong, like Gabriela, the reporters from the *Post* and *News*, and Grace Williams from *New York magazine*, gave his punches some extra oomph.

After about five minutes of good cushion pounding, he felt much more relaxed and ready to do some actual problem solving. One area of his marriage that certainly needed improving was his and Dana's sex life. They didn't do it nearly enough, and if he were his own therapist, he would tell his patient to schedule time for sex, make it a priority, and be more creative sexually. So before Adam left the office he called Dana and told her he wanted to make love tonight at ten o'clock.

'Why?' she asked.

Adam wasn't sure whether she meant why did he want to

have sex with her or why at ten o'clock as opposed to eleven or midnight. Deciding to take a less confrontational approach, he said, 'Because I love you very much and I miss being close with you.'

Okay, so maybe he was overdoing it a little, but he felt like he was communicating honestly, not apologizing for his emotions.

Later, on his way to the subway, Adam stopped off at a Ricky's drugstore where he remembered seeing an adult section and bought a sexy cheerleader's outfit in Dana's size. Several times she had told him about a fantasy she had of making love while dressed as a cheerleader, but they'd never explored it because he'd never had a cheerleader fantasy himself. That had been selfish of him, to flat-out reject her fantasy. He certainly wasn't opposed to her dressing as a cheerleader if it was a turn-on for her, and it was wrong of him to have stonewalled her like that.

At home, he noticed that Dana seemed to be in a much better mood than she'd been in this morning and the past couple of days. She was starting to believe that Gabriela had been the second intruder in their house the other night and that the threatening note had been left by some prankster. She was also encouraged by a new theory the police had, that Gabriela may have been killed by a drug dealer she was in debt to and who possibly had nothing to do with Carlos Sanchez.

'I thought she needed the money for her father,' Adam said.

'She did,' Dana said, 'but her sister doesn't think she would've robbed a house to pay for her father's operation, and I don't believe it either. I know she lied to us about a lot of things, but I can't imagine her actually coming into our house to rob us unless she was hooked on drugs and needed to pay off a drug dealer.'

This logic made sense to Adam, and he hoped it was a sign that things were on their way to returning to normal.

Dana cooked a nice dinner – chicken cutlets, rice pilaf, a salad – and they ate at the dining room table, finishing the merlot from last night. Marissa was out with her friends in Manhattan, seeing some band, so they had the whole house to themselves. Adam actually couldn't remember the last time he and Dana had a quiet, romantic dinner alone, and he made sure to ask her a lot of questions about her day and things that were going on with her in general, knowing that in the past she'd had the complaint that he didn't take enough interest in her.

At one point Dana asked, 'Why are you acting so nice?'

Her tone was vaguely accusing, but he answered honestly, 'I know I haven't been the greatest husband in the world lately. I want things to improve around here, that's all. I'd like it if we made the marriage more of a priority.'

He was purposely trying to use I-statements so she couldn't interpret anything he was saying as criticism. Her eyes started to tear, but he knew it was because she was so happy, realizing how much he meant to her. He reached across the table, held her hand gently, and said, 'Remember our date tonight.'

'I don't know,' she said. 'I'm a little tired.'

If she'd said this last week, he might've backed down, but instead he did what he would've instructed a patient to do in a similar situation – *don't be passive, be assertive; ask for what you want and you'll get it* – and he said, 'I like it when we make love and we're both tired. I think it's sexy.'

That was perfect – rather than accusing her of not wanting to have sex, he'd expressed himself in a positive way without getting confrontational.

'Okay,' she said, 'but I have to do the dishes first and clean up.'

'I'll help,' he said eagerly.

He hardly ever helped her clean up after dinner – another common complaint of hers – and he could tell how much she appreciated him making the extra effort.

Later, he entered their bedroom, holding the bag with the cheerleader's outfit behind his back. She was lying in bed in her bathrobe, reading some hardcover novel.

'I got something for you,' he said.

'What?' She seemed more worried than intrigued.

'You have to close your eyes,' he said.

She smiled as if she thought he was joking and went back to reading.

'I'm serious,' he said.

She looked at him again and asked, 'What is it?'

'You have to close your eyes,' he said.

She breathed deeply, as if it would take an enormous effort, then finally shut her eyes.

'No peeking,' he said as he took the blue and gold outfit out of the bag. Then he said, 'Okay, open up.'

Her reaction wasn't exactly what he'd expected. She seemed, if not shocked, then slightly offended.

'What is that?' she asked.

'What does it look like?' he said, smiling, waiting for her to join in.

'You don't expect me to *wear* that, do you?'

'What's wrong? I remember you said you had a fantasy about this, right?'

'When did I tell you that? When I was twenty-five? Do you seriously think I'm going to put that thing on?'

She'd told him about her cheerleader fantasy a few years ago, okay, maybe five years ago tops, but he didn't want to get into an argument about it. At the same time, he didn't want to keep his resentful feelings to himself.

Trying to express himself in a nonthreatening way, he said, 'I thought you'd be excited. But if you don't feel comfortable about it I understand, though I thought you'd be... I don't know... turned on by it.'

'What is that thing, a size *two*? Even if I wanted to put it on, I'd have to use a shoehorn to get into it. Come on, what did you expect me to do, get up on the bed and do a cheer for you?'

Actually that was exactly what Adam had expected her to do, but he was starting to feel attacked, belittled, and he said, 'I feel like you're getting upset with me for no reason. I feel resentful toward you right now.'

'Can you please stop talking to me like that?'

'Like what?'

'Like you're one of your fucking patients. I'm not your therapist, I'm your wife.'

He knew this was just more of her stonewalling, her typical way of deflecting conflict.

Validating her rather than confronting her, he said, 'I understand if you don't want to wear it. I just want to work on ways for us to get closer in this marriage.'

'This is how you get closer?' she said. 'We haven't made love in I don't know how long and then you come home with some outfit an anorexic sixteen-year-old would wear, talking to me like you're lying on a couch?'

'I feel like you're not being fair,' he said. 'I feel like you're purposely distorting everything I –'

'Oh, stop with that crap,' she said. 'What if I came home, out of the blue, with some slinky Speedo and made you put it on?'

She was acting defensive again, but he remained calm and objective and said, 'First of all, I'm not making you do anything. Second of all, if I'd told you I had a fantasy about wearing a Speedo, no, I wouldn't be upset at all.'

'Fine,' she said, 'I'll get you a Speedo tomorrow and you can wear it. I'll make sure it's four sizes too small, too.'

'Why do you always have to –' He caught himself using the word 'always,' which was disrespectful. He took a couple of deep breaths to subdue his anger, not wanting to get sucked into an argument, then said, 'If it's something you feel uncomfortable with, I understand. I can return it, it's no big deal.'

He put the cheerleader's outfit back into the bag and got into bed with her. He started kissing her neck and under her chin. She was stiff, not reacting at all.

Finally she said, 'Well, you really did a good job of setting the mood, didn't you?'

'I'm sorry,' he said. He always told his patients to compliment their lovers, so he said, 'You look so beautiful tonight.'

'You're just saying that,' she said.

'No, honestly,' he said. 'I know I haven't been telling you that nearly enough lately, but it's true, you look very beautiful.'

He started kissing her again, undoing her robe. During sex, he continued to kiss her and looked in her eyes as much as possible because in a marriage counseling session she'd said that it bothered her that he didn't look into her eyes when they made love and that made her feel distant. Maybe he was overdoing it because she seemed uncomfortable and kept looking away.

'Is something wrong?' he asked assertively.

'You keep staring at me,' she said.

'Sorry,' he said. 'It's just you're so beautiful, I can't stop looking at you.' Finally, after they switched from the missionary to the woman-on-top positions several times, Dana seemed to have an orgasm. He was starting to lose his erection, which had been happening a lot the last few years, so he did what sometimes worked – he blurred his vision and imagined Dana was Sharon.

'Is everything okay?' Dana asked.

Adam didn't know if she meant okay with his erection or if she'd noticed the weird look in his eyes.

'Fine,' he said and went back to imagining Sharon's full, heavy breasts, the scent of her perfume. At one point he almost blurted out Sharon's name, but he managed to restrain himself.

Adam lay in bed next to Dana, not touching her. She was sleeping soundly, snoring, but he was restless. Finally he went downstairs to get a snack and watch some TV.

It was past midnight, and Marissa wasn't home yet. Now that Adam was on his way to fixing his marriage, he wanted to make it two for two and improve his relationship with his daughter. He was tired of Marissa and all of her acting out and attention-seeking behavior; it was time for some serious tough love. From now on, for as long as she was living in his house, he wasn't going to let her come and go as she pleased. She was going to have to tell him where she was and who she was with and when she was coming home. He wasn't going to allow any more drugs in the house – that bong was going in the garbage pronto, that was for sure – and he wasn't going to let her parade strange boyfriends through the house anymore either. He was going to meet all her boyfriends first, and if she didn't like it she could pack her things and move out.

He started falling asleep on the couch, so he went back upstairs. As soon as he lay down he heard voices from outside, Marissa and somebody else, a guy. He went to the window and looked out. From his angle, he couldn't see them; they were probably right below him, near the front door. He couldn't make out what they were saying either, and then for a little while he couldn't hear them at all. The police car was still there, parked out in front, hopefully for the last night. Police protection seemed so unnecessary now.

Adam heard Marissa call out, 'Good night,' and then he saw a guy he'd never seen before – longish hair, a leather jacket – heading away from the house toward the sidewalk. The guy didn't exactly look like a doctor or a lawyer. God, where did she find these losers?

Adam heard Marissa's footsteps on the stairs. He waited until he heard the door to her room close; then he went down to make sure she'd set the alarm properly.

15

JOHNNY DIDN'T WASTE any time hooking up with Marissa. First thing Saturday morning he texted her:

> hey had great time last night wanna hang today?
> hope so! lemme know! xan

Xan. Just typing that stupid name cracked him up.

He knew there was zero chance she wouldn't get back to him. He didn't peg her as the game-playing type who would play hard to get. No, she was definitely an all-or-nothing girl, the type who decided she was into one guy and one guy only and blew off the rest of the world.

As usual, his instincts were dead-on because she texted back:

> I'd love to! Call me in a few!!

With exclamation points no less. Talk about being primed.

They spoke on the phone for about a half-hour. They could've gone longer – hell, all day – but Johnny knew how important it was to always leave phone conversations on a high point, to leave them wanting more. Nobody was better on the phone than Johnny Long. He knew exactly what to say to girls to get them – well, there was really no other way to put it – totally wet. He was so charming, so funny, so – what was the word? – personable, yeah, personable, and girls ate that shit right up. He knew he could pick a name out of the phone book, call the girl up, and there was a pretty good chance he'd be able to screw her. He'd actually done this one time just for fun, to see if he could pull it off. He called a couple of dozen women, pretending he was a cable guy from Time Warner. Well, that was the opening, but when the women starting talking, he turned on the Johnny Long charm. Yeah, a bunch of them hung up on him, and some were going to let him come over to check out their cable, but he wasn't convinced he'd score with them. But it was all about percentages and he finally hit pay dirt with a woman on Staten Island. She was in her sixties and had gone back for seconds on the ugly line, but what difference did that make? She invited him over to her house, where he checked out her cable – actually fixing a problem receiving premium channels – and then screwed her twice and got away with a few hundred bucks in cash and jewelry. It proved that Johnny Long wasn't just eye candy. He could use his voice and charm to seduce women, too.

Johnny invited Marissa to spend the afternoon with him at the Metropolitan Museum of Art, and naturally she thought it was an amazing idea. She'd actually said, 'Wow, that's an amazing idea.'

He met her at two o'clock on the top of the steps at the main entrance, and when he saw her approach he was impressed with how good-looking she was. In the bright sunlight her hair looked shinier than it had last night, and there was no doubt that she had a hot little body. She was in pre-ripped jeans, some trendy-looking black lacy top, and a short black leather jacket.

To sound like he knew his shit, before he'd met her he'd gone to Burger King and logged on to the Metropolitan Museum of Art's website and memorized info about twenty or so paintings. So when they went inside and she asked, 'So what do you want to see first?' he said, 'How about *The Storm*? That's one of my all-time favorites.'

'Oh my God, I love nineteenth-century French romanticism,' she said, obviously trying to impress him.

He'd only picked *The Storm* because it looked so sappy, so girly, with the guy and the girl running in the wind, their clothes coming off, and him trying to protect her. It looked like something that would be on one of those faggy books with Fabio on the cover, and he figured every girl in the world was looking for a guy like that, a guy who would save his girlfriend, do anything to keep her safe, even if she was kind of fat and not very hot.

As they looked at the painting, he told her some of the crap he'd read online about it, going on about the romance and passion in the painting and how he tried to get 'that feeling' into his own work. She said, all serious, '*The Storm* always reminds me of Rodin's sculptures, such as *Eternal Spring*.' He knew she was just repeating some uppity crap some uppity teacher at Vassar had told her or she'd read in some book. Johnny wondered how much Adam Bloom had spent to send Marissa to college – probably a hundred grand. A hundred grand and she didn't know any more than Johnny did after spending one morning in Burger King.

They went into one of the little rooms off to the side – 'the Impressionist wing' – and she showed him some of her favorite pictures, acting like she was a tour guide, going on and on about them, using big college-type words like 'symmetry,' 'aesthetics,' and 'illusionistic.' Johnny didn't understand half the shit she was saying, and he wondered if she did either. She took him to other 'wings' of the museum, walking him around until his feet hurt. All the pictures looked the same to Johnny, and the artists sounded the same, too – Monet, Manet, Pissarro, Picasso, how did anybody keep track of who painted what? While she was blabbing away, trying to impress him with how much she knew about paintings nobody except other uppity people gave a shit about, Johnny was looking at her with an interested expression, like he was totally gripped, but inside he was laughing his ass off, thinking about the things he was going to do to her and her family when the time was right.

After the museum, he was expecting her to invite him back to her place. Taking her up to see that *Storm* painting, showing his deep, sensitive side, had pretty much sealed the deal. Walking down Fifth Avenue, alongside Central Park, she even hooked her arm around his and said, 'It's amazing. I feel so normal around you, I feel like I can be myself.'

'Yeah, me, too,' he said, trying to look sincere.

She invited him out to some party later on, but he said he couldn't make it, that he had plans. His only actual plan for the night was to hit some bars and pick up a woman or two, but he'd already spent a couple of hours with Marissa today and didn't want to spend too much time together too fast. If he wanted this to turn out right, it had to be a slow build.

They stopped at a Starbucks for Frappuccinos; then he walked her all the way downtown to the subway at Fifty-ninth Street. He offered to ride with her back to Forest Hills, but she said it was okay, she could go alone, and he decided not to push it. He made out with her for a long time near the subway entrance, and when she was all worked up he said goodbye, leaving her wanting more.

He didn't suggest seeing her again on Sunday, figuring three days in a row might've made him seem too available, and a girl always wanted a guy to be a challenge even if she was dying to tear off his clothes. But they got together again on Monday, going to see a movie. He was hoping she'd ask him to pick her up at her place, so he'd have a chance to meet her father, but for some reason she insisted on meeting in front of the movie theater on Forty-second and Eighth. They saw a horror movie – her idea – which was perfect as far as he was concerned because they spent the whole time snuggled in the back, making out like teenagers, pawing at each other like they hadn't gotten any in years. Yeah, right.

At one point she whispered in his ear, 'God, I want to fuck you so bad.'

He was surprised – she was a raunchy little thing; he didn't expect that.

He knew he had to handle this right, and he whispered back, 'I want to take it slow.'

He saw her again on Tuesday, for lunch at Dojo in the Village. Yeah, it was a cheap place to take a date, but that was the whole point. He had to play up this starving-artist thing because he knew that was what turned her on. If he was trying to scam a Paris Hilton type, he would've been wearing Armani and it would've been Le Cirque all the way. But with a wannabe bohemian chick like Marissa, talking about how he couldn't pay his rent next month and how he'd been living on ramen noodles and macaroni and cheese was the way to go.

On Wednesday night something happened that nearly ruined everything. Johnny met Marissa in the East Village, and after a couple of drinks at a bar on Avenue A, they went to the Knitting Factory, where the Limons, some new retro Latin punk band she was into – she'd called them 'the Ramones meet Ricky Martin' – were playing. They'd been in the place for only a few minutes when Johnny felt a tap on his shoulder and heard, 'Frederick, is that you?'

Johnny looked over his shoulder and saw a woman – not so bad-looking, late twenties, maybe thirties, with straight brown hair and bangs. She didn't look at all familiar, but he'd used the name Frederick with various pickups.

'Sorry,' he said, 'you got the wrong guy.'

He turned back toward Marissa, rolling his eyes slightly, but he had a feeling the woman wouldn't let it go.

She didn't, saying, 'Like hell you don't, you son of a bitch. Where's my fuckin' money?'

He looked at her again and said, 'Look, I have no idea what you're talking about.' Actually, she was starting to look familiar, but he couldn't place her face yet.

As he started to turn away again, she grabbed his arm and said, 'You took two hundred fucking dollars from my pocketbook and, oh, yeah, some jewelry, too, but it wasn't worth shit.'

Now he remembered. A couple of months ago he'd picked her up at a bar, Max Fish on Ludlow, not far from where they were now, and he'd stolen some cash and some jewelry that had turned out to be gold plated; waste of his goddamn time. He usually didn't like to return to neighborhoods where he'd scored for at least six months for this very reason.

'I'm telling you, you have the wrong guy,' he said, shaking his arm loose. He noticed that Marissa was starting to look a little worried, but he couldn't tell if it was because he was being hassled or because she was starting to believe the woman's story.

'Give me my money back or I'm calling the fuckin' cops,' the woman said, flipping her cell phone open.

'You're out of your mind,' Johnny said. Then he took Marissa by the hand and said, 'Come on,' and led her toward the other end of the bar.

The woman followed them, shouting, 'I want my money back, Frederick!' A bouncer came over and asked what was going on. Johnny calmly explained that he had no idea who the woman was. The woman continued to go on about how Frederick had stolen money from her, sounding more and more crazed and hysterical. At one point she shoved the bouncer, and he grabbed her and pulled her out of the bar. Then the bouncer apologized to Johnny and Marissa for the 'inconvenience' and bought them a round on the house. Johnny, turning on his charm, bonded with the bouncer – they were both from Queens, around the same age – and after a few minutes they were like old buddies.

Johnny and Marissa bonded, too, talking about how 'weird' it was that the woman had mistaken him for that other guy and flipped out like that. It turned into a big joke, and Johnny knew that Marissa couldn't wait to tell her friends about it; he figured she'd probably blog about it, too. This was yet another example of how golden Johnny was, how he could do no wrong. Something that could've been a disaster and ruined his plans had turned into something that had scored more points with Marissa, bringing them even closer together.

Johnny was hoping that Marissa would invite him home with her tonight, but again she wanted to take the subway home alone. He insisted on going with her because it was past midnight and 'you never know what kind of maniacs are on the subways at this time of night.' She agreed, but when he was walking her back to her house, she was acting uncomfortable, not talking very much, and when they got to her house she barely kissed him goodbye and rushed inside. He had no idea what the hell was going on. He knew she was into him – that was obvious – so there had to be some reason she wasn't inviting him in. It wasn't like she'd never taken a guy home with her before. She'd talked about a couple of guys she'd had over to her house since graduating from college, including that skinny little dork Darren. Johnny wanted to ask her if something was wrong, but he figured it was better if she brought it up herself. He didn't want to push too hard and blow all of his plans.

The next day, Thursday, Johnny called Marissa in the morning and asked her if she wanted to meet him for lunch in Brooklyn. She said she'd love to – not exactly a surprise – and he met her outside the Smith–Ninth Street subway station and rode the bus with her to Red Hook, where they went to some trendy coffee bar where Johnny had seen a lot of artsy types go. They talked for a while, holding hands the whole time, and then he took her back to his place.

He'd been working hard to try to make his studio apartment look like a place where an artist would live. He'd picked up some more paintings from thrift shops and, a couple of days ago, had bought four paintings of bowls of fruit from some guy on Craigslist who lived about ten blocks away. He'd done a few more of his own paintings, too, in the Jackson Pollock style, and he thought they were at least as good as that shit in the Met.

On the way over to his place he gave her some BS about how 'nervous' he was about her seeing 'his work.' She told him how silly he was acting and said she was sure his paintings were amazing.

In the apartment, he watched her reaction closely as she looked around. He could tell she was seriously impressed.

'Wow,' she said. 'You really have a lot of range, don't you?'

'Thanks,' he said.

'You use oils and acrylics, huh?'

He had no idea what he was talking about, but he said, 'Yeah, I like to do a lot of everything. I mean, I don't like to limit myself. I want to blow the whole thing wide open.'

Wasn't that the line in *Pollock*? Eh, something like that.

Admiring the paintings he'd bought on Craigslist, Marissa said, 'Do you do your portraits from real life or photographs?'

'Real life,' he said.

'Wow,' she said. 'Impressive.'

She turned toward the wall where he'd hung up a couple of his own paintings and said, 'So you're into modern and abstract, too, huh?'

'Yeah,' he said. 'You see the Pollock influence, right?'

Influence. He was on a roll, all right.

'They're *very* Pollockesque,' she said. 'You and Pollock have a very similar controlled freedom in your styles. I love the use of gray – very Jasper Johns. I also see the homage to Picasso in your use of blue.'

'Yeah, that's exactly what I was going for,' he said. 'Johns and Picasso. Yeah, I'm so glad you noticed that.'

She continued to admire the paintings while he was thinking about how this whole art gig was so perfect for him. It was all about bullshitting, and nobody could bullshit better than Johnny Long.

When the love fest for his artwork ended, he cracked open a couple of Heinekens and sat with her on the couch.

A few minutes later, she was snuggled close, wrapping her leg over his legs, saying, 'I'd love to watch you work sometime.'

'That would be great,' he said, 'but nobody's ever watched me before. I might get nervous, you know?'

'You don't have to get nervous around me,' she said, and she put her beer on the coffee table. She kissed him, rubbing his chest with one hand, then said,

'Maybe I can… help you.'

'What kind of help do you have in mind?' he asked, playing along.

'Maybe some of this,' she said, kissing his lips. 'Or this.' She kissed his neck. After a while, she moved one hand over his crotch, then unsnapped his jeans and started to reach inside.

Naturally he was ready for her, but he shifted back a little and said, 'I think we should wait.'

'Wait for what?' she gasped, wanting him so badly.

'Until we get to know each other better.' It was so hard to

deliver these lines with a straight face. 'I mean, we've only known each other for less than a week.'

'So you've never slept with somebody you've known less than a week?' *Only about four hundred and fifty before you, baby.*

'But this feels… different,' he said. 'It feels… special.'

She smiled, blushing. 'You really mean that?'

'Yeah,' he said. 'Why? Doesn't it feel special to you?'

'It feels very special to me,' she said. 'I'm just not used to hearing guys say things like that to me. I'm used to guys trying to get into my pants.'

'I'm not most guys,' he said.

'You're *definitely* not most guys,' she said.

They kissed for a while longer. He was glad, because if he'd had to talk right then, not laughing would've been impossible.

When he was sure he'd composed himself he said, 'I guess I also feel a little uncomfortable.'

'Uncomfortable about what?' she asked.

'Well, you're living at home with your parents. I feel like I should meet them first before we… you know.'

That was the way – make out like he was too shy to say 'have sex.' That was him all right, Shy Johnny.

Marissa moved her leg off of him and shifted away a little and suddenly seemed upset. Johnny hoped he hadn't taken this playing-hard-to-get routine too far.

'What's wrong?' he asked.

'Nothing,' she said. 'It's not you, it's just… I'm not sure that's a good idea.'

Johnny held her hand, squeezing it tightly to show how much he cared, then said, 'I'm gonna have to meet them eventually, right? If my parents didn't live so far away I would've already brought you to meet them.' The other night he'd told her his parents lived in San Diego.

'It's just really complicated,' she said. 'God, I wish I wasn't living at home. It's just so hard, especially with my father and his mood swings.'

'Mood swings?'

'Not "mood swings," mood swings. I mean, he's not manic-depressive. But one day he's aloof, in his own world, and the next day he wants to be this involved father. Suddenly he has all these rules – I can't drink in the house, even a glass of wine, and he made me throw out my pot even though I barely smoked at home. Then I came home the other day from the museum and my freaking bong was gone – it was handmade, from Guatemala, and he threw it in the garbage. Oh, and I have to let him know when I'm coming home at night, the exact time, like I'm a teenager again. He knows I'm dating you, so the other night he made this big stink about how I can't bring you up to my room and you can't stay over or anything until he meets you.'

'So let me meet him,' Johnny said. 'What's the problem?'

She had that concerned look again. 'There's something I haven't told you,' she said.

He thought, *Uh-oh, VD.* Not that this really bothered him. He'd had crabs before, and he'd knocked out a case of gonorrhea last year. VD was part of the job when you wanted to be the next Casanova.

'I mean, you probably heard about it on the news,' she continued, 'but maybe you didn't make the connection.' She waited, as if trying to find the right words, then said, 'Our house was robbed last week.'

'It was?' Johnny thought he sounded convincingly surprised.

'Yeah, it happened when we were all asleep in the middle of the night,' she said. 'I heard the burglars in the house and woke up my parents, and then my father went and shot one of them.'

One of them, like he and Carlos had been what, two cockroaches? Isn't that what people said when they were trying to squash bugs: *I got one of them, but the other one got away?*

'Oh, that's right, yeah, yeah,' Johnny said, like it was all coming to him now. 'I think I read something about that in the paper. Yeah, the shooting in Forest Hills by that shrink. Wow, that was really your father?'

'I've been afraid to tell you,' Marissa said, suddenly talking faster, full of nervous energy. 'I've been afraid that you'd, I don't know, judge me. Maybe I was just being crazy – I do that sometimes, get all neurotic and paranoid, overthink everything

– but that's what I thought. It's not true, right? You won't hold it against me, will you?'

'Relax, baby,' Johnny said, squeezing her hand, letting her know that he'd always be there for her. 'You know I'd never do that to you.'

He held her and kissed her for a while; then she said, 'I'm still so pissed off at my father for doing what he did. It was so stupid, so totally thoughtless, and the thing is I don't even think he feels guilty about it.'

'Really?' Johnny asked.

'Yeah, he's been in this weird denial phase or something,' she said. 'I mean, even the morning after, he was just going about his life, acting like nothing happened. You would think a psychologist would be more in touch with his feelings, but with him it's the total opposite. I don't think he has any idea how he's feeling, ever.'

Johnny remembered being in the car outside Bloom's house, with the gun in his hand, seeing Bloom strutting down the block in his sweat suit, like he didn't have a worry in the world.

Well, you have something to worry about now, asshole.

'So you think what they were saying in the news was true?' Johnny asked. 'Your father wanted to kill the guy?'

'Between me and you,' Marissa said, 'yes, I do. I think my dad just lost it, in that moment and wanted to shoot him. I don't think he's a crazy person – I mean, he's not *psychotic* – but he holds stuff in, he's wound up, you know? It was also the middle of the night, he was tired, so, yeah, maybe he wasn't thinking rationally. He was angry that someone was in his house and he just went too far. He gets that way sometimes, does things without thinking.'

Johnny couldn't wait to kill Adam Bloom, watch him die in pain.

'That's rough,' he said. 'I'm sorry you had to go through all of that.'

'Yeah, I know, it was pretty scary and traumatic,' Marissa said. 'But the most terrifying thing was there was somebody else in the house that night.'

'There was?' Johnny was acting shocked.

'Yeah, the cops think it was our maid. Did you hear about what happened to her?'

'No, I don't think I... wait, wait, I did hear something. She was hurt, too, wasn't she?'

'She was *killed,* in her apartment.'

'Oh, man, that sucks,' Johnny said. He hoped Marissa didn't start crying, get all gushy and girly about it.

'Yeah, it was incredibly sad,' she said, 'but I don't know, that just doesn't make sense to me that our maid actually robbed our house. We were really, not like best friends, but really friendly, you know? Oh, and we got this note under our door, a kind of death threat.'

'Really? Who left it?'

'That's the thing, nobody knows. My dad's convinced it was a prank, but he's constantly making up stories, trying to rationalize everything. He's so screwed up, if you met him you'd never guess he was a psychologist. But maybe that's the way it works – maybe if you want to cure people's craziness, you have to be a little crazy yourself.'

Johnny put his arm around Marissa and said, 'It sounds like your family's going through a lot right now. If you don't want to bring me home to meet them, I understand, but I guess I should meet them eventually... I mean, if we're gonna be a couple.'

Her face brightened, and she said, 'You really mean that?'

'Of course,' he said. 'You think I'd want to go out every day and every night with every girl I meet?'

Finally he'd said something that wasn't a total lie.

She said, 'You're the most amazing guy I've ever met.'

He couldn't argue with that.

The next morning, Marissa texted Johnny:

my parents want u to come 4 dinner tonite can you make it at 7??

Johnny waited about fifteen minutes, not wanting to seem over eager, then replied:

Id be honored

215

This was it – the big night. He wanted to clean up his look a little, but not too much, so he trimmed his sideburns, but he left his hair long and wild and greasy. He chose his outfit carefully – black jeans, a black turtleneck, Doc Martens. He loved the idea of going in all black. He looked perfect for the occasion – like an artist but also like an assassin.

He arrived at the house – what did rich people say? – fashionably late, at ten after seven. As he expected, there was no sign of any cops. The robbery had been over a week ago, and it probably wasn't even a hot case anymore. He checked to make sure his .38 Special and his four-inch retractable switchblade were safely inside the inner pocket of his leather jacket, and then he rang the bell.

Several seconds later the door opened, and Marissa was there in a red dress, with a big scoop neck giving a nice view of her cleavage, and black leggings and black boots with heels that made her at least two inches taller. She was wearing more makeup than usual, including a bright red lipstick that she must've picked to match her dress.

She kissed him hello, lightly on the lips, and said, 'It's so good to see you,' and he said, 'Yeah, you too.'

'Can I take your coat?' she asked.

'Sure,' he said, and he took it off, watching her put it away in the hallway closet.

'Come on, I'll give you the tour,' she said.

She led him straight ahead, saying, 'Back here's the kitchen...,' but Johnny was looking over at the staircase, at the spot where Bloom had killed Carlos. It looked normal, like nothing had happened there. There was no damage on the stairs, no bloodstains or bullet holes in the wall. This was what rich people did, Johnny figured – they killed people in their houses and then did a little wall repair, a little paint job, and went on with their rich, happy lives. Yeah, they didn't care about *scum* like Johnny and Carlos. They thought they were so high and above everybody else, but now look who was in charge. They thought they'd gotten rid of their problem, they were safe, protected, but now Johnny was back in the house – even better, he'd been *invited* back to the house. Who else but Johnny Long could've pulled off a stunt like this? He'd already thought he was the greatest Casanova on the planet and the modern-day Jackson Pollock, but now he felt like there was nothing he couldn't do.

Johnny followed Marissa into the kitchen, then into the dining room. She made some joke about how he should 'try to ignore' her parents' decorating. Meanwhile, the house looked like a palace compared to the shitholes where Johnny had lived. The kitchen had all stainless steel appliances, with one of those refrigerators with an ice dispenser on the door. Johnny had always dreamed of having one of those, being able to have a Coke with ice whenever he wanted. Like it could be the middle of the night, whenever, and he wanted ice, and it would be there. He wouldn't have to deal with pouring water in trays, having to bend the tray to get the cubes out, and all that bullshit. The ice would just *be* there all the time, waiting for him. Yeah, he would've killed to grow up in a place like this and have half of what Marissa had. Didn't she know how lucky she was?

Well, it didn't matter because she was going to be dead soon anyway. After dinner Johnny planned to go up to her room with her and fuck her and then kill her. Then he was going to kill her parents – maybe torture them with the switchblade a little first just for the hell of it – and then rob the house and go on with his life.

As she went on, saying in that bored tone, 'And this is the living room...,' Johnny was looking around for things to steal. Those vases looked like they had to be worth something, and he had to remember to find that silverware Carlos had mentioned, and of course the diamond ring. It was too bad Johnny could only take things he could carry. Jesus, check out the leather couch and matching love seat and armchair. Johnny felt like he was in one of those showrooms at Macy's or Bloomingdale's. Sometimes he'd go in there to hang out for a while, just to imagine how rich people lived. He'd sit in one of those two-thousand-dollar massage chairs, wondering what it would be like to come back every day and get a nice massage, then go into his Jacuzzi. He bet the Blooms had an amazing bathroom upstairs, all marble, with a Jacuzzi or at least a big, roomy bathtub.

When they got back to the foyer, Adam Bloom was coming down the stairs. He looked even more stuck-up and into himself than the last time Johnny had seen him. Check him out in those jeans and a sport jacket, the black button shirt underneath, loose, not tucked in, to try to hide his gut. Johnny had a flashback to the night of the robbery on that same staircase, Bloom screaming, *Get the fuck out of here!*

'Hello,' Adam said, smiling widely when he reached the bottom of the stairs. 'You must be Xan.'

He sounded all uppity, like he thought he was so much better than the rest of the world just because he lived in this big house in Forest Hills and had *Dr* in front of his name. Did he think those letters made him better than everybody else? Did he think they *protected* him?

Yeah, probably.

Johnny saw Marissa roll her eyes a little; then she said, 'Xan, this is my dad.'

'Adam Bloom.' He held out his hand for Johnny to shake.

Johnny squeezed Adam's hand firmly – feeling sick, but not showing it – then said, 'It's an honor to meet you, sir.'

Sir. Man, Johnny was *on* tonight.

'You too,' Adam said. 'You too.' Was he going to let go of his hand already? Finally he did and added, 'I've heard a lot of great things about you.'

Johnny knew this was total BS. Marissa definitely didn't seem like she had the type of relationship with her father where she went and told him everything that was happening in her life. She'd probably barely mentioned him to her father.

Remembering how Marissa had bad-mouthed Adam yesterday, basically calling him a cold-blooded killer, Johnny said, 'Yeah, and I've heard a lot of great things about you, too.'

Then Johnny looked up and saw this extremely hot older woman coming down the stairs. He knew this had to be Marissa's mother – she kind of looked like Marissa, same skinny body type – but he was surprised because he didn't expect her mom to be so goddamn sexy. She was in a black top with tight jeans, showing off her shape, and there was a lot to show off. She must've been in her late forties, but she had nice toned arms, great legs, high tits. Well, at least they looked high with all the pushing up that was going on. Johnny had always had a thing for older women, and he thought Mrs Bloom was much hotter than Marissa.

She continued downstairs, and Johnny watched her the whole way. Then Marissa said, 'Xan, this is my mom. Mom, Xan.'

He could tell that Mrs Bloom was into him in a big way. If he was in a bar, looking for a pickup, she would've been the first woman he'd zero in on. The attraction was there, yeah, but there was more to it than that. A lot of women were attracted to Johnny – hell, just about every woman on the planet had the hots for him – but when they *really* wanted him, he picked up on a vibe of desperation, of longing. He could always spot an unhappy woman, a woman who had something missing in her life and was waiting for some guy to come along to give it to her. Mrs Bloom definitely had that look.

'Wow, Marissa,' Johnny said, 'you didn't tell me your mother was gorgeous.' This was the perfect opening because it made Mrs Bloom blush bright pink, and Johnny could tell that Adam took this as a compliment, too.

'I like him already,' Mrs Bloom said, totally flattered.

'It's a real pleasure to meet you, Mrs Bloom.' Johnny held her hand gently. He noticed she was wearing a wedding band but no engagement ring. The ring was probably upstairs in her bedroom, like Carlos had said.

'It's nice to meet you,' she said, smiling, looking into his eyes. 'You can call me Dana.'

Oh, yeah, she was definitely into him, there was no doubt about it. Maybe he'd bang her later just for the hell of it – tie Adam up, make him watch.

'Come on,' Adam said to Johnny. 'I'll get you a drink.'

Johnny let Adam walk ahead of him toward the living room. Marissa looked annoyed, but Johnny smiled at her and her mother – his two women – then followed Adam.

Adam asked, 'So what can I get you? A vodka and orange juice? A glass of wine?'

'Oh, I'm not a big drinker,' Johnny said.

'Really?' He sounded impressed.

'Yeah,' Johnny said, 'but I guess, since this is a special occasion, a glass of wine would be okay.'

Adam poured two glasses of wine – some cheap merlot, still had the $6.99 sticker on the bottle – then raised his glass and said, '*Za vas.*'

They drank, and then Adam said, 'So I understand you're from Russia.'

'Well, not *from* Russia. My father's father was Russian.'

'Our family's originally from Russia,' Adam said. 'Well, Belarus actually – Minsk.'

'Moscow,' Johnny said, smiling.

'Terrific, that's terrific,' Adam said. 'And the rest of your family?'

'French and German on my mother's side, Italian and Irish on my father's side. I even have a little American Indian on my dad's side.' Johnny hadn't prepared any of this; he was just winging it.

'Wow, so you have a real multicultural family,' Adam said. 'You must've had an interesting childhood.' Suddenly he sounded like a shrink.

'I did,' Johnny said, 'and I was a very happy kid, too.' Hey, he might as well go all the way with the bullshit.

'That's good,' Adam said. 'Unusual nowadays.'

He laughed in an uppity way, reminding Johnny of somebody, but who? 'Where's your family live now?' Adam asked.

'California.'

'Whereabouts?'

'San Diego.'

'And I understand you're an… artist.'

Artist, like it disgusted him to say it. Might as well have been saying 'bum' or 'faggot.'

'That's right,' Johnny said proudly.

'And this is something you plan to do full-time?'

'It sure is.'

'Can I ask how you support yourself?'

Johnny was tempted to say, *Well, you're gonna be supporting me for the next couple of years or so, Dr Bloom.* But instead he said, 'I have a benefactor.'

Thank you, *Pollock.*

'Really?' Adam said. 'That's wonderful. Anyone I might've heard of?'

'She's a big-time art collector on the Upper East Side, a friend of the Guggenheims. Yeah, she really loves my work.'

'Wow. That's very impressive.'

Marissa came into the living room and said to Johnny, 'He's not grilling you, is he?'

'No, no,' Adam said. 'Xan was just telling me about his burgeoning art career.'

'His art is *amazing*,' Marissa said proudly, putting an arm around Johnny's waist. 'He has so much range.'

'I'd love to see your work sometime,' Adam said. 'Do you have exhibitions, gallery openings?'

'*Dad*,' Marissa said.

'I'll probably have something going on in a couple of months,' Johnny said.

'Well, you'll have to be sure to invite us.'

'I definitely will.' Johnny was smiling at Adam, thinking, *I'm gonna be fucking your wife and daughter so hard later.*

Dana came into the room and announced that dinner was about to be served. Johnny immediately excused himself and went with Dana into the kitchen to help her serve the food. She'd made a salad, some kind of tomato vegetable soup, meatloaf, and mashed potatoes with gravy. He thanked her for going to all the trouble of cooking dinner for him and told her how much he loved the way the house was decorated. Dana seemed to appreciate the compliments very much, and at one point – when she thought he wasn't noticing – he saw her checking him out, looking him up and down. When she opened the refrigerator to get something, Johnny took a good, long look at her ass and was seriously impressed. Marissa had a flat ass, but Dana's butt cheeks were meatier and she had wider hips. Cool, tonight Johnny would get a little variety.

At the dinner table, Johnny was his usual charming, likable self. He had everyone laughing, and he could tell Marissa and Dana both wanted his body. Adam did a lot of talking, going on about himself, obviously trying to impress Johnny, and Marissa had been right before, using the word 'interrogation,' because that was exactly how Johnny felt when Adam started asking him questions again, like he was being questioned by a cop. And now Johnny realized who Adam reminded him of, not a cop but Father Hennessy.

Father Hennessy, Father *Fucking* Hennessy, used to rape Johnny every Thursday afternoon in his office at the church, telling him about all the trouble he'd get into if he ever finked on him, how Johnny would get kicked out of St John's and wind up living on the streets alone. Hennessy was an uppity guy like Adam Bloom, always asked a lot of questions. He lived in an apartment in Queens, but he owned a summer house, somewhere out on Long Island, maybe the Hamptons. He used to keep a picture of the house on the desk in his office, and when Johnny was bent over the desk with his pants down trying to 'stay quiet' he'd stare at the picture, imagining what it would be like to live there, how happy he'd be. Afterward, Hennessy would get all friendly. *What did you learn in school today? What's your favorite subject? What do you want to be when you grow up?* On and on with the questions. Johnny had planned to kill Hennessy one day, get revenge, but he never got the chance. Hennessy died of a stroke when Johnny was thirteen. All the other kids went to the funeral, but Johnny stayed in his room at St John's. Later that night Johnny snuck off to the cemetery and took a big fat shit on Hennessy's grave.

'More wine?' Adam asked, holding up the bottle of merlot. He was into his fourth glass and starting to slur.

'No, thank you,' Johnny said, still nursing his first glass. He had a lot of work ahead of him tonight, and he didn't want to be drunk during it.

As Adam added more wine to his own glass, he said, 'Xan says he's not a big drinker. That's very impressive. You must have a lot of discipline.'

'Well, I'm sure it takes a lot of discipline to be an artist,' Dana said.

'That's true,' Johnny said, smiling at her, *wanting* her. 'It takes a lot of passion, too.'

He let that one hang there, looking at her for an extra beat or two.

'But I think it's a bit unusual, isn't it?' Adam said. 'I mean, choosing a career in art when you say you had a happy childhood. Artists are generally brooding and unhappy and troubled – you know, tortured souls, like van Gogh.'

He said 'Gogh' in this weird, uppity way, like he was starting to throw up. 'Come on, Dad,' Marissa said. 'Can you just stop it?'

'What?' Adam said. 'It's a fact, and I'm just wondering how Xan overcame it.'

'How he overcame his *happy* childhood?' Marissa asked.

'Yeah,' Adam said. 'I guess that's exactly what I'm wondering about.'

'It was hard,' Johnny said coolly. 'I guess if I'd been an unhappy kid, the art would come easier to me, you know? But I don't think anyone's ever really happy. I mean, look at you, Dr Bloom. You have this great house here, a beautiful family, I'm sure you make a really good living, but I bet there are some things you're unhappy about, right? You're not one hundred percent happy, are you?'

Adam suddenly looked uncomfortable, and Dana was looking down at her lap, and Marissa had a little smile, like she was telling herself some private joke.

'No,' Adam finally said. 'I guess nobody's one hundred percent happy.'

'Exactly,' Johnny said. 'I guess all of us have darkness inside us somewhere. Some of us just have to dig a little deeper to find it, that's all.'

Johnny could tell Adam was impressed, and he'd impressed the women, too. He was such a deep, sensitive guy.

Throughout the rest of the meal, Adam continued drinking and asked more and more questions, and Johnny stayed on his game, giving the perfect answers, scoring points with the entire family. It was so easy to be liked; all you had to do was say the right things, tell people what they wanted to hear. When Dana mentioned that she'd done some gardening earlier in the day, Johnny told her how 'fascinating' that was and asked her a lot of questions about the type of flowers she grew – annuals or perennials? – and whether she grew fruits and vegetables and said he'd always loved to garden. At one point, Adam commented he'd strained his back playing golf, and then Johnny started bullshitting with him about golf, asking him questions like 'What's your handicap?' and 'What's your favorite course?' and lying about all the golf he'd played as a teenager. Whenever he could, he complimented the Blooms, telling them how nice and kind and interesting they were. Of course, at least four or five times, Adam dropped that he was a shrink – he was so freaking proud of himself – and Johnny stroked his dick, telling him how exciting his work sounded and how much respect he had for people 'who actually helped people.' Johnny could tell all this crap was going straight to Adam's head.

It was such a blast – getting the Blooms to like him, sucking them in, making them think he was this great guy. Meanwhile, only he knew the truth, the game plan, what was really going to happen. Only he knew that they all had only a few hours left to live. He felt so powerful, like God must feel – in total control, totally messing with their lives.

Johnny helped Dana clear the table and load the dishwasher, and then he helped her reset the table for coffee and dessert, blackout cake. Adam had an after-dinner drink – a shot of brandy – and was officially smashed. Dana and Marissa were a little tipsy, too, but Johnny wasn't even buzzed.

After helping Dana with the dessert dishes, Johnny returned to the living room. Adam must've gone to the bathroom or something; Marissa and Johnny were alone for the first time all evening. Marissa came over and put her arms around Johnny's waist. Her breath smelled like chocolate and wine.

'So how'd I do?' Johnny asked.

'You did amazing,' she said. 'My dad was just telling me how much he likes you, and he's never said that about any guy I'm dating.' She pulled herself in close to him and looked at his lips, whispering, 'You want to come up to my room?'

'Yeah, I'd love that,' Johnny said. In the foyer he added, 'Can you just get me my jacket? I need something in there.'

'Sure,' Marissa said, smiling, probably thinking he had to get condoms. She brought him his jacket, and then they went up to her room. As she went in ahead of him, he looked down the hallway, figuring that was her parents' room down there at the end.

She put on Enya's *Watermark* – did every woman in the world have this? – and then locked the door and took him by the hand and led him toward the bed. Like yesterday, when they started kissing her hand moved toward his crotch, and this time he didn't move away.

'Can you turn the music down a little?' he asked. 'It's distracting me.' Actually the music wasn't distracting at all – nothing ever distracted him when he was in the zone – but he wanted Adam and Dana to be able to hear all of the sex noises loud and clear.

Back in bed, Johnny gave Marissa the full Johnny Long lovemaking treatment. He took his time with her, using all of the techniques he'd mastered over the years. He worshipped her body, paid attention to what turned her on and what didn't. Finally, when she was practically begging for it, he went down on her. She was moaning softly at first, but when he really got into it, she lost control, probably forgetting where she was. He stayed down there for a long time, pleasuring her again and again.

When he was through with her, she was so blown away, so thoroughly satisfied, that it took her several minutes to recover, to be able to speak.

'My God,' she said. 'That was amazing. I've never come like that before… ever.'

Maybe women always said things like this to men in bed, but in Johnny's case they meant it.

'There's more where that came from,' he said.

They had sex, and Johnny got her off in a way no guy ever had before. After all, what was his competition? She was only twenty-two years old. She'd probably been with, at most, ten guys in her life, and they were probably all immature, unskilled lovers like that dork Darren. Yeah, like that weasel really knew how to satisfy a woman. She'd never been with a real man before, a true Casanova, and she couldn't get enough of him. As he built toward his own orgasm, he grunted louder and louder, until he was practically screaming, so Adam and Dana would have no doubt what was going on in their daughter's bedroom.

Lying in bed with Marissa afterward, Johnny was waiting for her to fall asleep so he could shoot her, put his plan in motion, when she whispered, 'I think I'm falling in love with you.'

Whenever Johnny heard that word, 'love,' he wanted to laugh. Love was such bullshit. It was just a word that people said to each other because they thought they were supposed to say it, because they'd heard people in movies say it.

'Really?' Johnny said, playing along. 'Don't you think it's too soon?'

'No,' she said. 'I know how I feel. It's different than it is with other guys. I feel really attached to you.'

Wow, Johnny was impressed – with himself. He'd really pulled this thing off perfectly. It was one thing to pick up a woman at a bar and screw her – practically any guy could do that – but how many guys could get a random girl to say 'I love you' in only a week?

'I feel the same way,' he said sincerely.

'You do?' Her eyes got big.

'Yeah,' he said. 'I mean, I know we haven't known each other very long, but I feel a really strong connection with you. I didn't think it was possible to fall in love with somebody so quickly.'

He didn't know how he was able to say all of this without throwing up. She was so excited that she started kissing him and rolling around with him on the bed, saying things like 'Oh my God' and 'I'm so excited.' Johnny didn't get it, how one word, 'love,' made people so happy. Sometimes he felt like he was the last sane person on the planet.

Johnny was pretty excited himself, but not for the reasons Marissa thought. He was just getting off on this whole situation – getting a girl to say she was in love with him and then killing her and her parents, ending all of their stupid, meaningless lives; it just didn't get any better than that. The only bummer was that very soon, within an hour or two at most, it was all going to end. He'd get away with the engagement ring, other jewelry, and whatever else he could carry out of the house, but he'd put so much work into this, getting Marissa to fall for him, getting her *family* to fall for him, that it felt like a waste not to get more. Johnny figured Adam Bloom had to be worth millions; the house alone had to be worth at least a couple of million. It seemed crazy to just walk away.

One thing about Marissa, she loved to talk, and she was so happy and 'in love' that she wouldn't shut up. She kept yapping away about all this boring stuff, about how she wasn't sure what she wanted to do with her life, how she loved art but she wasn't sure she wanted to work in a gallery, yadda, yadda, yadda. She'd been thinking about moving to Prague, but now that she'd met Xan she wasn't so sure about that anymore. She was thinking of just applying to grad school if a job at a museum didn't come through. Johnny acted like he was interested, occasionally giving her suggestions like 'You should do whatever makes you happy' and 'You have to follow your heart.'

'So what do you think of my parents?' Marissa asked.

'I think they're great,' Johnny said.

'Yeah, I don't know,' she said. 'I mean, they're good people, and I love them, but it's so hard to live here with them sometimes.'

He nodded, like he felt so sorry for her. Yeah, right.

'It was funny,' Marissa said, 'when you talked about them being happy, because they've been so miserable lately, fighting all the time. I mean, it's been pretty stressful, with the shooting and all the media attention, but they're definitely not the world's happiest couple.' Suddenly she looked like she had a big secret, and she said, 'You won't believe what I found out the other day.'

'What?' Johnny asked, looking across the room at his leather jacket, on the chair by the desk.

'My mom's cheating on my father,' she whispered.

'Really?' Johnny said it like he was surprised. Actually, he'd spotted her right away as the type who played around, who was always looking. Johnny Long was never wrong about a woman, ever.

Marissa told him she'd heard through a friend that Dana was cheating on Adam with this guy Tony, some trainer at her gym. So she went for the jocks. That wasn't very surprising to Johnny either. Cheating women always went for the opposite of what they had at home.

Marissa wanted to screw again, and Johnny thought, *Jesus,*

what was it going to take to make this girl fall asleep? Another mind-blowing orgasm seemed to do the trick. Marissa was curled up into Johnny, her head resting on his chest, starting to doze. It was almost midnight, so Johnny figured Adam and Dana were probably in their bedroom, asleep or falling asleep.

When Marissa started snoring slightly, Johnny knew he could kill them all right now. Put one in Marissa's head, then kill her parents; it could be all over in five minutes, ten tops. But if he killed them tonight all he'd get was the money and the jewelry in the house. He had a better idea – a way to get *all* of Adam Bloom's money, plus his cars, his house, and everything else.

The only downside was he wouldn't be able to kill them all tonight. No, to make this thing work he'd have to kill them off one by one.

16

DANA WAS IN the bathroom, looking in the mirror, putting on moisturizing cream, when Adam came in and said, 'Listen to them in there, it's ridiculous.'

'It's not *that* bad,' Dana said.

'Oh, come on,' Adam said. 'This is just more of her acting out, and I find it extremely inappropriate and passive-aggressive.'

'I don't think you're being fair,' Dana said.

'Really? So this is *my* fault?'

'It's not her fault either. She isn't making the noise, he is. What exactly is she doing wrong?'

Adam thought about this, then said, 'What's the matter with him anyway? Why does he have to be so loud?'

'Maybe he thinks the walls are thicker than they are, or maybe he, I don't know, can't control himself. But I really think you've been too hard on her lately. You said you wanted to meet her boyfriends before you let them sleep over, and you met her boyfriend. What more can she do?'

'There are some things a father shouldn't have to hear,' Adam said.

'Just try to ignore it.'

'How can I ignore it when I feel like I'm in the room with them?'

Dana was rubbing cream into the deep wrinkles in her forehead, thinking she might have to give in soon and get Botox.

'She's a beautiful twenty-two-year-old girl,' she said. 'You can't stop her from having sex.'

'Oh, yes I can.'

'Oh, really? What're you going to do, make her wear a chastity belt?'

'I don't have to allow her to have sex in our house anymore, that's what I can do.'

'Listen to you, *allow her*. So what do you want her to do, have sex in cars? In hotel rooms?'

Xan was grunting wildly.

'This is ridiculous,' Adam said and stormed out of the bathroom.

After Dana finished up with her moisturizing, she entered the bedroom, where Adam was pacing. They could still hear Xan's grunting and moaning.

'I feel like knocking on her door.'

'You can't embarrass her like that.'

'So I'm just supposed to listen to this all night?'

'Sleep downstairs or turn on Jay Leno if you don't want to hear it.'

'Why should I have to drown out the noise of my daughter having sex?'

'In the morning, we'll talk to her and ask her if she could talk to him about keeping it down from now on, but there's nothing we can do about it tonight. I mean, it's probably extremely awkward for her right now. What is she supposed to say to him? And I'm sure Xan isn't aware of how loud he's being, and after she talks to him about it everything'll be fine. You like Xan a lot, don't you?'

Adam stopped pacing, breathed deeply, as if he hated to admit it, then said, 'Yeah, I think he's a great guy.'

'Well, I like him, too,' Dana said. 'I think he's incredibly nice and charming and attractive, so I don't think we should complain. She could do a lot worse.'

Dana noticed Adam was staring at her in an odd way, squinting, like he was trying to figure something out.

'What's wrong?' she asked, and he said, 'Nothing,' then turned on the TV to *The Tonight Show*, Leno doing his monologue. The TV didn't drown out Xan completely, but it helped.

Adam sat at the foot of the bed, looking at the TV blankly. Dana, as she had several times during the past week or so, couldn't help feeling paranoid. Whenever Adam seemed particularly distant or gave her a funny look or acted in any way unusual, she couldn't help wondering if he'd somehow found out about her and Tony, or was at least suspicious.

'I just think it's... interesting,' he said.

'What's interesting?' Her heart was pounding.

'The way you described Xan. I haven't heard you talk like that in a long time, calling another man attractive.'

'What're you talking about?' Dana said, acting shocked, probably overdoing it. 'I was just commenting about him, that's all. He's a good-looking guy. He looks a lot like Johnny Depp, don't you think?'

'He was flirting with you a lot.'

'He was not.' She knew he had been; she just didn't want to get into it.

'Come on, it was so obvious.'

'I noticed he was paying attention to me, yes, but I wouldn't call it flirting. Come on, he's Marissa's boyfriend, for God's sake.'

'I was just making an observation, that's all, and wanted to let you know how it made me feel. It made me feel uncomfortable. It made me feel jealous.'

Adam was still in an annoying phase where he was constantly announcing his feelings, talking in I-statements. It was getting seriously wearing.

'I'm sorry you felt that way,' Dana said. Then, wanting to change the subject, she said, 'I still don't think you should be so hard on Marissa. You can't give her rule after rule after rule. At some point you just have to back off and let her live her life.'

As if on cue, they could hear Xan in the other room, practically screaming. 'I'm going out to take a walk,' Adam said and left the bedroom.

Dana got into bed and shut off the light. It was so strange for Adam to get jealous; she hoped that there wasn't more to it, that he wasn't catching on. She thought she'd been acting pretty normal lately, not nearly as depressed as she'd been after ending the fling with Tony, but maybe he'd picked up on something and was projecting it onto her. Oh, God, what was happening to her? She'd been listening to so much of his psychobabble lately that she was starting to think like him now.

Although Dana hadn't spoken to Tony since the night she left his apartment, she'd been missing him a lot, and it was hard to not have any contact with him. He'd texted her several times and had called her and left messages on her cell, and a few times she almost gave in and called him back. Yes, things had been better with Adam lately, but she wasn't sure what 'better' meant anymore. Better than what? Better than when she'd been miserable? Maybe being in a marriage that's slightly better than miserable was good enough for some women, but not her. She felt trapped with Adam, and the idea of staying in the same distant marriage, having the same fights over and over again for the rest of her life, seemed almost unbearable.

While she appreciated that Adam was making an effort to change, she didn't feel like it was a serious, heartfelt effort. Did he take her out to a nice dinner, or maybe surprise her with a weekend getaway? No, he brought home a cheerleader's costume. The psychologist, the so-called expert on marital conflict, tries to save his marriage by trying to encourage his wife to re-enact a scene from *Debbie Does Dallas*? Was that really the best he could come up with? It was pathetic with a capital *P*. The irony was that, while she'd told him she felt ridiculous putting on the outfit, the truth was she felt uncomfortable putting it on for *him*. During her fling with Tony, she'd dressed up many times – as a schoolgirl, a maid, a stewardess, and, yes, even one time as a cheerleader – but somehow living out her sex fantasies with a young sex object like Tony seemed much more normal than doing it with her middle-aged psychologist husband. And it definitely wasn't the magic pill that would resolve their marriage problems.

But the only alternative to staying with Adam was divorcing

him and the thought of being single again was terrifying. She knew a few women in the neighborhood who'd recently gotten divorces, and they were all miserable and lonely. What was she going to do, start dating again? She didn't remember how to date. Where did people meet nowadays anyway, on the internet? What would she do, post some picture of herself, retouched, in the perfect light, where she looked ten years younger, only to see the guys' disappointment and disgust when she met them? Her ego wouldn't be able to handle that. She seemed to get new wrinkles every day, and there was no way she could compete with women in their twenties and thirties who'd be interested in the same men. Then, in a few years, when she was in her fifties, it would get even harder to find someone. If she got very lucky, if she got incredibly lucky, then someday, maybe five or ten years from now, when she was pushing sixty, she'd have a chance to settle for someone who – at best – would be exactly like Adam, a decent enough guy with some very annoying qualities. What was the point of going through all of that pain, probably chopping years off her life because of all the stress, for the outside chance of winding up exactly where she was right now?

Adam returned from his walk, or wherever he'd been, and got into bed. 'Did they stop it in there?' he asked.

'Yes,' she said.

'Thank God,' he said and turned the other way and fell asleep without saying good night.

When Dana woke up, Adam wasn't in bed with her. She went down to the kitchen and saw that he'd brewed coffee, but, as usual, he'd left barely one cup for her. And *he* was the one who called *her* passive-aggressive? He knew full well that she liked to have two or three cups in the morning.

Dana was scooping coffee into the coffeemaker when she heard someone enter the kitchen. She turned, ready to confront Adam, and saw Xan standing there. He was in the same jeans he'd been wearing last night and a plain white wife-beater. His hair was messy from sleep, but on him it looked almost stylized. She noticed how good-looking he was – somehow he was even more attractive with morning scruff, like he could be an underwear model – and then she felt embarrassed because he was seeing her without her makeup.

'Sorry,' he said, smiling. 'Hope I didn't startle you.'

'No,' she said. 'I just, um, thought it was my husband.'

He looked at her the way he had last night, in that flirty way, kind of the way Tony looked at her sometimes, then said, 'It's a beautiful day today, isn't it?'

There was innuendo in his voice, especially in the way he'd said 'beautiful,' as if he wasn't only calling the day beautiful but calling her beautiful as well. This seemed especially apparent because it wasn't a particularly beautiful day. It was cloudy, a little chilly.

'Yes it is,' she said. 'So is, um, Marissa up yet?'

'Oh yeah, she is,' he said. 'She asked me if I could bring her up some coffee.'

'It's good timing then, isn't it?' Dana said. 'Should I make some for you, too?'

'No thanks, I don't drink coffee. I don't need anything to get me going in the morning.'

He smiled at her in a slightly suggestive way. With any other guy – especially any other boyfriend of Marissa's – Dana might've gotten offended, but somehow she didn't feel that way about Xan. His flirtatiousness somehow seemed appropriate, within his character – and, yes, she couldn't help feeling a little flattered by the attention. It felt good to feel sexy, even when it was early in the morning and she was wearing sweats and a baggy T-shirt.

While the coffee was brewing, Xan engaged her in small talk, asking her where she grew up and how she liked living in Forest Hills, and she liked the way he seemed interested in what she was saying, looking right at her and not seeming at all distracted like Adam always did when she was talking to him. She could see why Marissa liked him so much. Not only was he very attractive and intelligent and talented, he was sincere and seemed like a genuinely good person. He was the type of guy Dana could've easily fallen for twenty or thirty years ago.

Later, Xan was back upstairs with Marissa, and Dana was

alone in the kitchen, having yogurt with bananas and raisins along with her coffee, when Adam entered the house through the back door, sweat dripping down his face. He'd obviously been out jogging.

'Good morning,' he said, partly out of breath.

'Morning,' she said, trying to decide if she should mention anything about the coffee. She knew he'd blow it up into another whole 'discussion,' use it as another opportunity to 'express himself,' and she wasn't fully awake yet and didn't feel like she had the energy for all that. Then it occurred to her that this therapy phase of Adam's was really a way of shutting her up, getting her to not express herself at all. Maybe he thought he was bringing openness to their marriage, but the discussions were so tiresome that the end result was that she no longer wanted to discuss anything with him. In the end, his desire to 'communicate' had become a very effective way of cutting off communication entirely.

'Is Xan still here?' he asked.

'Yes,' she said, looking down at her yogurt.

He took a deep breath.

'Try not to think about it,' she said.

'It's just so inappropriate,' he said.

Oh, God, not again.

'She's had boyfriends spend the night before,' she said.

'Yeah, but she hardly knows this guy.'

Dana didn't feel like getting into another pointless argument; it was too early in the morning for drama. So without another word she picked up her coffee and her bowl of yogurt and fruit and went in the dining room, thinking, *You're not the only one who can do the shutting up in this marriage.*

After breakfast, Dana did some cleaning and laundry – she wanted to hire another maid, but she hadn't gotten around to looking for one yet – and then the sun came out and it was turning into a very nice day, so she went out to the backyard and did some gardening. She'd already planted most of the bulbs for next spring, but she added more tulips and narcissuses and did some pruning of the rose and forsythia bushes. While she was working with the hedge clippers, her cell rang. When she saw

Tony's number on the display, she couldn't help feeling turned on. This had happened whenever he'd tried to get in touch with her lately. Her first response was to become aroused – she'd actually get wet between her legs – but then logic interfered and she got upset, feeling like he was harassing her and wouldn't leave her alone. She let her voicemail pick up and switched her phone to vibrate, but a few minutes later he called again. She ignored this call, too, but when he called a third time she worried that he was crossing a line, that he was becoming obsessive. She remembered how he'd sent flowers to the house, and she was afraid he'd do something like that again or, worse, show up at the door. She turned off her phone, hating herself for letting things reach this point. Just because she was unhappy in her marriage didn't mean she had to go out and screw up her life. She could've talked to a therapist, tried to work things out. Her problems hadn't been so unsolvable.

She kept her phone off, but she was paranoid that Tony would try to call on the home phone or come by and ring the doorbell. Adam was around the house all day, reading and watching TV, and it was hard to be near him and act normal. A few times he asked her if everything was okay, and she said everything was fine, she was just feeling a little under the weather. Xan had left earlier in the day and then, at around five, Marissa left with her knapsack/overnight bag. Adam didn't exactly seem thrilled about this, but he didn't make a big stink about it either. Maybe he was starting to realize that Marissa was an adult, capable of making her own decisions, and he couldn't stop her from doing whatever she wanted to do.

Dana and Adam had dinner – leftovers from last night – and it was actually nice to have some time alone together. Maybe she was finally starting to get over Tony, because for the first time in months or longer she had a good time with Adam. They talked about minutiae – movies, TV shows, neighborhood gossip – but it was a relief not to talk about the robbery for a change and not be at each other's throats. She wondered if she'd been too critical of him lately, exaggerating his faults and ignoring the things she liked about him. He definitely seemed to be making an effort to change, taking much more of an interest in her than he had recently, and she wanted to change her behavior, too. After all, she certainly hadn't been an angel in this marriage.

She initiated sex with Adam. After their long drought, naturally it was awkward. The first time, he came too fast – he'd had an off-and-on problem with premature ejaculation for years – but she didn't let her disappointment show, because she knew how sensitive he was about his occasional malfunctions. She thought that was it – maybe she'd use her sex toy or they'd go to bed – but he was able to get another erection, surprisingly, and they made love again. Two times in one night – this had to be the first time in at least ten years that they'd done that. He lasted much longer in round two, and she enjoyed it as much as she possibly could. She'd never thought he was incredibly sexy, but she used to think he had a nice chest, so, although his chest was flabbier than it used to be, she focused on it, imagining that it looked like it used to look. Of course, fantasizing only took her so far. It was just hard not to compare Adam to Tony – and despite Tony's intellectual limitations, when it came to pure sexiness there was no comparison. Sex with Tony was always spontaneous and raw and intense, but sex with Adam was, well, sex with Adam. Like seeing a movie she'd seen dozens of times before, she always knew exactly what was coming next. But when she lowered her expectations, focused on the good rather than the bad – he was certainly gentler with her than Tony – the sex was actually okay.

The next morning Adam left early to make his tee-off time at the country club in Great Neck. Later on in the morning, she took the SUV to Costco and stocked up on food for the week. She spent some time browsing in the books section, skimming self-help books with titles such as *How to Survive an Affair* and *When Your Affair Ends*. A couple of other guilty-looking people were reading similarly titled books and Dana wondered, *Do publishers actually expect people to buy books with these titles*? The consensus was that affairs always ended badly for everyone involved, and the reading helped to convince her that she'd made the right decision in ending hers with Tony, nipping things in the bud before the situation had a chance to escalate.

When she returned home, the Mercedes was in the driveway.

Adam wasn't downstairs, so she figured he was upstairs, washing up or watching TV. Marissa was in her room, or seemed to be – her stereo was blasting. Dana carried all the cartons of groceries in from the car, making several trips. She began unpacking the cartons, which included twenty-four-count packages of toilet paper and paper towels and enough gargantuan boxes of Cheerios to last the whole year.

She was putting away two oversized jars of mango salsa when she heard the front door open, then slam. Moments later, Adam charged into the kitchen. His face was horribly bruised and bloodied, his hair was soaking wet, and he was screaming at her. 'You fucking bitch!'

Dana was completely confused and terrified. She stared at him for a few seconds, then said, 'My God, what... what *happened* to you?'

'Why?' he asked, spraying saliva from his bloodied mouth. 'Just tell me why? Why? Fucking why?'

Naturally she thought, *Uh-oh, it's Tony.*

'Why didn't you come talk to me?' he said. 'Isn't that what I always do? Don't I come talk to you?'

She didn't *know* it had to do with Tony, though. She couldn't make that assumption.

Playing innocent, she said, 'I don't know what the hell –'

Adam grabbed her arm hard and said, 'Why? Just tell me why. After all I've done. I've taken every possible step, done everything I can to save this marriage, and this is what you do to me? You *humiliate* me? Don't you think I've had enough humiliation lately? You think I needed *this*?'

'You're scaring me,' she said, her voice wavering. 'I have no idea –'

'I know, okay?' He was still squeezing her arm, staring hard into her eyes. 'You don't have to lie to me anymore, okay? I know, okay? I fucking know everything.'

Oh God, this was surreal. She felt like she was falling, plunging.

She stared back at Adam, who still looked crazed. His left cheek was badly bruised, and his left eye was partially closed. There was blood pooling on his lower lip.

Finally she said, 'I… I have no idea what you're talking about.'

'Oh, stop with your bullshit already,' he said. 'Can you just do that for me? Can you give me an ounce of fucking respect?'

'You're hurting me,' she said.

'Hurting *you*?' he said. 'That's a good one.' He squeezed her arm harder for a few moments, then let go.

She held her arm, looking down – anywhere but at Adam – thinking, *Maybe I'm wrong. Maybe it doesn't have to do with that at all.*

'Why're you doing this?' she said. 'What's wrong with you?'

'Why can't you just admit it?'

'Admit what?' she asked weakly.

'That you're fucking him!' he screamed, holding up a piece of paper in front of her face. His hand was shaking so much, there was no way she could possibly read it. It looked like it had been crumpled, and it had red, maybe blood, on it. Then she realized that it looked a lot like the other note that had been left at the house, the one that had threatened Adam. Now she was totally confused.

'Wh-what is that?' she asked.

'Read it.'

'I c-c-can't read it. Your hand's moving.'

'It's from the guy you've been fucking – Tony,' he spewed, spraying saliva. She felt beyond light-headed, like she had no blood in her head at all. Her legs felt like they were about to buckle, give way.

'How could you do this to me?' he asked. 'Just give me a reason. I want to know why. Why? *Why*?'

'It's not what you think,' she said.

'Oh, shut up!' he screamed. 'Just shut the fuck up!'

She'd never seen him this way, so angry and crazed. Thank God they were downstairs and not up in the bedroom. He still had that gun in the closet.

'Nothing happened,' she said desperately.

He glared at her like he hated her, like he wanted to kill her, then he said, 'You think you're the only one? Huh? You think you're the only one who's miserable in this marriage?'

'I never said I was mis –'

'You think you're the only one who ever wanted to cheat? You think when I dragged you into marriage counseling I was a happily married man?'

Dana started to cry, not because she was sad about herself but because she was starting to understand how badly she'd hurt Adam. 'I'm so sorry,' she said, 'but you don't –'

'What, you think you're the only one with bombshells, you're the only one with secrets? Well, I have a secret for you. I haven't exactly been faithful either. There, how does that feel? Does it feel good, or does it hurt?'

He stared at her, waiting to see her reaction, but she didn't have one. She thought he was lying, just to get a response from her.

'Please,' she said, 'you don't have to say things just to get even. If you'd just let me expl –'

'It was with Sharon.' His smile was gleeful, almost demented. 'That's right, your *friend* Sharon. We did it in my office, right on my therapy couch.'

Dana didn't believe him. 'Oh, stop it,' she said.

'What? You think I'm making it up?' Adam said. 'I swear on my father's grave, I swear on my life, I swear on Marissa's life that I am not making this up. I fucked your best friend. I fucked the hell out of her.'

'What's going on here?'

Dana looked over and saw that Marissa had entered the kitchen. She had no idea how long she'd been there.

'Nothing, just leave us alone for a few minutes,' Dana said.

'Oh my God, Dad, what happened to your face?'

Adam was still smiling in that strange way at Dana, looking like a mental patient.

'Just go upstairs,' Dana said.

'Why?' Adam said. 'It's all out in the open now, she'll find out eventually. Why not just tell her?'

'Tell me what?' Marissa asked. 'And what the hell happened to you?'

'It turns out your mother's been cheating on me with Tony,' Adam said, 'the trainer at New York Sports Club.'

'I have *not* been cheating,' Dana said.

'Why can't you just have the decency to fucking admit it?' Adam said.

'God, can you guys just stop it?' Marissa said. 'What's *wrong* with you two?' Now Dana was starting to wonder. Was he serious? Would he be taking it this far if he *wasn't* serious? She remembered that period – when was it? – about five years ago when she'd had a falling-out with Sharon. Sharon became distant, didn't want to get together as much, and Dana had never known why.

'Nothing happened with you and Sharon,' Dana said.

'Why would I make it up?' Adam said. 'Just to get even?'

'Wait,' Marissa said to Adam. 'You and Sharon Wasserman were having an *affair*?'

Dana was thinking about that New Year's Eve party, when she had walked into the kitchen and seen Adam with his arm around Sharon's waist, holding her close, and that time when she and Adam went to the movies with Sharon and Michael, and she had seen Sharon and Adam turn to look at each other a few times. It was all coming into focus, adding up, but she still didn't want to believe it.

'Sharon wouldn't do that to me,' Dana said. 'That's impossible.'

'You don't believe me? Go ask her for yourself, but I don't see what difference it makes now.'

He wasn't lying; they'd really done it. Suddenly Dana felt dizzy, nauseous.

'Oh my God,' Marissa said, covering her mouth.

Dana had to get outside, get some air. Maybe a few seconds later, she realized she was walking, then running along the driveway, toward the sidewalk. At first she just wanted to get away, breathe, but then she had a destination.

She went across the street, then around the corner. She rang Sharon's doorbell a few times and then started banging on the door as hard as she could.

Sharon's husband, Mike, answered, looking confused and concerned, and asked, 'What's wrong?'

'Where the hell's that slut? Where is she?'

'Excuse me?' Mike said as Dana pushed past him and went

into the house, saying, 'Where is she? Where the hell's that lying little bitch?'

Dana went toward the kitchen, didn't see Sharon there, and came back, knocking into Michael, who was saying, 'What's going on? What's wrong?'

'Dana?'

There she was, upstairs.

Dana ran up, screaming, 'You fucking slut! You fucking whore!'

Dana saw it in Sharon's expression – it was true, everything was true. When Dana was a few steps away, Sharon turned and started to run down the hallway toward her bedroom, but Dana was coming too fast. She grabbed the cheating bitch from behind and tackled her.

Sharon was screaming, 'Stop! Please, please stop it!'

Dana was punching Sharon, beating her on the back of her head and her neck. Then she put her hands around her throat.

Mike was behind Dana, trying to pull her off of his wife, but Dana was squeezing harder, digging her nails in, refusing to let go.

17

ADAM HAD PLAYED his best round of golf in years. He'd gotten off to a slow start on the front nine, blowing an easy putt on the third hole and needing three shots to get out of the sand trap on six, but on the back nine he really hit his stride. He got two birdies, including one on fifteen, where he used a three-iron from the rough and hit a two-hundred-yard drive and got a great – okay, *lucky* – bounce and wound up about five feet from the cup and then nailed the putt. He ended up with a ninety-two, only three strokes off his all-time best, which he'd gotten five or six years ago on a much easier course in Fort Lauderdale.

After a couple of beers in the club house with his friend Jeff and a few other club members, he drove back to Queens. He was still feeling upbeat, reliving that big shot on the fifteenth hole again and again. He really nailed that sucker, and the club tournament was coming up in a few weeks. He hadn't been planning to enter, but if he could hit shots like that...

When he arrived back at the house, he noticed that the SUV wasn't in the driveway, so he figured that Dana was still at Costco. He was going to call her to tell her about his great round but decided he'd wait till she got home. Besides, she wasn't interested in golf, and he doubted she'd really care. Instead, as he parked his Merc in the driveway, he called his friend Stu, whom he'd gone to college with but who lived in LA now. Stu was a big golfer and would appreciate the story.

When Stu picked up, Adam said, 'Wait till you hear this,' and proceeded to describe the entire round. He entered the house through the back door and was heading toward the front of the house, saying, 'So then on fifteen my second shot slices right into the rough,' when he saw the piece of paper near the front door. He went over and picked it up, not really thinking, saying mindlessly to Stu, 'And then I go for the three-iron.' Stu asked him why he didn't use a two from that far out, and he said, 'I was doing well with the three all day,' but he was getting distracted now as he read:

YOUR WIFE AND I HAVE BEEN FUCKING
I'M IN LOVE WITH HER
SORRY
TONY FROM THE GYM

Adam was still half-lost in telling the story to Stu and wasn't really processing what he was reading, but as he said, 'I knew it was heading right toward the pin,' it occurred to him that this note was on the same paper as the note that had threatened his life, and it was written in the same block letters and looked like the same handwriting. Stu was saying something, Adam had no idea what – the dog next door was suddenly barking like crazy, making it even harder to focus – and then Adam said, 'I gotta call you back' and shut the phone and read the note again, still trying to comprehend its meaning.

For years, Adam's patients had been describing to him the shock of finding out about their cheating spouses. They described initially feeling shocked and betrayed and then experiencing a tremendous rush of anger. Just a few months ago, Richard, a patient who had a history of alcohol abuse, suspected his wife was having an affair and said if he found out who the guy was he would kill him. Adam believed that

Richard was just acting out, trying to empower himself. Using standard cognitive-behavioral techniques, Adam questioned Richard's reasoning for wanting to confront his wife's lover and helped him understand that a confrontation leading to violence wouldn't accomplish anything other than causing even more pain for everyone involved, especially himself.

However, as Adam well knew, it was much easier to solve a problem when it wasn't his own. Now that he was experiencing all the emotions of a scorned lover himself, he was as clueless and helpless as any of his vengeance-seeking patients.

'Dana!' he screamed. 'Day-na!'

He started up the stairs, then remembered that she was probably still at Costco.

He looked at the note again, wondering if it could be some kind of prank; maybe the kids in the neighborhood playing another joke on him. It just didn't make sense that Dana would actually be having an *affair* with that young bodybuilder. He wasn't her type at all, and why would *he* be interested in *her*?

But he didn't see why a neighborhood kid would make up a story about Tony, and, come to think of it, Dana had been exhibiting the telltale signs of an adulterer. She'd been staying out late a lot with flimsy excuses, she'd been on that big fitness kick, losing about ten pounds over the past year, and she'd been taking better care of her appearance as well, going for those photo facials and laser hair removal treatments. Adam also knew that people often chose lovers who were the exact opposite of their spouses, and Tony was about as opposite from him as you could get.

Now Adam's rage was starting to hit hard, and he thought, *That goddamn son of a bitch*. Not only had that big goon been screwing his wife, he'd been screwing with his whole life, sending that threatening note, trying to scare him and his family. He was rubbing it in, not even trying to hide it.

Adam was so upset, so out of control, that as he headed toward the New York Sports Club it didn't even occur to him that going to confront a guy who was probably twice his size, with at least twice his muscle mass, probably wasn't such a great idea. Like his scorned patients, he was so caught up in his rage, so hell-bent on getting some kind of revenge, that all logic had been pushed aside.

He arrived at the gym, looking hardly menacing, still wearing his off-white, Izod-style golf shirt, with his scorecard and pencil sticking out of the front breast pocket. He went right to the weight room, where he saw a couple of other trainers but no Tony. Where the hell was that stupid son of a bitch? And let's face it, the guy was a moron. Was that Dana's way of acting out, sleeping with a retard?

'Where's Tony?' Adam asked one of the trainers, a blond guy.

'Dunno, check out the locker room,' the trainer said.

Adam burst into the locker room, pushing the swinging door very hard into a kid, a teenager. As he went to the locker area, he heard from behind him, 'What's your problem, stupid ass?' Adam went past the rows of lockers, looking for Tony. He imagined himself forcing Tony back against a locker and bashing his face in, pummeling the moron. It didn't even occur to Adam that he had zero chance of accomplishing any of this.

Adam didn't see Tony near the lockers, so he went into the bathroom. One of the stalls was occupied, and Adam banged on it and screamed something.

'Hey!' whoever was in there shouted. It definitely wasn't Tony.

Adam checked the sauna and steam room but didn't see Tony there either. He was on his way out of the locker room when he heard a guy singing off-key; it sounded like some corny pop song, something about how there was no air. It was coming from the showers, and Adam marched over there and saw Tony in the stall. First Adam looked right into Tony's eyes, registering his shocked yet knowing expression, and then he looked lower, at his oversized arms and chest, and then at his penis. He did this purposely – to humiliate Tony, the way a rape victim craves humiliating his or her attacker. He thought that staring at the cock of the man who'd been sleeping with his wife would give him satisfaction, empower him. If Tony had had a small penis, a pencil dick, maybe it would have boosted Adam's fragile ego, but unfortunately, even non-erect, Tony's penis was much longer and much thicker than Adam's, and looking at the cock only made Adam feel even more inadequate and intensified his feelings of self-loathing.

'Hey,' Tony said as Adam went after him, trying to punch him in the face, but he stumbled, maybe on the ledge leading into the shower, and fell hard onto his knees. If someone had walked in at that moment it would have looked like Adam was performing oral sex on Tony.

Adam was trying to get up as Tony said, 'The fuck're you doin'?'

Holding on to the soap dispenser, Adam was able to lift himself partway up. He was very close to Tony, practically squished against his wet, soapy body. Using his free hand, Adam tried again to punch Tony in the face, the way he'd fantasized doing it, but he was barely able to get any force into the punch, and he hit Tony weakly on the chin.

Tony pushed Adam back hard against the wall and said, 'Hey, take it easy, bro, okay, just take it easy.'

Then Adam spat at Tony's forehead. Tony shoved Adam and said, 'Hey, you fuckin' crazy?' and Adam spit again, hitting him in the left eye. This time Tony lost it completely and grabbed Adam and practically flung him out of the shower stall and Adam fell onto his side. Adam got up and went after Tony again, but Tony, outside the stall now, simply grabbed him and unloaded with a solid right to the face. Adam heard the loud crunch in his left cheek, and then the excruciating pain hit. But Adam was undeterred, and later he'd wonder if on some level he actually *wanted* to get hurt, if the desire to feel pain, to be *punished*, was his true motivation. Nevertheless, caught up in the moment, Adam was helpless, and he continued coming after Tony, who kept pushing him away and knocking him down onto the wet floor, like he was some minor annoyance.

When Adam returned from the gym, beaten up and bloodied, he confronted Dana in the kitchen, trying to get her to admit what she'd done, and when she wouldn't, he revealed his affair with Sharon. At that moment, he enjoyed seeing Dana's shock set in, watching her whole world fall apart. He felt like the playing field had been leveled – they were both in pain now, both suffering – and it was also a great relief to suddenly be unburdened of the secret he'd been keeping. Finally it was all out in the open; there was nothing left to hide.

Only after Dana ran out of the house – probably heading for Sharon's – did he realize the incredibly stupid, thoughtless, and hurtful thing he'd done.

He'd counseled many patients about the dangers of revealing a revenge affair to a spouse. He'd told them it might make them feel good initially, but in the end it would only compound the hurt for everyone involved. He'd even suggested that if his patients had the desire to get even they should leave, go away for a few hours to settle down, not act impulsively. But now, like before, he'd done everything he always told his patients not to do. He'd made a bad situation worse, not only further damaging his own marriage but potentially ruining Sharon's as well.

Marissa, who was still in the kitchen with Adam, said, 'Is it really true about you and Sharon? Were you really having an affair with her?'

It was time to finally start acting like a rational adult again, to get in control of this situation. Enough with the acting out and the childish, inappropriate rage. He had to own his feelings, take responsibility for his actions.

'It wasn't an actual affair,' he said. 'It was just a one-night stand… a one-*day* stand.'

Marissa looked at him in disbelief, and Adam realized how badly he'd hurt her, too. It would've been hard enough for her to reconcile her mother's cheating, but now she'd found out that both her parents were adulterers. What kind of examples had they set for her?

'You are such a fucking hypocrite,' she said. 'Telling me how to live my life, giving me all these rules, when your own life is so messed up. And how could you do that to Mom? With Sharon, of all people? My best friend's mother? What the hell is wrong with you?'

Adam knew she was right, about everything. She had every right to be angry at him, to hate him. After taking a few moments to absorb what she'd said, all he could say was, 'I'm sorry.'

'Un-fucking-believable,' she said and left the kitchen. He heard her heading up the stairs, then the door to her room slammed.

After all the yelling and drama, the sudden silence in the kitchen was glaring, but it also seemed foreboding. The way things were headed, the quiet seemed like a glimpse into the future, when he was going to be divorced, living alone in an empty house.

During the whole scene with Dana, his face hadn't been hurting him as much as it should've been, but now the agony was returning. He washed up in the kitchen, watching the pink water swirl down the drain, wincing when his hands touched the cuts and bruises. His face felt very swollen, and it was hard to see out of his left eye. It was probably too late to do anything for it, but he took a few Advils anyway and wrapped some ice cubes in a dish towel and held it against the most swollen areas with as much force as he could stand. He was afraid to look at himself in a mirror because he had a feeling it was even worse than he thought.

When his face started feeling numb and most of the ice cubes had melted, he left the dish towel in the sink and went upstairs. He couldn't believe what he'd done during the past half-hour, how he'd made one awful decision after another. The feelings of self-hatred and self-blaming were so familiar. He was aware that the way he felt right now was the way he'd felt as a child but also how he'd felt after the shooting. He didn't know why he behaved the way he did, why he almost willfully seemed to make the same mistakes over and over again. Why did his knowledge and training desert him at the worst times?

He realized that he should probably warn Sharon that Dana had found out that they'd had sex. He called Sharon's cell, but she wasn't picking up. It was probably too late anyway. Dana had probably gone over there to confront her and cause more drama; Adam didn't even want to imagine that scene. He knew Sharon would never speak to him again. He'd once told her that, no matter what, he'd never tell anyone about their affair. He'd done such a great job of keeping that secret.

As Adam was putting down the phone, he noticed he had a voicemail. He checked his incoming call log and saw it had only been Stu, calling back, wanting to hear the rest of the golf story. Adam remembered how happy he'd been after he made that last putt on eighteen. It felt like that had happened years ago.

The Advils and ice hadn't done anything, and his face was throbbing. He accidentally glanced in a mirror and was horrified by how awful he looked. The whole left side of his face was bruised and swollen, and his upper lip was badly swollen and looked purplish blue.

He was on his way down for more ice when the front doorbell rang, five or six times in rapid succession. It was probably Dana, who'd rushed out of the house without her keys. He hoped she hadn't actually gone to Sharon's house, that she'd done what he should've done earlier – taken a walk around the neighborhood to calm down and get hold of herself. He had no idea what he'd say to her, if there was anything left to say.

Without looking through the peephole, he opened the door and saw Sharon's husband, Mike.

Mike looked enraged – eyes widened, jaw clenched – and there was no mystery why. He was a big, stocky guy – he'd been on the wrestling team in college at Stony Brook – and Adam feared he was in for another beating.

'Please don't hurt me,' he said, resorting immediately to begging. 'I'm so, so sorry. Please, please don't hurt me.'

Mike looked slightly horrified now, as if he'd noticed what Adam's face looked like, and he said, 'How'd your face get like that? Your psycho wife do that to you?'

Adam didn't know why Mike thought Dana had beaten him up, but he didn't feel like getting into the actual explanation. 'No, it wasn't Dana,' he said.

'It was… I'm just so sorry. I don't know what else to say.'

Mike glared at Adam hard and then said, 'You're both pathetic. And you better tell your psycho wife to stay away from my wife, because next time she shows up at my house, next time she even rings the bell, I'm calling the fuckin' cops.'

'Oh, no, what did she do?'

'She tried to strangle my wife, that's what she did.'

'Oh my God,' Adam said. 'Is she okay?'

'Sharon's fine, but your wife should be locked up at fuckin' Bellevue.' Mike poked his index finger hard against Adam's chest. 'And *you* better stay the hell away from my wife, you son of a bitch, or I swear to God I'll kill you.'

He let that not exactly veiled threat linger for several seconds, keeping his index finger right where it was, jamming it in with more force for emphasis, and then he stormed away without looking back.

Adam remained there with the door open for a long time – he wasn't sure how long – and then he shut the door, feeling thoroughly distraught.

Marissa was still up in her room, blasting music now. Adam had no idea how he was going to rebuild his relationship with his daughter, how he'd ever regain her respect and trust. His relationship with Dana seemed even more hopeless. When she came home, if she came home, what could they say to each other? He felt like his marriage was almost certainly over. He knew from experience that when two people behave so hurtfully toward one another, they reach a point where reconciliation is impossible, and he and Dana had gone way, way beyond that point.

In the kitchen, Adam saw the note from Tony on the counter. He read it again, in a calmer, less emotional mood than he'd been in before. While the note still angered him and made him feel extremely manipulated and victimized, he was able to read it more objectively. Earlier he'd realized that the note looked almost exactly like the threatening note that had been left at the house – it was on the same plain white paper, was written in the same way – and he'd thought that Tony had only left the earlier note to scare him. But what if there was more to it than that? What if Tony really had been the second intruder in the house that night? Maybe there was some connection between Tony and Carlos Sanchez. Or maybe Tony had been over to the house sometime and met Gabriela and conspired to rob the house with Carlos.

The idea that Tony knew Gabriela and Carlos seemed farfetched, but the facts were that a note had been left at his house, possibly by the person who'd participated in the robbery, and now an identical-looking note had been left by Tony.

Adam did what he should've done right away, before he'd

confronted Tony and before he'd acted out so selfishly and thoughtlessly with Dana. He called Detective Clements to let him know about the possible lead.

Her dad and Sharon Wasserman having *sex*?

Marissa was at her desk in her room, staring blankly at her PC monitor, mindlessly scrolling through her iTunes playlist, trying to picture her dad and Sharon doing it. The idea of her dad having sex with *anyone* was hard to believe, and not just in the way all kids get disgusted by the idea of their parents having sex. With her dad it was actually hard to believe. He was such a serious, analytical person; Marissa just couldn't imagine him letting loose, having that kind of passion. Especially recently, the last several years, he'd seemed totally asexual. It was particularly hard to imagine him having an affair – *a one-day stand* – with Sharon Wasserman, of all people. Sharon was so laid-back, so outgoing, so cool, so totally unlike Marissa's father. And Sharon and Mike had always seemed like the perfect happy couple. Why would Sharon throw all of that away?

Marissa's cell rang. It was Hillary saying, 'Did you just call?'

'Yeah, I got your voicemail, but I didn't leave a message,' Marissa said. 'Where are you?'

'The city,' Hillary said, 'having drinks at Wetbar with Brendon. What's up?' Brendon was some supposedly very cute guy Hillary had met one night in the city whom Marissa hadn't met yet.

'Did you hear what's going on?' Marissa asked.

'What's going on with what?'

'I guess not then.'

'What is it?'

'I have some bad news for you,' Marissa said. 'Well, not bad news… weird news. Fucked-up news. Very fucked-up news.'

'Can you tell me already?' Hillary sounded very concerned.

Figuring she might as well just come out with it, Marissa said, 'My dad and your mom had sex.'

Saying it out loud, it seemed even more absurd, almost laughable.

There was a long silence, then Hillary said, 'No way.'

'Way.'

'This is a joke, right?'

'Swear to God, I just found out. It's so fucked up. My dad found out about my mom and Tony, too. My parents looked like they wanted to kill each other.'

'I don't believe you,' Hillary said, sounding a little edgy.

'Why would I call you up to lie about –'

'I don't know, but it's not funny.'

Marissa tried to sound ultraserious. 'I am not lying.'

'I have to go,' Hillary said coldly.

'Hill, come on, don't –'

'Bye,' Hillary said and ended the call.

Marissa was pissed off that Hillary had hung up on her like that – talk about shooting the messenger – but she could understand her reaction. The affair was hard to believe, and it had to be even harder for Hillary to accept because her life had always been so perfect. Her parents had always gotten along so well, and her family had always been one of the least dysfunctional families in the whole neighborhood.

'Welcome to the club,' Marissa said, and then the doorbell rang.

She went to the edge of the landing and kneeled down to get an unobstructed view of the front door, where her father was talking to – holy shit – Mike Wasserman, Hillary's dad. He sounded like he was threatening her father – oh no, this day was going from bad to worse. Marissa hoped her dad wasn't going to get even more beaten up; who'd beaten him up the first time, anyway? Did her mom do that to him? She'd seemed angry enough to beat him up, that was for sure.

Marissa returned to her room and clicked on a random song on iTunes – ironically and annoyingly, Hinder's *Lips of an Angel*, a song about a guy cheating on his girlfriend.

She turned down the music and called Xan.

'Hey,' Xan said.

It was so great to hear his voice, the voice of a rational person.

'I know you're busy painting, and I'm sorry to bother you, but there's some crazy stuff happening here.'

She told him about how her father had found out about her mother's affair with Tony the trainer and then had confessed his own affair.

'It's been a total mess,' she said.

'I'm so sorry,' he said. 'Man, that really sucks.'

'I've never seen my mother so hurt, and you should've seen the look on my father's face. He looked like he was enjoying it. It was so fucking sick.'

'Oh, shit,' Xan said. 'I'm really sorry, Rissa.'

'I know how busy you are,' Marissa said, 'and I really don't want to burden you, but I really don't want to be alone right now. Is it okay if I...'

'Yes, definitely, come over. Unless you want me to come there?'

'No, no, trust me, here is one place you do not want to be. But are you sure it's okay? Becau –'

'Yeah, I'm positive,' he said. 'You need to get away from all that craziness, and I want to be with you now.'

'Thank you,' Marissa said. 'You're so amazing.'

As she packed an overnight bag, she couldn't stop thinking about Xan, how thoughtful he was and how lucky she was that she'd found him. If Lucas hadn't hooked up with that other girl that night at Kenny's Castaways, Marissa might never have met him, and she didn't even want to imagine what things would've been like then. Right now Xan was the best thing in her life, the *only* thing, really.

Her attachment to Xan was weird because Marissa usually didn't fall for guys so quickly. In the past, when she was starting to get close to a guy, she'd be the one who'd freak out and say, 'I need some space' or 'I want to take it slower' or 'I don't want to be exclusive,' anything to avoid getting into an actual relationship. But with Xan she didn't feel trapped or pressured at all. Hanging out with him felt so normal, so natural, so right. Aside from being extremely cute, he was easygoing, sincere, attentive, kind, generous, and funny, and she had so much in common with him it was insane. She loved that he was an artist and that he liked to talk about art. Sometimes when she was with him she felt like he knew what she was thinking ahead of time, like their brains were wired the same way. But the most amazing thing about Xan was that they'd known each other for over a week now and no red flags had gone up; she hadn't had any what she called uh-oh moments. In just about every other relationship she'd ever been in, the guy would always seem great at first, maybe for the first date or two, but then there would be an uh-oh moment and he'd drop some bombshell, like she'd find out he was a hockey fanatic, a compulsive gambler, a drug addict, a Republican – something horrible.

The morning after they met, she did what every girl in the world did after meeting a new guy – she Googled him. She hoped to find old pictures of him or information about his art, hopefully even a blog. He'd told her his last name was something like Ivonov, but a search for 'Xan Ivonov' didn't bring up any information, nor did a search for 'Alexander Ivonov.' Maybe she was spelling Ivonov wrong or, since he was just an aspiring artist, there was no information about him online yet. She was trying a few other spellings – Ivonof, Ivonoff, Evonof – when he texted her, asking her if she wanted to spend the day at the Met. Was that the perfect first date or what? She had such a good time, taking him around, showing him all her favorite paintings. When he went on about how much he loved *The Storm*, she knew he was just saying this to impress her, but that was exactly what she loved about him, what made him stand out versus other guys. He made that extra effort; he actually cared.

During the week, he wanted to get together practically every night, something that would normally make her feel trapped, but she *wanted* to spend every second with him. When they weren't together she felt an incredible void and couldn't stop thinking about him, and then when they were together it felt so intense that she didn't want their dates to end. The timing of meeting Xan had been so perfect, because she'd needed to get away from her parents, distance herself from all of the fucked-upness at home, and he was the perfect distraction.

But she didn't want to sleep with him too fast. She wanted them to really get to know each other first, wait a few dates at least. When he invited her back to his place for the first time, she was ready for something to happen and had a pack of condoms in her purse just in case.

She knew he was worried and insecure about her seeing his artwork – it was so cute to see him get like that – and she kept reassuring him, telling him that his stuff was probably amazing. And she really did expect his work to be incredible. She'd been imagining that he was this major undiscovered talent, the next big thing, and would be hugely famous someday, so when she entered his apartment and saw his paintings it was hard to not feel a big letdown.

His work was extremely mixed. Some of it was very amateurish, bordering on plain awful, but a few of the paintings showed that he at least had some basic talent. His main problem was that his work was unfocused, that he had no singular vision. While he'd told her that he worked in a variety of styles, she was surprised by how vastly different the paintings were. His style ranged from realism to modern to abstract to postmodern, and his use of oils and acrylics seemed almost random. The painting he was currently working on was a total mess; it looked like he'd splattered the paint nonsensically onto the canvas, like a child's imitation of Jackson Pollock. The pictures looked so different from one another, in their styles and subjects, that his greatest talent as a painter seemed to be his ability to mimic other artists' techniques, and he didn't even do that very well. It was no wonder that she hadn't found any information about him online.

Of course, Marissa was careful to keep all her opinions to herself. She knew that, especially given how insecure Xan was about his artwork to begin with, voicing her true opinions would be an instant relationship killer. So she was very positive and upbeat, going on and on, exaggerating the few positives about his work and ignoring the many negatives. She knew she was taking it way too far – comparing his work to Picasso and Johns was about as overboard as it gets – but at least he didn't seem to catch on that she thought his work was mediocre. Assuming that things with Xan worked out and they continued dating, she'd have to tell him her true feelings about his paintings eventually, but she hoped by that time he'd realize for himself that he didn't have much of a future as an artist. Besides, the important thing – and one of the things she found most attractive about him to begin with – was that he was passionate about his art. So many people didn't have passion for anything these days; they just went along with their narrow, selfish lives without really caring about anything. But Xan was different. She knew that if he transferred the passion he had for art to something else he'd be hugely successful.

When they started kissing on his couch, she wanted to make love to him, but he wanted to wait until he met her parents. She thought this was very sweet, but she was also terrified that her parents would mess everything up for her. Her mother had been so depressed and moody lately, and her father had been incredibly annoying with all his rules. He'd told her it was 'time for some tough love,' but she felt like he was just doing it to annoy the hell out of her and make life at home so unbearable that she'd be forced to move out on her own and get a job. He was such a hypocrite, acting so high and mighty all the time, telling her that she was 'passive-aggressive' and 'acting out' and – the most ridiculous of all – 'exhibiting attention-seeking behavior.' Meanwhile, who was going around shooting people? Who was the new Bernie Goetz? Who was the one who'd made a fool of himself in that interview for Daily Intel?

Marissa was expecting dinner to be a total disaster. She knew her father would interrogate Xan, and she was afraid her mother would be in one of her down moods and just sit there and not say anything. But, thanks to Xan and his charm, dinner went amazingly well. Xan handled her father perfectly – taking him seriously, not getting too defensive – and by the end of the meal they were talking like old friends. Her mom was surprisingly conversational and seemed to like Xan a lot, too. Actually, she seemed to like Xan a little too much, getting a little too flirty with him. At least a few times Marissa caught her mother making googly eyes at Xan. She didn't know what was up with her mother and younger guys these days. Weren't men supposed to have the midlife crises? What was she going to do next, start buying sports cars?

After dinner, it was great to finally be alone with Xan in a bed. As they undressed each other and during foreplay, it felt different than it had with previous boyfriends. This wasn't just hooking up with some random guy. This was the beginning of something special.

But unfortunately, just like seeing his artwork, the sex itself was a major disappointment. It wasn't due to a lack of passion, because Xan was definitely trying. If anything, he was trying too hard, making so much noise. It was embarrassing with her parents so close by, and it was hard for her to relax and focus. She whispered 'Shh' a few times and said, 'We have to be quiet,' but it was like he couldn't control himself, and there was a limit to what she could say to him. She sensed that – like his art – sex was something he took very seriously and that any suggestions she made would be misinterpreted as criticism. She definitely didn't want to offend him their first time doing it. Besides, Xan seemed very inexperienced – he'd only mentioned a couple of past serious girlfriends – and she didn't want to make him feel self-conscious, like he was doing something wrong and needed coaching. She figured that once they got to know each other's bodies, and some of his nervousness and awkwardness faded, the sex would improve. Meanwhile, everything else about the relationship felt so perfect.

She left the house without bothering to tell her father where she was going and took the subway to Xan's in Brooklyn. On the way to his building, she imagined that she was living with him. She knew she was getting way ahead of herself, but so what? It was fun to fantasize. Xan's place was small, but it would be a good starter apartment, and with a little decorating and better use of the space it had a lot of potential. Living with a guy would be a blast, and she had a feeling that Xan would be very laid-back and easy to get along with. She had enough money to pitch in for rent for several months at least, and eventually she'd find some kind of job or go back to school or do *something*. When the timing felt right she'd gently persuade him to find a career outside of art. She wouldn't really care what he did for a living, because to her who he was was more important than what he was. She'd never been materialistic. She didn't want to marry some doctor and be miserable her whole life – she'd watched her mother make that mistake.

Xan buzzed her up to his apartment. Although it had only been a few hours since they'd seen each other, it felt like it had been days, and it was great just to be with him, to hug him, to feel close to somebody.

They got right into bed and lay side by side facing each other, kissing and giggling with their noses touching.

'So it sounds like it was pretty crazy over there, huh?' Xan asked.

'You have no idea,' Marissa said. 'I walked into the kitchen, and they looked like they wanted to kill each other. My dad's whole face was bleeding, my mother must've hit him or something, and then my dad said that *he's* been cheating, too. When my mother comes home it's gonna be a total disaster.'

She went on, venting, rehashing what had happened at the house. Xan didn't say much. Occasionally he said things like 'It sounds rough' and 'I'm so sorry' and 'Man, that sucks so bad.' But just having somebody to talk to, somebody who actually cared about her, made her feel so much better.

'I'm so lucky I have you in my life right now,' she said as they rubbed noses again. 'I think I must be the luckiest girl alive.'

18

DANA WAS AT the Starbucks on Austin Street in Forest Hills, into her second latte, contemplating her bleak future. It wasn't the first time she'd tried to imagine a life without Adam, but this time the idea of winding up divorced seemed more serious, more imminent, and the alternatives were as scary and as unappealing as ever.

She had no close relatives in the New York area, and she didn't want to burden any of her friends, so if she moved out she'd have to go to a hotel. She could stay there for a while, maybe a couple of months, then what? She knew that Adam would go all out, hiring Neil Berman, an old college friend and a high-priced, cut-throat divorce lawyer. Berman was as slimy as they came. She'd have to counter with her own pit bull, and she and Adam would wind up spending tens of thousands of dollars on nasty lawyer correspondence. She knew he'd fight like hell to keep the house and would probably be successful, given that the house had belonged to his family before they were married. She'd probably be able to get half their stock market account and savings – only a few hundred thousand dollars total, because they still hadn't recovered the money Adam had lost during the dotcom bust. They both had IRAs, and Adam had a 401(k) or a 403(b), but she wasn't sure exactly how much was in Adam's retirement accounts or whether she would be entitled to any of it. She would probably be able to work out some sort of alimony agreement, but Neil Berman was such a bloodsucking prick that Dana knew it wouldn't be much. And even if she was somehow able to work out a decent settlement, it wouldn't be enough to pay a New York City rent and all her expenses. She'd need some kind of job, and she doubted companies would be tripping over themselves to hire a forty-seven-year-old woman with limited skills who'd been out of the workforce for over two decades. Yeah, she'd try to meet another man, but would that even be possible? In a few years, she'd be fifty and single, struggling to pay her rent in some tiny, modest apartment.

Her future had never seemed so hopeless. Not only was she on the verge of being single, maybe for the rest of her life, but she'd also lost her best friend. Dana knew she'd never be able to forgive Sharon. This was a woman Dana had trusted, had confided in. Just the other day Dana had been over at Sharon's house asking for advice about how to end her affair with Tony. Dana had been asking *her* for advice. And what had the cheating bitch done? She'd gotten all holier-than-thou on her, telling her that 'affairs are wrong' and she had to 'think about Adam's feelings.' Meanwhile, that bitch had had Adam's cock in her mouth. Dana had never been angrier than she'd been when she'd had her hands around Sharon's neck. For the first time in her life she'd felt like she could actually kill someone, she could cross that line. It was an easy line to cross; it didn't take much effort. You didn't have to be crazy to kill. You just had to be a little thoughtless.

Dana was taking a long sip of her latte, finishing it, when her cell rang. It was fucking Tony.

'Son of a bitch, leave me alone,' she said, loud enough that the barista, a young black woman, heard across the store and looked over.

Dana couldn't believe he had the balls to call her now, after leaving that note and trying to ruin her life. She was going to let the call go to voicemail; then she thought, *Screw it,* and picked up and said furiously, 'What the hell is wrong with you? Why can't you just go the hell away?' He started to say something else, and she said, 'Just stay the hell away from me,' and hung up. A few seconds later he called back, and she said, 'Are you some kind of idiot or something? Are you demented?' and he said, 'I got no idea what the –' and she said, 'Like hell you don't,' and he said, 'Don't ha –' and she said, 'Fuck you, and I mean it' and clicked off.

Of course he called again, and this time she didn't answer. About a minute later her phone beeped, indicating a new voicemail. She was going to delete it but then thought about what Tony had just said, *I got no idea what the*, and for some reason she felt compelled to play the message with her thumb on the END button, ready to delete it at any point.

Look, I got no idea what the fuck's going on, okay? All I know is your husband showed up and tried to attack me in the shower. I didn't wanna hurt him, okay, but he spit in my face, and what do you want me to do, just take that shit? I don't know what's going on with you guys, if you told him about us or what, but I just called to make sure you were all right. I miss you, all right? Shoot me for saying that, but it's true. You know how much I love you, Dana. Do what you wanna do, but do me a favor – tell your husband to stay the hell away from me. I don't wanna have to hurt him again.

Dana deleted the message, deciding that Tony was officially insane and that she had to be insane, too, for getting involved with him in the first place. In retrospect he'd been unstable, obsessive, and prone to violence all along. The way he was rough in bed, the way he'd started telling her that he was in love with her when she'd let him know from the beginning that as far as she was concerned he was just a boy toy, the way he'd called her and texted her at inappropriate times, the way he'd sent flowers to the house, all should've been warning signs. He'd told her about fights he'd been in, people he'd beaten up at bars and clubs, and though she hadn't said anything to him, she'd thought, *Roid rage?* Then today, he dropped off a note at the house and beat the crap out of Adam, and he acted like none of it was his fault. Worse, he was still telling Dana that he was in love with her when she'd made it incredibly clear that she never even wanted to talk to him again.

'Jesus Christ,' Dana said, and the barista looked over again. Dana shot the woman a look back that screamed, *Yeah, I'm talking to myself. You got a problem with that?*

As if Dana didn't have enough to deal with, if Tony continued to harass her she'd have to look into getting a restraining order. It didn't help that now Adam had some kind of crazy vendetta against Tony. Had he really gone over there and 'attacked' him in the shower? That explained how he'd gotten so beaten up, and it was so like Adam to storm over to the gym and do something so insane. What had he been thinking, *Gee, I think I'll go beat up a bodybuilder?* Yeah, like that would work. It was just like when he went into the closet to get the gun that night. The man never learned.

Wired on caffeine, extremely agitated, Dana needed air.

On her way out, she saw the barista eyeing her again.

'What the hell're you looking at, *bitch*?' Dana said, not aware that she'd actually said it until she was halfway down the block.

When Dana entered, she braced herself, expecting Adam to lash out at her again, but the house was quiet. She went upstairs, and in the hallway outside her bedroom it suddenly hit her how much she'd lost. Her life had been so good, she'd had so much, and she'd given it all up, why? Because she was bored? Because she felt ignored?

She started crying, the tears flowing down her cheeks. She was leaning with her head against the wall at first, and then she sat on the floor with her head hanging between her legs. It had been years since she'd cried this hard, and she'd never felt so worthless, so helpless.

After maybe a half-hour of intense sobbing, she felt numb and dazed. She didn't want her marriage to be over. She knew things had gotten screwed up, beyond screwed up, but she didn't think it was unsalvageable. Until today, things had been getting better, and it wasn't like either of them had fallen in love, or was even in an active affair. She'd broken up with Tony and – apparently – Adam and Sharon had only been together that one time. In a way, her affair – and, yes, she was willing to admit that it had been an affair and not a mere fling – had been worse because, although he'd cheated on her with her best friend, she'd been with Tony dozens of times. He could rationalize what he'd done – *we got caught up in the moment; it just happened* – but what she'd done had been calculated and premeditated. If he could forgive her, then she didn't see why she shouldn't forgive him. Yes, they'd hurt each other, but a lot of married people hurt each other and worked things out; they didn't run away.

Thirsty and worn out from all the crying, she went down to the kitchen. She was about to open the fridge when she heard TV noise coming from the living room. She approached cautiously and then saw Adam lying on the couch. She was behind him and he was facing the other direction, so he probably didn't know she was there. She knew he wasn't actually watching TV because Rachael Ray was on and he couldn't stand Rachael Ray.

She was going to leave, give him some space, but she felt bad just standing there, not saying anything.

'How's your face?' she asked.

He didn't answer. She figured he was just ignoring her.

She waited a couple of minutes, watching Rachael Ray explain how to make 'extra-chunky salsa,' and then she said, 'I just want you to know it meant nothing to me. It was stupid, I have no idea why I did it. I think I should probably go back into therapy.'

She thought playing the therapy card would at least get a response, show him that she was willing to take responsibility for what she'd done, but he didn't have any reaction.

She continued, 'I still love you very much. I want to be together if you want to be together. I mean, we've been married twenty-three years. It's crazy to just throw that all away without even trying to fix things.'

He still wouldn't answer. She wondered if he was asleep, and she took a couple of steps into the room to get a better view of his face. Suddenly she had a horrible thought: *He's not asleep, he's dead*. For a few horrified moments she imagined the *next* few moments – touching his body, feeling his cold skin, her hysteria. Maybe he'd OD'd or slit his wrists. She expected to see a puddle of blood on the floor. Then she saw his eyes, and they looked wide open but lifeless.

'Adam.' She didn't scream it, but she said it suddenly, like she was saying 'Boo,' trying to scare him.

Adam's head turned toward her, and she said, 'Thank God.' Her pulse was pounding. 'Sorry, I thought you were... never mind.'

He turned back toward the TV and resumed staring.

Dana remained there until her heart rate returned to something close to normal, and then she started to leave.

'I talked to Clements,' Adam said.

Dana stopped. 'About what?'

Adam was still facing away from her, looking at Rachael Ray. 'I told him about the note that...' He paused, as if struggling to find the right words, then said with disgust, '... that Tony left.'

Again Dana realized how badly she'd hurt Adam.

'What about it?' she asked weakly.

'What do you mean, what about it?' he snapped, sounding like he hated her. 'It was almost exactly like the other note, the one that threatened to kill me.'

Dana hadn't thought about this before – or at all, really – because she'd had so much other crap on her mind. Why would Tony have left a note threatening Adam's life and claiming to be involved in the robbery? Tony might've been trying to harass Dana and her family, but leaving a note didn't seem like something he'd do.

'Are you sure the notes looked the same?' Dana asked.

'Yes, I'm sure. It was the same paper, same print. Everything was the same.'

'That would be weird,' Dana said.

'What?' Adam asked, though Dana knew he'd heard the first time and was trying to be harsh with her intentionally, to try to upset her.

'I don't see why he would've done that,' she said.

'Clements asked me if Tony had ever been to the house,' Adam said. 'Had he?'

265

Dana immediately thought about the bouquet of flowers. She didn't want to tell Adam about this, afraid that it would lead to more questions about the past and that he'd accuse her of having sex with Tony in their house, in their bed, and she didn't want to get into another big argument.

'No,' Dana said.

'Never?' Adam asked.

'As far as I know... no, never.'

'Did he know Gabriela?'

'How would he know her?'

'Did he know her or not?'

'I have no idea. I don't see how he could've –'

'Do you think he could've robbed the house or not?'

'No,' Dana said.

'Why not?'

'I just don't think it's something he'd do.'

'Why not?'

'Because I just don't.'

Adam was quiet for several seconds, then said, 'I'll call Clements and tell him. He said he's gonna send somebody by later to pick up the note.'

Another several seconds passed, and then Dana, still talking to Adam's back, said, 'So what do you want to do?'

'About what?'

Again she felt like he knew full well and was trying to agitate her.

'What do you think?' she said. 'I'm willing to work on it if you are. I feel awful about everything, and I know we have a lot to work out, but I think we can get through this. I mean, you see patients all the time in these situations, and you help them and they wind up staying in their marriages. People make mistakes, but it doesn't have to be the end.'

'Sometimes it is the end,' Adam said.

The coldness in his voice sent the clear message that as far as he was concerned the conversation was over; there was no room for discussion.

Dana stood there for a while, stunned, and then she left before she started crying again.

Adam didn't come to bed. Although he and Dana usually slept with a lot of space between them, barely touching, the bed still felt very empty without him, and she woke up several times during the night and cried into her pillow until she fell back asleep.

In the morning she woke up as Adam was closing one of the dresser drawers. He left the room immediately, probably going to shower in the guest bathroom. Later, when Dana heard the front door slam, she got out of bed.

She went downstairs. Adam hadn't left any coffee for her, but this time she didn't feel like it was passive-aggressive; it was just plain aggressive.

He'd also left bagel crumbs on the counter and hadn't bothered to put his dishes in the sink. Then Dana noticed that he'd written something on the blackboard in the kitchen where they sometimes left notes for each other. She went closer and saw *I want you to move out.*

Dana cried for a long time, knowing there was nothing she could do or say to change Adam's mind. She would try to talk to him again, but she knew it wouldn't help. *Sometimes it is the end.*

The worst part was that she was going through all of this entirely alone. Normally, Sharon would've been the only friend she'd feel comfortable talking to about something so personal and traumatic. She considered calling other friends, like Deborah, whom she'd grown up with in Dix Hills, Long Island, or Geri from the PTA, but she felt embarrassed and ashamed to actually say, 'I'm getting a divorce.' She felt like saying the words would make it real, there'd be no turning back, and as soon as she told someone, word would get around the neighborhood, and there would be more drama. Everyone would be talking about her, even people she hardly knew. *Did you hear Dana Bloom's getting a divorce? Oh, no, that's so terrible.* Everyone talking about her like she was this poor defenseless thing, a victim. Being divorced would become her new identity because, after all, what other identity did she have? She had no career, no young children. Her life had no meaning.

Dana got back into bed and didn't want to get up. She

was more scared than depressed, but she was aware that a depression was setting in and had a feeling it would only get worse. There was no way she'd be able to get through the stress of moving out, finding a new apartment, and the legal and financial nightmare all alone. She needed to get back on Prozac. Talking to someone, a professional, would probably be a good idea, too. She convinced herself to call her psychiatrist, Dr Feldman, whom she hadn't seen in what, three years? She took the soonest appointment Feldman had, this coming Wednesday afternoon.

Sometime in the afternoon Dana heard Marissa come up the stairs and go into her room. Dana hadn't really considered the effect the divorce would have on her daughter. Yes, Marissa was twenty-two, so it wasn't exactly like having to explain the situation to a young child, but it was still going to be a big deal in her life. Dana suddenly felt extremely guilty – for deserting Marissa and for being a bad mother, especially lately. Since Marissa had moved back home, had Dana been there for her at all? No, she'd been off in her fantasy world with Tony, thinking about herself, as usual. Dana couldn't believe that she'd been in such a fog, that she hadn't seen the effect that the affair had been having not only on Adam and her marriage but on her entire family.

Dana got out of bed sluggishly. She knocked on Marissa's door and then heard, 'What is it?'

'I need to talk to you,' Dana said.

After a long pause Marissa said, 'Come in.'

Dana entered and saw Marissa lying on her back in bed with her iPhone, texting someone. Suddenly she had a flashback of Marissa as a five- or six-year-old in the same bed, having a nightmare in the middle of the night and calling out, 'Mommy!' Dana would always get up – Adam was such a deep sleeper, he would've let her cry all night – and get into bed with Marissa and hug her tightly and assure her that everything was going to be all right. Sometimes Marissa would fall right back asleep, but other times Dana would get into bed with her and tell her made-up stories about the adventures of Marissel and Marissel's parents, Arthur and Diana. The characters were very thinly disguised versions of Dana, Adam, and Marissa, and at the end of each story, Marissel always wound up happy, home in bed, with her parents in the next room.

'What do you want?' Marissa asked, sounding irritated, like she often did lately.

'Can I sit down?' Dana asked.

'If you want to,' Marissa said. Then she added, 'You don't look good.'

Dana sat on the edge of the bed and said, 'First of all, I'm sorry.'

'Sorry for what?'

'That you had to see all that yesterday. I know how... disturbing this must be for you.'

'Disturbing?' Marissa laughed sarcastically. 'I just don't know what took you guys so long.'

'You know?'

'Dad called me before and told me.'

'Told you what?' Dana was afraid that Adam was already bad-mouthing her.

'That you guys are getting a divorce, and I think it's a good thing, to be honest. You two have been making each other miserable for years.'

'It hasn't been years.'

'It's been years,' Marissa said. 'So why stay together if you can't be happy? You should both go find people you're, I don't know, more compatible with.'

'It's not so easy,' Dana said, not sure if she meant going through a divorce, finding another man, or both.

'Oh, come on,' Marissa said. 'You're hot. Even Xan said so.'

'Really?' Dana needed the ego boost.

'Yes, really. His exact quote was "Your mom's hot."'

'Well, that was very nice of him, he's very sweet, but I'm not so confident about that. I think most men my age will be looking for women your age.'

'You didn't have any trouble hooking up with that guy Tony, and he's like, what, twenty years younger than you?'

'First of all, what happened between Tony and me was never serious, it's important for you to know that. I know Dad's going to make it out to you like I got into this actual relationship with another man, that that's why we're getting divorced, but that's not the way it is at all. I'm not *leaving* him. What's happening between us is mutual; it's not any one person's fault. And I want you to know how sorry I am that you had to find out about it the way you did. I know how upsetting that must've been for you.'

'Oh, pa-leeze,' Marissa said. 'You guys getting a divorce isn't exactly a bombshell. Besides, I already knew about you and Tony.'

'You did? How?'

'Hillary heard you and Sharon talking about it the other day. I still can't believe it, though, about Dad and Sharon. *That* was a real surprise. I mean, I just didn't see that one coming at all.'

Dana's eyes were getting teary, but she didn't want to start crying again, especially not in front of Marissa. She had to look away.

'Don't worry, Mom, it's gonna be okay. I told Dad that I think that was so wrong that he hooked up with Sharon. I mean, she's your friend, but Hillary's my friend, and it's just not right that he did that.'

Dana put an arm around Marissa and said, 'I just want to make sure you're okay with all of this. I don't want you to have resentment, toward me or your father.'

'Stop thinking about me,' Marissa said. 'Just do whatever you have to do, and I'll be fine.'

Dana couldn't hold back the tears now, and she leaned her head against her daughter's shoulder and sobbed.

Dana went back to her bedroom and got back into bed. She eventually dozed. When she woke up she was surprised that it was past six fifteen and that she'd been asleep nearly three hours, because she didn't feel at all rejuvenated.

Though she wasn't hungry and didn't feel like getting out of bed, she knew that eating something would probably be a good idea. She had mild hypoglycemia, and when she let her blood sugar get too low she got very anxious, irritable, and depressed.

Heading downstairs, she noticed that Marissa's room was empty. At the bottom of the staircase, in the foyer, she called out, 'Marissa!' but there was no answer. She probably went out to meet a friend or something.

Next door Blackie, the Millers' German shepherd, was barking loudly. Sometimes Blackie started barking at the mailman or at other delivery people.

Dana went to the kitchen and made a sandwich: turkey breast with lettuce and tomato on whole wheat. She really wasn't in the mood for food. She managed a few bites, then put the rest away in the fridge. She was loading the dishwasher when the back doorbell rang.

That was unusual. She and Adam and Marissa used the entrance occasionally, mainly when they parked in the driveway, but they almost always entered with a key. Her first thought was it was probably a delivery person, or Con Ed to inspect the meter. That would explain why Blackie was still barking so wildly. Dana wasn't expecting any deliveries, though, and didn't the Con Ed guy always ring the front doorbell?

She was too frazzled to think any of this through in any greater depth. She parted the curtain that covered the windowpane on the door and saw Xan. He was wearing dark sunglasses, and when he saw her peering through the glass he smiled widely and gave her a little wave.

She immediately let go of the curtain and thought, *Shit*. She couldn't let him in looking like this again. She was in a ratty T-shirt and baggy sweats and wasn't wearing a stitch of makeup.

'Um, one second!' she said, and she rushed upstairs.

As fast as she could she changed into jeans, a better bra, and a tighter long-sleeved black top, and then she put on lipstick and a little blush and pulled her hair back into a ponytail. She checked herself out in the mirror on the dresser. She still looked like crap, but it was better than nothing. Then she said, 'Shoes, shit,' and went for something with a little heel – black leather boots – and went back downstairs.

She opened the back door, and Xan smiled widely.

'Hey,' he said.

She'd forgotten how good-looking he was. He lifted his sunglasses and rested them on top of his head, and she was momentarily startled by the blueness of his eyes.

271

'Hi,' she said. 'I'm sorry about that. I was just, um, in the middle of something.'

Blackie was still barking like crazy.

'That's okay,' Xan said. 'I didn't mind waiting.'

'Marissa's not here right now,' Dana said. 'Would you like to come in?'

'If that's okay with you.'

'Of course it's okay.'

She let Xan by her and then closed the door and locked it.

'I don't know when Marissa left,' she said, 'or when she's coming back. Were you supposed to meet her soon?'

'Yeah, right about now, actually.'

'Oh, well, why don't you sit down? Can I get you something to drink?'

He remained standing, not far from the table, and asked, 'What do you have?'

'Whatever you'd like,' she said. 'Coke, Diet Coke, orange juice, water, iced tea…'

'Iced tea would be great.'

As she opened the fridge she had the same feeling she'd had the other night, that he was watching her, checking her out. She took out the jug of iced tea, and then, noticing that Xan was still standing, not sitting, she reached up to the cabinet to get a glass, saying, 'In the future, we usually use the front door.'

'Oh, sorry,' he said.

'No, no, it's no big deal at all,' she said. 'It's just sometimes hard to hear the back doorbell. I wish that damn dog would stop barking.'

'I rang the front bell, but no one answered,' Xan said.

'Oh,' Dana said, 'that's strange.'

She wondered if it was possible that he had rung the bell while she was still asleep. No, at least a couple of minutes had gone by from the time she woke up to the time the back doorbell rang.

Pouring the iced tea into the glass, she said, 'It really doesn't matter one way or the other.'

As she handed him the glass he said, 'Thank you.' He took a sip, then asked, 'So is Mr Bloom home?'

She wasn't sure why he was asking this, but she said, 'You

can call him Adam, but no, he's not here either.'

'And you said I can call you Dana, right?' He was smiling, looking right into her eyes.

'Yes,' she said, 'Dana's fine.'

'You didn't have to do all this for me, Dana.'

She was distracted momentarily by his intense gaze; then she said, 'All what for you?'

'Change, put on makeup,' he said. 'You didn't have to change just for me.' Now she felt embarrassed, on the spot, and she said, 'Actually I was in the middle of getting dressed when you rang and –'

'I'm just saying,' Xan said. 'You're the type of woman who doesn't have to do anything. You look beautiful no matter what.'

She was aware that he was being inappropriately flirty, but in the state she was in – on the verge of divorce, with her self-esteem in the toilet – it was hard not to feel flattered.

'Thank you,' she said.

'Can I ask you a personal question?' he asked.

Had he taken a step or two closer to her without her realizing? It seemed like he had.

'Um, sure,' she said.

'Are you attracted to me?'

'Excuse me?' She had an edge in her voice, wanting to let him know he'd crossed a very thick line.

'I'm not trying to offend you,' he said. 'I'm just making an observation. I'm just an artist, that's what I do – observe. I see the way you look at me, the way you were looking at me the other night, and the way you're looking at me right now. I know what's going on in your head.'

She was extremely uncomfortable and more than a little scared. This was not the same charming Xan from the other night. There was something creepy, even menacing, about him.

'I think you should wait for Marissa in the living room,' she said.

'I'm not trying to offend you, Dana.' He took another step toward her, but he was still a few feet away. He said, 'I just think it's, I don't know, exciting.'

'I want you to wait in the living room,' Dana said firmly.

'Why're you so nervous?' he asked.

'I'm not nervous,' she said, but she was trembling.

He took another step toward her and said, 'Relax.'

She noticed that she couldn't see one of his hands. It was behind his back; was he holding something?

An instant later he was grabbing her hard, turning her around, pushing her back facing the sink. She couldn't believe this was actually happening to her. She felt his hands grabbing her ponytail, pulling on it hard. She might've said, *Stop it*; she wasn't sure. She was dazed, shocked, too panicked to actually think the word 'rape,' but she knew that was what was happening, was about to happen. She was expecting him to take down her jeans when he grunted loudly and she felt an enormous stunning pain in the middle of her back and then her legs felt like they were gone and she was on the floor, and that red puddle, *God*, that must be her blood. The pain in her chest and back and neck was awful at first and she wanted to scream but she couldn't because something was suddenly clogging her throat. She saw him standing very far away, it seemed, watching her, saying, 'It's okay, baby, just let it go… let it go, baby… just let it go.'

19

THIS HAD TO be some kind of high point of Johnny Long's life. Maybe other great things would happen to him – hey, he was still young, right? – but it was hard to imagine living to eighty or ninety or whatever and looking back at his life and having a better memory than the time he totally fucked Dr Adam Bloom and his whole uppity family.

Everything had been going perfectly, even better than Johnny had planned. On Saturday Marissa had come over to his place, and they'd spent the day and night screwing and getting 'closer' to each other. They talked a lot, too. He was casual about it, but he picked up some important info about her and her parents and their habits that he hoped he could use later on. Like when she was talking about her father he slipped in questions like, 'Does your dad work every day?' and 'What time does he usually come home from work?' Not being obvious about it, just acting like he was curious, making small talk. She told him that Adam Bloom usually left for work at 'like eight o'clock' and came home 'like around seven or eight.' It turned out he'd need this info a lot sooner than he'd thought.

Marissa left his place at around eleven thirty on Sunday

morning. After two straight nights together, they were planning to spend the day and night apart to give him 'time to paint.' Johnny already knew that Adam was planning to play golf in the morning – the other night during dinner he'd mentioned he had a seven-thirty tee-off time – and Marissa had said that her mom was planning to go shopping at Costco, like she did every other Sunday. So Johnny figured that today could be the perfect opportunity to make his first move.

About twenty minutes after Marissa left, Johnny left. At 12:52 Johnny exited the Forest Hills subway station and headed toward the Blooms' house. He knew he was taking a risk. He was gambling that Dana had already left for Costco and wasn't home yet, and that Adam hadn't finished playing golf, and that Marissa had beat him to the house. If one of them saw him he'd have to make up an excuse for why he was at the house. If they all believed him, he could go on to plan B, but if they started getting suspicious, his whole plan would be in trouble.

The Blooms' Merc and SUV weren't in the driveway – a good sign. Johnny had already written a note from 'Tony from the gym,' and he slid it under the Blooms' front door. He was walking away when he saw Adam Bloom's Merc coming down the block, heading right toward him.

It was a good thing Johnny was paying attention, because if he'd taken another step or two, Bloom probably would've seen him. But Johnny turned quickly and went up the driveway.

Shit, now what? The backyard had tall picket fences on all sides with no real place to hide, and Bloom's car was going to turn into the driveway in maybe five seconds.

As a kid, Johnny had learned how to run away from the cops and kids who'd wanted to kick the shit out of him. He'd always been a great climber – fences, trees, he could climb anything. He leaped onto the fence and hoisted himself up. If he'd had more time he could've gotten over easily, but he couldn't find any good support for his feet, and the top of the fence had pointy wooden spikes. He could hear the car getting close, probably right about to turn into the driveway. Using all his strength, he pulled himself up and in the same motion managed to lift his legs up and swing them over the top of the fence. Then he let go with his hands, but he wasn't over yet. His leather jacket got caught on the top of the fence. He reached up, freed himself, and fell down hard on to his ass right as Bloom's car was heading up the driveway.

His ass and lower back killed, but he was fine. More important, he'd managed to make it over the fence just in time, without Bloom seeing him.

What did see him was a German shepherd in the house next door to the Blooms. The stupid mutt was on its hind legs, clawing at the window, trying to break through the glass. Johnny was going to stay where he was – the dog was in the house; it couldn't come after him – but, shit, what if somebody was in the house and came over to see why the dog was barking? The person would see Johnny in the backyard, huddled on the ground, in plain view.

Johnny got up, ran to the driveway of the house with the dog, and stayed as close to the house as he could, without moving at all, but the dog, the son of a bitch, had come to the side of the house and was barking, clawing against the window.

Then Johnny heard a woman's voice inside the house – there must've been a screen on the window – saying, 'What is it, Blackie?'

Johnny didn't think the woman would be able to see him, but he wasn't sure. She would definitely see him if she opened the screen and looked out. He couldn't run away, because he didn't know if Bloom had gone into his house yet, so he had to stay where he was and hope for the best.

'What? Where? I don't see anything,' the woman said, but the dog was still barking insanely. Then the woman said, 'Come on, just stop it… I said stop it right now.'

The dog wouldn't shut up, but the barking sounded farther away, like the woman was pulling the dog away from the window.

Johnny stayed there for a couple of minutes longer, just to make sure Bloom had gone into the house, and then he went to the sidewalk and turned left, away from the Blooms' house, and went back toward the commercial area of Forest Hills.

All in all, Johnny was happy with the way things had gone.

He'd accomplished what he'd wanted to, anyway, and now it was just a matter of going back home and seeing how it played out.

And it played out all right.

At around two o'clock, as he was getting off the subway in Brooklyn, Marissa called him, sounding like a mess, saying that her parents were in the middle of a big fight. Johnny acted confused, saying, 'A fight? What about?' Marissa said that her father had found out that her mother had been screwing her trainer and – get this – it turned out her father had been screwing somebody, too, the mother of Marissa's best friend. Johnny thought, *Man, what a fucked-up family*. The parents were cheating on each other, and the daughter was an unhappy spoiled brat. It was like they were all just begging for somebody to come along and put them out of their misery.

Johnny insisted that Marissa come back to his place to 'get away from all of that craziness.' Ah, was this beautiful or what? She was already so dependent on him, and they'd only known each other about a week. Johnny had pulled off some great hustles, but this time he was outdoing himself.

When Marissa arrived she hugged him tightly, like she never wanted to let go, and said, 'I'm only happy when I'm with you.'

Later, after screwing a couple of times, Marissa was sleeping, resting her head on Johnny's chest. But he was hyped up, wide awake, thinking about his plan, trying to work out every detail. This was so great, with Dana and Adam; now he had to make his big move, as soon as he could.

In the morning – it was Monday – Johnny suggested meeting Marissa later in Manhattan.

Johnny could tell Marissa loved the idea, but she said, 'Are you sure? I mean, I don't want you to get sick of me.'

'How could I possibly get sick of you?' he asked.

She blushed, then said, 'Seriously, maybe it's not such a great idea.'

'I want to see you again,' he said, 'and I think it's a good idea to give your parents some space, you know?'

This line had been unrehearsed, but it was so perfect.

'Yeah, you're probably right,' she said, 'and I'd like to be around them as little as possible myself, but I just don't want to impose on you.'

'Are you kidding?' he said. 'I want to spend as much time around you as I can. I'd spend every second with you if I could.'

She loved this. After they kissed for a while, she said, 'But I have to go home and shower and change and take care of some stuff first. I can meet you back here at around five.'

He knew she'd want to go home first. He said, 'I have an idea. Let's meet in the city at six thirty. We can grab a bite to eat, then go to a movie.'

She said this sounded great, and they arranged to meet outside the subway station at Fifty-ninth Street and Lexington Avenue.

Marissa left Johnny's at a little before one o'clock. He wanted to make his move today, but he needed to find out her parents' schedule. He didn't want to do this half-assed. He wanted to take care of every last detail.

He went to a phone booth about ten blocks away – he didn't want to make the calls from too close to his apartment – and called information and got the number of Dr Adam Bloom, PhD, in Manhattan. He called and asked the woman who answered if he could speak with Dr Bloom. The woman said that Dr Bloom couldn't come to the phone, he was with a patient. Of course Johnny would've hung up if Adam *had* been available; he said, 'That's okay, I'll call him later. What time will he be there till tonight?'

'His last patient's at five.'

Shit, that was too late. That meant Bloom might leave at six and be home at seven.

'Okay, thanks,' Johnny said.

The woman was saying, 'If you want to leave a number I'll –' as Johnny hung up.

Later, back at his apartment, Johnny called Marissa and asked if they could meet at seven thirty instead of six thirty.

'That's totally fine,' Marissa said. 'I was just about to call you. My friend Hillary wants to meet me for drinks at five thirty, and I thought six thirty was cutting it too close.'

This was so perfect. *She* was pushing back the plans.

'Cool,' Johnny said. 'There's an eight thirty movie so that's no problem at all.'

Actually, he had no idea what the movie schedule was, but he figured he could cover for this later if he had to.

'Great,' she said. 'Oh, God, I can't wait to see you. It's been another nightmare day here.'

She told him that she'd found out her parents were getting divorced – more great news as far as Johnny was concerned.

'So is your mom home now?' Johnny asked.

'Yeah,' she said. 'She was just in here asking me if I was okay with the divorce, if I was going to be traumatized by it.' She laughed, then asked, 'Why?'

He didn't think she was suspicious, she was just asking.

'Just curious,' he said, but he needed some explanation, so he added, 'I mean, do you think she and the trainer are still... getting together?'

'I don't know. She didn't look like she was going anywhere today. She looked like shit actually.'

'So you think she's staying in today?'

'Yeah, why?'

Now there was a little suspicion, and Johnny had to be careful. He didn't want this to be something that Marissa would look back on later and wonder about.

'I was just saying,' Johnny said. 'It would be bad if your father caught her and the trainer together.'

'Yeah, bad for my father,' Marissa said. 'But honestly I don't see how things could get any worse between them. It's about as worse as it can get right now.'

Yeah, right, Johnny thought, but he said, 'You've done a great job handling all of this so far. I'm so proud of you.'

At about four o'clock, Johnny left his apartment. He had everything he needed in his black backpack. He hunted around a while and finally found an older Saturn with no LoJack or alarm. He broke in, hot-wired it, and was on his way.

The drive to Forest Hills took longer than he expected because of rush hour traffic, but he was still doing okay on time. He parked in the closest spot he could find, about half a block away from the Blooms' house. From the car, he called Marissa to confirm that she was actually in the city with her friend Hillary, but he told her it was because he missed her and just wanted to hear her voice. He looked around carefully, and when he was pretty sure that no one was watching, he got out of the car and headed toward the Blooms'.

It was 6:22, and Adam was probably on the subway on his way home. Adding on fifteen minutes for rush hour and assuming he didn't stop off anywhere, he should arrive at the house in Forest Hills around seven o'clock. Johnny wanted Adam to come home after he killed Dana. If for some reason he came home much earlier it could be problematic.

Johnny was wearing black leather gloves and a black wool cap. It wasn't exactly hat-and-glove-wearing weather – it was in the fifties – but he wanted to disguise his appearance as much as possible. Besides, he knew Dana would be too distracted by his good looks and charm to notice anything else.

Nearing the house, he was especially careful to make sure no one was noticing him. A man at the far end of the block was leaving his car and heading into his house, but the man wasn't looking in Johnny's direction. Still, Johnny hesitated, walking at a slower pace, until the man went into his house, and then Johnny continued toward the Blooms'.

The SUV and the Merc were in the driveway – Johnny hoped this meant that Dana was home. He didn't want to ring the front doorbell and risk someone seeing her letting him into the house, so he went down the driveway toward the backyard. Johnny wouldn't have done this if he'd remembered about the dog. That crazy mutt must've heard him or sensed him or something, because when he was about halfway up the driveway the barking started. Johnny didn't see the point in turning back and ringing the front doorbell, and he wasn't concerned with the barking itself – he was worried about someone next door looking out the window and seeing him, then remembering this later and telling the police.

Going as fast as he could, he went to the Blooms' backyard, then up onto the small deck. From this position he was out of view from the house next door, and he didn't think he'd been seen.

He rang the doorbell, and several seconds later he saw Dana looking out. *Baby,* he thought, as he smiled wildly and gave her a little wave. But she held up one finger, like she'd be back in a second, and before he had time to say anything she was gone.

Shit, this was a complication Johnny didn't need. The dog was barking even louder, and although he was out of view of the house with the dog, he was in clear view of the backyard of the house of the Blooms' other next-door neighbor. If someone in that house heard the fuss the dog was making and came out onto the back porch, the person would see Johnny standing there.

What the hell was taking Dana so long? He knew she was probably changing, putting on makeup or something. It seemed like she'd been gone for ten minutes, but it probably hadn't been nearly that long.

He told her he was supposed to meet Marissa at the house. Of course she said Marissa wasn't there, but he didn't know if Marissa had told her mother about her plans to go into the city. If she had, Johnny was going to say they'd changed their plans, but Dana seemed totally clueless and invited Johnny in to wait.

He was glad to be inside the house, and the damn dog's barking was finally dying down. He turned on the charm so she wouldn't notice his gloves or that he looked like, well, like someone who was going to kill her. The way she was looking at him, acting all flirty, he knew she wanted him, and he could've seduced her. He would've loved to have added her to his long list of conquests. Man, would that have been a trip, to screw Adam Bloom's wife before he killed her? But Johnny wasn't an idiot. He knew that banging her would get him into all kinds of trouble with DNA, and he wanted to play this thing right.

Still, he wanted to have a little fun with this thing – if he couldn't actually screw her, at least he could make her think he was going to. Meanwhile, when she went to get him some iced tea, he grabbed a chef's knife, one that had about an eight-inch blade, from the knife rack on the counter. This was part of his plan, as he'd seen the knives when he was in the kitchen the other night. When she asked him to sit down he didn't, but she didn't seem to notice that he had the knife there behind his back. Then, what the hell, he told her how attracted he was to her, and he could tell she wanted him so badly, even if she was acting like she didn't. But he didn't want her to flip out, start screaming, so he decided to just get it over with.

He'd never killed with a knife before, but he'd killed with a switchblade and once with a shank that time at Rikers. He knew that the key to killing with any type of blade was to not be half-assed about it. Anybody could stick a knife a few inches into a body – hell, a weak old lady could probably give you a nice little wound. But to do serious damage you had to go all the way with it. You had to fight through that next inch or two of muscle and maybe bone so you could cut up the major arteries and organs. So when Johnny stabbed her in the middle of the back, he made sure he did it hard enough to get most of the blade in; then he pushed even harder, feeling it cut through something, and it went in easier. When he'd gotten about five or six inches of the blade in and it wouldn't go any farther, he let go of her.

He backed away, watching her squirm around in her blood on the kitchen floor. He hated watching her suffer. He would've loved to yank the knife out of her back and slit her throat or stab her right in the heart, get it over with, but he didn't want blood to splatter everywhere, especially on him. From what he could tell, he only had a little blood on his gloves and on the edge of the right sleeve of his sweatshirt, and he wanted to keep it that way.

The important thing was that although Dana was still alive and moaning and trying to crawl away, she wasn't actually screaming in pain, maybe because she was too weak and couldn't get the air into her lungs. The knife had probably gone into one of her lungs – or maybe there was too much blood coming up out of her mouth. So Johnny just stood back, waiting for her to bleed out, trying to make her feel better by saying things like 'Just let it go' and 'Stop fighting it.'

It really sucked that it was taking her so long to die. Eventually she stopped moaning, but she was still squirming. The suffering was hard to watch, but there was something about the blood that Johnny found, well, beautiful. Maybe he was starting to take this art shit too seriously, but the, what was that word, contract? No, contrast. Yeah, he loved the contrast of the bright red blood on the white tiled floor. Also, he loved the way the blood was spreading away from the body, the puddles expanding very slowly but keeping their perfect rounded shape. When he got home later he was going to try to re-create this scene, try to get this same shade of red. He'd probably have to mix a little white into the red, and he'd use oils, not acrylics. Maybe he'd do a whole series of paintings, call them his Bloodworks. Oh, man, was he a genius or what? He could see his paintings hanging at the Met – or what was that one across the street, the Prick? – and all the uppity art lovers going on and on about what a genius he was. Yeah, they would all be talking in big words about the 'message' of the paintings. He could hear them saying they were a comment on society, on 'our times.' They'd probably invite him to all their parties, all the rich people tripping over themselves, wanting to talk to the man who'd painted the Bloodworks.

Finally she stopped moving. He went up to her, getting as close as he could without stepping in the blood puddle, and looked at her face and saw her wide-open eyes and thought, *Yeah, she's dead. Finally.*

He left the knife right where it was, in her back, and then he took another knife from the rack. This one had a bigger blade – maybe closer to ten inches – and he stood back, waiting for Adam to show up.

It was 6:52 according to the clock on the stove. Hopefully Adam had left work at six after his last patient. If he came right home by subway he would be here any minute. When Johnny heard him coming in through the front door, he'd stay off to the side, in the nook between the table and the entrance to the dining room. Adam would see his wife on the floor and be distracted, and then Johnny would attack him. He would try to stab him as few times as possible, though he knew this would be harder with Adam because he'd fight back and it might be hard to get the blade deep enough into the heart or lungs. The key would be to kill him as fast as possible, before he had a chance to scream too much. If Johnny had to stab him three, four, five times or more to get this done, then so be it. The bottom line was he needed Dana and Adam to both be discovered dead, slashed to death, on their kitchen floor. Then the police would look to the obvious suspect – 'Tony from the gym.' Johnny felt sorry for fucking up the poor sucker's life, but what could you do?

Although Johnny didn't think he'd gotten any blood on his shoes, he didn't want to risk walking around the house. He looked at the body for a while, still loving that shade of red; then he looked over toward the blackboard where someone – probably Adam – had written *I want you to move out*.

This was almost too perfect. It was like the Blooms were helping, not only to get themselves killed but to give Johnny the perfect alibi. Their marriage was such a mess that the cops would go right to that Tony guy and arrest his ass. Johnny wanted to stay cool and in control, but it was hard not to feel excited. He was so close to the big prize, to getting everything he'd ever wanted, that he didn't feel like he was in the Blooms' house anymore. It was *his* house, and he couldn't wait to get rid of all the Blooms' stuff and then go on a spending spree, spend fifty grand – hell, why not a hundred or two hundred? – and fill it up with everything he'd ever wanted.

The only problem was that Johnny needed Adam dead and Adam wasn't showing up. Johnny figured Adam must've left his office at about six, and even if he walked very slowly to the subway, the trip to Forest Hills wouldn't take him more than an hour. He hoped nothing was wrong with the subways and that Adam didn't have other plans this evening. Johnny had done everything he could to make this plan go as smoothly as possible, but some things were beyond his control.

At seven o'clock, about fifteen minutes since Dana had died, there was still no sign of Adam. To keep his alibi, Johnny had to meet Marissa at seven thirty. He could be a few minutes late, but he didn't want to arrive any later than seven forty, seven forty-five the absolute latest. If he was too late, it could be something Marissa would wonder about, and he didn't want any complications.

Johnny was staring at his watch, telling himself that he'd

give it another ten minutes, till ten after seven, and then he'd take off, when the phone rang. The noise startled him, and for a second he even thought that the house's alarm had gone off. After four rings, either the caller hung up or the answering machine answered. Johnny waited till seven ten, then gave it another five minutes, but he couldn't wait any longer. He decided to look at the bright side – the day hadn't been a total bust; at least he'd gotten rid of one of the Blooms. One down, two to go.

Johnny had brought a full change of clothes in his backpack, including another pair of shoes, his leather jacket, and another pair of leather gloves. But since he didn't think he'd gotten any blood anywhere except on his sweatshirt, all he needed was the jacket.

He put the unused knife back in the rack. As he took off his sweatshirt, pulling it up over his head, he thought about hairs and fibers from his hat and DNA evidence. He tried to be as careful as possible, but even if a piece of hair fell out onto the floor he didn't see why this would be any big deal. It wasn't like he hadn't been in the house before. Why couldn't the hair have fallen out the other day?

Just in case, when he had the sweatshirt off he crouched down and looked around. Nope, no hairs.

He put on his leather jacket and leather gloves and then put the sweatshirt away in the backpack. Walking around the body and the blood, he left the kitchen and went through the house toward the front entrance. It sucked that he couldn't leave through the back, where he was much less likely to be noticed, but he didn't want to risk the dog making a racket again.

Outside it had gotten totally dark. He opened the front door cautiously. If Bloom was there, Johnny would have to do something to get rid of him. He'd have to strangle him, crack his head open, something like that. He had his gun with him, but he didn't want to shoot him. If the cops found Dana with a knife in her back and Adam with a bullet in his head, they might not focus on Tony as the suspect. Johnny needed the cops to think that Tony had taken the knife and impulsively stabbed Dana. But if Adam got shot the cops might think, *Why didn't*

Tony use the gun on Dana? See, Johnny was always thinking, he was always one step ahead.

When Johnny looked out toward the street, Adam wasn't in sight. The coast seemed clear in both directions, and he didn't hear any cars coming, so he calmly left the house and then turned right and headed down the block to the Saturn. He pulled out and turned onto the main street and, son of a bitch, there was Adam, walking along the sidewalk, holding two bags of groceries.

Johnny hoped the asshole knew how lucky he was.

20

ON HIS WAY to work Adam made an emergency appointment with Carol. Reaching her on her cell – she was on a Metro North train, en route from her home in New Rochelle – he told her that he was in the midst of a 'major crisis' and had to meet with her immediately.

'My schedule's full today,' she said.

'I have to see you,' he said desperately. 'My life's falling apart.'

She called him back a few minutes later, saying that she'd postponed her ten o'clock appointment so that she could meet with him.

It was the most difficult session Adam had had in years. As he described to Carol everything that had happened yesterday after he returned from his golf game, he broke down crying several times, especially when he described how 'enraged' and 'out of control' he'd felt. Naturally Carol was very detached and supportive. When patients were in the midst of a crisis it was important to let them express themselves, and it was no time for a therapist to intrude with 'solutions.' Carol mainly listened, maintaining the constant highly concerned expression that all therapists mastered, as he went on, except during the times he was most upset, when she gave him generic tidbits of support, telling him that it was 'natural' to act the way he did and that he didn't have to 'apologize for his feelings.' When he was through with his venting she challenged him a bit more, but still remained very supportive, telling him that he'd felt hurt and betrayed and assuring him that he'd acted the best he could under the circumstances.

As the session continued, Adam became increasingly agitated, frustrated, and annoyed. This was one of those situations where Adam was hyperaware of the therapeutic process, so much so that he felt it was impossible to make any true inroads. He didn't want to be coddled and manipulated by his analyst. He didn't want to buy into the idea that his behavior had been justified, that he'd done the right thing. He knew he'd acted like a total schmuck yesterday. He'd been out of control, in a reactive state, and had expressed his anger extremely poorly. Picking the fight with Tony had been bad enough, but then he'd made another extremely poor decision by revealing his affair with Sharon. There had been no reason to drag her into it, possibly damaging her marriage and compounding the hurt for Dana and even Marissa.

'This isn't working,' Adam announced.

Carol, completely unfazed, giving her patient the room to express himself, asked, 'What isn't working?'

'This,' Adam said. 'What you're doing right now. I know what you're doing, because I'd be doing exactly the same thing. You're trying to treat me, and I don't want to be treated.'

'What do you want?'

'I want solutions, I want answers, but I'm never going to get them this way.'

'How can you get them?'

'See? You can't stop analyzing me, not even for a second. Analysis won't work on me. I can help other people, I *know* I've helped other people, but I need to be told what to do, I need to be fixed. I'm screwing up my whole life right now, and I feel like I can't stop myself. I feel like I'm addicted to very negative behavior.'

'You know I can't tell you what to do, Adam.'

'Can't you just talk to me like a normal human being?'

'If you wanted to talk to a normal human being you wouldn't've called me this morning.'

There was a long pause; then they both laughed, a nice icebreaker.

'Fine, you want me to help you. You don't need my help. How's that for help?'

'I'm not a victim, right? I'm in control of my life, it's not controlling me.'

'See? You have all the answers.'

'But knowing this doesn't help me.'

'That's a decision you're making. Do you really want your marriage to end?'

'No,' he said without hesitation, and at that moment he felt he'd made a breakthrough. True breakthroughs were rare in the therapeutic process, but in his experiences with his own patients he'd seen them come at the least expected times. In his case, by confronting Carol about his lack of progress he'd ironically made more progress than he had in years.

Adam desperately needed a day off to process his feelings, but he couldn't go home. Although he'd gotten more cancellations and no-shows, he still had several patients scheduled. In his current mindset, it was difficult to take on the role of therapist and counsel other people, but he did his best to be attentive, and he managed to get through the day.

After his last patient, he did some insurance paperwork, then left his office at about six fifteen. When he left the subway station in Forest Hills he called home. He wanted to apologize to Dana for giving her the silent treatment and for leaving that note on the blackboard, but the machine answered. He wondered if she was home but was screening his calls. He was going to leave a message or say something like 'If you're there, pick up, I need to speak to you,' but he ended the call, figuring he'd see her in a few minutes anyway.

He stopped at a grocery store and did some shopping for the house. There was a long line at the checkout counter, and then the woman ahead of him disputed the price of a canister of coffee, so the cashier – who seemed new – had to do a price check. She paged the manager, but it took several minutes for him to come over and then several more minutes for him to find the actual price and remove the overcharge. Finally Adam checked out and headed home.

He couldn't wait to see Dana, to start communicating with her again. He'd had enough of the childish behavior of the past couple of days and it was time to act like an adult and confront this situation head-on. He knew it wouldn't be easy. He planned to apologize to her for his inappropriate behavior – while not blaming her for hers – and suggest that they go into counseling. He still felt angry and betrayed, but he felt like he was ready to reach out to Dana and make a recommitment to the marriage. If it turned out they couldn't resolve their differences, then so be it, but he felt it was important to at least make a serious attempt.

He entered the house, noticing that the lights were on upstairs and in the kitchen but the rest of the house was dark.

'Dana!'

No answer.

He called out, 'Dana!' a little louder, but there was still no response. He figured she probably heard him loud and clear and was just giving him the silent treatment to get back at him for the way he'd treated her last night and this morning. She often played childish revenge games, though in this situation he couldn't blame her.

But then, as he was hanging up his coat in the hall closet, he thought, *What if she's with Tony*? It certainly wasn't beyond the realm of possibility that they'd decided to continue their affair. People in full-blown affairs often found it extremely difficult to break up with their lovers. A patient had once told Adam that having to end an affair was one of the most painful experiences of his life, on par with the deaths of his parents.

'Dana!' he called upstairs. 'Dana, are you there?'

The house was almost completely silent; the only noise was the wind rattling the dining room windows.

He tried not to get too upset. After all, nothing had actually happened. He'd simply made up a scenario in his head and was reacting to it. He had to be aware of his anger and monitor its effect. As he often reminded his patients, feelings were fleeting.

No one stayed angry forever, and no one stayed happy forever, so if you became too attached to your emotions you were setting yourself up for disappointment.

Feeling in control, in what he sometimes referred to as an even-keel state, he entered the kitchen.

At first, he didn't know what he was looking at. He just knew that it was something strange, something he'd never seen before. He registered the bright red liquid and the body – a woman's body – and the knife in her back.

It took at least another ten seconds before it hit him that he was staring at his dead wife.

He didn't even know how the police had gotten here. He didn't remember calling them; he could barely remember anything since discovering Dana's body. It was like trying to remember a dream he'd almost forgotten.

'Dr Bloom?'

Adam focused on Detective Clements's face. Clements was standing, and Adam was sitting on the living room couch next to a guy in a navy hospital uniform.

'I need to talk to you, just for a few minutes,' Clements said. 'Is that okay?' Then he said to the guy next to Adam, 'Is it okay if I talk to him now?'

'His pressure's still high, but he should be all right,' the hospital guy said, getting up, then heading out toward the foyer.

Like on the night of the robbery, the house was filled with cops, detectives, and crime scene technicians. Now Adam remembered calling 911, screaming into the phone, frustrated that the woman on the other end didn't seem to understand him.

'I appreciate you taking a few moments to talk to me,' Clements said. 'I know how difficult this is for you right now, but we have to move fast on this thing, and what you tell me right now could be crucial to our investigation. So I'm just gonna ask you a few very brief questions, okay?'

Adam nodded. He felt like he was barely there.

Clements asked a question, and Adam actually couldn't process what he was saying. He watched his lips moving and heard the words, but the only words he actually understood were 'time' and 'discover.'

'What was that?' Adam asked.

'I said, what time did you discover your wife's body?'

'Oh.' Adam was still confused. 'I don't know.'

'You have to focus on this, Dr Bloom... I know how hard this is.'

'You know how hard this is,' Adam said flatly.

'Excuse me?'

'You said you know how hard this is.' Adam laughed, but not in an amused way. 'Sorry, but I doubt you know how hard this is, Detective.'

'You're right,' Clements said. 'I have no idea how hard this is, but you have to bear down now, focus as well as you can just for a few minutes and tell me what I need to know. Do you think you can do that for me, Dr Bloom?'

Adam hated the way Clements was talking down to him.

'I told you about him yesterday,' Adam said. 'I told you he left the notes, I told you he might've robbed our house. Did you even bother to look into any of this?'

'Yes, we did, Doctor.'

'You could've prevented this from happening,' Adam said. 'You could've arrested him, you could've done something.'

'I understand your frustration, but we can't simply go arrest somebody because we *think* he might've done something.'

'I told you about the notes, and look what he did to me, for chrissake. How do you think I got these bruises on my face?'

'I was going to ask you about your face.'

'Tony did this to me yesterday at the health club. I was angry when I saw the note, so I went over there to... to talk to him, and this is what he did to me.'

'You didn't mention he hit you when you called me last night.'

'I didn't?' Adam thought he had, but maybe he hadn't. It was hard to think clearly about anything right now.

'Maybe if you'd mentioned that, we could've held him on assault or at least would've had a reason to question him longer than we did. But I did talk to him yesterday, went to his apartment actually. I asked him where he was last Thursday, the day you received the first note, and he claimed he was on Long Island that whole day, helping his brother-in-law paint his house. We checked this out, and I didn't think there was any reason to believe he was lying. Also, he claimed he didn't leave any note at your house yesterday.'

'Come on, that's bullshit.' Adam was practically yelling. 'He left the note, he left both notes, and then he came over here and killed my wife.'

'Okay, try to stay calm, Dr Bloom. We're one step ahead of you, okay? We're picking Tony Ferretti up right now, and we're gonna check him out thoroughly, okay? If he's our guy we're not gonna let him get away, okay?'

'He is the guy,' Adam said. 'I know he is.'

'What I need to know from you,' Clements said, 'is do you have any evidence that Tony was in the house today? I mean, did your wife tell you she was expecting him? Do you know if he called her at some point or came by to talk to her?'

Adam suddenly felt dazed and disoriented.

'You okay, Doctor?'

'Yeah, fine,' Adam said. 'What was the question?'

Clements repeated it; then Adam said, 'I don't know, I have no idea.'

'We'll be looking at the phone records, et cetera,' Clements said. 'I just thought you might've heard something, or overheard someth –'

'I didn't hear anything,' Adam said, 'but I know he did it. How could it be any more obvious?'

Clements didn't seem convinced. He asked, 'Where's the note you think Tony left yesterday?'

'It's upstairs… top drawer of my dresser.'

Clements called another detective over and told him to go up and get the note. 'Handle it like it's evidence,' he said.

'I'm feeling very anxioius,' Adam said. 'I need more Valium.'

'You're going to be okay,' Clements said.

'I need a higher dosage,' Adam said. 'I'm telling you, he didn't give me enough before.'

The EMT guy overheard Adam and was about to come over, but Clements held up his hand, making the stop signal, and said to Adam, 'You're going to be fine, okay? Just relax, try to stay focused, okay? When was the last time you saw your wife?'

'This morning,' Adam said, 'when I went to work. She was still asleep.'

'And did you talk to her during the –'

'No,' Adam said, 'but I was planning to.' He suddenly felt incredibly guilty for treating Dana so harshly yesterday. He was aware of why he'd treated her the way he had, but this didn't make it seem any better. He had to take a few moments to compose himself before he said, 'I was planning to try to talk to her and I… I made a mistake yesterday, confronting Tony, and I said some incredibly hurtful things to her and… can I please have some more Valium? I'm telling you, the dosage was too low.'

'What time did you come home this evening?' Clements asked, ignoring Adam.

'I'm not sure,' Adam said.

'You called nine-one-one at seven thirty-five,' Clements said. 'So did you discover the body as soon as you came home?'

Adam remembered the shock of entering the kitchen, seeing the body on the floor, not knowing what it was at first.

'Yes,' Adam said weakly.

'Yes what?' Clements asked.

'I discovered the body right away. Can't you get me some more –'

'Did you drive to work today?'

'No… I never drive. I took the subway.'

'Did you notice anything suspicious on your way home from the subway? Anything that just didn't seem right?'

He thought about it, or tried to, anyway, then said, 'No, nothing.'

'So let me get this straight,' Clements said. 'You came home, discovered the body, then called nine-one-one.'

'Right,' Adam said, aware of his heart racing. He needed more Valium – now.

'So when did you go over and touch the body?'

Adam was confused. 'Touch it?'

'You told the nine-one-one operator you checked to see if

your wife was dead. That's how you got that blood on your sleeves, isn't it?'

Adam looked at his shirt's sleeves, surprised to see the smears of blood – *Dana's* blood. He felt dizzy and thought he might even pass out.

'I really need more Valium,' he said. 'I'm having an anxiety attack.' Clements waved over the EMT guy, who gave Adam another couple of milligrams of Valium.

Adam had barely finished swallowing the pill and still felt very dizzy when Clements said, 'So, about the blood…'

Clements's total lack of empathy astonished Adam. He waited a few seconds, then said, 'I think it was right after I saw her. I was in shock, naturally, and I went over to her, just to, I don't know, see if there was something I could do.'

Adam realized he hadn't cried at all since discovering the body and that he should be crying, releasing tension.

'I know it's upsetting,' Clements said. 'But the sooner we can get through this, the sooner I can leave you alone to deal with your grief, okay?'

Deal with your grief, like grief was something you could simply deal with – cross it off your checklist and ta-da, you could move on. Did they teach heartlessness at the police academy? Adam didn't bother responding. His head hurt, and he was still dizzy; when would that damn Valium kick in?

'There was a message on the blackboard in the kitchen,' Clements said. 'It says, "I want you to move out." Who wrote that?'

'I did,' Adam said.

'So you and your wife were planning to split up?'

Again Adam felt extremely guilty for the way he'd treated Dana over the past couple of days, for handling the whole situation so poorly. If he hadn't confronted Tony, maybe Tony wouldn't have come over here tonight and maybe Dana would still be alive.

'I was very upset this morning, about her and Tony,' Adam said, 'but I was planning to…' He cleared his throat, took a couple of breaths, then continued, 'I was planning to try to work things out with her. I didn't want to leave her. I wanted to stay in the marriage.'

'Did you come straight home from work tonight, Dr Bloom?'

Was Adam imagining it or was there a change in Clements's tone? Did he sound harsher, even vaguely accusing?

'Yes, I did,' Adam said. 'Why?'

'What time did you leave your office?'

'After my last patient.'

'When was that?'

'About six. No, it was later, six fifteen.'

'So you left at six fifteen and called nine-one-one at seven thirty-five, shortly after you discovered the body. Is that correct?'

'Yes, but I stopped off to go shopping at the grocery store on my way home.'

'I thought you came directly home?'

Now there was nothing vague about it.

'Excuse me?' Adam asked.

'I'm just trying to get all the facts, Dr Bloom.'

'Why does it matter if I stopped to go shopping or I didn't stop to go shopping?'

'Please just answer my questions.'

'This is absurd,' Adam said. 'It's bad enough that you guys never solved the robbery and you removed the cops who were doing surveillance or protection or whatever, but now you come in here, knowing what's happened to me today, and you have the balls to accuse me of...' He couldn't say it, so he said, 'Are you out of your mind? Are you fucking insane?'

It felt great to scream, to vent, to curse. This wasn't necessarily the most productive way to express anger, but sometimes it was necessary.

'You're going to have to calm down, Dr Bloom.'

'Calm down? How can I calm down when you won't even give me enough goddamn Valium?'

'If you'd just relax –'

'You know, instead of wasting my time talking to me you should be talking to Tony, the guy who killed my wife. I'm the victim here –'

'And I'm running this investigation,' Clements said, raising his voice authoritatively. He paused, letting this sink in, obviously getting off on the power trip, then said, 'I'll decide what questions I ask and to whom I ask them, okay? Now, I'll ask again, how long were you at the grocery store, Dr Bloom?'

Adam answered the rest of Clements's annoying questions. He told him that he'd been at the grocery store for about fifteen minutes and that he didn't speak to anyone while he was shopping and that after he finished shopping he went directly home.

'So I just want to make sure I'm getting all of this. You left work at six fifteen and, taking into account the length of the subway ride and the time you were shopping, would you say it took you about an hour to get from work to your house?'

'That sounds about right.'

'So then there's about a twenty-minute gap between the time you got home and the time you called nine-one-one.'

Adam remembered that after he'd discovered the body he'd sat on the floor in the hallway outside the kitchen, staring straight ahead, stunned. He had no idea how long he'd been there.

'It might've taken me longer than an hour to get home,' Adam said.

'But you said you didn't call nine-one-one right away,' Clements said.

'I was in shock,' Adam said. 'I couldn't react right away.'

'You were in shock for twenty minutes?' Clements sounded incredulous.

It took a few extra seconds for Adam to register Clements's question. Maybe the Valium was finally working.

'It might not've been twenty minutes,' Adam said. 'It might've been only five... or ten.'

'Well, thanks for your patience,' Clements said. 'I'll be in touch a little later, and I really am sorry for your loss.'

Clements left, and Adam sat alone on the couch, watching the activity in the house. Clements was talking to another cop, and there was a technician nearby who seemed to be looking around for fingerprints or other evidence. For a while, Adam felt like an observer, completely removed, like he was watching a movie. He thought, *This has nothing to do with me. This isn't even happening.*

Then, after a few minutes, he realized that although the scene was surreal, he was very much a part of it. Dana was dead, and, even worse, he was a suspect. Maybe not the prime suspect, but still a suspect. Adam couldn't blame Clements for focusing on him, as there was certainly plenty of circumstantial evidence. His marriage had been on the verge of imploding, he'd been behaving erratically lately to say the least, and, oh, let's not forget the blood on his shirt – that really made him look great. As far as the police were concerned, Adam already had exhibited homicidal tendencies by shooting and killing Carlos Sanchez the other night, so why not explore the idea that he'd murdered his wife? Besides, when a woman is killed, the husband always has to be ruled out as a suspect, so it was completely understandable that Clements was questioning him.

But it amazed Adam that he'd reached this low point in his life. How had it happened? Just a couple of weeks ago things had been going so well for him. Okay, he and Dana had had some unresolved marital issues, but so did practically every other couple in the world, especially people who'd been married for longer than twenty years. And, yes, Marisssa had been going through her own age-appropriate problems, but for the most part they'd been a happy, together family up until the night that Marissa woke them up and told them that someone had broken into their house. That, in retrospect, had been the big turning point, the moment when everything had begun to go to hell.

Marissa, Adam thought. He had to tell her.

He took out his cell but couldn't make the call. How do you tell your daughter that her mother's been killed? *Violently* killed. Her life would never be the same; she'd have to go through years of therapy just to begin to deal with it, and he felt awful for compounding the hurt, giving her such a hard time with all of that tough love crap. It was clear to him now how inappropriately he'd been behaving toward her lately. He'd been displacing his emotions, punishing her rather than punishing himself. Why had it bothered him so much that she'd had a bong in the house when she barely smoked? Had that really been such a monumental issue? Adam actually regretted that he'd thrown the bong out the other day. He could've used a few hits himself right now.

He wasn't sure he could handle making the phone call and was going to ask a cop to make it for him, but then he forced himself to do it on his own. She deserved to hear the news from her father rather than a complete stranger.

He couldn't reach her and didn't want to leave a message, so he ended the call and figured he'd try again in a little while. She was probably out with Xan. He was glad she had a boyfriend now, a good solid guy. She'd need him to help her get through this.

Adam walked slowly through the house, for some reason hearing in his mind the chorus of Pink Floyd's *Comfortably Numb*. Maybe he had chosen this song because the lyrics reminded him of his current state of mind, or perhaps it was because it reminded him of being a teenager, when he'd lived in this very house, in a much safer, more comfortable time in his life. Jesus Christ, could he stop being an analyst for one minute? Why did everything have to mean something else? Why couldn't he just accept things for what they were?

He peered into the kitchen, looking beyond the crime scene tape, and saw the investigators at work. Dana's body was still there, on the floor, and a photographer was busy, taking pictures. Adam barely felt anything, and as he drifted semi-aimlessly back toward the front of the house, he was aware that he was still in shock. He had counseled many patients during their grieving processes and was a proponent of Kubler-Ross's five stages of grief. Still, it hadn't even begun to set in, truly set in, that Dana had been murdered. Now her death was simply a concept. It was something he could say and think, but he was unable to actually feel it or comprehend the consequences.

In the living room, he lifted a venetian blind and peeked outside. He expected to see reporters, but he was astonished by how many there were. It was like a presidential news conference. One reporter spotted Adam and shouted, 'There he is!' and there was a sudden frenzy of reporters talking at once, some yelling for Adam to come outside. Horrified, Adam dropped the blind and moved away from the window. Unlike after the robbery, he had no interest in attention from the media. He had no desire for fame; he hoped he never had to see his name in print in any publication ever again. But he knew they wouldn't just leave him alone, and it didn't matter if he made a statement or not. Their stories were probably already written. The wife of Adam Bloom, the crazed vigilante, had been found dead with a knife in her back in the middle of her kitchen floor. What more did they need to know?

Adam was suddenly dizzy again. As he made his way back through the house a cop asked, 'You okay?' but Adam ignored him and sat at the dining room table. The Valium wasn't working; he needed Xanax or Klonopin. He was through thinking that he was superhuman, that he could handle crises better than the average person. Just because he was a psychologist, because he was aware of his thought processes, didn't make him immune from normal human emotions. These last couple of weeks had humbled him, taught him that he was no better off than his most troubled patients. He was a weak, confused man, and he wasn't going to make it through this nightmare without some serious drugs.

301

21

MARISSA WAS WITH Xan in the movie theater on Third and Fifty-ninth, watching the new Matthew McConaughey comedy, when her phone vibrated. She saw DAD on the display and rolled her eyes and turned off the phone. She figured he was just checking up on her, being Mr Controlling again, trying to make her life as miserable as possible. She snuggled closer to Xan and resumed making out with him.

After the movie, Xan went to use the bathroom. Waiting for him in the lobby, Marissa checked her phone and saw her father had left two messages. She was starting to read texts her friends had sent her when her dad called again. She picked up and said, 'I was just about to call you.'

'I have some awful news,' he said.

She thought, *What now? More about their freaking divorce?* She didn't understand why she had to be constantly dragged into the middle of her parents' marital problems, why she had to be updated on every single development.

'Look, I really don't want to get involved,' she said. 'You two do whatever you want to do.'

She was about to end the call when her father said, 'It's about Mom.'

He was probably calling to tell her that her mom was moving out, or had already moved out. And of course he had to speak in that grave, serious tone, trying to scare her, acting like this was some kind of life-and-death situation.

And to think, this was coming from a man who'd been telling her that *she* liked to cause drama.

'Yeah, I know it's about Mom, and it's really none of my business, Dad. Is that why you had to call me three times in the middle of a movie? Because Mom's moving out? Couldn't you've just waited to tell me at home, or not at all?'

'Mom's dead,' her father said.

'What?' She thought she must've misheard him.

'She's dead,' he repeated. 'You have to come home right away, the police're still here. Is Xan with you?'

'What the fuck are you talking about?' She seriously didn't get it. Dead? What the hell did that mean? Did he mean their marriage was dead?

'You have to come home, Marissa. Right away.'

Xan was back from the bathroom.

Marissa yelled into the phone, 'Tell me what the hell is going on! Just tell me! Tell me!'

People were looking at her. A security guard in a red jacket tapped Marissa on the shoulder and said, 'You're gonna have to keep it down, ma'am.'

'She was stabbed,' her father said. 'You have to come home. Have Xan take you. I don't want you to be alone.'

In the cab to Forest Hills, Marissa was out of control, crying and screaming. She still didn't believe any of this was actually happening. It had to be a misunderstanding – had her dad really said 'dead'? Maybe he'd said some other word that sounded like 'dead.' She always got shitty reception on her cell phone; yeah, it had to be something like that.

Thank God Xan was with her. He kept reassuring her, telling her 'Everything's gonna be okay' and 'You'll get through this no matter what, I promise.' He was so calm, so in control, so supportive; without him she would've completely lost it.

When the cab approached the house and she saw all the police cars, the ambulance, the news trucks, the swarm of reporters, reality hit hard. She was crying uncontrollably, and even with Xan's arm around her she lost her balance a few times and stumbled on her way toward the house. When the reporters spotted them, they rushed over and surrounded them, shouting questions. She kept her head down, unable to speak, as Xan continued to steer her toward the house, asking the reporters to 'stay back' and to 'please respect the girl's privacy.'

Finally they made it inside. She thought she'd feel relief, but, Jesus, it was like the night of the robbery all over again. Cops, strangers, were everywhere. Then her dad came over, and her first thought was *He's like a child*. There was something about him that reminded her of a picture she'd seen of him as a little boy. It was the one of him on the beach, maybe Fire Island, where he had just been crying about something and he looked so weak, so sad, so vulnerable.

He held her tightly and they cried in each other's arms for a long time. She was thinking about how much she missed her mother, how she couldn't believe she was actually gone; she'd never see her again, and her father was all she had now. Her mom's family was scattered around the country and had never been very involved in her life, and on her father's side her closest relative was her grandma Ann, who was in her eighties and had serious heart trouble. So her dad was pretty much it. She was hugging her entire family.

'We'll be okay,' her dad said. 'We'll get through this.'

She was aware of how appropriately upset her father sounded. There was none of that weird self-delusion and denial. He was having a normal reaction.

They sobbed on each other's shoulders, and then her father said, 'I love you, Marissa. I love you so much.'

After a while, Marissa looked over and saw that Xan was standing a few feet away, and he was crying, too. She went over and hugged him, and then he went over to her father and gave him a big tight hug.

'I'm so sorry, Adam,' Xan said. 'I'm so so sorry.'

Marissa was watching her father and Xan consoling each other when one of the cops left the kitchen. As the door swung open, she caught a glimpse of blood on the floor and part of her mother's leg, and she wailed uncontrollably, 'No, Mommy, no, no! No, no, no, no, no!'

It took a long time before her father, Xan, and some EMT guy could calm her down. They took her into the living room, and she was sitting with Xan on the couch when that asshole Detective Clements came over and said he had to talk to her. This was the last thing she was in the mood to do, but she knew she had no choice.

'Can my boyfriend stay with me?' she asked.

'Yeah, that'll be fine,' Clements said. Then he turned toward her father, who was standing nearby. 'But I'd rather you wait in the other room, Dr Bloom.'

Her father seemed pissed off, and Marissa didn't get why Clements was dismissing him. It was probably some power trip; the guy was such a prick.

Her father left, and, with Xan holding her hand, Marissa answered Clements's questions. At first, it was pretty much stress-free because she didn't have much to tell him. She explained that the last time she saw her mother was at about three this afternoon before her mother went to take a nap, and that when she left her mother was still sleeping. No, she hadn't heard her mother talk to anyone on the phone, and no, no one had been inside the house when she left.

But then he asked about her parents, if they'd been fighting a lot lately. She told him that there had been a lot of their usual bickering until they'd revealed their affairs.

'Affairs?' Clements asked. 'Plural?'

'Yeah, they both cheated on each other.'

'Really?'

Marissa didn't get why Clements was interested in this or what this had to do with finding out who'd killed her mother.

'You know about my mother and Tony, right?'

'Yes, your father told me about that, but I didn't know he was having an affair as well.'

'Yeah, with my friend Hillary's mother, Sharon.'

'Sharon what?' Clements had a pad out.

'Wasserman,' Marissa said.

'Do you know how I can get in touch with her?'

Marissa gave him her phone number, then asked, 'But why do you care about my father and Sharon?'

'It's important for us to know everything that was going on in your mother's life,' Clements said.

Marissa didn't buy this and felt like Clements was really trying to find a motive for her father killing her mother. She was shocked and looked over at Xan, who she could tell felt the same way she did. It was great the way they could communicate without speaking. They were like an old married couple already.

Clements asked her if her mother had seemed worried or had mentioned anything about her life being in danger, and she said, 'No, definitely not. She seemed normal. Well, depressed and upset about the divorce, but normal.'

'And today she didn't tell you about any plans to see Tony Ferretti? Or express any fears about seeing Tony Ferretti?'

Marissa was shaking her head. 'No, there was nothing like that at all.'

'Getting back to your father,' Clements said. 'During their arguments, did you ever get the sense that your mother was, well, afraid of your father? Or did she ever tell you she was afraid of him, or tell you that he threatened her in any way, or that she felt threatened?'

'I don't believe this,' Marissa said. 'You're not seriously asking me this, are you?'

'Did she or didn't she?' Clements asked.

Slack-jawed, Marissa looked at Xan, then back at Clements and said, 'No, she didn't.'

'Have you ever seen your father hit your mother or threaten to hit her?'

'No, never,' she said firmly. Then she remembered a time when there had been some violence between her parents.

Clements must've noticed her change in expression, because he asked, 'Did he or didn't he?'

'No, not really,' Marissa said. 'I mean, I think he pushed her once.' Clements's eyes widened. 'Really? When was this?'

Why had Marissa brought this up when it meant absolutely nothing? What was wrong with her?

'It was nothing,' she said. 'It's just when I was in high school. My parents were arguing one time and my father pushed my mother and she fell. But it was an accident. He wasn't trying to hurt her or anything.'

'What about more recently?' Clements asked.

'No, and this is crazy. My father didn't kill my mother, okay? He loved her. I mean, I know they were getting divorced, but he still loved her. He cared about her – very, very much.'

Marissa's voice trailed off as she started crying again. Xan quickly had his arm around her and was holding her tightly. After a few more questions, Clements told her she could go.

Later, in the foyer, when Clements was in another room, Marissa's father came over to her and asked her how the questioning had gone.

'Fine,' she said. It was hard to maintain eye contact. 'I mean, I didn't really have anything to tell him. He wanted to know if I knew if Mom talked to Tony today, and I said I didn't think so.'

'Well, I just heard that the police took Tony in for questioning, so hopefully we'll have a confession soon.'

'Yeah, hopefully,' Marissa said.

She and her father hugged, but she didn't feel as close to him as she had before.

'You should go lie down, try to get some rest,' he said.

'I can't stay here tonight,' she said.

'I was thinking about going to a hotel, too,' Adam said, 'but do we really want to deal with all of the reporters out there? Besides, Clements said the cops'll be here all night. Until we figure out what's going on, the house is the safest place we can be.'

'Whatever, I guess I'll stay,' Marissa said. Then she said to Xan, 'If you have to go home, I understand.'

'Are you kidding me?' Xan said. 'There's no way I'm leaving you alone tonight.'

Marissa managed a smile and said, 'I have no idea what I would've done without you here.'

'I want to thank you, too,' her father said, 'for taking such good care of my daughter.'

'No thanks necessary,' Xan said. 'It's the least I could've done.'

Not surprisingly, Marissa didn't sleep. Xan held her all night as she stirred, cried, and occasionally wailed. The world had never seemed more random and more insane. In her head, she kept telling herself, *My mother's dead, my mother's dead,* hoping this would help her accept what had happened, but she kept reliving the shock, as if she were still at the movie theater, hearing the news for the first time.

Around dawn, Marissa was still awake, feeling miserable. Xan hadn't slept at all either, and he'd held her all night. Looking into his beautiful, kind blue eyes, she said, 'I'm so lucky I have you,' and he said, 'I was just thinking the same thing.' She wanted to feel him inside her so badly, to be closer to him, as close as she could possibly be.

'Make love to me,' she said. '*Please* make love to me.'

He did, and even though she was crying throughout, it was still very nice. Afterward, when they were lying on their sides facing each other, Marissa said, 'So do you think that Tony guy did it?'

'It must've been him, right?' Xan said softly.

'I don't know,' Marissa said. 'That asshole detective kept asking me about my father.'

'That's just the way cops are,' Xan said. 'I mean, I imagine they have to look at these things from every different way, you know?'

'I know, but that's what scares me. I mean, he's a cop, he knows what he's doing. Why would he keep harping on it if, I don't know, there wasn't some basis to it? Why would he waste his time like that? You know what I mean?'

'Your father's an amazing guy,' Xan said. 'He'd never do something like that to your mother.' He was running his fingers back and forth along the inside of one of her arms. It felt so good. 'I mean, would he?'

'What do you mean?'

'I'm not saying this is what I think or anything, so don't take it the wrong way – but it's true that your parents were having serious problems lately, right?'

'Right,' Marissa said, remembering her father gleefully telling her mother that he'd slept with Sharon Wasserman.

'I'm just saying, from where I'm at, just kind of being, like, an outsider to all of this, it seems kind of, I don't know, coincidental to me.'

'I know,' Marissa said.

'I mean, think about it,' Xan said. 'Your parents announce to you that they're getting divorced, and the same day your mother's killed? It does make you think, you know? You don't *want* to think it, but you still think it.'

That word, 'killed,' gave Marissa a jolt. She shifted away and sat up, then said, 'Yeah, but that's why I think Tony probably did it. Maybe my mom told him she was splitting up with my dad but didn't want to be with him and he got pissed off and came over here and lost it. The guy's crazy, a total psycho. You saw what he did to my father, right?'

Xan kissed her softly on the lips – God, she was dying to feel him inside her again. He said, 'I know, and you're probably right, but you said your father went over to the gym the other day and started the fight with Tony. You said he got in that big fight with your mother, too –'

'But I heard my father saying something about how the note that Tony left, the one about him and my mother, looked like the note he got last week, the one that threatened him about the robbery.'

'Just because Tony left the notes doesn't mean he killed your mother.'

'But it shows he's crazy, that he might've robbed our house, for God's sake. Maybe he was angry because my father shot that other guy, what's his name, Sanchez, so he came back here and killed my mother to get even. Or maybe it was like I said before, because my mother was breaking up with him.'

'Like I said, I think you're right, it was probably Tony,' Xan said, 'but – and I'm just throwing this out there, so don't get upset – what if your father left the notes?'

'Why would he do that?'

'To set Tony up. Maybe he found out your mother was cheating on him, then left the notes and then went to start a fight with Tony, knowing he'd get beat up, knowing it would make Tony look bad. You see what I mean?'

'But would my father really think it through that much? Would he really do all that planning?'

'I have no idea,' Xan said, 'but he did kill somebody before, right? And if he killed before, I guess that means he could do it again.'

Marissa couldn't deny it anymore – what Xan was saying was making a lot of sense, too much sense. She could easily see her father, especially the way he'd been acting lately, losing control and snapping. He could've been arguing with her mother and impulsively grabbed the knife just like he'd impulsively gone into the closet the other night to get the gun.

'Oh my God,' Marissa said. 'He did it.'

'Whoa, come on, I didn't say *that*,' Xan said.

'It's like I've been in this deep denial or something. Oh my God, I can't believe this is happening.'

Xan moved on top of her, resting on his knees and elbows, looking down directly into her eyes, and said, 'Nothing's happening. You don't know anything, the police don't know anything.'

'I won't be able to handle this,' she said. 'I'm warning you right now, I won't be able to get through this.'

'Don't worry, I'm here,' Xan said. 'No matter what, you'll be okay, I'll make sure you're okay. But if it turns out that Tony didn't do it, I mean he has an alibi, I just want you to be ready for the police to start looking at your father, you know? I don't want it to be a shock to you.'

She imagined her father grabbing the knife and sticking it into her mother's back.

'Oh, God, no, no, no,' Marissa said as she wrapped her arms and legs around Xan's warm body as tightly as she could.

Later, Marissa didn't want Xan to leave. She was afraid to be home alone with her father.

'I'll stay with you as long as you want me to,' Xan said.

'But you don't have any clothes or –'

'I don't care. You're the only thing I care about right now.'

Xan was blowing her away. He was just so perfect.

They took turns going to the bathroom, and when Marissa went she heard her father talking downstairs on the phone.

'You should probably go down,' Xan said.

'I don't want to,' Marissa said. 'I just want to stay here in bed with you all day.'

'I'd go down with you, but this is a family thing, and you two should be alone right now, have some time to yourselves.'

'I don't want time with him.'

'I'll be right here,' Xan said. 'If you need me, just call for me and I'll be right down, okay? You don't have to worry about anything.'

Figuring she'd have to face her father eventually, Marissa decided to just go down and get it over with.

From the staircase, she heard her father talking on the phone in the dining room. She didn't know how they were ever going to use the kitchen again because she sure as hell wasn't going in there anytime soon. She'd order in Chinese food for every meal if she had to.

When she went into the dining room, her father, sitting at the table, made eye contact with her as he finished a phone call. By his tone, she knew he was talking to his friend Stan.

She stood there, watching him talk, searching for some sign that would tell her whether he was guilty or innocent. He seemed appropriately upset, but did that mean anything? Wouldn't he be acting upset either way? Either he was upset because her mom had been murdered or he was pretending to be upset to keep the act going. And if he was really crazy, if he was an actual psychopath, he'd be very good at faking his grief.

After about a minute he ended the call and said to her, 'That was Stan. Jesus, this is so hard.'

For a few moments Marissa couldn't think of anything to say – it was weird, she was actually *scared* to be near her father. Then she said, 'I can make some calls, too, if you want me too.'

'No, no, it's okay. Actually, I've almost called everybody I have to. Some friends are calling other friends, and I've gotten in touch with most of the relatives, grandma's coming up tonight. I was afraid to tell her, with her heart condition, but what can you do? Oh, the funeral's tomorrow morning at ten, by the way.'

Marissa wasn't surprised that the funeral would be so soon. Although they were hardly a religious family, they followed some Jewish traditions, like burying the dead as soon as possible. Marissa's grandfather had also been buried only a couple of days after he'd died.

Her father went on about how her mother would be buried in the family plot on Long Island and about the arrangements he'd made with the rabbi and the funeral home. 'The only relative I'm not inviting is Mom's brother,' he said. 'I don't think she'd want him here.'

'Yeah, I don't think so either,' Marissa said.

Marissa had only met her uncle Mark a few times and hadn't seen him in years, but apparently Mark had abused her mother when they were kids, and her mother had pretty much cut off all contact with him.

'This is still so surreal,' her father said. 'I'm still expecting her to walk in here any second. When I heard your footsteps on the stairs before, at first I thought it was her.'

He looked like he was on the verge of tears, straining very hard to maintain his composure. Marissa still didn't see any sign that this was a put-on, and she was feeling guilty for suspecting him, for losing faith in him, when he said, 'Oh, so Clements called before, and unfortunately they haven't made an arrest in the case yet.'

'What about Tony?' Marissa asked.

'He has an alibi, and apparently it's airtight. I don't know all the details, but Clements said he was with a friend at the time Mom was... anyway, Clements said it rules him out, but I don't believe it. If it's a friend, how do we know the friend isn't covering for him? But Clements said they're looking at other possibilities, and what do you think that means? I can't believe I have to deal with this while I'm in the middle of planning Mom's funeral. I'll tell you one thing, I'm not talking to him alone again. I'm not saying another word to him without my lawyer sitting right next to me. If I'd been thinking straight last night I would've hired a lawyer right away, put an end to this ridiculousness.'

Marissa was looking at her father closely, focusing on his eyes, trying to figure out if he was lying.

'And then I'm gonna have to deal with all of that media crap again,' her father continued, 'with all of the sensational articles they're writing.'

'It's in the papers?' Marissa asked. She hadn't even thought about this yet.

'I only checked the *Post,* the online edition, and yeah, it's front page, and I'm sure it's on the front page of all the other papers, too. In the *Post* story Clements called me a person of interest in the case. I understand why he has to check me out, but it's so awful to lose your wife and then have to read that crap. Do you have any idea what this is going to do to my practice, to my career? I don't even want to think about that yet or I won't be able to get through the funeral and everything else. The reporters are still out there, and they can stay out there all day if they want to, but I'm not saying a word to them, and I don't think you should either. This is total harassment now, and I'm gonna talk to my lawyer about this, too, see if there's any kind of action I can take. You always hear about the media exploiting people, celebrities. You become immune to it, like it's part of our culture, because you don't think it can happen to you. You think it's only something that happens to other people, that you're protected, but you're not. The thing is it can happen to anybody... why're you looking at me like that?'

'Like what?'

'I don't know, you're looking at me... strangely.'

'I was just thinking.'

'About what?'

'About how awful all of this is.'

Her father seemed incredulous, like he wasn't buying this explanation, but then he said, 'Oh, Clements talked to the Millers next door, and JoAnne said their dog was barking like crazy yesterday at around six thirty.'

'So?' Marissa asked.

'So,' her father said suddenly agitated, 'the other day, before

I found the note from Tony, when I came in the house the dog was barking, too. I thought it was a little unusual at the time. I mean, the dog knows us, right? He never barks at us.'

Marissa, distracted, barely paying attention, said, 'I don't get it.'

'It means Tony was here again.' Now her father was practically yelling, and Marissa, frightened, backed away a few steps. 'The dog was barking both times, and we know Tony was here once, right? Clements said this sounds interesting, but I don't think he really gets it. This is another thing I'm talking to my lawyer about, though. There have to've been other witnesses; somebody must've seen Tony coming or going. What's wrong? Why're you moving away from me?'

'I'm not,' Marissa said.

Her father glared at her, something in his eyes reminding her of the way he'd looked when he'd gleefully revealed his affair to her and her mother. Then he said to her, 'You do believe me, don't you?'

'Of course I believe you,' she said.

'I can't believe it,' he said. 'You don't believe me, do you?'

'Hey,' Xan said.

She hadn't seem him enter the dining room from behind her, and she was so startled she might've shrieked.

'Sorry,' Xan said. 'Just wanted to see how you two were doing.'

Marissa held his hand, relieved he was here. 'We were just… talking about the funeral,' she said. 'It's tomorrow morning.'

'If there's anything I can do to help you out, just let me know,' Xan said to Adam.

'Thanks, but I think we're okay,' Adam said, looking at Marissa. 'At least I hope we are.'

Marissa and Xan went upstairs.

In her room, she whispered to him, 'Oh my God, he did it. He really fucking did it.'

22

JOHNNY WATCHED THE couple get off the Coney Island–bound F train, and then he followed them down the long escalator and out to the street. The couple went past the convenience store at the corner and turned right. Johnny hung back for a block or two, until the couple reached an area that was darker and more deserted, and then he made his move.

He pulled down his black ski mask and started walking faster, until he was about twenty yards behind them; then, right when the guy looked back over his shoulder, Johnny sprinted toward them, holding his .38. Before the couple could run or yell for help or react at all, Johnny was pointing the gun at the guy's face, saying, 'Gimme the fuckin' ring.'

Johnny had spotted the woman's ring on the subway. It was a sparkly diamond engagement ring, looked like at least one carat. The woman was blond, blue-eyed, and, like most people in this part of Brooklyn nowadays, probably not a native New Yorker. She was probably from the Midwest, Kansas or some shit. No girl who grew up in the city would wear her engagement ring, diamond up, on the subway at eleven o'clock at night.

'Please... don't shoot him,' the woman said.

Yeah, definitely not a New Yorker.

'Just gimme the fuckin' ring, bitch,' Johnny said. He hated that he had to be so disrespectful, that he couldn't talk like the charming woman-lover he normally was, but he knew that in a robbery situation it was a good idea to act as little like your normal self as possible.

'Take it easy,' the guy said. He was tall and thin and had the same bumpkin accent as the girl. 'We don't want any trouble, yo.'

Yo. Like he thought he was talking street and that would, what, save him? Johnny pressed the gun into the guy's cheek and said, 'Tell the whore to gimme the fuckin' ring.'

'Give him the ring,' the guy said to the woman.

'I can't. It's my grandmother's.'

'Give it to him, goddamn it.'

'Please,' the woman said to Johnny, 'take our money. I have two hundred dollars in my purse, and my fiancé has money, too. You can have it all, but please, I can't give you the –'

Johnny pistol-whipped the guy across the side of his head. He fell to his knees, and then Johnny hit him with the gun again, on the front of his face, and heard something crunch. The woman started screaming. Jesus, what the hell was wrong with these people? Did they *want* to die?

Johnny grabbed the woman's left hand and started to pull off the ring. Would you believe it, she was still trying to resist? She was screaming in Johnny's ear, trying to break free. Johnny was ready to shoot her in the head and shut her up, but then the ring slid off.

'Thanks, guys,' Johnny said.

He'd got what he wanted. No reason not to be polite now, right?

He walked away quickly. After he turned the corner he jogged a few blocks, and then continued home at a normal pace.

He wished he could sell the ring right away. He knew he could get a thousand for it, maybe more, from any pawnshop, and he didn't like to hold on to the things he stole, especially jewelry.

Jewelry, especially rings, was the type of stuff that people wanted back. Sometimes he'd dump stolen jewelry for a fraction of what it was worth just to get rid of it. After all, he wasn't an idiot. That was the difference between him and every other criminal in the world.

But he needed the ring, to give to Marissa when the time was right. Then when she was dead, like her parents, he could pawn it off and make his thousand bucks. Not that a thousand bucks would mean anything to him then.

Yeah, it would've been nice if Adam Bloom had come home on time and Johnny had killed him like he'd planned to, but everything else had gone so well since then that he couldn't exactly complain. After he left the house on Monday evening, he dumped the stolen car in a supermarket parking lot way out in Flushing and got rid of the backpack and the sweatshirt that had gotten blood on it. Then he washed up in the bathroom of a gas station and hailed a livery cab and had the driver drop him off around the corner from the movie theater on Fifty-ninth at about eight o'clock. He was only about a half-hour late, and he told Marissa the subways were running slow and he couldn't call her from underground. She wasn't upset, because she'd been running late, too, and had just gotten there. The movie was about to start, so they decided to go in and get something to eat afterward. Not that she seemed interested in actually *watching* the movie. While they were in the back of the movie theater, making out, he was replaying the murder in his head. Were there any loose ends? He couldn't think of any. He'd gotten rid of all the evidence, and the cops had probably already arrested Tony. Hopefully Tony would go to jail for the rest of his life or get the death penalty. If Tony had an alibi, the cops might try to pin the murder on Adam. That would work out really well for Johnny, too. Johnny needed to get rid of Adam for the rest of his plan to work, and it didn't really matter if Adam was rotting in a jail cell or six feet underground as long as he was gone for good.

After the movie, Johnny took a leak, and when he met Marissa back in the lobby and saw her looking so upset, talking to somebody on her cell, he knew she'd heard the news. Johnny lived for moments like these. He got to play a role, be another person and, even better, be this great guy everybody loved.

Johnny knew that Marissa needed him to take charge, and he handled it beautifully, putting her in the cab, telling her all the right things. At the house, Adam was totally buying into his shit, too, and Johnny played it just right, hugging him, literally giving him a shoulder to cry on about three hours after killing his wife. Seriously, did it get any better than that?

While Adam and Marissa were hugging and slobbering like babies, Johnny was listening in on a conversation between a gray-haired detective – later he'd find out his name was Clements – and some other cop. Although Johnny was only catching bits and pieces, it sounded like they weren't sold on the idea that Tony had killed Dana Bloom. Johnny didn't know why this was, but he didn't waste a second and started working on his backup plan. See, this was what set Johnny apart from the two-bit criminals who were crammed into jails all over the country – he never got complacent; his mind was always working, thinking ahead.

Naturally Marissa asked him to sit next to her while Clements was questioning her. She needed him so badly now, she couldn't bear to be without him for even a few minutes. Johnny loved it when Clements asked Adam if he could 'wait in the other room;' the look on his face was priceless, like he already knew what was about to go down and how screwed he was and how there was nothing he could do to stop it. Then Clements asked Marissa about Adam, if she'd ever seen him threaten Dana, and it was beautiful how Marissa mentioned Adam had pushed Dana that one time and knocked her down. Now Clements was really starting to believe that Adam was his man.

When Johnny finally got alone with Marissa in her room, and she was telling him how lucky she was to have him and saying she wanted to feel him inside her, Johnny knew she was officially *his*. He'd hooked her so good, there was no way she was getting away now. He made love to her, slowly and passionately, the way only Johnny Long could, and then he picked up where Clements had left off, trying to get her to believe that her father had killed her mother. He knew he had to handle this carefully, not come on too strong, blaming her father. He had to let her think that it was her idea, that she'd come up with it on her own. It worked, and it was incredible – he felt like he was in total control of this girl, like he could get her to do or think anything he wanted her to. And with Adam's own daughter believing he was guilty, who would he have to defend him?

When Adam was gone, Johnny would ask Marissa to marry him, and, come on, at this point how could she not say yes? She was already dependent on him, and when *both* her parents were gone she'd be desperate to start a new family. When they were married – and the way things were going, that could only be a few months from now – he'd make sure he was in her will, as her sole beneficiary, because who else would there be? She sure as hell wouldn't want her father, that murderer, to get anything. Then Marissa would die in some 'unfortunate accident' – the poor Blooms, they'd had so much tragedy in their lives – and Johnny would have everything he'd ever wanted.

Marissa was so convinced that her father was guilty, she was afraid to be in the house with him alone. Johnny said he would stay with her for as long as she wanted him to – 'forever if I have to' – but then her grandmother, Adam's mother, arrived, and Johnny wanted out. He got a bad vibe from the old lady from the get-go and knew she wouldn't be as easy to win over as the other Blooms.

'I think she hates me,' Johnny had said to Marissa.

'No, that's just the way she's been with all my boyfriends,' Marissa said. 'It's because you're a *shagetz*.'

'A what?'

'Because you're not Jewish. My grandmother has always had this stupid thing in her head about me having to marry a Jewish guy someday even though we're not at all religious.'

'How does she know I'm not Jewish?'

'She *knows*,' Marissa said, and that was exactly what Johnny was worried about. If the old lady could tell he wasn't Jewish, what else could she tell? Johnny didn't want to take any chances, especially when everything was going so well.

With her grandma staying in the guest room next door, Marissa didn't seem as worried about being in the same house with her father, so Johnny came up with a good excuse to go back to his apartment – he needed to get his suit for the funeral. Marissa wanted to go with him but decided she should probably stay and be with her family.

When Johnny left, the reporters, who'd been camped out there all day, swarmed him, shouting questions. Johnny told them he was just 'a friend of the family,' and he didn't stop to talk to them. At the subway station, he bought the *Post* and *News*. Marissa had already told him that Tony had an alibi for the murder and might be off the hook and that Adam was the main suspect now, but even the papers that had come out early this morning were slamming Adam. Each paper had about two or three pages on the story, focusing on how Adam Bloom, the crazed vigilante who had shot and killed an intruder in his house less than two weeks ago, was now a suspect in his wife's murder. While the articles focused on Tony as a suspect, the *Post* called the Blooms 'the philandering couple' and said that the Blooms' marriage had been 'in crisis' since the break-in and that Adam Bloom might have 'snapped again' and killed his wife. And Johnny loved that Clements had called Adam 'a person of interest' in the case. Reading this on the subway to Brooklyn, he couldn't help laughing out loud. For years, Johnny had been running away from the cops, and now, in a weird way, a cop was actually helping him get the biggest score of his life. He almost felt like Clements deserved a cut of the action.

Later on during the subway ride, Johnny spotted the couple with the engagement ring. He wouldn't need the ring for a while, but he'd learned a long time ago that when an opportunity comes along to get what you want, go for it, because you don't know when you'll get that chance again.

At his apartment, he was checking out the ring – it didn't have any noticeable flaws; maybe it was worth more than he'd thought – when he got a text from Marissa:

I miss you so so much!!

Man, Johnny loved his life.

In the morning, Johnny met Marissa outside the funeral home in Forest Hills. She was already a mess – dark circles under her bloodshot eyes, streaks of mascara on her cheeks – so he had to shift right into supportive boyfriend mode. This might've been hard to pull off for some guys, but not for Johnny. He even managed to squeeze out some tears.

The funeral seemed to take forever, the rabbi going on about what a wonderful, caring person Dana had been and how much she'd be missed. At one point the rabbi called her 'a loving wife.' And Johnny – probably like everybody else in the chapel – was thinking, *Yeah, but loving to who?*

Everyone was sobbing, especially Marissa and Adam. But Adam was almost crying too much. It seemed to Johnny that a lot of Adam's crying was for show, not because he was faking it – he was probably actually upset – but because he knew other people, including Marissa and any reporters who'd gotten into the chapel, were watching him to make sure he was crying as much as a grieving husband should be. A couple of times Johnny saw Marissa look over at her father, and Adam would immediately start crying or blow his nose extra loud or do something to prove how upset he was.

Johnny rode with Adam, Marissa, and Marissa's grandmother – Grandma Ann – to the cemetery. Johnny was doing a great job with the whole grieving act, but, man, it took a lot of work. In the back of the limo, the old biddy kept looking over at him, giving him the evil eye, glaring through her Coke-bottle glasses. He knew it wasn't just because he wasn't Jewish; there was more to it than that.

At the grave, Johnny actually felt sad for the first time all day. It was a shame that Dana had died before Johnny had a chance to screw her, before she had a chance to experience the orgasms that you could only experience with Johnny Long. Talk about tragedy.

Johnny had to continue to console Marissa, and he was running out of bullshit to say to make her feel better. How many times could he tell her 'I know' and 'She's in a better place' and 'It's gonna be okay'? Meanwhile, Adam was still overdoing it. When they lowered the coffin into the ground he collapsed, crying, but then he started beating the ground with his fists, like a baby having a fit. Johnny was thinking, *Fists? Come on, gimme a break.* At one point, Johnny even saw Marissa look over at her father and roll her eyes slightly.

During the ride back to the Blooms' house, Marissa looked away the whole time, staring blankly out the window. Johnny left her alone, giving her her space.

Marissa didn't say a word until they got back to the house. She took him up to her room, shut the door, and said, 'I think you were right – he definitely did it.'

'I never said I thought he actually *did* it,' Johnny said.

'But that's what you thought, that was your first instinct, and first instincts are usually right.'

Johnny wasn't going to argue with this. He blinked once, very slowly, to show her how concerned he was, and squeezed her hand tightly.

She continued, 'Everything about him today was so fucking fake. Did you see the way he was punching the ground? He thinks he's gonna get away with it, but he won't because I'm not gonna let him. If he did this he's gonna pay for it. He's not just gonna go on with his life while my mother's rotting away underground.'

Johnny loved how she was ready to turn on her father, to, well, bury him. The Blooms were having some Jewish thing called a shiver sitting, something like that, where all their friends and relatives were going to come over with food and drinks and sit around and mourn with the whole family. It sounded like hell; even worse, it was going to last a whole week. What was it with Jews anyway? Did they want to drag out their misery for as long as they possibly could?

Maybe people were staying away because of the 'rumors' about Adam in the news, because only about ten people showed up at the house all day even though there had been at least a hundred people at the funeral. Adam seemed out of it, wandering in and out of the living room, occasionally checking his BlackBerry, shaking his head and mumbling to himself. Grandma Ann continued to give Johnny dirty looks. Johnny tried to start a couple of conversations with her, asking her about Florida, but the old lady wouldn't even make eye contact with him. Later, Johnny saw her go over and whisper something to Adam; then Adam looked over at Johnny, trying to be casual about it. Johnny didn't care what Marissa said; he knew that the old lady wasn't only treating him like this because he wasn't Jewish.

Marissa wanted Johnny to spend the night with her, and he couldn't turn her down, could he? In bed, she told him that she loved him, and he said he loved her, too, 'more than anything in the world.' He knew it was way too early to ask her to marry him, but he thought the timing was right to test the waters, to see if she was as primed as he thought she was, so he asked, 'Do you want kids someday?'

'Someday,' she said. 'Definitely. What about you?'

'Yeah,' Johnny said. Then he added, 'And I think you and me could make great-looking babies.'

If she seemed at all freaked out by this, he would've backed off, changed the subject, said he was only joking.

Instead she said, 'I know, I was thinking about that today actually.'

'You were?'

'Yeah. I mean, I know it's early, but I definitely feel strongly about you.' Wow, Johnny was impressed with himself. He knew Marissa would be especially vulnerable today, on the day of her mother's funeral, but she was about as attached to him as a person could possibly get.

'I want to show you something,' he said.

He went over to his suit jacket, which he'd laid over the chair at her desk, and took the diamond ring out of the inside pocket.

'I know this isn't the right time to do this,' he said. 'And I'm not sure you'll even want me to do it, but if you do... someday... look at what I have.'

He opened his hand and watched her eyes widen. It was amazing the way women shit themselves over diamonds.

'Wow, it's beautiful,' she said.

'My grandmother gave it to me when she was dying of cancer. She told me to propose to the girl I love someday.'

Marissa was smiling, and Johnny knew she was thinking, *Please let that girl be me. Please let me be Mrs Xan Evonov.*

323

Then her expression changed and she said, 'It was your grandmother's ring?'

'Yeah,' Johnny said.

'Oh,' she said, 'that's weird. It doesn't look like a very old setting.'

'That's because I had it reset. Yeah, I wanted it to look more modern, and it's the stone that's really important to me.'

Good thing Johnny was a fast thinker.

'That's so sweet,' she said, 'and the stone is so beautiful.'

He could tell she wanted to try the ring on, but he took it away, thinking, *Always leave them wanting more.*

He was kissing her tenderly when there was a knock at the door.

'Yes?' Marissa said.

'Dinner's on the table.' It was Grandma Ann.

'Okay, coming,' Marissa said.

'It's getting cold.'

'We'll be right down.'

Johnny didn't hear Grandma Ann's footsteps. He pictured her at the door, trying to listen in.

'Maybe I should go,' Johnny said, talking low, almost whispering.

'Why?' Marissa asked, concerned but talking very quietly, matching Johnny's tone.

'I just think your family needs some time alone.'

'Please don't go. I need you here tonight.'

Johnny decided he would electrocute Marissa. It wouldn't happen for a long time, for months, and he'd have to work out the details, but when the time was right, that was how he'd get rid of her.

Moving a few strands of hair away from her eyes, Johnny said, 'I really think your grandmother doesn't want me here.'

'I'm telling you that's just the way she is.'

Now Johnny heard Grandma Ann walking away down the hallway. Johnny gave Marissa a look that said, *See what I mean?*

'She's totally harmless, I'm telling you.'

Johnny didn't believe her, but he decided to focus on the positives. Dana was dead, and Marissa was in love with him and, even better, was practically ready to marry him. Everything was falling into place. It was time to move ahead with the next phase of the plan, and this would be the most enjoyable phase, the part that would give him the biggest rush.

Yeah, it was time to kill Adam Bloom.

23

Hello, Dr Bloom, this is Lisa DiStefano. I'm very sorry to tell you this, but... but I'm going to have to discontinue my treatment... I'm really sorry, Doctor, but I just feel like I have no choice. I appreciate everything you've done for me and –

ADAM COULDN'T LISTEN to any more. He deleted the message, as well as the other messages he hadn't even listened to yet, and shut off his BlackBerry. He didn't know how many patients he'd lost so far – ten, fifteen? And those were only the ones who'd bothered to call, the ones he'd been seeing for years, who felt indebted to him. The others probably just wouldn't bother to show up to their appointments.

It wasn't like the situation would ever improve, either. Even if the police announced that they'd made an arrest in the case, if Adam was completely vindicated, the damage had already been done. His name had been permanently scarred, and people would always believe that there had to be some truth in there somewhere. Maybe he really did kill his wife and the police botched the evidence. Or if he didn't kill his wife, he'd shot that guy in his house, hadn't he? He was still unstable, still crazy.

Maybe if he was a plumber or a carpenter he could've continued his career at some point, but as a psychologist, people needed to trust him with their mental health; they needed to know that the person treating them wasn't potentially crazier than they were.

All funerals are like nightmares, but for Adam, Dana's funeral was especially horrific. It was bad enough that he had to bury his wife, a woman whose life had been tragically cut short – she'd only been forty-seven years old, for God's sake – but he had to suffer through the indignity of being scrutinized and judged, not only by the media and the public but by his own family. Even Marissa didn't believe he was innocent. This made Adam feel horribly sick whenever he thought about it, and he wasn't sure their relationship could ever recover from this. At the chapel and at the cemetery, people kept giving him looks and acting generally suspicious. Even when people came up to pay their respects, he knew that they weren't being sincere. They were sorry for Dana, but they had no sympathy for him – and these were the people who supposedly cared about him the most. These were people he'd grown up with, gone to school with, worked with. He'd been there during the difficult times in their lives, when their loved ones were sick or had died, but now, when he needed them the most, they deserted him. He felt bitter and betrayed. He felt completely alone in the world.

Well, almost completely alone. He was glad his mother was there. Like every other person in the world, Adam had mother issues. Despite his best attempts over the years to achieve resolution, to reach closure, he had petty, unresolved resentments toward his mother that he'd harbored for years and that led to constant bitterness toward her. Although he always tried to confront his feelings and express himself fully, it was usually hard for him not to act irritable when he was around her for an extended period of time – well, for more than a day or two. But today he needed support and unconditional love from his mother, and he'd appreciated it when, shortly after she arrived from Florida, she took him aside and said, 'I know my son isn't a killer.'

This was exactly what he needed to hear. Finally he had an ally.

'Thank you, Mom,' he said. 'You don't know how much it means to me to hear you say that.'

As his mother held him, he felt like he was a child again and he'd just scraped his knee on the sidewalk and run home to his mommy.

'Don't worry, everything's going to be okay,' she said.

For a few moments, he actually believed her.

Then, maybe because he was with his mother and felt safe and protected, he suddenly felt the need to cleanse his soul. He said, 'I made a mistake the other night, Mom. I didn't have to shoot that guy.'

Adam had talked to his mother on the phone a few times since the shooting, but he'd only given her the general details because he didn't want to upset her too much.

'Oh, stop it, you did what you had to do,' his mother said. 'Somebody was in your house in the middle of the night. What were you supposed to do, let him shoot you first?'

'But I didn't have to shoot him so many times.'

'So, who cares?' his mother said. 'Stop feeling so guilty about everything. You always make yourself feel guilty, you drive yourself crazy. Give yourself a break.'

Her advice wasn't bad. Forgiving yourself was always a good idea, though it was hard to feel innocent surrounded by people who were convinced he was guilty. It was also hard not to let what the media was saying get to him, especially that crap about how he was a 'person of interest.' He didn't even want to think about the very real possibility that the police could somehow put together a case against him, actually charge him with his wife's murder. He knew that if he let his thoughts go there he wouldn't be able to function at all. As it was – maybe because he hadn't taken enough Valium – during the entire funeral he'd felt extremely disoriented. He wasn't exactly sure who'd been there or what he'd said or how he'd behaved. He remembered Carol coming over to offer her condolences, and holding Marissa's hand while he cried, and falling to the ground in front of the grave, but that was about it.

When he got back to the house, he was experiencing major anxiety symptoms – rapid heart rate, severe dizziness, a pounding headache. He called a psychiatrist he'd once seen, Dr Klein, and Klein called in a prescription for Klonopin to the local Duane Reade. Adam thought he'd have to get the medication delivered – what with all the reporters out there, he would be a prisoner in his house for days – but Xan volunteered to go pick it up.

After his first dose, Adam started feeling better. Well, he was still a mess, but at least he didn't feel like he was on the verge of having a heart attack anymore. He joined his friends and family who had come over for the shivah, aware of notable absentees, like Sharon and Mike. Adam didn't really mind, though. He'd rather be alone than around a bunch of people who were judging him.

When Adam went to get a glass of water, his mother came over to him and whispered, 'I don't like him.'

'Who?' Adam said.

'Who do you think? Her boyfriend.'

Adam looked over at Xan, who was looking right at him. Adam shifted his eyes back toward his mother, then rolled his eyes slightly and walked away, shaking his head. His mother had always been critical of Marissa's boyfriends, especially the ones who weren't Jewish.

But his mother wouldn't let it go. Later, when Marissa and Xan had gone upstairs, she picked up as if she'd never left off and said, 'I don't care, I don't like him.'

'Come on, he's a nice guy,' Adam said.

'Where did she meet him?' his mother asked.

'In the city. I think at a bar or a club, I'm not really sure.'

She gave him a look.

'A lot of people meet in bars, Ma, and Marissa seems happy with him. He's been great, actually – very supportive throughout all of this. I mean, I had my doubts at first, too, but he's a good guy.'

'What kind of doubts did you have?' His mother was squinting seriously.

'I don't mean *doubts*. I mean I was just a little skeptical, about his career mainly. He's an artist, a painter, and I didn't want Marissa to get involved with some flaky guy. But that doesn't seem like the case at all. He seems very dedicated, very passionate.'

'He reminds me of Howard Gutman.'

'Oh, come on,' Adam said.

His mother had told the story of Howard Gutman dozens of times before, but that didn't stop her from retelling it again and again.

'He sat at our table at your dad's cousin Sheila's wedding,' she said. 'Everyone was talking to him and thought he was this great, wonderful guy, but I knew something was off about him. There was just something about the way he looked at people. It was as if he wasn't really looking at them at all. A couple of months later we heard he killed his wife. He took a hammer and pummeled her to death while she was sleeping.'

'And what does this have to do with Xan?' Adam asked.

'I don't like the way he looks at people,' his mother said. 'I can't put my finger on it, but there's something just off about him.'

'Whatever you do, please don't mention any of that to Marissa,' Adam said. 'Just try to give her a break, okay? She's going through a lot, obviously, and she seems very happy with Xan.'

'Xan,' his mother said with disdain.

'A lot of kids shorten their names these days,' Adam said.

'It's not his name I'm worried about,' she said.

About an hour after he took the first dose of Klonopin, Adam felt like it was wearing off, so he took another pill and a couple of Valiums, too. He didn't bother to check for warnings about drug interactions, as at this point his health wasn't exactly his top priority.

In the morning, when he went downstairs to the kitchen, his mother was already preparing for the second day of the shivah. It was hard to be in the kitchen and not think about what had happened there – that the floor around where the body had been was stained lightly pink didn't help – and it was still hard to be on the front staircase and not think about the shooting and all the blood.

'How did you sleep?' his mother asked.

'I didn't,' Adam said.

'Oh, you poor thing, why don't you take a nap?'

'If I could sleep I would've slept last night.'

'At least go lie down on the couch. You need your rest.'

What he needed was some more Klonopin.

'I'll just have a cup of coffee. Can you do me a favor and bring it out to me in the dining room? It's hard for me to be here with the floor like that.'

A couple of minutes later his mother brought his coffee and said, 'So I didn't go to bed till after midnight, and Xan was still here.'

'I know, he slept over,' Adam said.

'He sleeps over already? How long has he known her?'

Adam took a sip of coffee and winced. His mother always made coffee too strong.

'Do you need another sugar for that?' she asked. 'I put two packets in, but –'

'It's okay, I'm fine.'

'Are you sure, becau –'

'I said it's fine.' He managed another sip, then said, 'Dana and I had discussed it. We didn't feel comfortable with her bringing boyfriends home we hadn't met, but we met Xan and we approved him.'

'Approved him?' she said.

God, she was already starting to annoy him, trying to say everything she could possibly say to aggravate him. Not surprising – they were at the two-day mark. When she got like this it was hard for him to believe that she wasn't being passive-aggressive and doing this intentionally. The fact was, in this case he was actually on her side – he didn't like the idea of Marissa having guys stay over either – but his mother had the uncanny ability to force a person into taking an opposing point of view.

'Do we really have to discuss this?' he said. 'Sorry, but I really don't think Marissa's boyfriend situation is the most important thing in the world right now.'

They sat across from each other in silence for several minutes, but Adam knew his mother wouldn't let it go. He could tell that her brain was churning, and he even saw her lips moving as she mumbled silently to herself.

'What can I tell you?' she finally said. 'I feel the way I feel.'

'You never had problems when I had girlfriends over,' Adam said.

'What're you talking about?'

'You and Dad,' he continued. 'I had girls up to my room all the time and you never had a problem with it.'

'When did you have girls over?'

'All the time. Come on, don't you remember my girlfriends? Stacy Silverman? Julie Litsky?'

His mother looked lost. She'd done it again, hit on another of his issues, how he'd felt ignored and emotionally neglected as a child. He'd always felt like his parents were too wrapped up in their own problems and didn't pay enough attention to what was going on in his life. Was it possible that he'd re-created this dynamic in his relationship with Marissa?

'You really don't remember Julie Litsky?' he asked, suddenly very agitated.

'Did she have red hair?'

'She had brown hair.'

'Oh, okay, I think I remember her now,' she said, but it was obvious she still had no idea who Julie Litsky was.

'And you don't remember that you and Dad let girls sleep over in the house when I was in college? I used to have my girlfriends over all the time over the summer, for spring break, the holidays –'

'That was different,' his mother said. 'They were girls you knew, who you went to school with, who came from good families. Who is this Xan? Some stranger off the street?'

'You don't know anything about his family.'

'Neither do you.'

'Okay, I'm serious now, I really don't want to discuss this anymore.'

Adam left the dining room. He went into the kitchen, just to get away from his mother, but then he noticed the pinkness on the floor and went back out toward the front of the house, avoiding looking at the staircase. Jesus, could he feel any more trapped? Then he peeked outside, saw a couple of news trucks, and thought, *Yes, I can.* There were fewer reporters than yesterday, but it was still early. There would probably be more later on, and then they'd start ringing the bell, trying to get him to come out and comment. One thing was for sure – this story wasn't going to go away on its own. Until the police arrested Tony or someone else for the murder, Adam knew there would be constant speculation about his possible involvement. There would be newspaper and magazine articles, TV features, you name it. Actually, the real nightmare scenario would be if the police didn't make an arrest and the case went unsolved. If that happened, no one would care about the evidence or facts in the case – Adam would be presumed guilty for the rest of his life.

Adam went upstairs and took a Klonopin and a couple of Advils. He felt nauseous several minutes later, and he wasn't sure whether it was from anxiety or some side effect of the medication. He lay in bed for a while but decided this was making him feel even worse and returned downstairs.

His mother was alone in the living room, and the trays with bagels and doughnuts were untouched.

'I think it's disgusting,' she said.

He knew she was referring to the lack of friends and family who had shown up for the shivah. Fewer than ten people yesterday and no one so far today.

'Eh, it's expected,' Adam said. 'People read the papers, they watch TV.' He noticed that the TV was on and picked up the remote and turned it off. 'Sorry, but I'd rather live in a plastic bubble for a while, if you know what I mean.'

'But it's not about you, it's about Dana,' his mother said. 'These are people who loved her, who supposedly cared about her, and they can't be here for her now?'

His mother had pushed yet another button as he felt a pang of guilt for the way he'd treated Dana before she was killed. It was bad enough that they hadn't been speaking to each other and had been on the verge of divorce, but even before then, over the last several months, he hadn't treated her very well. She'd obviously been suffering, going through whatever internal conflicts had caused her to cheat on him, and she'd tried to talk to him so many times, but he'd been oblivious. He was the psychologist. He should have recognized the signs of the failing marriage and insisted that they go into counseling. There was no excuse for it, none at all.

'You can't control what other people do,' he said, mindlessly ripping a bagel in half and then biting into one of the halves. Actually, he didn't mind that no one had shown up today. He wasn't in the mood to make phony conversation, especially with people who hated him.

Adam took another bite of the bagel, then realized he didn't have an appetite and put the rest on the plate. He started pacing the living room, and then Marissa and Xan entered. They all exchanged good mornings, but when his mother spoke he noticed that she was looking at Marissa but not Xan.

'Can I talk to you a sec?' Marissa asked Adam.

'Sure,' he said.

'In private,' she added.

'I'll wait in the hallway,' Xan said. Clearly he didn't want to be left alone with Adam's mother.

Adam and Marissa went into the dining room, and she said, 'Sorry, but I have to get out of here today.'

'Where are you going?'

'Xan's place. I just need some space, I need to breathe. I just can't be around here.'

'I understand,' Adam said, wondering if 'around here' really meant 'around you.'

'I might come back to sleep here tonight, or I might stay at Xan's and come back tomorrow morning,' she said. 'Did you hear anything new?'

'No, nothing yet,' Adam said.

Marissa wouldn't make eye contact with him, and he could tell that she still thought he was guilty. He couldn't hide his frustration and let out a deep breath, as if signaling that this conversation was over. She took the cue and went ahead of him back into the living room. While she said goodbye to her grandmother, Xan came over and hugged him tightly and said, 'I'll be thinking about you, man.'

'Thank you,' Adam said. 'I appreciate that.'

As Marissa and Xan started to leave, Adam's mother said, 'Call us later,' and Marissa said, 'I will.'

His mother remained on the couch, and Adam picked up the other piece of bagel and bit into it and chewed it harder than necessary. He was still upset at Marissa for treating him that way. He wondered if she knew how badly she'd hurt him.

Then Adam became aware of a dog barking. It sounded like Blackie, the Millers' dog, and the noise seemed to be coming from the street in front of the house. The dog was really barking wildly, the way he'd been barking the other day when Adam had returned from playing golf and found the note from Tony under the door.

'Do you hear that?' Adam asked his mother, but he was really talking to himself, thinking out loud.

'Hear what?' she asked.

Adam went to the front of the house, to one of the windows facing the street, and peered through a space in the venetian blinds. He saw JoAnne Miller holding the taut leash, trying to restrain Blackie, who looked almost rabid as he tried to escape to attack Xan.

24

IN THE EARLY afternoon, when it became clear that no guests were going to show up, Adam's mother paused the movie she'd been watching, *Notting Hill*, and put away the bagels and cream cheese and other food. Although Adam had been sitting next to his mother, he'd been very distracted, not paying any attention to the movie, getting up every few minutes or so to pace.

When his mother returned from putting the food away, she said, 'Okay, you can unpause it now.'

'Go ahead, I'm not watching,' Adam said.

'Are you feeling okay? Do you want to lie down?'

'I'm fine, just watch.'

'I can tell, since Marissa and Xan left, you seem very upset about something.' Adam hadn't wanted to discuss it with his mother, partly because he was confused and wasn't sure there was anything to discuss, and partly because he knew that if he told her she would flip out and cause a whole scene.

But he really needed to talk to *somebody* about this, and maybe she'd have some advice or a rational opinion. In his current state he didn't trust his ability to make decisions.

'I'm concerned about something,' he said.

'About what?'

'Did you hear the way our neighbor's dog, Blackie, was barking before?'

'I knew it had to do with that dog. What about it?'

Adam told her that he'd heard Blackie barking when he'd found the note from Tony and that JoAnne Miller had reported that her dog had started barking like crazy the night Dana was killed.

'So what does that have to do with the dog barking before?'

'The dog was barking at Xan and Marissa, but Marissa has known the dog for years, she used to walk him when the Millers went on vacation.'

'So you think the dog was barking at Xan?'

'I have no idea what I'm saying,' Adam said.

'Didn't I tell you about Xan?' his mother said.

Adam knew his mother would use this to get in an I-told-you-so jab.

'I just think it was strange the way the dog was going so crazy like that, that's all,' he said. 'I've known that dog for years, and I've never seen him bark like that, just at somebody on the sidewalk for no reason. I mean, reporters have been out there for the past couple of days, and you didn't hear the dog barking at them, right?'

'So the dog doesn't like Xan,' his mother said. 'Smart dog. I don't like him either.'

'I don't think you get what I'm saying,' Adam said.

His mother stared at him, then said, 'You think the dog was barking other times at *Xan*.'

'I'm sure I'm being ridiculous, but –'

'But you said the note was from Tony.'

'It was from Tony. It was the same writing, on similar paper, as another note I got, I think from Tony, that was kind of threatening.'

He told his mother about the other note, and then she said, 'So you're saying you think Xan could've left *both* notes and not Tony?'

'I don't *think* that… I'm just wondering, that's all.'

'Why would he do that? And how would he even know that Tony and Dana were having an affair?'

'I don't know. That's why it doesn't make any sense.'

'I said I didn't like Xan, but I didn't say I think he killed Dana.'

'I don't think that either.'

'Of course you think that. That's why you're bringing this all up.'

Adam, suddenly hyped up, full of energy, said, 'Xan is not a killer. Tony killed Dana. His alibi's gonna fall apart, you'll see. This is probably just a ridiculous waste of time.'

'I don't think it's such a waste of time. I think you should call the police anyway just to let them know.'

'Let them know what? That a dog started barking at my daughter's boyfriend? They'll think I'm insane, more insane than they already think I am.'

'I'm worried about Marissa.'

'There's nothing to be worried about.'

'What if you're right and Xan's a killer?'

'Can you stop it? He's not a killer, all right? I wouldn't've even started thinking about this if you didn't put the idea in my head.'

'So now you're blaming me?'

'No, I'm just saying there's no basis to it. He had no reason to want to hurt Dana. They got along great, and she liked him a –'

He had a realization, a sudden moment of clarity, and his mother noticed the change in his expression.

'What is it?' she asked.

'She liked him a lot,' he said.

'So? What're you talking about?'

'The other day, after Xan came to dinner and we met for the first time, Dana and I had an argument. Well, not really an argument, just a little spat, you know? It seems ridiculous now, but she told me that she thought Xan was handsome, and I got jealous about it. But the real reason I was jealous was because of the way they were acting the night before at dinner. Xan, you know he's a smooth guy, you know, a charmer, likes to compliment everyone, play up to people, that's just his style. But I could tell how much Dana liked the attention.'

'Oh my God,' his mother said. 'So you think they were having an affair?'

'No, that's impossible,' Adam said.

'Why is it so impossible? She was having an affair with that other guy.' This was a good point – and Xan was a younger guy, just like Tony.

Feeling sick, realizing he couldn't totally rule this out, Adam said, 'I don't think she'd do that, not with Marissa's boyfriend. She wouldn't do that to Marissa.'

'You never know what somebody'll do,' his mother said, letting the implication hang there.

Adam was shaking his head. 'No, she wouldn't do that, I'm positive.' He wasn't positive at all, actually, but it made him feel better to say it. Then he added, 'But I guess that doesn't mean he felt the same way.'

'You mean you think he –'

'I'm just saying, what if Xan was interested in her? I mean, more interested in her than she was in him.'

'Then why would he kill her?'

'Maybe he came over here hoping to find her alone. Maybe that was why JoAnne next door heard her dog barking like crazy, probably around the time Dana was killed.'

'Call the police,' his mother said, panicked.

'No, wait, that doesn't make any sense,' Adam said. 'Xan was at the movie that night with Marissa. And just because he and Dana were flirting a little, if you could even call it flirting, doesn't mean he'd come over here to try to sexually assault her. I'm taking a huge leap there. There was no sign of sexual assault; the police would've jumped on that right away. All of this is ridiculous, really, when you think about the facts. There's no basis for any of it.'

'Call the police anyway,' his mother said. 'Let them decide if it's ridiculous or not.'

'Maybe, I'll have to think about it,' he said. 'It all seems very confusing right now.'

Adam went upstairs, even more stressed out than earlier. He took a hot shower, thinking the whole thing through every which way. While some parts of it seemed to fit, he still couldn't come up with any logical motive for Xan to come over to kill Dana, a woman he hardly knew. Only a total psychopath would do something like that, and Xan wasn't a psychopath. If Xan was mentally unstable or had psychopathic tendencies, Adam certainly would've noticed it immediately. Detecting abnormal behavior was his profession, after all. And Adam wasn't even sure if it was physically possible that Xan could've done it. Would he have had time to kill Dana and then meet Marissa at the movie theater? Probably not. Adam tried to forget about the whole thing, think about something else, but the dog barking so ferociously at Xan kept nagging at him, and what his mother had said earlier about how Xan was basically a total stranger kept repeating in his mind as well.

When he got out of the shower, just to reassure himself, he went online to see what he could find out about Xan Evonov. He expected to find a lot of information, even Xan's own website – the guy was an artist, after all – but a Google search for the phrase 'Xan Evonov' turned up zero results. Adam thought this was pretty strange. Why wouldn't an artist have any information online? He'd said he hadn't exhibited his work yet, but it seemed like everybody marketed themselves online nowadays, especially people in the arts – and didn't he say he had a benefactor? There were hundreds of results for 'Alexander Evonov,' but they were mostly in Russian, and the few in English had nothing to do with Xan.

Adam was trying another search engine when the doorbell rang. He figured it was reporters again, harassing him, and several seconds later when his mother called, 'Adam!' he mumbled, 'Goddamn it.' He'd told her not to answer the door for reporters under any circumstances; what was she doing? He headed downstairs, ready to explode.

It wasn't a reporter, though. Detective Clements was standing there, and Adam had a feeling that went way beyond déjà vu.

'What's going on?' Adam asked, hoping there was good news. Maybe there'd been a break in the case – Tony or someone else had been arrested.

But Clements, looking cold and serious, said, 'I need to talk to you, Dr Bloom,' and Adam thought, *Jesus, not again.*

Adam said, 'If you have news I'd appreciate it if you just told me what it is. This is a very difficult time for me, obviously.'

'I understand, and I promise it won't take long.'

'If you're going to question me I don't want to do it without my lawyer here.'

'That's up to you,' Clements said, 'but this isn't formal questioning. I'm just doing some more information gathering. If you want to call your lawyer, you can, but I can't hang around here waiting for him to show up. You'll have to come down to the station with me.'

That was all Adam needed – if the reporters saw a detective taking him in for questioning, what stories would they write then? Adam figured he'd see how it went. If they were just basic questions, he'd answer them. If not, he'd call his lawyer.

They went into the dining room and sat in the same seats they'd sat in during Clements's other interrogations – at the middle of the table, Clements directly across from Adam.

'You're getting to be a pro at this, huh?' Clements asked.

'I guess it's to be expected when I'm a person of interest.'

Adam's tone was dripping with sarcasm, but Clements either didn't get it or wasn't amused; he didn't crack a smile.

'Don't worry,' he said, 'you're not a suspect in the case.'

Adam didn't believe him. 'Really?' he said. 'Do the reporters out there know that?'

'Like I said, this won't take long. I just need to go over your whereabouts on Monday evening, from the time you left your office to the time of the nine-one-one call.'

'Are you kidding me?' Adam said. 'We've been through all this how many times?'

'I understand, but we're doing this with everyone involved in the case. We just need to make sure there are no discrepancies.'

'What about Tony's whereabouts? Are you double-and triple-checking his alibi?'

'Yes, we're still talking to Tony, and we're talking to a lot of other people. So you said you left your office at around six fifteen, is that correct?'

Adam told Clements pretty much verbatim what he'd told him the other day – he left his office, rode the subway to Forest

Hills, stopped at the grocery store, discovered the body, and after several minutes called 911. He gave Clements the same estimated times he'd given during the previous questioning.

'Is it possible you shopped for less than ten minutes?' Clements asked. 'No,' Adam said. 'It was at least ten minutes, maybe closer to fifteen or twenty. There was a woman complaining at the checkout counter.'

'So you're saying that you got home no later than seven twenty-five or seven thirty?'

'That's an estimated time, but yes, that sounds about right.'

Clements wrote this in his pad.

'Can I ask why my whereabouts are so important if I'm not a suspect?' Adam asked.

'Everything's important in a murder investigation,' Clements said, not answering the question. Then he added, 'We have to create an accurate time line for Monday night. Forensics has given us a probable time of death of between six thirty and seven thirty, so we think your wife was dead for less than an hour before the time you say you discovered her body. We have the reports of your neighbors' German shepherd barking very loudly at approximately six thirty, which also fits into the time your wife was killed. We're also talking to your neighbors and other people in the neighborhood to see if anyone saw –'

'I have to talk to you about that,' Adam said excitedly.

'About your neighbors?'

'No, the dog,' Adam said. 'I think I have some information you might find pretty... well, pretty damn interesting.'

He told Clements that the dog had barked at Xan earlier today and when he'd found the note from Tony, and that Xan had flirted with Dana a few nights before she was killed, and that there was strangely no information about Xan on the internet. As Adam spoke, he thought the whole scenario sounded so flimsy, so outlandish, so circumstantial, that he was convinced Clements was going to laugh the whole thing off.

So he was surprised when he was through and Clements asked very seriously, 'So why do you think Xan would forge notes pretending to be Tony?'

'That part I can't figure out,' Adam said. 'I admit there are holes in all of this, but I wanted to tell you anyway because there're other things that seem... I don't know, it's just I hardly know this guy. My daughter's only been dating him for about a week.'

'If I'd known this the other day I would've questioned him. He was the long-haired guy who was here when I was interviewing your daughter, right?'

Adam nodded and said, 'If I'd even remotely thought about any of this, of course I would've told you about it then.'

'Did she start dating him before or after you received the first note?' Adam thought about it for a few seconds, then said, 'After, I think.'

'Well, this definitely sounds like something we should look into. It might go nowhere, but throughout my career dogs have sometimes given me my biggest leads. In fact, I used to work for the canine unit.'

'Really?' Actually, Adam couldn't care less about Clements's career, but he was glad to be on his good side and not be treated as a suspect, at least for the moment.

'Yeah, for five years,' Clements said. 'You really get attached to dogs, and they're great to work with, a lot easier to work with than the human partners I've had, I'll tell you that much. They're even easier to get along with than a couple of my ex-wives.'

Adam forced a smile.

Clements went on, 'The interesting thing is that Tony has continued to deny writing either of those notes so, yeah, everything's worth looking into. Where's Xan now?'

'With my daughter. They should be back at his place in Brooklyn by now.'

'Do you have a phone number or an address for Xan?'

'No, I'm sorry, I don't. But Marissa said he lives in Red Hook.'

'That's okay, we'll get his info. Can you just spell his name for me?'

Adam spelled Xan's full name for Clements and told him to also look under the first name Alexander. As Clements was writing that down, Adam said, 'So if the same person wrote both of the notes and that person wasn't Tony, it's possible that the same person who wrote the notes broke into my house.'

'Anything's possible,' Clements said.

'So maybe you should see if there's a connection between Xan and Carlos Sanchez. I think that's pretty remote, but –'

'Don't worry, we'll check out everything,' Clements said, getting up and putting the pad away. 'By the way, Dr Bloom, are you right-handed or left-handed?'

'Right-handed.'

'Thanks very much, Doctor. I'll be in touch with you again soon.' Clements left, but his last question lingered. Adam figured it must've been forensics related; maybe they'd figured out, or were trying to figure out, whether the killer was a righty or a lefty. Well, so much for not feeling like a suspect. That had lasted for, what, a minute?

Adam's mother had been eavesdropping on the conversation from the other room – why wasn't Adam surprised? – and she said, 'See, he doesn't think checking out Xan is so crazy. I told you, I got a bad feeling about him.'

'What can I say?' Adam said. 'Maybe you should become a cop.'

'Maybe I should,' she said seriously. 'But what about Marissa?'

'What about her?'

'I don't like that she's alone with Xan.'

'Yeah, me neither, but as soon as the police find his address I'm sure they won't dilly-dally. They'll send somebody right over there.'

'I think you should at least call her and let her know what's going on. Better yet, tell her to come home. Tell her we want her here.'

'How'm I supposed to do that?'

'Please, just do it. I really want her here with us right now.'

While Adam knew his mother was overreacting, he was concerned about her getting too upset, what with her heart condition. Besides, he'd rather have Marissa home with them right now, too.

From his BlackBerry, he called her cell.

'Hello,' Marissa said.

'Where are you?' Adam asked.

'At Xan's, what's up?'

'Is he there with you right now?'

'Yeah, why?'

'Can you go into another room for a second please?'

'Why? What's going on?' There was panic in her voice.

'Nothing bad,' he assured her. 'I just need to talk to you in private for a second.'

Marissa took a deep breath, then another. 'What is it?'

'Are you in another room?'

'Yes.' She was annoyed.

'We want you to come home,' Adam said.

'Why?'

'Because Grandma and I want you here, that's why.'

'What for?'

'We just do, okay?'

'Look, I told you, I need some space –'

'Please don't argue with me about this, Marissa. I want you to come home – without Xan.'

'Why can't I bring Xan?'

'Can he hear you?'

'No, but why did you –'

'Please try to keep your voice down. I just want you here, okay? I want the whole family to be together. Just the family.' He knew this explanation was flimsy, but it was the best he could come up with.

'I'm not coming home, and I can't believe you. You scared me. I thought there was some emergency or something.'

Adam shook his head and looked at his mother, who stage-whispered, 'Tell her.'

'Look, you can't tell Xan about this, but there's something going on with the police, okay?'

'Why can't I tell Xan?'

'Keep your voice down.'

'Why're you being so mysterious?'

'They want to talk to him, okay?'

'To Xan?'

'Yes.'

After a short silence, Marissa asked, 'Why?'

'I'm sure it'll all be routine, but we'd rather you were here, so please don't argue with me.'

Adam's mother said, 'Come home, Marissa,' probably loud enough that Marissa could hear.

'I don't understand what's going on,' Marissa said. 'What does Xan have to do with anything, and why're you both freaking out?'

'We're not freaking out,' Adam said. 'There're just some things I've been concerned about, and –'

'Wait, *you* did this?'

'I didn't do anything –'

'What did you tell the police about Xan?'

'Can he hear you?'

'You'll say anything, won't you? Now what're you trying to do, say that Xan killed Mom?'

'I said keep your goddamn voice down,' Adam said, raising his own voice.

'You're pathetic, you know that? I can't believe you're doing this.'

'There're things you don't know, okay? Things that seem very strange –'

'Strange, that's a good one. You know what seems strange to me? You. Yeah, you. The way you acted last week, on your big ego trip, then everything that happened with Mom, and now trying to blame my boyfriend, who I'm in love with. You're the one I should be staying away from.'

'Marissa, plea –'

'Just leave me the hell alone.'

'Marissa... Marissa?... *Marissa?*' He realized she wasn't there. 'Damn it.'

'What is it?' his mother asked.

'She hung up on me.'

'Call her back.'

Adam tried but got her voicemail.

'Shit. Goddamn it.'

'What?'

'I think she turned her phone off.'

'Oh my God, so now how're we supposed to get in touch with her?'

'Okay, let's try to stay rational here. You're getting very carried away, okay? There's nothing to panic about. It's not like she's in any danger.'

'How do you know?'

'Let's just wait, okay? Clements is probably on his way over there. The police have ways to –'

Adam's landline rang. The display read RESTRICTED.

'Who is it?' Adam's mother asked.

'I don't know,' Adam said. He picked up and said, 'Hello?'

'Dr Bloom.'

'Hi, Detective Clements,' Adam said so his mother would know who was calling.

'Is it possible Xan has a roommate or uses another name besides the one you gave me?' Clements asked.

'Not that I know of,' Adam said. 'Why?'

'We can't find any listing for him in the entire city. There's an Alexander Evonov in Brighton Beach, but you said he was living in Red Hook, right?'

'That's what I understood.'

'It's probably a different guy, but we'll check it out. In the meantime, can you call your daughter?'

'I'm trying to reach her.'

'When you do, can you get Xan's address and let me know it right away?' Adam said he would.

With his mother hovering over him, Adam called Marissa several times and kept getting her voicemail before the first ring. There was no doubt her phone was off.

'Okay, let's not panic, okay?' Adam said. 'It didn't sound like Clements was panicking. He probably knows that this whole idea of Xan having anything to do with any of this is very far out.'

'And what if you're wrong? What if Xan killed Dana? What if he's some kind of maniac?'

'Don't worry, she'll be fine,' Adam said. 'I'm absolutely sure of it.'

25

'OH, GOD, THAT man is beyond annoying,' Marissa said to Xan. 'Can you believe he told the police to talk to you? What is *wrong* with him?'

They were on Xan's couch, in the middle of the afternoon. He was holding her hand, caressing the inside of her wrist with his fingertips.

'Why would he tell the police to talk to me? I mean, I was with you when you talked to that cop, and if the cop wanted to ask me anything he would've asked me right then.'

'I know,' Marissa said. 'But I have to admit it, it scares me.'

'Scares you how?'

'I think my dad's getting desperate. Why else would he bring you, of all people, into it? Next thing he'll be telling the police to talk to my freaking grandmother.'

'So you think he's trying to take the blame away from himself?'

'Exactly. I don't know how I'm going to be able to handle this – if my father really killed my mother.'

'Shh, don't worry, you'll get through it,' Xan said, squeezing her hand.

'I don't want to see him again,' she said. 'The sound of his voice just… just disgusts me.'

'Does he know where I live?' Xan asked.

'My father? I'm not sure. Why?'

'I just wonder if he gave the police my address, that's all.'

'I didn't tell him,' Marissa said, 'but I guess the police will find you anyway. I'm so sorry my father's dragging you into this, after all you've done for me, just being here for me. You've been so great.'

'Don't worry about me,' Xan said, 'you're the only thing I'm concerned about. Is your phone off?'

Marissa nodded.

'Good,' he said. 'Keep it off. You don't need any more stressful phone calls today.' He kissed her gently on the cheek and then said, 'How about something to drink? Water, Diet Coke?'

'Diet Coke would be great.'

He kissed her on the cheek again and then went to the kitchen area. She remained on the couch, ruminating about the phone call with her father, and then her gaze drifted toward the easel and one of Xan's latest paintings. It was a large, abstract piece, and he'd used only red paint. He'd done a few other similar ones and had hung them on the wall. Maybe it was because he'd arranged the paintings in a group, but they really seemed to make a statement. For the first time she thought he actually had potential as an artist.

'I love your new paintings,' she said.

'Really?' he said as he poured the soda into a glass.

'Yeah, especially the one you're working on now. It has so much emotion and passion. When did you paint these?'

'A couple of nights ago, before your mom's funeral. Yeah, I'm pretty happy with them, too. I guess I was just inspired.'

'Inspired by what?'

'I guess by what happened to your mom. It's been very intense.'

Marissa was looking at the painting on the easel, noticing the deep shade of red. 'It's weird, isn't it?' she said. 'I mean, the way something awful can bring out art, the way art comes out of tragedy… I don't know what I'm saying. I'm such a total mess right now.'

'Here you go,' Xan said, handing her the soda and then sitting back down next to her.

She took a long sip, then said, 'I don't know why everybody's picking on you when you're so great.'

'Who's everybody?' Xan asked.

'Well, you said my grandma was giving you the evil eye, right?'

'Yeah, but I wouldn't say she was picking on me. You said it was because I'm not Jewish, right?'

'Yeah, but still. And then there's what Darren said at the funeral.'

'What did *he* say?'

'I didn't tell you?'

Xan shook his head.

'Oh,' Marissa said. 'I was such a mess that day I didn't know where I was half the time. But, yeah, he came up to me, I think in the chapel, before the service started and paid his respects, you know, told me how sorry he was. I don't think you were there. I think you were with my father.'

'And then he said something?' Xan asked.

'Yeah, but don't get upset or anything. It was just Darren being Darren. He can be so annoying sometimes. Anyway, he said something to me like "So you're still with that crazy guy, huh?" Or, no, maybe it was like "You're still with that lunatic, right?" If I wasn't so upset, already, grieving, I would've gotten really pissed off. I mean, first of all, there I was at a *funeral*, my *mother's* funeral, so why is he talking about you at all? It's so disrespectful. And I knew he was just saying it because he was jealous, because I haven't talked to him in days but he read on my blog and heard from other people about how into you I am.'

'So what did you say to him?'

'I don't remember really,' Marissa said. 'Something like "What're you talking about?" And he was like "You want to know what he said to me the other night?" He being you. So then he said it was when he kept bothering me at the bar and you went over to talk to him, you know, the night we met. He said you said to him that if he didn't leave me alone you were going to cut off his dick and feed it to him.'

Marissa smiled, trying to show how ridiculous she thought the whole thing was, but Xan remained deadpan and said, 'You didn't believe him, did you?'

'Of course I didn't believe it. I knew he was just saying it to upset me, but that makes it even more disturbing because he was trying to upset me at my mother's funeral.'

'What I told him was that he was causing a scene and he should leave the club before the bouncer kicked him out.'

'Yeah, I know, I figured you said something totally innocuous like that. But can you believe how pathetic Darren is that he'd actually make something like that up?... is it hot in here?'

'I don't think so,' Xan said. 'Have some more soda.'

Marissa drank some more, then said, 'I feel a little dizzy.'

'Want me to open a window?'

'Yeah, can you? Maybe it's talking about Darren, it's getting me sick.'

Xan opened one of the windows. The breeze felt good.

'I'm sorry if I upset you,' Marissa said. 'I knew it was ridiculous, but I just wanted to tell you.'

'I'm not upset at all.' He sat back down next to her. 'Feeling any better?'

'No, not really. I didn't eat yet today, that's probably it.'

'Drink some more soda, that'll help.'

She took a few sips, then said, 'It's so weird.'

'What is?'

'I don't know.' She felt very disoriented. 'Just how my father and Darren are picking on you, of all people. You're the best thing in my life right now.

Honestly... I don't know what I'd do without you... wow, I feel really dizzy.'

'Here,' he said. 'Lean on me.'

It was hard to see clearly. She wasn't sure where she was.

She was looking at a painting. It was very red.

Everything had been going great for Johnny until that damn dog started barking at him. He couldn't believe it when he left the house with Marissa and saw the woman walking the mutt. She had to be walking it right then? What were the odds? He was hoping the dog wouldn't notice him, but no luck there. As soon as he saw Johnny, he went after him, like he wanted to bite his head off.

The woman struggled, pulling on the leash with both hands like she was trying to win a game of tug-of-war. Walking away down the sidewalk, Marissa said to Johnny, 'That was so weird. I've known Blackie for years and I've never seen him get like that before.'

'I know, it's always been that way for me with dogs,' Johnny said, trying to make it into a joke. 'I think they think I smell like a cat or something.' He was hoping that Marissa would forget about the whole damn dog thing and that no one else would make any connection about it either.

But what was that old saying, bad things come in threes? Well, number two was when she got the phone call from her father. She went into the kitchen area to talk to him, but Johnny, sitting on his couch, heard the whole conversation – well, her part of it, anyway – and it was enough to tell him that something else had gone wrong. Her father wouldn't have gotten suspicious about him for no reason, and it sounded like the police believed her father, which was even worse. Johnny wondered if there was something he'd overlooked, some evidence he'd left behind or something.

Johnny wasn't about to take any chances. He wasn't going to just hang out in his apartment and hope the cops didn't show up to bust him. No, Johnny wasn't a gambling man, especially when it came to the safety of his own ass. He knew he wasn't above screwing up and getting caught, and he was smart enough to know that sometimes shit happens that you can't control, which was why he always had a backup plan – and not just a plan B. He had plans C, D, E, and F, too.

It was a good sign that Marissa hadn't told her father where Johnny lived. The name Xan Evonov wouldn't help the cops out, and it would probably take days for them to figure out that his real name was Johnny Long; by then he'd be long gone, living under a new name, somewhere far away from New York. Although he would have to give up the fantasy of living in the Blooms' house, he could still get all the money and still watch

Adam Bloom die in pain. Hey, like Meatloaf says, 'Two out of three ain't bad.'

When Marissa ended the call with her father, Johnny made sure she'd turned her phone off. It was an iPhone, and he knew those had GPS. He didn't know how badly the cops wanted to talk to him, but he didn't want to take any chances that they'd try to track him down by tracing Marissa's phone. Next, he needed to subdue Marissa, so when he poured her a glass of Coke he slipped a roofie into it. Johnny occasionally had to drug the women he hustled, so he always had plenty of Rohypnol and chloroform on hand. He only used drugs to rob women, though, never to rape them. Every woman Johnny had ever seduced had gone to bed with him willingly. Johnny knew that rape was the worst thing you could possibly do to a person; murder was a favor compared to rape. When you kill somebody, they're gone, they're done feeling pain. But when you rape somebody, the pain goes on and on. Besides, he didn't want to scar his record as a Casanova. Someday, when somebody wrote a book about him, or they made a movie, or mov*ies,* when Johnny Long became a *legend,* he didn't want to be like those athletes who were caught using steroids. He didn't want there to be any doubts about his achievements.

When Marissa passed out, Johnny carried her to his bed and tied her up and taped her mouth shut. Yeah, he had the rope and tape ready – you always had to be prepared. He made sure her nose wasn't covered by the tape and she was breathing. He needed to keep her alive, for a little while anyway.

He went out, stole a Toyota, and parked it in front of his building. He'd been gone less than an hour, and Marissa was still unconscious. He went around his apartment and packed a backpack with clothes, toiletries, and whatever else he could fit into it. He was bummed that he'd have to leave his Bloodworks behind. He hoped when the landlord cleaned out the place he was smart enough to save the paintings, or at least give them to some gallery or art dealer. When Johnny Long became the world's most famous Casanova, how much would those pictures go for? A few hundred thousand each? More? Yeah, probably.

When it got dark out, Johnny untied Marissa and removed

the tape from her mouth; she moaned when he did this but remained unconscious. Then he walked her – well, really *carried* her – out of the apartment and down the stairs to the street. It was perfect because if anyone noticed it would look like she was drunk and he was helping her get home.

He had her in the car, ready to go, but he couldn't bear to leave the paintings. He rushed back up and took all six of the Bloodworks. They wouldn't fit in the trunk but were just barely able to fit in the backseat area, thank God. He couldn't think of anything else he needed and, with Marissa passed out next to him, he headed happily out of the city.

26

A DAM MUST'VE TRIED calling Marissa fifty times, and he still couldn't get through. He'd left a few messages, but the other times he ended the calls as soon as he heard her voicemail greeting.

'Something awful's happening,' his mother said. 'I know it is.'

Adam was getting sick of his mother and her psychic hunches. He knew that if he were alone he wouldn't be nearly as panicked, but with his mother lurking nearby, on the verge of hysteria, it was impossible to stay calm.

'Call Clements again,' she said.

'I left a message for him ten minutes ago.'

'Maybe he didn't get it.'

'He got it.'

'How do you know?'

'Because he did, okay?'

'Maybe he found out where Xan lives. Maybe he knows *something.*'

'If he did he would've called us.'

'You don't know that. Maybe he –'

'Okay, that's enough,' Adam said. 'Let's just calm down.' Unconsciously he called Marissa again, reached her voicemail, and clicked off, then said, 'The problem is we're too caught up in this, okay? Chances are none of this has anything to do with Xan and we're getting hysterical for –'

Adam's cell started ringing, and he nearly jumped. He checked the display and said to his mother, 'Clements.' Then into the phone he said, 'Hello?'

'How many times did you call me?' Clements asked.

'A few,' Adam said. 'Did you find out –'

'There's no reason for you to call me more than once,' he said. 'You just have to leave one message and I'll get back to you. Leaving more than one message just wastes my time and yours.'

Adam resented the lecture. He asked, 'So did you find out where Xan lives or not?'

'He doesn't seem to be listed anywhere in Brooklyn,' Clements said. 'We checked out the Alexander Evonov from Brighton Beach, but he died three weeks ago. What about you? Did you reach your daughter?'

'I've been trying. I'm pretty sure her phone's off.'

'Why's it off?'

Adam didn't feel like explaining the whole thing, so he said, 'I don't know, maybe it ran out of charge or something.'

Adam's mother was saying, 'Give him her number. Give him her number.'

'Do you want her number?' Adam asked Clements.

'Yeah, okay,' Clements said. Adam gave it to him, and then Clements added, 'But you keep trying her, too, and when you get through, call me back. But don't call me just to leave messages, because that only wastes time on my end, okay?'

During the next few hours, Adam tried to watch TV with his mother, but every five minutes or so he called Marissa. He kept getting her voicemail, and his mother's nervous agitation was driving him crazy. He had to get away from her, so he went upstairs to the PC in his office and did more searches, trying to find Xan's address or any information about him, but he couldn't find anything. Then his phone started vibrating, and he saw that he'd received a text message from MARISSA CELL.

'Thank God,' Adam said.

Then he read the message:

**if you wannna see the little bitch again call me in
one minute clocks ticking**

For several seconds he was confused, unable to compute the words' meaning. Then it set in that Marissa hadn't sent the message, that the message was *about* Marissa. He read it a few more times but couldn't focus. Finally he realized that someone was threatening to kill his daughter, but Adam, still scattered, didn't know how he was supposed to call back when there was no number to call. Was he supposed to call back on Marissa's phone? Adam frantically clicked SEND, knowing the minute was probably already up.

'Barely made it,' Xan said.

Jesus Christ, they'd been right about him.

'Where the hell's my daughter?' Adam nearly shouted.

'Hey, take it easy, Doc. You don't want me to do something I'd regret, do you?'

'I want to talk to her.'

'I think we need to talk about what *I* want.'

'Put her on the phone, damn it.'

'Are the cops there?'

'I said put her on the phone.'

'Hey, you wanna see your little bitch alive again? Do you? Huh? Do you?' Adam was suddenly aware of how absolutely terrified he was. He was shivering.

'Please don't hurt her,' he said. 'Please, *please* don't hurt her.'

'That's all up to you right now, Doc. If you do what I tell you to do and you stop interrupting me, you'll see her again. If not…'

'You goddamn son of a bitch,' Adam said.

He couldn't believe this was actually happening, that Xan had done this to him, to *them*.

'See?' Xan said. 'That's what I'm talking about right there.'

'I'm listening, okay?' Adam said. 'I'm fucking listening.'

'That's good, but if the cops are listening in, or you're recording this conversation, or you even tell the cops you spoke to me, then you'll never see your daughter again. Sorry, but that's just the way it is. If I see one cop at the meeting spot they'll never find your daughter's body. I guarantee that.'

'Meeting spot? What meeting spot?'

'Hey, didn't I say I'm gonna be asking the questions?'

Adam heard his mother's footsteps in the hallway.

'Just tell me what to do and I'll do it,' he said. He went to the doorway, leaned his head into the hall, and whispered to his mother, 'It's just a friend of mine from college.'

'What friend?'

He could tell his mother didn't believe him.

'I'll be right off,' he said and shut the door.

'Was that the old biddy?' Xan asked.

Adam wanted to scream at Xan, but he said as calmly as he possibly could, nearly whispering in case his mother was trying to listen in, 'I'll do whatever you tell me to do.'

'Yeah, you *will* do whatever I tell you to do because this is *my* thing, I'm calling the shots here. You're not used to that, are you, Doc? You're used to being the big shot, the man in charge. I bet you don't let your patients talk a lot. I bet you like to do all the talking. You know, I saw a shrink once. Yeah, when I was at the orphanage, they thought I was "troubled" so they had me talk to this old man shrink – well, he seemed old at the time, but he was probably about your age. Man, I hated that guy, acting like he was so above me, acting like just because he was in the chair and I was on the couch he had all the power, and I could tell he was getting off on it. But now the tables are turned, now I'm in the chair and you're on the couch. How does it feel to be on the couch, Dr Bloom?'

'It doesn't feel good,' Adam said, trying to placate Xan, the way he would a patient. He remembered something Carol had once told him. *If the patient wants to feel powerful, let him feel powerful.*

'You're damn right it doesn't feel good. It feels like shit, and that's how I want you to feel, like the piece of shit you are.'

'I understand,' Adam said.

'You understand? What do you mean, you understand? What the hell's that supposed to mean?'

'It means I understand how you feel.'

'You don't understand how I feel. Nobody understands how I feel.'

Xan was raising his voice. He sounded unstable, insane. Adam couldn't believe that this was the same guy who'd been over to the house for dinner, whom he'd accepted and liked.

'I want to give you what you want,' Adam said. 'Just tell me what you want and it's yours.'

'Yeah? And what if I told you I want to see your daughter's head on a plate? Could I have that?'

Adam was squeezing the phone so hard he heard it starting to break. 'Don't hurt my daughter,' he said as calmly as he could, but he knew it probably sounded like a threat.

'There you go, talking down to me again, telling me what to do. Is that any way to talk to a man who has a gun to your daughter's head?'

'How do you want me to talk to you?' Adam asked, shaking again, starting to cry.

'I want you to shut your mouth and listen to me when I tell you what to do. You think you can do that?'

Adam knew Xan didn't want him to answer, so he didn't.

'Good,' Xan said. 'You're learning. Twelve noon, tomorrow, I want one million dollars in cash, in unmarked fifties and hundreds. You're gonna bring it to the parking lot of the ShopRite on Miron Lane in Kingston, New York. If the bills are marked or if I see a cop, a single cop, or a detective, or anyone I don't like, I'm not gonna show up and the little bitch dies.'

'I don't have a million dollars,' Adam said.

'Then get it.'

'How'm I supposed to do that by noon tomorrow?'

'Your problem, not mine.'

'I need more time.'

'That's all the time you're getting.'

'Please just –'

'Shut the fuck up. You know, you're lucky I'm even giving you the chance to see your daughter again. You killed Carlos, he was part of *my* family. For that I should kill your wife *and* the little brat.'

Adam had been so absorbed with Xan's threatening Marissa that it hadn't registered that he was talking to the man who'd killed his wife. Why the hell had he done it? Just for revenge? For fun? And why did he start dating Marissa? How did he meet her? None of it made any sense.

'I'm begging you,' Adam said. 'Give me more time, another day, just one more… hello, are you there?… are you *there*?'

The call had disconnected. He tried to call back and listened to the voicemail: 'Hey, this is Marissa's cell. Sorry I missed your call. Leave a –'

He pressed END. He sat at his desk, holding the phone, shaking worse than before. He had no idea what to do next. He'd never felt so terrified and alone.

'Adam?'

His mother entered the room, and he immediately swiveled away so she couldn't see his face.

'Please leave me alone, Ma.'

'Who was that on the phone?'

'I told you, it was just an old friend.'

'Why're you –'

'I'm just upset about Dana, okay? Please just give me a little while, okay?'

His mother stood there for several seconds, then said suspiciously, 'Okay,' and left the room.

Adam knew that if he told his mother what was going on she'd insist that he call the police, and he wasn't sure that was the right thing to do. Xan was obviously psychotic and probably extremely paranoid, and Adam believed that he meant what he said – if he saw a cop, or even if he believed the police would get involved, he'd kill Marissa without hesitation. He'd already killed Dana, so what would stop him from killing somebody else?

But Adam wanted to make sure he was making the right decision. After all, this wouldn't be the first time he'd acted impulsively. Although it was still difficult to fully concentrate, he imagined calling the police. He'd tell Clements exactly what Xan had said, but what if Clements misjudged Xan and showed up in Kingston with a whole SWAT team? Then what if Xan

killed Marissa like he said he would? How w
with himself?

There was no doubt about it – calling the
huge mistake. His best chance to save Marissa was
Xan, give him exactly what he wanted, but how was he supposed
to get one million dollars by noon tomorrow? He'd lied; he had
the money – well, he could raise it, anyway. The problem was
he only had access to a couple grand in cash and money market
funds, but if he sold stock, mutual funds, liquidated part of his
401(k), he could get the million. But it would take time to do
this; he sure as hell couldn't get it done by noon tomorrow *and*
make it all the way up to Kingston.

Then Adam had a thought that scared the hell out of him.
What if he gave Xan the money and Xan killed Marissa anyway?
Why wouldn't he? What would there be to stop him?

Adam was feeling completely hopeless when he had another
idea. It was risky, very risky, but it seemed to have a better
chance of working than any of the other plans. He thought it
through, deciding he had no choice but to go for it.

27

JOHNNY DROVE THROUGH northern New Jersey toward upstate New York. In Tuxedo he pulled over on the side of the road and turned on Marissa's cell. In her DIALED call log he found DAD CELL and clicked MESSAGE. He sent Adam Bloom the text saying he'd kill the little bitch if he didn't call back within a minute. Johnny wouldn't've really killed her – why kill her before he got paid? – but, man, it was a rush to mess with Adam like that, to be in total control.

Naturally Adam called back, sounding desperate. Yeah, Johnny could hear the terror in his voice, and he knew he had him by the balls. Man, it felt so great to have all the power, to be the guy calling the shots. Knowing how much Bloom hated him made it even better. Johnny was the last person in the world Bloom wanted to talk to, but he had no choice but to stay on the phone and listen and do whatever Johnny told him to do.

After he gave Bloom the instructions, he ended the call while Bloom was still talking and turned off the phone. Then he wiped off all the prints and tossed the phone into the woods as far as it would go.

He drove another hour or so to a small town called Accord.

When he was growing up at St John's, Father Hennessy would take Johnny and the other kids up to an old bungalow colony called Max's for one weekend every summer. Although the bungalows were falling apart and the grass was overgrown, the kids loved getting out of the hot city and running around all day and breathing in fresh air. Johnny loved it, too, except when Hennessy took him on long hikes in the woods and raped him. He told Johnny that if he didn't keep it a secret God would punish him. Johnny never told anyone, but not because he was afraid of God. He just didn't want the other kids to make fun of him and call him a faggot.

Johnny figured that one of the bungalows would be the perfect spot to hide out with Marissa. He remembered Hennessy telling him the place was always empty during the off-season and there was no one around for miles.

They drove along the narrow, winding country road. There were so many weeds and overhanging trees in front of the MAX'S sign that Johnny missed the turnoff and had to make a U-turn and go back. The road going up the hill to Max's used to be gravel, but it had become almost completely overgrown, and it was hard to even tell that it was a road. Johnny had thought the orphanage was still using Max's, but it seemed like the whole bungalow colony had been abandoned, like no one had been up there for years.

Johnny parked where Father Hennessy used to park the mini school bus, at the bottom of the hill near the old barn. The barn had been dilapidated and bat-infested back then, but it was where Johnny and Carlos and the guys used to hang out at night and watch TV and play poker and blackjack.

When Johnny cut the headlights it was pitch-dark; he couldn't see Marissa or the dashboard or anything. Then he turned on the flashlight he'd brought, and maybe the light startled Marissa or she just happened to wake up at that moment because she started moaning, 'Where... where am I?... where am I?' and Johnny said, 'Someplace safe, go back to sleep.' Then she said, 'How come we're –' and Johnny said, 'Just shut the fuck up and sleep,' which was probably a mistake because she suddenly started screaming. Johnny wasn't very concerned – they were in the middle of nowhere, and no one had been to Max's probably for years – but the screaming was loud, hurting his ears, and he just wanted her to shut up.

'Shut the fuck up!' he yelled, but she was fighting back, trying to scratch his face. Then she knocked the flashlight out of his hand, which really pissed him off. He fumbled around on the floor while she continued screeching in his ear, 'Help me! Help me!' and then he grabbed the flashlight and smashed her in the face with it. He hit her harder than he meant to – he heard bone, probably her nose, breaking – and it didn't shut her up at all; it made her scream even louder.

He found a rag he'd brought on the floor and poured some more chloroform onto it and then pressed it over her face. He was pushing down hard, right on her probably broken nose, which had to kill, but after about ten seconds she stopped fighting back and then passed out again.

He waited several seconds, enjoying the sudden silence, and then he put on his backpack and dragged Marissa out of the car. It was about ten degrees cooler up here than in the city – it felt like it was in the low forties, maybe the upper thirties. He should've brought a warmer jacket or a sweater and blankets and, oh yeah, food and water. But, come on, he couldn't think of everything, right? Besides, they were only going to be here one night.

He dragged her up the hill and then the rickety steps to the porch of one of the bungalows. It was the one he used to stay in with Carlos and a couple of other guys. Some of the floorboards were so loose, probably rotting away and eaten by termites, that he thought the whole floor might cave in. When he pulled on the handle of the front door it was stuck at first, and when he yanked on it the upper part of the door came off its hinges.

It was freezing in the bungalow; it seemed colder than outside. It was musty, too, like air hadn't circulated in this place for years. Coughing, he shined the flashlight ahead of him as he dragged Marissa along toward the bedroom in the back of the bungalow. His feet were crunching against something. He'd thought it was gravel or sand, but then he shined the flashlight downward and saw that the floor was covered with mouse shit.

The mattress on the old single bed, the one he used to sleep on, was covered with mouse shit, too, but what could you do? He rested Marissa on the bed, got the rope from the backpack, and tied her up so tightly that the rope was probably cutting into her arms, but he didn't want to take any chances. He was about to tape her mouth shut again, but there was so much blood from her broken nose he was afraid she'd suffocate or choke to death. What he really wanted to do was shoot her right now. Yeah, she was a spoiled brat, and she'd tried to scratch his eyes out a few minutes ago, but he really had nothing against her. His grudge was against her father, so the best thing he could do for her was to put a bullet in her head.

But he knew he had to be smart about this, not humane. Besides, she'd be out of her misery soon. If everything went as planned, she had fourteen hours to live. Fifteen, tops.

Johnny woke up thinking, *Note to self – next time you kidnap somebody, don't hide out in a freezing, mouse-shit-covered bungalow.* He'd barely slept. He had to get up to chloroform Marissa a few more times during the night, but he probably wouldn't have been able to sleep much anyway because of the cold and because he was so excited, thinking about the million dollars he'd get and how he'd spend it. He was definitely gonna go somewhere warm, somewhere there were beaches, there was no doubt about that. If he couldn't get out of the country, he'd get a new identity and hide out in California or Florida, probably Florida. He had dark skin, could probably pass for Cuban, and he'd clean up with all the girls down there in Fort Lauderdale and South Beach. Put Johnny Long on a South Florida beach and there was gonna be trouble.

It was a cloudy day. It didn't look like it would rain, but it didn't look like the sun would come out either. Johnny was on the stoop in front of the bungalow, breathing in some fresh air, trying to get all that stuffy mouse-shit air out of his lungs, when Marissa started making noise again.

'Pain in my ass,' he said as he went inside.

She was screaming, her face red, trying to get loose but not making any progress. Her nose was swollen to about twice its normal size, and there was a lot of blood, some of it brown and crusted, around her nostrils and upper lip.

'Hey, can you shut up?' Johnny said. 'I said shut the fuck up!'

She wouldn't, and Johnny grabbed the rag with the chloroform and said, 'You have two choices – shut the fuck up or I chloroform you again. Which is it?'

'P-p-please,' she begged, sobbing. 'P-pl-please…'

'That's better,' he said. 'I mean, why waste your voice screaming? Nobody's gonna hear you, and you're just gonna give us both headaches.'

'Where… are… w-w-we?' she asked.

'It doesn't matter where we are,' he said. Then he added, 'We're someplace safe.'

'Why?' she asked, crying. 'Why?… why?'

'It's complicated, baby,' he said. 'But don't worry, if you stay calm and do everything I tell you to do I won't hurt you.'

He'd been lying to her since the second he met her; why stop now?

She was sobbing harder, and then he smelled something awful. At first he thought it was something rotting, maybe under the bed, and then he realized she'd shit in her pants during the night. Maybe that was what all the screaming had been about.

'Oh, you had an accident, huh?' he said. 'I'm so sorry. Man, that really sucks. I wish I could let you clean yourself up, but you're nice and tied up now and I don't want to risk you trying to get away. I mean, I know you wouldn't get anywhere, because there's no place to get to, but still.'

'You fucking asshole!' she screamed. 'You motherfucking lunatic!'

'You won't scream again,' he said, dangling the rag over her face to show he was serious. She looked away from him, toward the wall, and started crying again.

'Sorry you feel so shitty,' he said.

He laughed about that one all morning. He really had to start writing this stuff down so he could put it in the Casanova book. It was always good to have a little humor in a story; he couldn't just go on and on about his sexual conquests for five hundred pages. Well, he could, but still.

At around eleven o'clock he chloroformed Marissa for the last time. She struggled, screaming and trying to bite his hand – and to think, just a couple of days ago she'd had such good manners. Finally she gave in and passed out. He hoped she'd stay unconscious for a couple of hours. By then he'd have the money, and he could come back and shoot her. If things worked out, she'd never wake up again.

Johnny left the bungalow and walked down the hill to the car. Looking over at the barn, he had a flashback to one night when a couple of guys were picking on him, taunting him with switchblades, and Carlos came over with a gun and ordered the guys to go away. It reminded Johnny of why he was going through all of this. It wasn't really about the money. It was about revenge, getting even.

At about eleven thirty, Johnny pulled up just outside the parking lot of the ShopRite in Kingston. He didn't see Adam Bloom's SUV or his Merc in the lot, but he was mainly looking out for cops. He knew if they were here they'd be undercover and hard to spot, but that was why Johnny had arrived a half-hour early. There was a good chance that anyone who was hanging out in the parking lot was a cop. So far the only person who looked suspicious was the gray-haired older woman in the double-parked Lexus. She didn't look like a cop, which made her even more suspicious. Then an old guy, probably her husband, got in with her and they drove away.

Johnny didn't think Bloom would bring the cops into this. He wouldn't want to take the chance of his daughter winding up dead, and besides, it wasn't Bloom's style. No, Bloom had showed his cards early, the night of the robbery. He was a take-matters-into-his-own-hands type of guy. He wanted to be the big shot, the hero, and Johnny knew that driving upstate to rescue his daughter from the 'maniac' who was holding her hostage would be too big an opportunity for him to resist.

At noon, Johnny didn't see any sign of cops, but where the hell was Bloom? At ten past, he still hadn't shown. Johnny didn't think he'd come late and risk his daughter's life, but what other explanation was there?

Johnny spotted a phone booth near a pizza restaurant at the

other end of the strip mall. He drove over there, left his car running, and called Bloom's cell – he'd memorized the number before he'd tossed away Marissa's cell last night. Bloom's voicemail picked up before the first ring. Had he really turned his phone *off*?

Johnny got back in the car and waited about ten more minutes, until it became clear that Bloom wasn't showing. This Johnny hadn't expected at all. He'd thought Bloom might show up with less money, try to bargain the price down, but he didn't think he'd get stood up. Who the hell did Bloom think was in charge of this thing, anyway? Who did he think was calling the shots?

Suddenly furious, Johnny drove out of the lot. It was time for plan C, or D, or whatever the hell letter he was up to. He'd go back to Max's and shoot Marissa. Killing a guy's wife and daughter was good enough revenge. Yeah, the million dollars would've been nice, but Johnny knew money wouldn't matter once the Casanova book sold, and he'd get hundreds of thousands of dollars, maybe millions, someday from the Bloodworks. Yeah, he'd have to let Adam live, but maybe that was a good thing. Living was so much worse than dying. Why give the guy a break?

Then, a few minutes later, Johnny looked in his rearview and saw a red midsize car about a hundred yards behind him. There was another car in between, and it was hard to see the driver of the red car, but then, as they went around the bend, Johnny caught a glimpse of the guy, and he couldn't believe it. Who the hell did he think he was kidding?

Around sunrise, Adam left Forest Hills. The reporters were finally gone, but he had a feeling that, no matter what happened upstate, they'd be back very soon.

He'd left a note for his mother on the kitchen table: *Running some errands.* He knew she'd get worried when he didn't come home and was unreachable, but he had no choice. If he told her he was driving up to the Catskills to try to rescue Marissa single-handedly, she would've called the police and possibly gotten Marissa killed.

Adam drove to La Guardia Airport, parked in long-term

parking, and then rented a Taurus at Budget. He knew Xan would be looking out for the SUV or the Merc, and he wanted to be as incognito as possible.

Several times, he almost stopped and turned back. He knew he was taking a huge risk by going up alone, but he didn't see any alternative. If he called the police it would be the equivalent of gambling that the police would bust Xan before he had a chance to kill Marissa or that Xan had been lying about how he'd kill Marissa if the police got involved. He'd misjudged Xan from the beginning – they all had – and he wasn't going to do it again.

Adam exited the New York State Thruway in Kingston and, using directions from a map he'd printed, found the ShopRite. It was early, before ten o'clock, but he was glad he was here, relieved he'd avoided the nightmare scenario of getting stuck on the road and missing the noon meeting time. He didn't want to stay in a static position, though, and risk being spotted by Xan, so he drove around the area and then parked for a while in the lot of a nearby strip mall. At eleven thirty, he headed back to the ShopRite. As he entered the lot he spotted Xan in his parked car just outside the lot. He was pretty sure that Xan hadn't seen him, but it was a close call – too close. If Xan had spotted him that would've been it; the whole plan would've been shot to hell. He should have waited across the road and watched with binoculars or something. He was angry at himself for making that slipup, and he was aware of his raging pulse. In his rush to leave the house he'd forgotten to take the Klonopin with him, and he hadn't had a pill since last night. Klonopin was supposed to have a long half-life but, maybe because he'd double-dosed yesterday, he was already aware of possible withdrawal symptoms – severe anxiety, irritability, panic. He once had a patient who'd had a seizure when he went off Klonopin too quickly. That was all Adam needed right now, a goddamn seizure.

He pulled into a spot between a pickup truck and an SUV. This was perfect because, while most of his car was out of sight from where Xan was positioned, he could still see the back third or so of Xan's car and he'd know when he pulled away.

Adam didn't stop staring at Xan's car, not even to look at his watch. He was trying to blink as little as possible, to the extent that after a while his eyes started to feel irritated.

Adam had no idea what time it was, but it had to be after twelve o'clock. Xan was probably starting to get impatient, slowly realizing that he was getting stood up.

Then Xan left, pulling away suddenly. Adam had been idling the engine of his car, but a woman was walking by in front of him, pushing a large wagon full of groceries and holding a little girl's hand. She had another child in a BabyBjörn.

'Move it!' Adam yelled. 'Come on, move it already!'

He would've been better off saying nothing. His tantrum made the woman stop and stare for a couple of moments, like she was looking at an insane person.

'Come on, come on!' he yelled, waving his arms frantically, and then the woman finally moved out of the way and Adam peeled out of the lot, nearly colliding with a car that was backing out of a space near the exit.

Adam spotted Xan's car up ahead and followed from a distance as Xan made several turns. Then Xan sped up as he entered US-209. Adam entered as well, but he couldn't see Xan's car any longer, and there was a limit to how fast he could go because there were cars ahead of him on the two-lane road. He weaved in and out, into the opposing lane, but there was too much oncoming traffic to risk trying to pass the other cars. Even more troubling, he couldn't see Xan's car. If Xan had turned off the road that would be it – Marissa could wind up dead.

'Please, God, no,' Adam begged. 'No, no, no…'

Klonopinless, Adam took deep breaths, trying to get hold of himself.

There was a break in the oncoming traffic, and Adam accelerated past three cars, barely making it back into the right lane and avoiding a head-on collision with a van. His heart was beating furiously when he spotted Xan's car, about one hundred yards ahead of him.

It was hard to feel any real relief, though, as he knew that this was probably the riskiest part of his entire plan. He had to stay far enough behind that Xan didn't realize he was being followed, but at the same time he couldn't lose him again. It didn't help that US-209 was a winding road and around every bend Xan's car seemed to disappear. After about thirty minutes, Xan turned right onto a narrower, bumpier, even curvier road. Adam lost track of Xan's car as they passed what seemed to be an old bungalow colony. He went past a run-down tennis court and over an old, very small wooden bridge but didn't see Xan's car anywhere. He had a hunch that Xan had turned off the road, and he made a fast U-turn and headed back past the tennis court. He knew if his hunch was wrong it could turn out to be a fatal error, as he could have lost Xan for good, but then up ahead to the right, on top of the hill, near several decaying bungalows, Adam spotted Xan's car.

Suddenly Adam was confident again. Following Xan rather than paying the ransom or calling the cops had been the right move after all. Everything was going the way he'd planned it last night and early this morning. He was going to save Marissa and drive her back to the city. Tonight she'd be home, safe in bed where she belonged.

Adam parked off to the side of the road at the bottom of the hill. He checked to make sure his Glock was loaded and he had more ammo, three more clips in his jacket pocket, and then he got out of the car, closing the door as softly as possible.

He didn't want to go up the hill in plain sight along the dirt road, so he walked through the shrubbery alongside the road, crouching to stay low. He knew time was a huge factor now. He hadn't shown up at the meeting spot, and, for all he knew, Xan was going to do exactly what he'd said he was going to do and kill Marissa. Adam had a vision of Xan with a knife, like the one he'd used to kill Dana, and he started moving fast, jogging and then running up the hill while still staying low, trying to remain out of view.

He reached the edge of the shrubbery; his arms were cut up by thorns, but he barely noticed. He took a quick look around and didn't see Xan by his car or anywhere else, so with his right hand in his jacket pocket gripping the handle of the Glock, he jogged through the high grass and weeds toward the bungalow near where the car was parked. He went up to the side of the bungalow and waited a moment. He didn't hear anything – not a bad sign, as anything was better than hearing Marissa's screaming – but he hoped that he was in the right place, that Xan and Marissa weren't in some other bungalow or someplace else. There was also a possibility that Marissa wasn't even here, that Xan had come to this decrepit bungalow colony for some other reason. This would be awful, because if Xan returned to his car alone now and drove away, Adam wouldn't be able to make it down the hill to his own car in time to follow him.

Adam took a few steps toward the back of the bungalow and then peered through a dirty, cobwebbed window. He looked in at an old kitchen but didn't see anyone. Then he heard a noise – it sounded like a floorboard creaking inside the bungalow – and he backed away.

He knew someone was inside, and he didn't want to waste another second. He went back to the front, holding the gun out ahead of him. He hadn't fired the Glock, or any gun, since the night he'd killed Carlos Sanchez. He saw a flash of the scene – the sound of the shots in the dark, the way the recoil had felt – but he shook it off quickly.

The front door was ajar. He opened it farther, just wide enough to get into the bungalow. He was making noise, the floorboards were creaking, but it didn't matter anymore. His index finger was on the trigger, ready to fire.

'We're back here, Doc.'

It was Xan's voice. At least he was here, in the bungalow – and he'd said 'we're,' which seemed to be a good sign, too. But he sounded very casual, almost like he'd been expecting Adam. That wasn't a good sign.

'Marissa, are you there?' Adam said. 'Marissa?'

After a short pause, he heard Marissa say softly, 'Yes, Daddy.' Her voice was very weak. She sounded terrified.

'Don't worry, honey. You're gonna be okay, I promise.'

He approached the back room slowly, knowing this was probably some kind of trap. He knew Xan wouldn't have told him where they were if he didn't have something planned. Whatever it was, Adam was ready for it. There was no way he was going to let this son of a bitch hurt his little girl.

Suddenly Xan appeared ahead of him. Adam nearly fired, but just as his finger was about to squeeze the trigger, he realized that Xan wasn't alone. He was holding Marissa in front of him, as a shield, pressing a gun up to her head.

'Hey, take it easy there, Doc,' Xan said. 'Now's not the time to get trigger-happy, if you know what I mean.'

Marissa looked absolutely terrified. Her eyes were bloodshot, her lips were trembling, and her nose was bloodied.

'Let her go,' Adam said.

'There you go again,' Xan said, 'telling me what to do. When're you gonna learn that that's not the way this thing works? *I'm* the one who tells *you* what to do.'

Adam was aiming his gun at Xan's head, or at least he was trying to. It was hard to keep his shooting hand steady.

'Don't worry,' Adam said to Marissa. 'It's okay. You're gonna be okay.'

'Where's my money?' Xan asked.

'Let her go first, then I'll give it to you.'

Xan pressed the barrel of his gun harder into Marissa's cheek. Marsissa started to scream, then seemed to stop herself.

Xan said to Adam, 'Don't make me ask you again.'

'It's in my motel,' Adam said, 'down the road. If you let her go we can go together, you and me, take your car if you want. Just let her go. That's all I care about.'

'You must think I'm a real idiot, don't you?' Xan said. 'I'm some kind of moron, right? Just because you got those letters in front of your name, that makes you, what? Better than me?'

'Just give him the money!' Marissa yelled. Then she said in a quieter, shakier voice, 'Please, Dad… just give him the money. Please… please just give it to him.'

'He can't give it to me,' Xan said. 'You know why? Because he didn't bring it, that's why. Why don't you tell her the truth, Doc? You didn't bring any money, did you?'

Trying to aim his gun between Xan's eyes, Adam said, 'I told you, the money's in my room.'

'You're a lying bastard,' Xan said. 'You didn't bring any money because you wanted to handle it your way, didn't you? You thought you could get off cheap, save your spoiled brat daughter, be the big hero. Now give me one reason why I shouldn't kill her right now. Give me one reason.'

'Give him the money, Dad,' Marissa said, crying. 'Just give it to him... please, just give it to him... please... please...'

Part of Xan's head was now behind Marissa's head. Adam wasn't sure he had a clear shot anymore.

'The police know I'm here,' Adam said because he was desperate and couldn't think of anything else to say.

'Now *that* I seriously doubt,' Xan said. 'If you called the cops they would've been here a long time ago, and they sure as hell wouldn't've had you follow me in a bright red rental car. You really thought I wouldn't notice you, huh? You should've just had a big sign on top of it – *It's me. Here I am.*'

Marissa was sobbing.

'The cops,' Xan continued, smiling. 'Come on, I knew you'd never call the cops. That isn't your style, is it, Doc? Nah, you're a handle-it-yourself type of dude, right? Who needs cops? Get your gun, get your name in the paper – Dr Bloom saves the day. Except it doesn't always work out the way you want it to, does it? Yeah, it's just like that night in your house all over again, when you killed my brother, Carlos. He wasn't really my brother, but he was part of my family. You know what it feels like to lose part of your family, Doc? Well, maybe you do.'

Adam wanted to shoot him, squeeze off a whole round like when he killed Sanchez, but he remained calm, as calm as he possibly could, and said, 'You can't get away. The cops'll be here any second. Just let her go – this is between you and me. It has nothing to do with her.'

'I've listened to enough of your bullshit,' Xan said. 'Drop your gun or I shoot the little bitch in the head.'

Xan had shifted a little. Adam had a clear shot at his right eye.

'Let her go,' Adam said.

'Listen to you, still thinking you can tell me what to do,' Xan said. 'It doesn't matter that your daughter's about to die. You just have to be right, don't you?'

'Drop your gun, Dad!' Marissa shouted. 'Just fucking drop it!'

Adam knew he couldn't drop his gun. If he did, Xan would

shoot him, then shoot Marissa. He was sure of it.

'If you shoot her, I'm gonna shoot you,' Adam said.

'So you really think I give a shit about that?' Xan said. 'What kind of shrink are you anyway? You really have no idea who I am, do you?'

Adam thought about all those times in the range when he'd hit the bull's-eye, and the targets were much farther away than Xan was right now. All he had to do was hit that bull's-eye one time...

'You think I'm messing with you?' Xan said. 'As you know, I had no problem killing your wife, who really wanted me, by the way. Man, she was so hot for me. I really wish I had a chance to –'

Adam fired. During the millisecond between when his finger pressed the trigger and when the bullet left the gun, he was aware of his shooting hand shifting slightly downward and to the right. But it was too late to do anything about it, and he had to watch helplessly as the bullet entered Marissa's chest.

The rest seemed to happen in super slow motion – Marissa falling, all of that blood, his realization that he'd shot his daughter. Maybe Adam had started to scream, *No,* or maybe he was just thinking about screaming it, when he heard the second shot.

Marissa had been thinking one thing all along: *Stay alive.* On the way to wherever she was now, most of the time she didn't know whether she was asleep or awake – everything was blurred, part of the same nightmare. A few times the confusion lifted and she realized what was going on, that for some reason, Xan, *her* Xan, had drugged her and was taking her someplace. *What the fuck?* She also knew that he'd probably killed her mother, but this concept was impossible for her to comprehend. She had no idea what the hell was wrong with him, how any of this could possibly be happening, but she knew she had to do whatever she had to do to stay alive.

In the car, she tried to beg him to let her go, but he put that rag over her face, and when she woke up again, tied to a bed, she screamed and he hit her and drugged her again. She had to go to the bathroom so badly, she could barely breathe, her nose was probably broken, and he still wouldn't let her go. She knew it was pointless to try to fight it anymore. He was too strong and she was too weak – there was no way she could possibly win. Her only option was to stay alive, to wait. Either he would kill her or someone would come to save her, but nothing she did would change the situation.

She woke up alone, dazed, tied to the bed, her nose hurting like hell, lying in her own feces, the ropes cutting into her arms, and she was afraid that he'd left for good – that he was going to let her die like this. Her throat was already dry as hell from all the screaming and crying she'd done, but she yelled for help until she could barely make any sound.

Then, finally, Xan returned. Weirdly, she was actually glad to see him. At least he hadn't abandoned her.

Then she saw he had a gun, and she screamed, or tried to scream, 'Don't shoot me.'

'I'm not gonna shoot you, baby. Relax.'

He was such a total maniac, the way he sounded so calm, so detached. How could this be the same guy who she'd thought was so great, who – Jesus Christ – she'd said 'I love you' to?

He started untying her, saying, 'You wanna live, just do what I say, you think you can do that? I don't think that's so hard, just to keep your pretty little mouth shut.' Then he winced and said, 'Man, you stink. If there was a shower here I'd let you clean yourself off. I'm really sorry. I know how uncomfortable this must be for you.'

His face was near hers as he untied the rope over her chest, and she wanted to bite into his cheek, hear *him* scream. But she restrained herself, thinking, *Stay alive. Just stay alive.*

As he finished untying her, she asked, 'Where are we going?' and he said, 'Nowhere.'

His tone was ominous, threatening. He lifted her out of bed and held the gun to her head. Was he going to shoot her now? Why untie her just to shoot her?

Then she heard a noise, a door opening.

'We're back here, Doc,' he said.

Was it really her *father*? Then she saw him, aiming the gun.

She figured he must've called the police. The whole building was probably surrounded. In a few minutes, even seconds, this nightmare would be over.

But why did Xan still seem so cocky? And why would the cops have sent her father in here alone? With a gun?

It started to hit her that her father had done it again. There were no cops. Xan told her father to drop the gun or he'd kill her. She knew he meant it, and she screamed at her father as loud as she could to drop his gun.

Of course he didn't listen. Her father never listened.

Then he shot her. It happened so fast. One second she was standing, the next she was on the floor, bleeding, pain ripping through her chest.

Then she heard another shot and with blurry vision saw her father, part of his head missing, lying on the floor.

Was this really happening?

The pain was getting worse and she was getting weaker, but she was thinking, *Stay alive. Just stay alive.*

She knew if she moved or screamed or said anything, Xan would kill her. She saw him walking away, past her father. He probably thought she was dead. With the pain she was in, it took all her strength to stay still, to not even moan. She was shivering, and the blood, *her* blood, was spreading closer toward where her face was pressed against the floor.

Stay alive. Just stay alive.

She heard the front door open, then close. She spotted her father's gun a few feet away from her, still partially in his hand.

Marissa crawled through her blood, through her father's blood, toward the gun. Every moment and every breath was total agony.

She heard noise from outside, footsteps on the porch, and then the door opened. She grabbed the gun. There was blood on the handle, and it was hard to get a grip. She dropped it once, as she heard footsteps getting closer, and then she grabbed it again.

She looked up and saw Xan looking down at her. He was aiming his gun at her face.

'Going somewhere?'

377

Johnny took another couple of steps toward her, stopping at the edge of the blood puddle.

'Oh, man, look at you,' he said, smiling. 'You look so beautiful right now. I really hate to do this.'

This was going to be perfect – finishing off the family. It would be just like he'd planned. Well, almost.

'I'm gonna paint a picture of you tonight,' he said, 'the way you look right now. I want to remember you like this forever.'

He was still smiling when she squeezed the trigger and a bullet struck him in his right shoulder. What the hell? His gun fell, and Marissa kept shooting. Then she hit him in the upper thigh, close to his crotch. As he started to keel over, she held the gun steady with both hands and shot him in the middle of his chest. He fell to his knees facing her, blood dripping and then gushing from his still smiling mouth.

'Come on, baby, I know you love me.' She tried to fire again but was out of bullets. It didn't matter, though. He collapsed face-first onto the floor.

28

MARISSA WAS SICK of everybody telling her how lucky she was. All the doctors and nurses at Mount Sinai Hospital in Manhattan had been going on about it for weeks, making comments like *If the bullet had been just an inch to the left you would've been killed instantly* and *If you hadn't gotten to your father's cell phone and called for the ambulance and if the ambulance hadn't gotten there so quickly you wouldn't be alive right now.* This made her *lucky?* If she was lucky, her parents never would have hired Gabriela as their maid. If she was lucky, that tropical storm wouldn't have been approaching Florida and they wouldn't have been in the house the night of the robbery. If she was lucky, she never would have gone with her friends to see Tone Def that night and met Xan, aka Johnny Long. Lying in the hospital bed, she ran through everything that had gone wrong in her life leading up to the nightmare in the bungalow in the Catskills, and she kept coming to the same conclusion: she'd been anything but lucky.

Although she'd been trying to avoid reading the newspapers and watching the news on TV, she knew that the media was calling her a hero, overglorifying everything she'd done. She'd just been trying to stay alive; how did that make her a hero?

While the media was praising her, they were blasting her father, calling him 'Adam Bloom, the psycho therapist of Forest Hills.' They portrayed him as a crazed vigilante, who'd driven up to the Catskills to try to rescue his daughter, hell-bent on avenging the murder of his wife and restoring his own tarnished reputation. The media also criticized the police, particularly Detective Clements, for not pushing for a full mental evaluation of Dr Bloom or revoking his gun license and for giving him the opportunity to go upstate on his own. Marissa enjoyed seeing Clements get attacked, and she agreed with what the media was saying about her father, too.

One day a couple of weeks after the shootings, Grandma Ann came to the hospital to visit and said, 'You can't blame your father forever. You can't go through life with that kind of anger.'

Her grandmother looked worn and frail. Marissa was worried about her.

'I really don't want to talk about it anymore, Grandma.'

Marissa had been through two surgeries to remove the bullet and repair the deep tissue damage and several broken ribs, and she was still in severe pain, despite all of the painkillers they were giving her.

'Your father loved you,' her grandmother said almost desperately. 'He just wanted to do the right thing.'

'The right thing?' Marissa said. 'He fucking shot me.'

'He was trying to save your life.'

'Yeah, and he did such a great job of it.'

'You're alive, aren't you?'

'No thanks to him.'

'He was scared, he panicked. And if he didn't go up there that Xan, I mean *Johnny*, might've killed you.'

It had come out in the news that Xan had actually been a career criminal named Johnny Long. He'd grown up in the same orphanage as Carlos Sanchez, and the police believed that Johnny had been the second intruder in the robbery and that he'd killed Marissa's mother and Gabriela. Marissa knew it was her fault for letting Xan into their lives, but everything else had been her father's fault.

'I know what your father did was wrong,' her grandmother said, 'but imagine, just imagine, what the last seconds of his life were like, how awful that must've been for him. He had to die, thinking he'd killed you, thinking he'd killed his daughter. That's the last thing he thought, the last thing he saw...'

Her grandmother was sobbing. Marissa gave her a couple of minutes to get hold of herself, then said, 'Look, I know it's hard for you to accept, Grandma, but my father made a huge mistake, okay? I wish he'd been a better man, I really do. I wish I could defend him, I wish I could justify what he did, but I can't. He was a selfish asshole who went around like he was wearing a red cape and he didn't care about me or my mother or anybody but himself. If he'd called the police they might've saved me and I might not've gotten shot, and if he'd called the police when our house got robbed maybe my mother would still be alive and I wouldn't've had sex with that son of a bitch Johnny Long. Don't you see? My father caused it all, and I don't care what you say, I'll never forgive him for that, ever.'

The day of Marissa's discharge, Grandma Ann returned to the hospital. She looked extremely frail, like she'd lost ten, maybe fifteen pounds since Adam's death.

'Are you okay, Grandma? I'm really worried about you.'

'I'm fine,' she said flatly. 'Are you ready to go?'

The plan was for them to ride in a Town Car to the Mansfield Hotel in midtown, where Marissa had booked a suite. Marissa intended to never set foot inside the house in Forest Hills again. It was already up for sale, and at some point she'd arrange for someone to sell off all the furniture and clothes and move everything else into long-term storage. Her parents' life insurance policies, the proceeds from the sale of the house, and their other assets would make her a multimillionaire. She didn't know what she was going to do with her life, but she sure as hell wasn't going to waste it working. She was planning to move to Prague after all of the financial details were worked out. She'd live there for a while and then maybe move to Paris or Barcelona or some other city. She just wanted to get away – from New York, from America, from everybody who'd ever heard of Adam Bloom. The thought of having to live the rest of her life as Adam Bloom's daughter disgusted her so much that she'd already started doing the paperwork to legally change her last name to Stern. It was her mother's maiden name and she thought it would be a nice tribute.

She got out of the bed and into a wheelchair. She could walk fine, but it was hospital policy that all patients, no matter what their condition, had to be wheeled out when they were discharged. The orderly wheeled her very slowly so Grandma Ann, next to them, could keep up.

At the hospital doors, Marissa stood and walked next to her grandmother toward where the Town Car was waiting at the curb.

Reporters rushed them. One of the loudest shouted, 'Ms Bloom, how does it feel to be a hero?'

Marissa stopped for a moment, glared at the guy, who was a little older than her, and said, 'I'm not a hero, and my last name isn't Bloom, it's Stern. I'm Marissa Stern. You got that?'

They moved on toward the car. Now the reporters were shouting, 'Ms Stern! Ms Stern! Ms Stern!'

Marissa helped her grandmother in and then got in after her. As they drove off down Fifth Avenue, she could still hear the reporters screaming.

'I swear to God,' Marissa said, 'I better not see the name Marissa Bloom in the papers tomorrow morning.'

Her grandmother, looking away, didn't say anything. Now the reporters were running alongside the Town Car, banging on the windows.

'I mean, seriously,' Marissa said. 'What's wrong with people anyway?'

Acknowledgements

For their enormous impact on this novel and my career I'd like to thank Ken Bruen, Bret Easton Ellis, Lee Child, Kristian Moliere, Shane McNeil, Charles Ardai, John David Coles, Sandy Starr, Brian DeFiore, Nick Harris, Diogenes Verlag, Ion Mills, and Steven Kelly.

About Us

In addition to No Exit Press, Oldcastle Books has a number of other imprints, including Kamera Books, Creative Essentials, Pulp! The Classics, Pocket Essentials and High Stakes Publishing > oldcastlebooks.co.uk

For more information about Crime Books go to > crimetime.co.uk

Check out the kamera film salon for independent, arthouse and world cinema > kamera.co.uk

For more information, media enquiries and review copies please contact > marketing@oldcastlebooks.com